Praise for
*New York Times*

# RACHEL VINCENT

"*Twilight* fans will love it."
—*Kirkus Reviews* on *My Soul to Take*

A high-octane plot with characters you can really care about. Vincent is a welcome addition to this genre!"
Kelley Armstrong on *Stray*

"I liked the character and loved the action. I look forward to reading the next book in the series."
Charlaine Harris on *Stray*

"Fans of those vampires will enjoy this new crop of otherworldly beings."
—*Booklist*

'*My Soul to Take* grabs you from the very beginning."
—*Sci-Fi Guy*

"Wonderfully written characters… A fast-paced, engrossing read that you won't want to put down. A story that I wouldn't mind sharing with my pre-teen… A book like this is one of the reasons that I add authors to my auto-buy list. This is definitely a keeper."
—*TeensReadToo.com*

*Also available from* **Rachel Vincent**

*Published by*

**Soul Screamers**
MY SOUL TO TAKE
MY SOUL TO SAVE
MY SOUL TO KEEP

*Coming soon…*

IF I DIE

# RACHEL VINCENT

## my SOUL to *Steal*

Published in Great Britain 2011
MIRA Books, an imprint of Harlequin (UK) Limited,
Eton House, 18-24 Paradise Road, Richmond, Surrey, TW9 1SR

© Rachel Vincent 2011

ISBN 978 0 7783 0478 4

47-1111

Printed and bound by
CPI Group (UK) Ltd, Croydon, CR0 4YY

# ACKNOWLEDGEMENTS

Thanks first of all to my editor, Mary-Theresa Hussey, who knew just what this book needed. Her suggestions challenged me to find better solutions, and the book is *so* much better for it.

Thanks to Natashya Wilson, for so much enthusiasm and support.

Rinda Elliot, for the lightning-fast critique, and for being the first to love Sabine.

Thanks to #1, who made fajitas and helped me figure out how to hurt a hellion.

Thanks to Ally, Jen, Melissa, Kelley, and everyone else in the YA community for advice, camaraderie, and for making me feel so welcome.

And most of all, thank you to the readers who have given Kaylee and her friends a place in this world. Without you, none of the rest of it would matter.

To all the real life couples, exes, and unrequited romantic interests, tangled up in love and nightmares. Sometimes that frayed knot is the best lifeline in the world. Other times, it works more like a straitjacket…

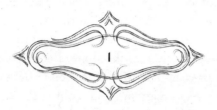

1

BY THE TIME the second semester of my junior year began, I'd already faced down rogue grim reapers, an evil entertainment mogul, and hellions determined to possess my soul. But I never would have guessed that the most infuriating beast of all, I had yet to meet. My boyfriend's ex-girlfriend was a thing of nightmares. Literally.

"I WON'T BITE." Nash looked up at me with a green bean speared on his fork, and I realized I was staring. I'd stopped on the bottom step, surprised to see him at school, and even more surprised to see him sitting alone at lunch, outside in the January cold, where I'd come to get away from the gossip and stares in the cafeteria.

Obviously he'd had the same idea.

I glanced over my shoulder through the window in the cafeteria door, looking for Emma, but she hadn't shown up yet.

Nash frowned when he noticed my hesitation. But I wasn't worried about him. I was worried about me. I was afraid that if I got within touching distance of him—within reach of the arms that had once been my biggest comfort and those gorgeous hazel eyes that could read me at a glance—that I would give in. That I would forgive, even if I couldn't forget, and that would be bad.

I mean, it would *feel* good, but that would be bad.

The past two weeks had been the most difficult of my life. In the past few months alone, I'd survived horrors most sixteen-year-old girls didn't even know existed. But a couple of weeks without Nash—our entire winter vacation—had nearly been enough to break me.

Whoever said it is better to have loved and lost than never to have loved was full of crap. If I'd never loved Nash in the first place, I wouldn't know what I was missing now.

"Kaylee?" Nash dropped his fork onto his tray, green bean untouched. "I get it. You're not ready to talk."

I shook my head and set my tray on the table across from his, then sank onto the opposite bench. "No, I just... I didn't think you'd be here." I hadn't gone to see him, because that would have been unfair to us both—being together, when we couldn't really be together. But I knew he'd been very sick from withdrawal, because my father, of all people, had called regularly to check on him.

And based on his brief reports, withdrawal from Demon's Breath—known as frost, in human circles—was hell on earth.

"Are you...okay?" I asked, poking at runny spaghetti sauce with my own fork.

"Better." He shrugged. "Still working toward okay."

"But you're well enough for school?"

Another shrug. "My mom was giving me a sedative made from some weird Netherworld plant for a while, to help with the shakes, but it just made me sleep all the time. Without dreams," he added, when he saw my horrified expression. The hellion whose breath he'd been huffing had communicated with Nash through his dreams sometimes. And through me, the rest of the time. By hijacking my body while I slept.

I'd been willing to work through the addiction with Nash—after all, it was my fault he'd been exposed to Demon's Breath in the first place. But his failure to stop the serial possession of my body—or even tell me it was happening—was the last straw for me. I couldn't be with him until I was sure nothing like that would ever happen again.

Unfortunately, what my head wanted and what my heart wanted were two completely different things.

"I still don't have much appetite, but what I do eat is staying down now." Nash stared at his full tray. He'd lost weight. His face looked…sharper. The flesh under his eyes was dark and puffy, and he hadn't bothered to art-fully muss his hair that morning. The bright, charismatic Nash I'd first met had been replaced with this dimmer, somber version I barely recognized. A version I was afraid I didn't know on the inside, either. Not like I'd known *my* Nash, anyway.

"Maybe you should have stayed home a little longer," I suggested, slowly twirling noodles around my plastic fork.

"I wanted to see you."

The fissure in my heart cracked open a little wider, and I looked up to find regret and longing slowly twisting the greens and browns in his irises. Humans wouldn't see that, even if we'd had company. But because Nash and I were both *bean sidhes*—banshees, to the uninformed—we could see the colors swirling in each other's eyes, and with a little practice, I'd learned to interpret what I saw in his. To read his emotions through the windows of his soul—when he let me see them.

"Nash…"

"No pressure," he interrupted, before I could spit out the protest I'd practiced, but hoped not to have to use. "I just wanted to see your face. Hear your voice."

Translation: *You didn't visit me. Or even call.*

I closed my eyes, trying to work through an awkwardness I'd never felt with Nash before. "I wanted to." More than I could possibly express. "But it's just too hard to…"

"To see, but not touch?" he finished for me, and I met his rueful gaze. "Trust me, I know." He sighed and stirred a glob of mass-produced peach cobbler. "So, what now? We're friends?"

Yeah. If friends could be in love, but not together. In sync, but out of touch. Willing to die for each other, but unable to trust.

"I don't think there are words for what we are, Nash." Yet I could think of at least one: *broken*.

Nash and I were like the wreckage of two cars that had hit head-on. We were tangled up in each other so thoroughly that I could no longer tell which parts of us were him and which were me. We could probably never be truly untangled—not after what we'd been through together—but I had serious doubts we could ever really recapture what we'd had.

"I just… I need some time."

He nodded, and his eyes shone with the first flash of hope I'd seen from him in ages. "Yeah. We have time."

In fact, we had lots and lots of time. *Bean sidhes* age very slowly from puberty on, so while I'd likely be carded until I was forty, if Nash and I actually managed to work things out, we'd have nearly four hundred years together, barring catastrophe.

Although actually barring catastrophe seemed highly unlikely, considering that since the school year began, my life had been defined by a series of disasters, barely held together by the beautifully strong thread of Nash's presence in my life. At least, until recently. But now I was clinging to the wreckage of my existence, holding the pieces together on my own, trying to decide if I would be helping us both or hurting us by letting him back in.

"So, how's Em?" Nash asked, his voice lowered as he glanced at something over my shoulder.

I twisted to see Emma Marshall, my best friend, heading toward us across the nearly deserted quad. Everyone with half a brain—or nothing to hide—was eating inside, where it was warm. Em carried a tray holding a slice of pizza and a Diet Coke, content to eat with us outside, not because she couldn't face the crowd ready to judge her, but because she didn't care what they thought.

"Em's strong. She's dealing." And though she didn't know it, in many ways, Emma was my hero, based on her resilience alone.

Doug Fuller, Em's boyfriend of almost a month, had

died from an overdose of frost two weeks earlier, and though they'd been connected at the crotch, rather than at the heart, she'd been understandably upset by his death. Especially considering that she couldn't comprehend the Netherworld origin of the drug that had killed him.

Nash lowered his voice even further as she walked toward us. "Did you go to the funeral?"

"Yeah." Doug had been one of Eastlake High's starting linebackers. Practically the whole school had shown up at his funeral—except for Nash. He'd been too sick from withdrawal to get out of bed. And Scott, their third musketeer. Scott had survived addiction to frost—but at a devastating price. He'd suffered brain damage and now had a permanent, hardwired mental connection to the hellion whose breath had killed Doug and mortally wounded my relationship with Nash.

"Hey." Emma came to a stop on my right and glanced from me to Nash, then back before taking a seat next to me. "Someone bring me up to speed. Are we making up or breaking up? 'Cause this limbo is kind of driving me nuts." She grinned, and I could have thanked the universe in that moment for the ray of sunshine that was Emma.

"How low can you go?" I asked, then crunched into a French fry.

"Lower than you know..." Nash replied, with a hint of an awkward grin.

Em rolled her eyes. "So...more limbo?"

Nash looked just as ready for my answer as she did. I exhaled heavily. "For now."

He sighed and Emma frowned. Like I was being

unreasonable. But she didn't know the details of our breakup. I couldn't tell her that he'd let a hellion take over my body and play doctor with him—to Nash's credit, he hadn't known it wasn't me that first time—without even telling me I was being worn like a human costume.

I couldn't tell her because the same thing had happened to her, and for her own safety and sense of security, I didn't want her to know that her body had been hijacked by the hellion responsible for her boyfriend's death. Her friendship with me had already put her in more than enough danger.

"Oh, fine. Drag out the melodrama for as long as you want. At least it'll give everyone around here something else to talk about." Something other than Doug and Scott.

If they hadn't already had two weeks to deal with grief and let off steam, the whole school probably would have been reeling from the double loss. The looks and whispers when we passed in the hall were hard enough to deal with as it was.

"So, did you see the new girl?" Emma asked, making a valiant attempt to change the subject as she tore the crust from her triangle of pizza.

"What new girl?" I didn't really care, but the switch in topic gave me a chance to think—or at least talk—about something other than me and Nash, and the fact that there was currently no me and Nash.

"Don't remember her name." Emma dipped her crust into a paper condiment cup full of French dressing. "But she's a senior. Can you imagine? Switching schools the last semester of your senior year?"

"Yeah, that would suck," I agreed, staring at my tray, pretending I didn't notice Nash staring at me. Was it going to be like this from now on? Us sitting across from each other, watching—or pointedly not watching— each other? Sitting in silence or talking about nothing anyone really cared about? *Maybe I should have stayed in the cafeteria. This isn't gonna work....*

"She's in my English class. She looked pretty lonely, so I invited her to sit with us." Emma bit into her crust and chewed while I glanced up at her in surprise.

First of all, Em didn't have other girlfriends. Most girls didn't like Emma for the same reason guys couldn't stay away from her. It had been just the two of us since the seventh grade, when her mouth and her brand-new C-cups intimidated the entire female half of the student body.

Second of all...

"Why is there a senior in your junior English class?" Nash said it before I could.

Emma shrugged while she chewed, then swallowed and dipped her crust again. "She got behind somehow, and they're letting her take two English classes at once, so she can graduate on time. I mean, would you want to be here for a whole 'nother year, just to take one class?"

"No." Nash stabbed another green bean he probably wasn't going to eat. "But I wouldn't want to read *Macbeth* and *To Kill a Mockingbird* at the same time, either."

"Better her than me." Em bit into her crust again, then twisted on the bench as footsteps crunched on the grass behind us. "Hey, here she comes," she said around a full mouth.

I started to turn, but stopped when I noticed Nash staring. And not at me. His wide-eyed gaze was trained over my head, and if his jaw got any looser, he'd have to pick it up off his tray. "Sabine?" he said, his voice soft and stunned.

Emma slapped the table. "*That's* her name!" She twisted and called over her shoulder. "Sabine, over here!" Then she glanced back at Nash. "Wait, you've already met her?"

Nash didn't answer. Instead, he stood, nearly tripping over his own bench seat, and when he rounded the table toward the new girl, I finally turned to look at her. And instantly understood why she wasn't intimidated by Emma.

Sabine was an entirely different kind of gorgeous.

She was a contrast of pale skin and dark hair, where Em was golden. Slim and lithe, where Em was curvy. She swaggered, where Emma glided. And she'd stopped cold, her lunch tray obviously forgotten, and was staring not at me or her new friend Emma, but at *my* boyfriend.

My kind-of boyfriend. Or whatever.

"Sabine?" Nash whispered this time, and his familiar, stunned tone set off alarm bells in my head.

"Nash Hudson. Holy shit, it *is* you!" the new girl said, tossing long dark hair over one shoulder to reveal a mismatched set of hoops in her double-pierced right ear.

Nash rounded the table and walked past me without a glance in my direction. Sabine set her tray on the nearest table and ran at him. He opened his arms, and she flew into them so hard they spun in a tight circle. Together.

My chest burned like I'd swallowed an entire jar of hot salsa.

"What are you doing here?" Nash asked, setting her down, as she said, "I can't believe it!"

But I was pretty sure she could believe it. She looked more thrilled than surprised. "I heard your name this morning, but I didn't think it would really be you!"

"It's me. So...what? You go to school here now?"

"Yeah. New foster home. Moved in last week." She smiled, and her dark eyes lit up. "I can't believe this!"

"Me, neither." Em stood and pulled me up. "What is it we're not believing?"

And finally Nash turned, one arm still wrapped casually around Sabine's waist, as if he'd forgotten it was still there. "Sabine went to my school in Fort Worth, before I moved here."

"Yeah, before you ran off and left me!" She twisted out of his grip to punch him in the shoulder, but she didn't look mad.

"Hey, you left first, remember?" Nash grinned.

"Not by choice!" Her scowl was almost as dark as her grin was blinding.

What the hell were they talking about?

I'd already opened my mouth to say...something, when Tod winked into existence on my left. Fortunately, I was still too confused by the arrival of Nash's old friend—*please, please* just be a friend!—to be surprised by the sudden appearance of his mostly dead grim reaper brother.

"Hey, Kaylee, you..." Tod began, running one hand through pale blond curls, then stopped when he saw

Sabine and Nash, still chatting like long-lost relatives, while the rest of us watched. "Uh-oh. I'm too late."

"Too late for what?" Emma asked, but I could tell from the lack of a reaction from either Nash or Sabine that Em and I were currently the only ones who could see Tod. Selective corporeality was one of several really cool reaper abilities, and now that Emma knew about him, Tod rarely appeared to me alone. For which I was more than grateful—Em was one less person who thought I went around talking to myself when I was really talking to the reaper.

"To warn you," Tod continued. "About Sabine."

"She comes with a warning label?" Em whispered.

I crossed my arms over the front of my jacket. "Well, it can't be sewn into her clothes, or we'd see the outline." Sabine's black sleeveless top was so tight I could practically count her abs.

Emma raised one brow at me. "Catty, much?"

"Well, look at her!" I whispered, both relieved and very, very irritated that neither Nash nor Sabine had given us a second look. A strip of bare skin showed between the low waist of her army-green carpenter pants and the hem of her shirt—an obvious violation of the school dress code—and she wore enough dark eye shadow to scare small children. And—most grating of all—the look worked for her. And it obviously worked for Nash. He couldn't look away.

"I don't think it's her you have a problem with," Emma whispered. "It's *them*."

I ignored her and turned to Tod. "I take it they were involved in Fort Worth?"

Tod nodded. "Yeah. If you're into really dramatic understatements."

Great.

"Hey, you two, care to introduce those of us on the periphery?" Emma called, betraying no hint of Tod's presence. She was a fast learner.

Nash looked up in surprise. "Sorry." He guided Sabine closer. "I'm guessing you've already met Emma?" he said, and the new girl—his *old* girl—nodded. "And this is my..." Confusion flashed in Nash's swirling eyes, and he dropped his hand from Sabine's waist. "This is Kaylee Cavanaugh."

Sabine truly looked at me for the first time, and I caught my breath at the intensity of her scrutiny. Her eyes were pools of ink that seemed to see right through me, and in that moment, the certainty—the terror—that Nash would want nothing to do with me now that she'd arrived was enough to constrict my throat and make my stomach pitch.

"Kaylee..." Sabine said my name like she was tasting it, trying to decide whether to swallow me whole or spit me back out, and in the end, I wasn't sure which she'd chosen. "Kaylee Cavanaugh. You must be the new ex."

Resisting the overwhelming urge to take a step back from Sabine, I shot Nash a questioning look, but he only shrugged. He hadn't told her. He hadn't even known she was there until she walked into the quad.

"I..." But I didn't know how to finish that thought.

Sabine laughed and fresh chill bumps popped up on my arms, beneath my jacket. "Don't worry 'bout it. Happens to the best of us." Then she turned—pointedly dismissing me—and grabbed her forgotten tray in one hand and Nash's arm in the other. "Let's eat. I'm starving!"

He glanced back at me then, and a flicker of uncertainty flashed in the swirling greens and browns of Nash's irises before he turned with her and headed for our table.

As they sat, I turned to find Tod watching them warily. "How long ago did they break up?" I asked, without bothering to whisper. Nash and Sabine no longer knew we existed.

"Well…" Tod hesitated, and I frowned at him. Like Emma, he was usually blunt bordering on rude.

"What?" I demanded.

Tod exhaled heavily. "Technically speaking, they never did."

2

"So, how serious were they?" I handed change and a receipt to a balding man in his forties. He shoved them both into his front pocket, then took off toward the north wing of the theater with a greasy jumbo popcorn.

"You sure you want to hear this?" Tod sat on the snack counter in his usual jeans and snug white tee, invisible and inaudible to everyone but me and Em. Not that it mattered. Monday afternoons were dead at the Cinemark. But then, so was Tod.

Emma leaned over the counter next to him. "I'm sure *I* want to hear it." She was on a break from her shift in the ticket booth, but Tod and I were obviously much more entertaining than anything going on in the break room.

"I didn't come to rub your face in it," the reaper insisted, watching me as he snatched a kernel from Emma's small bag of popcorn.

"No, you came because you're bored, and my problems obviously amuse you."

Tod had just switched to the midnight-to-noon shift reaping souls at the local hospital, and since reapers didn't need sleep, he was now free every afternoon to bug his still-living friends. Which consisted of me, Em, and Nash.

Tod shrugged. "Yeah, that, and for the free food."

"Why are you eating, anyway?" Emma pulled her paper bag out of his reach. "Can you even metabolize this?"

Tod raised one pale brow at her. "I may be dead, but I'm still perfectly functional. More functional than ever, in fact. Watch me function." He reached around her and grabbed another handful of popcorn while she laughed. "And that's not all I can do..."

"Can we save the live demo for later, please? *Bean sidhe* in angst, here." But the truth was that it felt good to laugh, after what we'd all been through in the past few months. "Seriously, tell me about Sabine."

Emma grinned. "Does she have a last name, or is she a superstahh? Like Beyoncé, or the pope?"

I threw a jelly bean at her, from the open box I kept under the counter. "You know that's not his name, right?"

Em threw the jelly bean back.

"Anyway..." Tod began. "Vital stats—here we go... Her name is Sabine Campbell, and she's probably seventeen by now. She likes long walks down dark alleys, conspicuous piercings, and, if memory serves, chocolate milk—shaken, not stirred." Tod paused dramatically, and the good humor shining in his eyes dulled a bit. "And she and Nash were the real thing."

My grape jelly bean went sour on my tongue, and I had to force myself to chew. But he'd said *were*. They *were* the real thing. As in, past tense. Because I was Nash's present tense. Right? We were taking a break so he could get clean, and I could come to terms with what had happened, but that didn't mean he was free for the taking!

"Wait, the real thing, like hearts and candy and flowers?" Em asked, wrinkling her nose over the cupid cliché.

Tod started to laugh, but choked off the sound with one look at my face. "More like obsession and codependence and…sex," the reaper finished reluctantly.

I rolled my eyes and poked through my box of jelly beans for another grape. "I know he's not a virgin."

"Well, he was when he met Sabine."

"Ohh," Emma breathed, and I dropped my jelly beans into the trash.

"Okay, so what?" I opened the door to the storage closet and grabbed the broom. "So she was his first. That doesn't mean anything." I swept up crushed popcorn kernels and smooshed Milk Duds in short, vicious strokes. "She didn't save lives with him. She didn't risk her soul to rescue him from the Netherworld. Whatever they had can't compete with that, right?"

"Right." Emma watched me, her eyes wide in sympathy. "Besides, we don't even know that she's still interested in him. They were probably just surprised to see each other."

I stilled the broom and raised both brows at her.

Emma shrugged. "Okay, she's totally still into him. Sorry, Kay."

"It doesn't matter. So long as *he's* not into *her*." I resumed sweeping, and accidentally smacked the popcorn machine with the broom handle.

Tod hopped down from the counter and held one blessedly corporeal hand out. "Hand over the broom, and no one will get hurt." But I found that hard to believe. Sabine was making me doubt everything I'd thought I knew. And I'd spent less than fifteen minutes with her.

I gave Tod the broom and he put it back in the closet. "He hasn't seen her in more than two years. Give him a chance to get used to her being here, and everything will go back to normal."

*Normal.* I could hardly even remember what that word meant anymore. "You really think so?"

Tod shrugged. "I give it a fifty-fifty chance."

"Doesn't that mean I have a better chance of being struck by lightning at least once before I die?"

Em laughed. "Knowing your luck? Yeah."

I pulled a plastic-wrapped stack of large cups from under the counter and began restocking the cup dispensers. "So, what's the deal? How did they hook up?"

"I was limited by real-world physics at the time, so I don't know the whole story," Tod said, leaning back with his elbows propped on the counter.

"Just tell me what you do know."

The reaper shrugged. "Nash was only fifteen when they met, and still coming into his full *bean sidhe* abilities—Influence doesn't come on full-strength until puberty."

"Really?" Emma said, a kernel of popcorn halfway to her mouth. "I didn't know that."

I hadn't, either. But I was tired of sounding ignorant about my own species, so I kept my mouth shut.

"Yeah. Otherwise, the terrible twos would turn any little *bean sidhe* boy into a tyrant. Can you imagine Nash ordering our mom around from the time he could talk?"

Actually, I could, having had a taste of what out-of-control Influence looked and felt like.

"So, anyway, Nash was coming into his own, but he didn't have our dad around to teach him stuff, like I did, so he was kind of mixed up. Sabine was abandoned as a kid, and she'd been through a bunch of foster parents. When they met, she had it pretty rough at home, and she'd gotten into some trouble. She had a temper, but nothing too serious. She and Nash just kind of fell into each other. I think he thought he could help her."

Yeah, that sounded like Nash and his hero complex. We'd gotten together the same way.

I stared at the gritty floor, trying not to feel sorry for Sabine. Something told me she wouldn't welcome my sympathy any more than she'd welcome my currently undefined presence in Nash's life.

"Did Harmony like her?" I asked, unable to deny the queasy feeling my question brought on. I didn't want Nash's mother to like any of his exes better than she liked me, but the new fear went beyond that. Harmony and I shared *bean sidhe* abilities. We'd bonded beyond our mutual interest in Nash, and I wanted her for myself, just like I wanted Nash.

Tod shrugged. "Mom likes everyone. The two of them

together scared the shit out of her, though, the same way you and Nash being together probably gives your dad nightmares."

"So what happened?" Em asked, while I was still trying to process the fact that Nash and Sabine's bond had been strong enough to worry Harmony.

When Tod didn't answer, I looked up and he shrugged again. "I died."

Emma blinked. "You...died?" She knew he was dead, of course, but that didn't make his proclamation sound any more...normal.

"Yeah. I died, and Mom and Nash didn't know I'd be coming back in my current incarnation." He spread his arms to indicate his existence as a reaper—and his completely unharmed-by-death physique. "So they moved for a fresh start, just like we did after my dad died. We'd lived around here when Nash and I were kids, so this probably felt a little like coming home for my mom. It made everything harder for Nash, though. Because of leaving Sabine."

"And he and Sabine never broke up?" I moved on to the jumbo plastic cups, fascinated in spite of myself by Tod's story.

"He couldn't get in touch with her. She was kind of... in state custody at the time. No email. No phone calls, except from family. Which she doesn't have."

Emma stood straight, brown eyes wide. "She got arrested?"

"I told you she got into some trouble."

"Yeah, but you didn't mention that she was a criminal." I shoved the cups down harder than was probably necessary. Nash's ex-girlfriend—his former "real thing"—was a convict? *That's* not scary or anything.

Obviously at some point his tastes had changed. Dramatically.

"What'd she do?" Emma said, asking the question I most wanted answered, but refused to ask myself.

Tod shrugged. "Nash never told me. But she got probation and a halfway house instead of prison, so it couldn't have been too bad."

"I'm guessing that's a matter of opinion." I twisted the end of the cellophane around the remaining cups and shoved them under the counter. "Maybe I should call him after work."

"What are you gonna say?" Emma asked. "'I'm not sure I want you back, but I'm sure I don't want your ex-con ex-girlfriend to have you, either'? Yeah. That'll start this little triangle off on the right foot."

"This is not a triangle. This is—" *a disaster* "—nothing. Exes turn into friends all the time, right?" Emma and Tod exchanged a glance. "Right?" I demanded, when neither of them answered.

"I don't know, Kay." Emma crumpled her empty popcorn bag and tossed it into the trash can from across the counter. "But on the bright side, according to Mrs. Garner, the triangle is the most stable geometric shape. That has to count for something, right?"

"This is not a triangle," I repeated, turning my back on them both to check the number of nacho cheese containers lined up beneath the heat lamp. I couldn't afford to let my decision about me and Nash be influenced by

Sabine's arrival. Or her criminal record. Or her prior claim on my boyfriend.

When I turned back around, Em was still watching me. "Maybe you shouldn't start grilling Nash about his ex until he's back on his feet for sure."

"Yeah." Except by then she could have swept him off of them. Or knocked them out from under him. Either way, Nash off his feet would be bad.

"Marshall, your break's over!" the new assistant manager called from across the lobby, fleshy hands propped on his considerable gut. "Back in the ticket booth!" His name was Becker, but when she made fun of him after work, Em replaced the capital *B* with a *P*. She'd called him Pecker to his face once, by accident, and he'd been yelling at her ever since.

Emma rolled her eyes, pushed the remainder of her soda toward Tod, and headed backward across the lobby. "See you after work." We'd ridden together, as we usually did when we had the same shift. But now, more often than not, we had a third carpooler.

As if he'd read my mind—not a reaper ability, as far as I knew—Tod glanced around the snack bar as a group of junior high kids came through the front door, wearing matching aftercare shirts. "Where's Alec?"

Tod, Nash, and Harmony were the only ones—other than my dad—who knew the truth about Alec, that he'd spent a quarter of a century enslaved by a hellion in the Netherworld. Until we'd rescued him in exchange for his help saving my dad and Nash from that same hellion.

I glanced at the clock. "He's on his break, but he should be back any minute." I'd given him my keys so he could eat a bag of Doritos in the car, by himself. Alec had grown comfortable with me and my dad, but the same could not be said for the rest of the general populace.

For the most part, Alec had adjusted well to being back in the human world. He was fascinated with the internet, DVDs, and laptops, none of which had been around in the eighties, when he'd become Avari's Netherworld proxy—a weird combination of a personal assistant and snack food. I hadn't even seen my iPod in days.

But he was still sometimes overwhelmed by crowds, not because of the numbers—he'd regularly faced large groups of terrifying monsters in the Netherworld—but because of the culture shock. He was getting to know the twenty-first century at his own speed through TV, newspapers—evidently people still read them in his day—and all the movies he saw for free at the Cinemark. But he got nervous when he had to actually interact with groups of people who didn't understand his cultural handicap. So far, "Medium or large?" and "Would you like butter on your popcorn?" were the most we'd gotten out of him at work.

"Want me to find him?" Tod asked, as the gaggle of kids descended on Emma in the ticket booth. But before I could answer, Alec rounded a corner into the lobby, tucking his uniform shirt into his pants.

"Sorry. Fell asleep," he said, then ducked into a small hall leading to the break room and service entrance. When he stepped into the snack bar a second later, scruffing one brown hand over short-cropped, tight curls, I couldn't help noticing that he still looked only half-awake.

"Just in time. We're about to get hit hard." I pointed to the swarm of tweens, and his dark eyes widened. "Don't worry, kids usually get Slurpees, candy, and some popcorn. Nothing complicated."

Alec just stared at me as I dumped a bag of popcorn seeds into the popper, careful not to burn myself. "Hey, you missed the inside scoop on Sabine." Em and I had told him about her on the ride to work, but his confused frown said he obviously hadn't been paying attention. Not that I could blame him. After twenty-six years spent serving a hellion in the Netherworld, high school drama probably felt trite and irrelevant.

But Sabine was anything but irrelevant to me.

"It turns out she's an ex-con. Or something like that. Tod doesn't know what she did, but…" I turned around to look for the reaper and wasn't surprised to realize he'd disappeared. I think the temptation to put a couple of the prepubescent punks out of their misery was a little too strong.

"Anyway, she definitely wants Nash back, and…" But before I could finish that thought, the kids descended on the snack bar, and my pity party was swallowed whole by the universal clamor for sugar and caffeine.

I pointed to the other register. "You take that one, and I'll cover this one."

Alec nodded, but when the first of the tween mob started shouting orders at him, he stared at his register screen like he'd never seen it before.

*Great. Awesome time to succumb to culture shock.* He'd been fine taking orders twenty minutes earlier, when there was no crowd. "Here. I'll take orders, you fill them." I stepped firmly between him and the register and shoved an empty popcorn bucket into his hands.

Alec scowled like he'd snap at me, then just nodded and turned toward the popcorn machine without a word.

I took several orders and filled the cups, but when I turned to grab popcorn from Alec, I found him staring at the machine, holding an empty bucket, like he'd rather wear it on his head than fill it.

"Alec…" I took the bucket from him and half filled it. "This is really not a good time for a breakdown." I squirted butter over the popcorn, then filled it the rest of the way and squirted more butter. "You okay?"

He frowned again, then nodded stiffly and grabbed another bucket.

I handed popcorn across the counter to the first customer and glanced up to find Emma jogging across the lobby toward me. "Hey, Pecker sent me to bail you out," she said, and several sixth graders giggled as she hopped up on the counter and swung her legs around to the business side. She thumped to the floor, and I started to thank her—until my gaze fell on four more extralarge buckets of popcorn now lined up on the counter.

*What the hell?*

I turned the register over to Emma and picked up a medium paper bag, stepping close to Alec so the customers wouldn't hear me. "They're not all ordering extralarge, Alec. You have to look at the ticket." I handed him a ticket for a medium popcorn and a large Coke, then scooped kernels into the bag. "Didn't they have tickets in the eighties? Or popcorn?"

Alec frowned. "This job is petty and pointless." He

dropped into a squat to examine the rows of folded bags and stacked buckets.

"Um, yeah." I filled another bag in a single scoop. "That's why they give it to students." And forty-five-year-old cultural infants.

Alec had been nineteen when he crossed into the Netherworld—the circumstances of which he still wasn't ready to talk about—but hadn't aged a day while he was there.

"What's his problem?" Emma asked, as I handed her the medium bag.

"He's just tired." Em didn't know who he really was, because I didn't want her to find out that he'd once possessed her body in a desperate attempt to orchestrate his own rescue from the Netherworld. She thought he was a friend of the family, crashing on our couch while he saved up enough money for a place of his own and some online college classes.

When I turned back to Alec, I found him leaning with his palms on the counter, staring at the ground between his feet.

"Alec? You okay?" I put one hand on his shoulder, and he jumped, then stared at me like I'd appeared out of nowhere. He shook his head like he was shaking off sleep, then blinked and looked around the lobby in obvious confusion.

"Yeah. Sorry. I didn't get much sleep last night. What were you saying?"

"I said you have to look at the ticket. You can't just serve everyone an extralarge."

Alec frowned and picked up the ticket on the counter

in front of him. "I know. I've been doing this a week now, Kay. I got this."

I grinned at his colloquialism. He only used them on his good days, when he felt like he was fitting into the human world again. And honestly, in spite of his fleeting moments of confusion, some days, Alec seemed to fit into my world much better than I did.

3

THE HALLWAY IS COLD *and sterile, and that should be my*
*first clue. School is always cluttered and too warm, but*
*today, cold and sterile makes sense.*

*I walk down the hall with Emma, but I stop when I*
*see them. She doesn't stop. She doesn't notice anything*
*wrong, but when I see them, I can't breathe. My chest*
*feels too heavy. My lungs pull in just enough air to keep*
*me conscious, but not enough to truly satisfy my need*
*for oxygen. Like satisfaction is even a possibility with*
*them standing there like that. In front of my locker, so I*
*can't possibly miss the act.*

*I can't see her face, because it's sucking on his, but I*
*know it's her. It's her hair, and her stupid guy-pants that*
*look hot on her the same way his T-shirts probably look*
*hot on her when that's all she's wearing. And I know*
*she's worn his shirts. Hell, she's worn* him, *and if they*

*weren't in the middle of the school, she'd probably be wearing him now. She practically is, anyway.*

*I stop in front of them so they can't ignore me, and she peels herself away and licks her lips, like she can't get enough of the taste of him, and I know that's true. My teeth grind together, and when I glance around, I realize there's a crowd.*

*Of course there's a crowd. Crowds gather for a show, and this is one hell of a show.*

*I say his name. I don't want to say it. I don't want to acknowledge him and what he's doing, but I can't stop myself. It won't be real unless he says it, and part of me believes he won't say it. He'll say the right words instead. He'll say he's sorry, and he'll look like he's sorry, and he'll be sorry for a very long time, but then everything will be okay again.*

*Instead, he shrugs and glances around at the crowd, grinning at the faces. The faces leer and blur together. I can't tell them apart, but it doesn't matter, because the crowd only has one face. Crowds only ever have one face. Et tu, Brute? It's the mob mentality, and I am Caesar, about to be stabbed.*

*Or maybe I've already been stabbed, and I'm too stupid to know I'm bleeding all over the floor. But I know I'm dying inside. He's killing me.*

*"Sorry, Kay," he says at last, and I hate him for using my nickname. It sounds intimate and friendly, but he just had his tongue in her mouth, and now I want to cut it out of his head. "Sorry," he repeats, while my face flames, and my world blurs with tears. "She knows what I like. And she delivers…"*

*They're laughing now, and even though the crowd only has one face, it has many jeering voices. And they're all laughing at me. Even Emma.*

*"I told you," she says, shaking her head as she tries to hold back a giggle, and I love her for trying, even if, in the end, the laughter can't be denied. It's not her fault. She's just playing her part, and the lines must be spoken, even if each word burns like an open wound.*

*"I told you it wasn't worth saving. You can't win the game if you won't even play. You have to deliver...."*

4

I SAT UP IN BED, sweating and cold, my heart beating so hard it practically bruised my sternum. I took a deep breath, threw the covers back, and stepped into my Betty Boop slippers, then padded silently down the hall and into the living room, where Alec lay on the couch with the blanket pulled over his head. His exposed feet were propped on the armrest at the opposite end, brown on top, and pale on the bottom. When I walked past him, his toes twitched, and I nearly jumped out of my skin.

In the kitchen, I got a glass of water, and I was on my way back across the living room when Alec folded the blanket back from his head and blinked up at me.

"Okay, that's starting to get creepy," I said, as he sat up.

"What?"

"You. Lying there awake but covered." I sank into my dad's recliner and tucked my feet beneath me. "It's like watching a corpse sit up in the morgue."

"Sorry." He ran one hand absently over his smooth, dark chest. Twenty-six years in the Netherworld may have scarred him on the inside, but his outside still looked good as new. "I can't sleep. Can't get used to the silence."

"What, did Avari sing you to sleep in the Netherworld?"

"Funny." Alec leaned forward with his elbows on his knees, his head sagging on his shoulders. "Once you get used to all the screaming at night, it's hard to go to sleep without it. Not that I actually slept every night."

"Are you serious?" The fresh crop of chill bumps on my arms had nothing to do with my bad dream, and everything to do with his living nightmare.

Alec shrugged and sat up to meet my gaze. "Hellions don't sleep, so I passed out whenever I got a chance. Whenever Avari was busy with someone else."

I started to explain that I was horrified by the screaming, not by his irregular sleep patterns, then decided I didn't want to know any more about either. So I kept my mouth shut.

"What about you?" he asked, as I sipped my water.

"Bad dream." I set the glass over the existing water ring on the end table.

"What about?"

My exhale sounded heavy, even to me. "I dreamed Nash dumped me for his ex-girlfriend, in front of the whole school, after eating her face in front of my locker."

"Literally?" Alec frowned, and I realized that where he'd spent the past quarter century, literal face eating might have been a real concern.

"No. That might actually have been better."

He leaned back on the couch, arms crossed over his bare chest. "I thought you dumped him."

"I did. Kind of." Nash and I were too complicated for simple explanations, and something told me that would only get worse, with his ex suddenly in the picture.

"But now you want him back? Even after what he did?"

Alec knew exactly what Avari had done with my body when he'd possessed me, because he'd been there in the Netherworld with the hellion when it happened. I couldn't blame Nash for what Avari had done, but I couldn't help blaming him for not telling me. And for not even trying to stop it from happening again. And again. And for lying to me about taking Demon's Breath. And for using his Influence against me.

Alec knew all of it—even the parts Emma and my dad didn't know—because I'd needed to talk to someone who knew about things that go bump in the Netherworld, but who wouldn't hate Nash on my behalf before I'd decided how I felt about him myself. Alec had been my only option for a confidant. Fortunately, he'd turned out to be a good one.

"Well, yeah. I never stopped wanting him." Trust was our new stumbling block, and as much as Nash meant to me, I couldn't truly forgive him until I knew I could trust him again. I sighed and ran one finger through the condensation on the outside of my glass. "And I guess I kind of assumed that when we were both ready, we'd get back together. But now, with Sabine back in the picture…" I swallowed a bitter pang of jealousy. "It hurt to see them together."

They shared a history I hadn't even known existed. A connection that predated my presence in Nash's life and made me feel…irrelevant. And it wasn't just sex. She'd known him before Tod died. That was practically a lifetime ago. Was Nash very different then? Would I have liked him?

Would he have let a demon possess Sabine, when they were together? Would he now?

"And the dream…" But I couldn't finish. Being publicly humiliated and rejected like that by someone who claimed to love me—that was a whole new kind of terror, and even the memory of the dream left me cold.

"Tod says they were, like, *obsessed* with each other, and now she's back, and it turns out they never really broke up. She's not just gonna bow out gracefully, is she?"

Alec shrugged. "Honestly, I don't have a lot of experience with human girls—you're the first one I've really talked to in twenty-six years. But I do know a bit about obsession—you might recall Avari's ongoing quest to possess your soul?"

"That does ring a bell…" My hand clenched around my glass, and I gulped from it, trying to drown the pit of lingering terror that had opened up in my stomach.

"Well, whether she's obsessed with him or actually in love with him—or both—she's probably not gonna just walk away," Alec said, when I finally set my glass down. "But really, that's a good thing, in a way."

I gaped at him. "In what universe does Nash's ex wanting him back qualify as a good thing?"

Alec leaned back against the cushions. "Think of it as a

second opinion on his value. If he wasn't worth the fight, wouldn't she just let him go? Wouldn't you?"

Hmm... Would I? *Should* I?

"How did you get so wise? You're like a giant Yoda, minus the pointy ears and green skin." I hesitated, eyeing him in curiosity. "They had *Star Wars* in the eighties, right?"

Alec laughed, and his deep brown eyes lit up. "Only the original trilogy. You sure know how to make a guy feel old." Then he frowned. "But I guess that makes sense. It's weird." He met my gaze again. "Physically, I'm still nineteen. But I'm old enough to be your dad."

I shook my head and grinned. "No way. My dad's a hundred and thirty." Though he didn't look a day over forty. "Why? Do you feel forty-five on the inside?"

Alec shook his head, holding my gaze with a serious, heavy sadness. "I feel way older, most of the time. Every day in the Netherworld was like a year, and I was there for something like twenty-six years. Doesn't even seem possible. Then, suddenly I'm out, and I'm here, and everything's different and fast and hard and shiny. I'm old and wise, according to some—" his eyes flashed in brief good humor on my behalf "—and in some ways, I feel ten thousand years old, because after everything I've seen, and everything I had to do to survive, shiny new Blu-ray disks and stereos that fit in your pocket seem so...irrelevant."

Alec shrugged again, looking lost. "But then sometimes I feel like a little kid, because these shiny bits of irrelevance are everyday parts of my life now, and half the time, I don't have a clue what they do."

"Wow." I grinned, trying to lighten the mood. "That was deep."

He returned my grin and raised a challenging eyebrow. "Isn't it past your bedtime?"

"You're sayin' I should listen to my elders?"

His smile died, and he glanced at the hands clasped in his lap, then back up at me. "I'm saying I wish I wasn't your elder." Another sigh. "I wish I hadn't lost twenty-six years of my life, and I wish to hell that it wasn't so hard to take advantage of what I have left."

Unfortunately, everyone he'd known before he left the human world was a quarter century older now, so he couldn't just show up on old friends' doorsteps—assuming he knew where to find them—with a smile and a suitcase. My dad and I were all Alec had at the moment, and we had no intention of cutting him loose.

But deep down, we all three knew that we couldn't replace his real family any more than my aunt and uncle had been able to replace my parents.

"I just wish I could turn back the clock and undo everything that went wrong."

I knew exactly how he felt.

TUESDAY MORNING, the second day of the spring semester, I was waiting in front of Nash's locker when he arrived, walking down the hall alone for the first time since I could remember. His two best friends were gone, and we'd broken up. He was alone and probably miserable. And I couldn't help wondering how he'd gotten to school, considering he didn't have a car and no longer had anyone to bum a ride from.

Surely he hadn't taken the bus with the freshmen.

"Hey." His voice was casual, and completely Influence free, but his eyes swirled slowly in genuine pleasure. He was happy to see me.

My pulse spiked a little at that knowledge, and I resisted a relieved smile, trying to think of a way to ask him about Sabine without admitting that I wanted to nail her into a crate and ship her to the South Pole. Even though I'd just met her. "Hey. Can we talk?"

"Yeah." Nash opened his locker, then unzipped his backpack. "Actually, I need to tell you something. I wanted to say this yesterday, but then we got interrupted, and…" He set his bag down without taking anything out of it and looked right into my eyes, so I could see the sincerity swirling in his. "Kaylee, I just want you to know that I'm clean. It sucks, and it's hard, especially when I'm home by myself with nothing else to think about. But I'm totally clean. And I'm going to stay that way."

My heart ached. Part of me wanted to hug him and forgive him and take him back right then, because I was afraid that if I didn't, I'd lose my chance. Sabine would move in, and the time-out that was supposed to give Nash a chance to get better and me a chance to deal with what happened would only end up giving her a way into his life.

But I couldn't just forget about everything he'd done. If I took him back before I was sure we were both ready, we could fall apart for real. Forever. Rushing in could ruin everything for both of us.

Of course, so could Sabine.

"I'm glad. That's really good, Nash," I said, hating how

lame I sounded. Did Hallmark make a card for former addict ex-boyfriends who were trying to stay clean?

"So…what did you want to talk about?" he asked, as I clung to the strap of my backpack like a life preserver. Why was I so nervous?

"I just…" I closed my eyes and took a deep breath, then made myself look at him. "How worried should I be about Sabine?"

At the mention of her name, Nash's irises exploded into motion, swirling so fast I couldn't interpret what he was feeling. And with sudden, frightening insight, I realized that was because he didn't *know* what he was feeling. Probably several conflicting emotions. But whatever they were, they were strong.

"Worried about her?" His irises went suddenly still, as he slammed the lid shut on his emotions, blocking me out. I couldn't blame him. Who wants to walk around looking like a giant mood ring? But I was desperate for a hint of what he really felt about her. And about me. I needed to know where I stood. "Why would you…"

But before he could finish, she was suddenly there, down the hall, shouting his name like she didn't care who heard. Or who turned to stare.

Sabine was fearless.

"Nash!" She jogged down the hall toward us, bag bouncing on her back, low-cut khakis barely hanging on to her hips. As she came to a stop, she reached into her hip pocket and pulled out a cell phone. Nash's cell phone. "You left this in my car. You know, you should really set it to autolock. Otherwise, all your information's just there for the taking…" Instead of handing him the phone, she stepped close and slid it slowly into his front left pocket, letting her fingers linger until he actually had to pull her hand from his pocket. Right there in the hall.

My face flamed. I could feel my cheeks burning and could see a scarlet half-moon at the bottom edge of my vision.

"Um...thanks," Nash said.

"Anytime," she purred, then finally seemed to notice me standing there. "Hey, Katie, what's up?" Her black eyes stared into mine, and I flashed back to my dream from the night before. Chill bumps popped up beneath my sleeves, and if I didn't know any better, I'd swear the fluorescent light overhead flickered just to cast deep shadows beneath her eyes.

It was everything I could do not to shudder. Something was wrong with her. How could Nash not see it? Looking into Sabine's eyes was like taking a breath with my head stuck inside the freezer.

"It's Kaylee," I said through gritted teeth, forcing the words out when what I really wanted was to excuse myself and walk away. Fast. "And we were talking."

"Oh, good!" She turned back to Nash, grinning like she'd just made a clever joke and I was the punch line, and I was ashamed of how relieved I was to no longer be the focus of her attention. "What are we talking about?"

"It's private," I said, my hand clenching around my backpack strap.

"Oh. Speaking of *private,* I actually slept pretty well last night, for once. I think I just needed to be *really* worn out to make it happen, you know?" She raised one brow at me, and I fought another chill as she turned to Nash. "Good thing your mom works nights now."

I reeled like I'd been punched in the gut. My breath deserted me, and my lungs refused to draw in more air.

"Kaylee..." Nash tried to reach for me, but I pushed him away and stumbled backward into the lockers. When I could finally breathe, I looked right into his eyes, silently demanding that he let me see the truth.

"You were with her last night?"

"More like early this morning," Sabine said casually, like she couldn't tell I was upset. But she knew exactly what she was doing. I could tell from the way she watched for my reaction, rather than his. She was studying me. Sizing up the competition. And deep inside, I knew I should have been happy about that—that she considered me serious competition.

But closer to the surface, I was thoroughly pissed. Warm flames of rage battled the chill that resurged every time I glanced at her, until I felt half frozen, half roasted, and thoroughly confused.

"We had a lot to catch up on," she added, while Nash's jaw clenched. "That's not a problem, is it? I mean, you guys broke up, right? That's what Nash said..."

"Sabine," he said at last. "I'll see you at lunch. I need to talk to Kaylee before the bell."

She shrugged and smiled like she hadn't just ruined my whole day. Or like she'd meant to. "I gotta head to class, anyway. I'm trying out this punctuality thing. The guidance counselor says it's all the rage." She winked at him—actually winked!—then turned to squint at my cheek, like I'd suddenly grown a wart. "Hold still,

Kay…" My pulse spiked at her unwelcome use of my nickname. "You've got an eyelash…."

Sabine reached out and brushed one finger slowly, deliberately across my cheek, but her gaze never left mine. In fact, it strengthened, as if she was trying to see through my eyes into the back of my skull.

I wanted to pull away, but I couldn't. I could only stare back as that instant stretched into eternity, and I stood frozen.

And for a second—just a single moment—her eyes suddenly looked darker, and that horrified, humiliated pain from my dream flashed through my head and throbbed miserably in my heart.

"Sabine…" Nash whispered, in the warning tone he usually saved for Tod.

She blinked, then smiled. "There. Got it." She held her finger up, then let her hand drop too fast for me to see the alleged eyelash. "Later, Kay…" she said, and I stood in shock as she sauntered down the hall without a glance back.

For a moment, Nash and I just looked at each other. I couldn't think past the surreal second that his ex-girlfriend's finger had lingered on my cheek. "What the hell was that?"

Nash sighed. "She's… Kaylee, Sabine's had it pretty rough. She doesn't remember her real parents, and she's been in more than a dozen foster homes, and she's never had many friends, so—"

"Maybe that's because she's a creepy bitch!" I spat, and Nash's eyes widened. He was almost as surprised by my snap judgment as I was. It usually took much longer than that for me to decide I didn't like someone, but Sabine had definitely found a shortcut.

"She's rough around the edges, I know, but that's not her fault."

"Tod told me her sob story," I snapped. "He also said she's a convicted criminal."

He frowned and his eyes narrowed slightly. He was looking for more. "He say anything else?"

"Yeah," I said, and Nash's eyes swirled in panic. "He said she was your first, and you two practically shared the same skin for, like, a year."

"Oh." Nash sagged against his locker, but he looked oddly relieved. "That was years ago, Kaylee. I haven't seen her since the summer before my sophomore year."

"You were with her last night," I reminded him, hating the warble in my voice.

"We were just talking," he insisted. "I swear."

"All night?"

He shrugged. "We had a lot to catch up on."

"Like, her latest felony and your latest conquest? Did you two laugh about me?" My heart throbbed, and suddenly I was sure that's exactly what they'd done. They'd laughed at me all night long. "Am I your little inside joke? 'Poor, frigid Kaylee has to be *possessed* before she'll let anyone touch her.'"

I started to walk away, tears forming in my eyes in spite of my best effort to stop them. But Nash grabbed my arm. "Kaylee, wait." He pulled me back, and I let him because I wanted him to deny it. Desperately.

What the hell was wrong with me? I wanted to be

wrong, but I was terrified I was right. So scared of the truth that I could hardly breathe.

Nash looked down into my eyes, like he was looking for something specific in the shades of blue that were probably twisting out of control at the moment. "Damn it, Sabine…" he mumbled. Then, to me, "I'll talk to her. She doesn't mean anything by it. It's just habit."

"What's habit?" I was obviously missing something.

He closed his eyes and exhaled. "Nothing. Never mind." When he looked at me again, his eyes were infuriatingly still. "Look, Sabine and I haven't seen each other in a long time, and we were just getting caught up. Nothing happened, and nothing's going to happen. I know I messed up with you, but I'm trying to make it right, and I'm not going to let anything get in the way of that. Not even Sabine. Okay?"

"I…" I wanted to believe him. But I was so scared that he was lying. And if he was, I'd never know it. "Yeah. I just… I have to get to algebra."

"I'll see you at lunch?" he asked, as I walked away.

"Yeah." But he'd see her, too.

I dropped into my chair in Algebra II and stared at the wall, trying to ignore the whispers around me. No one knew the truth about what had happened to Doug and Scott, but they all knew that Nash and I had been involved. And that we'd broken up. And half of them had probably seen him getting out of Sabine's car.

Emma thought our classmates' theories were hilarious, and probably much worse than what had actually happened. But she was wrong. They couldn't begin to imagine anything as awful as how Doug had died. How Scott was now living.

After wallowing in unpleasant thoughts for a while, I looked at the clock. Class should have started eight minutes ago, but Mr. Wesner hadn't shown up. And neither had Emma. But just as I glanced toward the door, Emma came in from the hall, eyes wide, cheeks flushed.

She dropped into the chair next to mine, and I started talking, eager to share my misery with someone I knew I could trust. "You're not going to believe what just happened," I said, leaning in so no one else would hear.

"You're not going to believe this, either," she interrupted. "Mr. Wesner's dead. The custodian found him this morning, slumped over his desk." She turned and pointed toward the front of the class. "*That* desk."

5

AT FIRST, I JUST SAT THERE. Stunned. Staring at Mr. Wesner's desk. And before I could ask for details, a crowd had formed around us, everyone looking at Emma.

"Wesner's dead?"

"He died here?"

"No way," one of the girls from the pom squad—Leah something or other—insisted. "I was here early to sell raffle tickets, and I didn't see anything. No police. No ambulance. No body. It's just a stupid rumor."

Em shook her head and gestured for silence. "It's true. I heard Principal Goody telling Mr. Wells in the office when I went in for a late slip. One of the custodians came in at six this morning to let a repairman into the cafeteria before breakfast, and he found Mr. Wesner. Right there." She pointed at the desk again, and every head pivoted, all voices silenced now, except for Emma's.

"Goody said the custodian called her, and the

ambulance was already here by the time she got here at, like, dawn. They took him before any of us got here, but they're still in the office scrambling for a sub."

"Damn," someone said from behind me, and while I watched, the same stunned, vaguely frightened expression seemed to spread from face to face.

"How'd he die?" Brant Williams asked, clutching the back of my chair.

Emma shrugged and glanced at the desk again, and again, all eyes tracked her gaze. "I don't know. A stroke or something, I'm guessing. He was probably here all night."

"Ugh. That is *so* morbid," Chelsea Simms said, yet never paused in the notes she was taking for the school paper. But I couldn't help wondering if they'd actually let her run the story.

"This whole *year* has been morbid," Leah added, eyes round and a little scared, and everyone else nodded.

*You have no idea….*

Ironically, Mr. Wesner's stroke, or heart attack, or whatever, was the only normal death our school had experienced so far. Yet it was the one that most creeped people out.

Before anyone could ask any more questions, Mr. Wells, the vice principal, came in and officially announced Mr. Wesner's unfortunate, unexpected demise, then said that he'd be watching the class until a substitute could be found.

Wells seemed disinclined to dig through Mr. Wesner's desk for his lesson plan, though, so he gave us a free period. Which meant we were free to spend the period imagining Mr. Wesner slumped over the desk our vice principal obviously didn't want to sit behind.

"Can you believe this?" Em whispered, scooting her desk closer to mine. "Yesterday he was fine, and today he's dead. Right here in his own classroom."

"Weird, huh?" And I couldn't help wondering why Tod hadn't told me someone was scheduled to die at my school, just as a courtesy. If I'd been there when it actually happened, I'd have been compelled to sing—or scream—for his soul.

"And sad. Makes me feel bad about not bothering with homework for most of last semester. Do you think he was grading midterms when he died?"

I frowned when I realized she was serious. "Emma, your test did *not* give him a stroke."

"I think you underestimate my incomprehension of sign, cosign, and tangent," she said, obviously trying to lighten the mood. And failing miserably. Her eyes narrowed as she watched me. "Everyone else is completely weirded out by this. Why isn't this freaking you out, Kaylee?"

I could only shrug. "It is. It's just that…" I lowered my voice and leaned closer to her. "I've seen a lot of death in the past few months, and every bit of it has been weird and *wrong*. After all that, it's actually kind of good to know that Mr. Wesner died at his own time and that his soul isn't being tortured for all of eternity. For once, death worked the way it was supposed to, and honestly, that's kind of a relief." Even if it did happen at school.

"I guess I can understand that," Emma said at last. But I had my doubts. "Okay, enough of this. I'm depressing myself." Emma shook her head, then forced her gaze to meet mine. "So...what were you going to say earlier?"

My news didn't seem quite as catastrophic as it had before I'd found out my algebra teacher died, but the very thought of Nash and Sabine alone at his house still made my blood boil. "Nash spent most of the night with Sabine."

"With her? Like, *with* her, with her?"

I shrugged. "He says they were just talking, but she's on the prowl, I swear. She actually reminded me that Nash and I broke up. Like that gives her some prior claim or something."

"Well, yeah, technically. You're both his exes now, so..." Em hesitated, obviously wanting to say something I wouldn't want to hear. "Does he seem interested in her again?"

"His mouth says no, but his eyes... His irises churn like the ocean every time I say her name. There's definitely something still there, but I can't tell exactly what it is. It's strong, though. And she was spewing innuendo like some kind of gossip geyser, saying how great it is that Nash's mom works nights. She's making up for more than just lost time. Plus..." I felt like an idiot, saying it out loud, but it was the truth. "She's creepy."

"What do you mean, creepy?"

I scratched at a name carved into the corner of my desk. "I don't know. She gives me chills. I think there's something wrong with her. And Nash knows about it, whatever it is. He told me he'd talk to her. Like, he'd *take care* of her. I think she's seriously unstable."

Em raised both brows at me, and I rolled my eyes. "I

know, that sounds hypocritical coming from me." Usually I was hypersensitive to references to mental instability, because I'd spent a week locked up in the mental health ward a year and a half ago. "I don't mean she's crazy. I mean she's...unbalanced. Dangerous. She's a criminal, Em."

Emma shrugged. "Tod says she did her time."

"Yeah. A few months in a halfway house. I'd hardly call that paying for her crimes."

"You don't even know what her crimes are."

"I'm guessing theft. She probably stole someone's boyfriend."

Emma laughed, and I gave in to a grin of my own. "I don't think you have anything to worry about, Kaylee. Whatever they had can't compare to what you and Nash have been through together. I mean, she's human, right? How well can she possibly know him?"

I sat a little straighter. Emma was right. Sabine was a nonissue. I'd faced down two hellions in the past four months, not to mention assorted Netherworld monsters. Compared to all that, what was one stupid ex-girlfriend?

Right?

BY LUNCHTIME, news of Mr. Wesner's death had already been chewed up and regurgitated by the masses so many times that it bore little resemblance to the story Emma originally reported. In any other school, during any other year, a teacher's death would have been a headline all on its own. But we'd already lost four students, and the yearbook's In Memoriam page was getting regular updates. So while some of the snippets of conversation I overheard were flavored with either disbelief or morbid curiosity, most people sounded kind of relieved that life now made a little more sense than it had the day before.

After all, Mr. Wesner was pretty old and overweight enough that he'd wheezed with practically every breath. In a weird way, his death seemed to be giving people a sense of security, as if the world had somehow been shoved back into alignment with the natural order of things, wherein old, unhealthy people died, and young people talked about it over nachos and cafeteria hamburgers.

I paid for my food, then grabbed a Coke from the vending machine and made my way outside, where I found Nash sitting at a table on the far side of the quad. Alone. Again.

I felt bad for him. With the rest of the football team still reeling from their double loss, no one seemed to know what to say to the last surviving musketeer. But Nash's solitude was a definite advantage to me. I headed his way, hoping Emma would be late again and that Sabine would walk off the edge of the earth so he and I could talk.

His eyes lit up when I sat on the bench across from him, and some of my tension eased. "Hey, did you hear about Mr. Wesner?" he asked. "Don't you have him this year?"

"First period." I twisted the cap off my bottle. "Em's the one who broke the story."

After that, he seemed at a loss for what else to say.

I knew exactly what *I* wanted to say—what I wanted to

know—but I questioned the wisdom of actually asking. What's that they say about beating a dead horse?

But after a few sips of my soda and a lot of awkward silence from Nash, my curiosity overwhelmed my common sense. "So…what'd she do?"

"What'd who do?" Nash asked, around a mouthful of burger.

"Sabine. What'd she get arrested for?"

Nash groaned and swallowed his bite. "Kaylee, I don't want to talk about Sabine. Not again. Not now."

"Well, you sure had plenty to say *to* her." And in that moment, I hated Sabine for turning me into a paranoid, desperate shrew. Even more than I already half hated her for coming between me and Nash. But that wouldn't stop me from asking what I needed to know. "How late was she at your house?" I'd never been there past midnight when his mom wasn't home. If she was there after one, I was going to lose it. You don't stay at your ex's house alone with him past one in the morning to *talk*.

Nash exhaled, long and low. "Burglary and vandal-ism."

It did not escape my notice that he'd answered my first question, rather than the latest one. Not a good sign.

"What'd she steal?" I took the top bun off my hamburger and squirted ketchup onto the naked patty, just to have something to do with my hands.

"Nothing, really." Nash hesitated, poking his limp fries with a fork. "She took a baseball bat, but she didn't actually leave with it."

"What does that even mean?" I dropped the bun back onto my burger and tried to pin him with my glare. "She took something, but she didn't really take it. What happened? She hit someone with it?" The poor, defenseless girlfriend of some guy she had a crush on, maybe?

"Not a person. A car. Thus, the vandalism charge."

"She beat up someone's car? Why?"

Nash dropped his fork onto his tray, exasperated. "Kaylee, that's really her business. If you want to know any more, you'll have to ask her." He hesitated again, then met my gaze across the table. "Only don't, okay? That's all in her past, and she's seriously trying to make a fresh start here. You wouldn't want some stranger asking questions about your week in mental health, would you?"

*Damn.*

"Okay, fair enough. So long as she didn't assault some-*one.* I mean, if your ex hates me and is dangerous, you'd tell me that, right?"

Nash flinched, and my stomach pitched.

"What? I thought she just beat up a car?"

He set the remaining half of his burger down. "The assault charge came later, when she got picked up for violating probation."

"She hit a cop?" My horror knew no bounds. Why on earth would he have ever gone out with a creepy, violent thief and vandal, much less slept with her?

"No!" He leaned forward and lowered his pitch when the cafeteria door opened behind me and new voices came into the quad. "Kaylee, you're making this into a much bigger deal than it really is. Some asshole from our school in Fort Worth tried to make her do something she didn't want to do. If she'd told me about it, I'd have taken care of him."

The flash of pure fury in Nash's eyes told me how badly he wished he'd had that chance.

"But she's stubborn—like someone *else* I know—and she wanted to handle it herself. So she pounded on his car with his own bat. She got probation for that, but a few months later she missed curfew and was picked up for violating her parole. While she was in the detention center, waiting to see the judge, some idiot picked a fight with her in the cafeteria. Sabine broke her jaw with a lunch tray."

Words utterly deserted me. Concepts were even a bit iffy for a minute there. Then, suddenly, I couldn't speak fast enough.

"She broke someone's jaw with a lunch tray." I leaned forward, whispering fiercely. "She hates me, Nash—I can see it when she looks at me—and in case you haven't noticed, we all share a lunch period. Where there happens to be an abundance of lunch trays."

"She's not..." Nash stopped, closed his eyes, then started over. "She doesn't hate you, Kaylee. She's jealous of you. But she's not gonna hit you. Even if she wanted to, she wouldn't, because she knows that'd piss me off."

"Exactly what part of that is supposed to make me feel better?" Though, honestly, hearing that she was jealous of me did make me feel a *teeny, tiny* bit better.

He shrugged, but still looked pale and miserable. "I'm just answering your questions. What more do you want?"

What did I want? I wanted Nash. The old Nash, who'd loved me and wanted to protect me, and had risked both his life and his soul to help me. But I didn't know— couldn't *believe*—he'd had time to truly get himself back together. I wanted Sabine to transfer back to wherever she'd come from. I wanted to turn back time and make things right again.

"This isn't about what I want," I said at last. *When in doubt, change the subject.* "This is about what *she* wants. She wants you, Nash. You know that, right? Or is there some kind of testosterone-powered mind shield that prevents you from seeing her for what she is?"

Nash frowned and let a moment pass in tense silence before he answered. "I know what she wants, Kaylee. But that doesn't mean she's going to get it."

I should have been relieved. I should have been dancing on the table in joy. But something in his eyes said my celebration would have been premature. "She will if you keep letting her hang out in your room till two in the morning." *Please, please correct me. Say she wasn't there that late.*

But no correction came.

"You're not going to stop hanging out with her, are you?" My voice held a numbing combination of anger and disbelief.

For a moment, he watched me, studying my expression. "Are you asking me to?"

*Damn it, why is this conversation so hard?* I didn't have any right to tell him who not to hang out with! How pissed would I be if he told me to stop hanging out with Emma or Alec?

The answers were there, and they were clear, but I didn't like them.

"Nash, I just… I can't see any way for this to play out

without one of the three of us—or maybe all three of us—getting hurt." And possibly actually injured.

Nash exhaled heavily and stared at the table for several seconds before finally dragging his gaze up to meet mine. "Kaylee, I still love you, and I still want you back. I miss you like you wouldn't believe, and I swear that not seeing you for the past couple of weeks—not even hearing your voice—hurt worse than the nausea and headaches combined. It kills me to sit here knowing I no longer have the right to lean over this table and kiss you. I want to be the first person you call the next time something goes wrong. I want to know that you're eventually going to be able to forgive me. And I'm not gonna do anything to jeopardize that possibility." He took a deep breath and held my gaze. "But Sabine needs me…"

"No…" I shook my head, but he spoke over me, refusing to be interrupted.

"Yes, she does. You may not like it or understand it, but that doesn't mean it's not true. And right now, I need her, too."

"You *need* her?" My nightmare came roaring back like a train about to run me over, and suddenly I wondered if it was more premonition than dream. I summoned anger to disguise the deep ache in my chest. "In what way do you *need* her exactly, and do *not* tell me she scratches the right itch, or I swear I will walk away right now, and this time I won't look back, Nash."

He exhaled again and his features suddenly looked heavy, like he couldn't have formed a smile if he'd wanted to. "I'm not sleeping with her, Kaylee. I swear on my soul."

I would have been relieved by his admission—and the confirmation I saw in his slowly swirling eyes—but I was too confused to process much of anything in that moment. "Then why would you possibly need her?"

Nash closed his eyes and inhaled deeply. Then he met my gaze over our forgotten lunches. "I'm two weeks clean, and every single day feels like starting all over. It never gets any easier, but yesterday truly sucked for me. Seeing you and not being able to touch you—hardly getting to talk to you... That made everything harder. Including willpower. Last night, I was one breath away from paying someone to cross me into the Netherworld."

I opened my mouth to ask who he could possibly have hired as a Netherworld ferry, but he continued before I could.

"Don't ask. There are places you can go. People—kind of—who will do it for the right price."

Fresh chill bumps crawled over my skin, followed by a bitter wash of revulsion. I hated it that he even knew things like that.

"But my point," Nash continued, "is that I was trying to talk myself out of it when she showed up on my porch. And we just talked. I swear that's all that happened, but it was enough. She gave me something to think about, other than how badly I wanted a hit, or an hour alone with you."

"So she's a substitute for me?" Suddenly my throat felt thick and hot. Bruised by the words I made myself swallow. How was I supposed to trust the two of them alone together, knowing that? "That's not fair, Nash. I can't..."

"I know. You're not ready to be alone with me, and I

understand that. I deserve it. But I need *someone*, Kaylee. I need a friend. And in case you haven't noticed, no one else is exactly beating down the door to talk to me right now." His wide-armed gesture took in the entire table, still empty except for us.

"They just don't know what to say," I insisted. "People never know what to say when someone close to you dies, and it's even worse this time, thanks to the rumors about Scott." Half the student body thought he and I were cheating on Nash and my cousin, Sophie, and that we'd been caught the day of Scott's infamous breakdown.

"I know, but that doesn't change anything. I've been alone and sick from withdrawal for two weeks, and when I get back to school, people just stare at me and whisper."

"I get it." How could I not? But I had Emma and Alec to help distract me from Nash's absence. And even Tod had been coming around more lately... "What about Tod?" I asked, as the thought occurred to me. "Why can't you just hang out with your brother?"

"Because he won't talk to me. I haven't even seen him since that night. After the Winter Carnival." When he'd punched Nash for letting Avari possess me over and over. "Since he can't do anything else for Addy, he's decided that he's your white knight, and I don't think he's going to forgive me until you do."

Wow. "I had no idea."

Nash leaned forward and crossed his arms over the table, staring directly into my eyes. "I'm not making a play for your sympathy. I know I got myself into this. But I need someone to talk to—someone to just hang out with—and I know you're not ready to play that role for me yet. But Sabine is. And she needs me for the same reason. She's new here, and she doesn't know anyone else, and she's trying to pull herself together. Just like I am."

I held his gaze, my next question stalled on my tongue, where I wanted it to wither and die. But I had to know. "Did you love her, Nash?"

His pause was barely noticeable. But I noticed. "Yeah. We were only fifteen, but yeah, I loved her." He blinked, then met my gaze again, letting me see the truth swirling in his. "But that was years ago. She's just a friend now, Kaylee."

My leg bounced under the table, uncontrollably. "Have you told her that?"

"Yeah. And eventually, it'll actually sink in. Look, I know she makes you uncomfortable, and I'm sorry about that. And if it's going to mean losing my second chance with you, I'll tell her to go away. But I'm asking you not to make me do that."

I bristled. "I can't make you do anything, Nash." Though the same could not be said for him and his Influence.

He frowned. "You know what I mean."

"You want my blessing to strike up a friendship with your ex-girlfriend. The first girl you ever slept with, who's still in love with you and doesn't even deny it. Does that sum it up?"

Another long exhale. "Yeah. I think that covers it."

If I said yes, I'd be giving him permission to spend time with his hot, willing ex. If I said no, I'd be denying him what he needs to work through his addiction.

*How did I even get into this mess?*

He'd left me no real choice, unless I was ready to let him go. Or willing to pretend that the past six weeks of my life had never happened. And I couldn't do that, even if I wanted to. Not yet.

"Fine. Hang out with Sabine. But if this thing goes beyond friendship and support—"

*I'll what?* Leave him to find solace in her arms? Or her bed? That's exactly what she wanted, and in spite of Nash's good intentions, it wouldn't take him long to get over me, considering the kind of comfort she'd offer. I had no doubt of that.

"It won't," Nash insisted, saving me from grasping for a viable threat, and I hated the sudden surge of relief in his eyes. How could he not see what she was really like?

"Whatever. But don't expect me to spend time with the two of you." Though maybe Tod would, if I asked him. He couldn't watch them every second, but surely he'd see enough to report back on the true nature of their relationship….

*Great, now I'm spying on Nash.* I should have been ashamed. Instead, I was just…scared. Scared of losing him—even though I'd pushed him away—because now she was there to catch him.

"Just…be careful, okay? You may be looking for some kind of Netherworldly AA sponsor, but she's looking for trouble. I saw it in her eyes."

Nash's brows shot up, and a smile tugged at one side of his mouth. "That's not what you saw in her eyes. There's something else we need to talk about, but I don't want to do it here."

However, before he could elaborate, footsteps sounded

at my back. A second later, Sabine appeared on my right, then settled onto the bench next to Nash. Her silverware clattered as she dropped her tray on the table.

"I don't know how you guys can eat this shit. It's an open campus, right? Let's go get some real burgers."

"It *is* an open campus," Nash said, both brows raised. "I almost forgot." The prohibition against off-campus lunch—the result of a wreck in the parking lot the second week of school—had expired with the fall semester.

"There's only twenty minutes left in lunch." It was all I could do to speak to her civilly. Every time I looked at her, I saw her making out with Nash in front of my locker, and that bitter, acrid fear from my dream sloshed around in my stomach, rotting the remains of my breakfast.

"Yeah, but you have study hall next, right?" Sabine said, ignoring me in favor of Nash. "And a decent burger would totally be worth a tardy in Spanish."

Nash glanced at me for an opinion, but I only shook my head. I couldn't afford another tardy in English. "Maybe tomorrow," he said at last, and Sabine scowled.

"Fine. But I'm not going to eat this crap." She shoved her tray across the table, and one corner of it knocked my open soda over. Coke poured from the bottle and splash-fizzed all over the front of my shirt. I jumped up to avoid getting drenched, and Sabine stood, too.

"Here, take my napkin." She plucked a single, thin cafeteria napkin from her tray and dropped it onto the table, where it was instantly soaked.

I glared at Nash and would have been appeased a bit by

how miserable he looked—if I weren't busy blotting my shirt, while Coke pooled where I'd sat a second earlier.

"I'll get more napkins," he muttered, then jogged toward the cafeteria, leaving me alone with Sabine.

"Sorry about the mess." Sabine stepped calmly around the table and added Nash's napkin to the puddle on my bench seat, apparently oblivious to everyone else in the quad now staring at us. "I just needed a chance to talk to you, girl-to-girl," she said, stepping too close to me so no one else would hear. "I figure it's best to get this out in the open."

"What?" I couldn't think beyond the cold, sticky spots on my shirt.

"It's cute, how he still thinks he loves you. Very chivalrous. Very Nash. But if you're not gonna make your move, don't blame me for making mine." She shrugged, and I saw that dark flash of...something in her eyes again. "Love, war, and all that. Right?"

Was she serious? Was this an open declaration of her intent to take my boyfriend? My kind-of boyfriend? Just like that?

My mouth opened and closed. *Say something!* I couldn't let her have the last word—that first little victory.

"So...which is this?" I asked, frustrated to realize that I sounded shell-shocked. "Love, or war?"

Sabine's smooth forehead wrinkled in surprise. "Both!" She smiled, a glaring ray of sunshine beneath storm-cloud eyes. "When it's good, it's always both. And Nash is so very, very *good*." Her eyes widened in mock regret, like she'd just let some vital secret out of the bag. "Oh, but you wouldn't know, would you?"

My face flushed. "He told you…?" Hadn't he already humiliated me enough?

Sabine shook her head slowly, exaggerating a show of sympathy. "He didn't have to. You may as well have a shiny white *V* stamped on your forehead."

Suddenly I hated her. Truly hated her, in spite of my generally forgiving temperament and everything Nash swore she'd been through.

Unfortunately, my abject hatred saw fit to express itself in utter speechlessness.

"Anyway, I don't have many girlfriends, so when this is all over, if you wanna hang out, I'm totally willing to let bygones be…well, bygone." She watched me expectantly—completely seriously—and I could only stare until Sabine blinked and shrugged again. "Or not. Either way, good luck!"

She reached out with her right hand and shook mine before I recovered the presence of mind to jerk away from her grip. When my skin touched hers, Sabine blinked, and her eyes stayed closed just an instant too long. When they opened and focused on me, her smile swelled, her irises darkened, and my chill bumps returned with a vengeance.

I pulled away from her and almost backed into Emma. "What happened?" Em asked, holding out a handful of napkins.

"I knocked her Coke over," Sabine said, as Nash jogged across the grass toward us. They soaked up the mess while I carried the soggy remains of my lunch to the trash can against the wall, desperate to put some distance between me and my new least favorite person in the whole world. In either world.

At least Avari'd never invaded my school.

"What the hell was that?" I whispered under my breath, as I dumped my empty bottle and my ruined hamburger into the can.

"*That* was Sabine," Tod said from my left, and I jumped, nearly dropping my sticky tray.

"Something's wrong with her," I whispered, when I'd recovered from the surprise. "If she wasn't human, I'd swear that…"

"Human?" Tod's brows rose. "She's not human, Kay. Not even close. Nash didn't tell you?"

*Crap.* He'd tried to tell me something about Sabine. Tried twice, but she'd suddenly shown up to prevent him both times. "What is she?" I said, turning to watch the cleanup effort under way at our table as my heart tried to sink into my stomach.

"She's your worst Nightmare, Kaylee," Tod said, his frown widening. "Literally."

I STOMPED THROUGH the empty hall, each step putting the cafeteria farther behind me. But I couldn't outrun anger and humiliation.

Sabine wasn't human. The one advantage I'd thought I had over her was that Nash and I had bonded through a mutual lack of humanity, which set us apart from everyone else at school. I knew what he really was and what he could do. I knew things about him that he could never tell anyone else.

But evidently, so did she. And Nash hadn't bothered to tell me.

Oh, he'd started to a couple of times, but I couldn't help thinking that if he'd really wanted me to know, he wouldn't have let Sabine's timely interruptions stop him.

Tod had started to tell me everything, but I'd cut him off. I wanted to hear it from Nash, when we had enough time and privacy for me to demand real answers. I needed to yell at him, but I didn't want to do it in front of Sabine. I couldn't let her know that her declaration was getting to me, nor was I willing to let her see me mad at Nash. She would only take that wedge and drive it deeper.

I turned the corner and stomped past two open classroom doors, ignoring the chair squeaks and whispers from inside as my thoughts raced, my cheeks flaming with anger. The door to the parking lot called to me from the end of the hall. There were only five minutes left in lunch, and then I could escape into my English class, where no one could challenge me, lie to me, or threaten to take my boyfriend.

I had both hands on the door's press bar when Nash shout-whispered my name from behind. "Kaylee, wait!" I froze, then turned slowly. So much for escape.

He jogged to catch up with me and I crossed both arms over my chest, displaying my anger, in case he hadn't picked up on it yet.

"She's not human?" I demanded softly, when he came to a stop inches away. "Is that what you were going to tell me?"

"Along with some specifics, yeah." He shrugged apologetically. "I tried to tell you earlier, but…"

"Sabine got in the way, right? I have a feeling that's about to become routine."

Nash exhaled slowly. "Can we go somewhere and talk? Please? I want to explain everything, but I need to be able to speak to you alone for more than a few minutes at a time." And from the frustrated twist of color in his eyes, I knew he wanted to talk about more than just

Sabine's species. We hadn't really spoken—not like we used to—in more than two weeks.

I missed talking to him.

"Please," he repeated. "Skipping one English class won't hurt anything."

Talking to him without Sabine around was *exactly* what I needed. I opened my mouth to say yes—then snapped my jaw closed before I could form a single word, terrified by the sudden, familiar thread of pain and primeval need winding its way up my throat.

*No!*

"Kaylee?" Nash whispered, while I glanced around the hall frantically. It was empty, but the dark panic inside me continued to swell. Someone nearby was going to die. Soon, based on the strength of the scream clawing its way up my throat.

I clamped one hand over my mouth and aimed a wide-eyed, desperate look at Nash. He knew the signs. His brow furrowed and his irises began to swirl with brown and green eddies of distress. "Who is it? Can you tell?"

I rolled my eyes and gestured with one hand at the empty hall at his back, trying to swallow the raw pain scraping its way toward my mouth as the scream demanded its exit.

Nash whirled around, and when he reached for my free hand, I let him have it. We raced past first one closed classroom door, then another, stopping to peek through the windows, but found nothing unusual. Until we got to the third door. I peered through the glass over Nash's shoulder to see Mrs. Bennigan slumped over at her desk, where she'd obviously fallen asleep during her lunch break. Her back rose and fell with each breath.

"Is it her?" Nash whispered, but I couldn't tell with the closed door separating us. So he pushed it open softly.

Shadows enveloped the sleeping teacher like a cocoon of darkness, where there'd been nothing a second before. Panic crashed over me, cold and unyielding. The scream reverberated in my head with blinding pain. A thin ribbon of sound began to leak from between my sealed lips, then spilled between the fingers covering them.

My hand clenched Nash's. Mrs. Bennigan was going to die. Any minute. And there was nothing we could do without condemning someone else to her fate instead. Because while Nash and I—a male and a female *bean sidhe*—could work together to restore a person's soul, we couldn't save one life without taking another.

"Come on." Nash took off down the hall, and I let him tug me all the way into the parking lot, one hand still clamped over my mouth. The urge to scream faded a little with each step, but even when the school door closed behind us—locking us out—the demand was still there, the unvoiced scream still scratching the back of my throat and reverberating in my teeth.

"Are you okay?" he asked, and I shook my head, clenching my teeth so hard my jaw ached. Of course I wasn't okay. Someone was dying—another teacher—and there was nothing I could do but wait for her soul to be claimed by whichever reaper had come for her, so the screaming fit would pass.

"Can I…? Will you let me help?" He stepped in front of me, blocking my view of the hall through the glass door, but I shook my head again. He couldn't help without using his Influence, and I couldn't let him do that to me again. Even with the best of intentions.

And anyway, I didn't need any help. I'd been handling it on my own just fine.

But when he pulled me close and silently wrapped his arms around me, I let him hold me. He felt so good. So warm and strong, as I battled the dark need trying to fight its way free from my body. So long as he didn't talk, holding me was fine. Holding me was *good*. It reminded me of the way things used to be between us, and that gave me something to think about, other than the fact that Mrs. Bennigan sat alone in her empty classroom, dying. And no one else had any idea.

The bell rang while Nash still held me, and for a moment, the shrill sound of it battled the ruthless screech still ringing inside my head. He pulled me to one side, out of sight from the hall, and I twisted in his grip to peek through the door.

The hall filled quickly, but I saw no faces. I couldn't tear my focus from that open doorway, waiting for someone to go inside and find her. And finally, as the excruciating pain began to fade in my throat and my jaw began to loosen, someone did. A freshman girl I knew only by sight stepped into the classroom.

I opened my mouth and inhaled. Nash's grip on me tightened from behind, offering wordless comfort. And maybe taking a little for himself.

And only seconds after she'd entered the room, the girl raced back into the hall. Her shout was muted by the glass between us and was only a fraction of the shrill sound I could have produced, but the crowd in the hallway froze. The dull static of gossip went silent. Everyone turned to look.

Nash pulled me away from the door as the first teacher came running, and I slid down the brick wall, my jacket catching on the rough edges. For the first time, I noticed the cold, and that my nose was running. "Are you okay?" he asked again, dropping to the ground in front of me, and that time I could answer.

"No. And neither is Mrs. Bennigan."

"What are the chances that this is a coincidence?" he asked, and I sucked in a deep breath, as if I'd actually emptied my lungs on the unvoiced scream.

"I don't believe in coincidence." Not anymore. "And even if I did, this is too much. Two teachers in one day? Something's wrong." I looked up to find a steady, tense swirl of green snaking through his irises. "Any idea what?"

He shook his head. "And I'm not sure I want to know. We've had enough to deal with this year, and I'm not..." His voiced faded into pained silence and he blinked, then started over. "Besides, this has nothing to do with us. Something's obviously going on, but it could be bad bean dip in the teachers' lounge, for all we know. Or some weird virus Wesner passed to Bennigan. Don't they sing in the same church choir, or something?"

I nodded slowly, trying to convince myself. Just because we'd lost four classmates to Netherworld interference didn't mean Mr. Wesner's and Mrs. Bennigan's deaths involved any extrahuman elements, right? Surely

I was just letting my own fears and past experiences color my perception.

*Please, please let me be overreacting....*

But what if I wasn't?

"We better go in," Nash said, shoving himself to his feet.

"Yeah." Still half-stunned, we started around the building toward the cafeteria doors, which were kept unlocked during all lunch periods. And it wasn't until nearly an hour later, as I sat in my English class, that I remembered what Nash and I had been discussing when my *bean sidhe* heritage got in the way.

Sabine's species.

We'd been interrupted again.

AFTER SCHOOL, I STOOD in the parking lot next to my car with my keys in my hand, dialing up my courage as I waited for Nash to come out of the building. Most of my afternoon teachers had been reeling from the death of two colleagues in one day, and they'd made no attempt to actually involve students in their lesson plans. Which gave me plenty of time to avoid thinking about Mrs. Bennigan by planning my first move in Sabine's sadistic little game of love and war.

She'd laid down the challenge, and I could either rise to it or slink home alone and call Nash later for the scoop on his ex's inhuman specifics. And after the day I'd had, I just didn't feel like slinking anywhere.

I knew I'd made the right decision when they came through the double glass doors together. Sabine was laughing and Nash was watching her, and even from across the lot, I recognized the light in his expression.

That was the way he used to look at me.

I got into my car—newly made over by the local body shop, after Doug Fuller had totaled it a week before his death—and dropped my books onto the rear floorboard. Then I cranked the engine and took off across the lot as fast as I dared, one eye on potential pedestrian casualties, the other on Nash and Sabine, as he said something I couldn't hear. Something that made her laugh harder and made him watch her even more closely.

My car squealed to a stop in front of them as they hit the end of the sidewalk, two feet away. Nash looked surprised, but Sabine actually jumped back, and a tiny granule of bitter satisfaction formed in the pit of my stomach, like a grain of sand in an oyster. If I nourished it properly, would it grow into a pearl?

I didn't have automatic windows, so I had to shift into Park and lean across the passenger seat to shove the door open. The awkward movement dulled the sharp edge of my dramatic gesture, but I made up for that when Nash leaned down to see me beneath the roof of the car.

"Get in," I said, and he raised one brow.

"He came with me," Sabine said, before he could make up his mind.

"And I'm taking him home. Get in the car, Nash. We need to talk."

Sabine looked impressed in spite of herself, until he glanced from her to me, then back to her. "What did I miss?"

"This is about what *I* missed," I said, shifting into Drive while the engine idled. "Get in the car."

Nash turned back to Sabine. "What did you do?" His voice held a single blended note of caution and curiosity, which made the hair stand up on the back of my neck. He wasn't even surprised to know she'd done something.

She grinned, one hand propped on a half-exposed hip that evidently felt no cold. "You don't really want the answer to that. Not yet."

"What do I really want?" Nash asked, humoring her, whereas I wanted to roll my car over her foot.

"You want to know why Kaylee's suddenly grown a pair."

He frowned. "Enlighten me."

She twisted one mismatched earring and shrugged. "I laid the cards out on the table. It's only fair that she knows the stakes, right?"

Except she'd left one of those cards out of her disclosure. They both had.

"Damn it, Bina."

"What?" She rolled her eyes, like *I* was the one being unreasonable. "I told her the truth. You can't get mad over the truth."

Oh, yes, we could. The truths between me and Nash hurt as badly as the lies.

Nash dropped his bag on my passenger's side floorboard and turned back to Sabine. "I'll see you later."

Sabine—Bina? Really?—scowled, then leaned in with one hand on the roof of my car, wearing an ironic, almost respectful smile. "Well played, Kaylee."

Nash got in and closed the door, and I drove off, leaving her standing there alone.

"I'm not playing her game, no matter what it looks like," I said, as I turned left out of the parking lot.

"Good. The only way to win is by refusing to play. Trust me." But he was smiling as he said it, like she was a toddler whose antics were still cute and harmless.

I did not find Sabine cute. Or harmless.

"Advice from your days in Fort Worth?"

Nash ran one hand through his thick brown hair, leaving it tussled in all the right places. "Based on observation, not experience. She doesn't play games with me. She doesn't need to."

"She's been back in your life for one day, and you sound like she was never gone." I braked at a red light, and unease crawled up my spine. How deep must their connection have been, if they could pick up right where they'd left off more than two years before?

He exhaled heavily. "How am I supposed to answer that?"

"It wasn't a question."

Nash twisted in his seat to face me, and his expression made my stomach churn. "We got caught up last night. And I'm sure once she gets used to the fact that I want you in my life, she'll—"

"No, she won't." I'd just met her, and I understood that much. My hand tightened on the wheel and I took a right at the next light. "She threw down the gauntlet, Nash. Like I'm gonna fight her for you."

"I know. I'm sorry, Kay. But it's not a physical fight she wants."

"What do *you* want?" I demanded, taking the next curve a little too fast. "You want us to fight over you? You get off on this—two girls, no waiting?"

He sighed and stared out his window. "Days like this I wish I had a car."

I rolled my eyes, though he wasn't watching. "Days like this I wish you'd tell me the whole truth for once, instead of leaving little bits of it lying around for me to follow like a trail of bread crumbs."

A moment passed in silence, except for the growl of my engine. Then he exhaled slowly and turned to look at me. "I'm guessing Tod told you?"

"He shouldn't have had to."

"I know. I tried to tell you, but Sabine…"

My pulse spiked in irritation. "You're going to be saying that a lot now, are you? 'But Sabine…'?"

"Do you want to talk, or are you just going to throw barbs at me?"

I exhaled deeply as I turned the car into his driveway. "I haven't decided. How's my aim?"

"Dead-on." He pushed his door open and hauled his backpack out of the car, and I slammed my own door, then followed him into the house. I hadn't been there in two weeks, but nothing had changed, except that someone had taken down the holiday decorations.

"You want something to eat? Mom made blondies." Nash dropped his backpack on the worn couch, then pushed through the swinging door into the kitchen.

"Just a Coke." I followed him into the kitchen, where Harmony Hudson glanced up from the breakfast table in surprise.

"Kaylee!" She crossed the small kitchen and wrapped her arms around me in a warm hug, her soft blond curls brushing my face. "I'm so glad you're back." Then she pulled away from me, frowning with her hands still on my shoulders. "You are back, aren't you?"

Nash groaned with his head stuck inside the fridge, then emerged with two cans. "*Laissez faire* parenting, Mom. We talked about this." He handed me a soda, and Harmony let me go to scowl at her son.

"That was before I spent two weeks nursing you through withdrawal from a substance more dangerous and addictive than anything the human world has ever even seen. I think that's earned me a little latitude, even if you are old enough to vote."

"Fine." Nash's jaw clenched in irritation, but he'd never disrespect his mother. That much had not changed. "Kaylee's just here to talk. Let's try not to scare her away."

Harmony gave me a hopeful smile, then handed me a paper plate piled high with blondies and shooed us out of the kitchen.

I followed Nash to his bedroom, where he sat on the bed and leaned back on the headboard, leaving the desk chair for me.

"Was Sabine in here?" I set the plate on his nightstand, glancing around his room as if I'd never seen it.

Nash popped open his can, his posture tense and expectant. He watched me like I was a bomb about to explode. "Does it really matter?"

"Yeah." I set my can on his desk and faced him, fighting through suspicion and fear so I could focus on my anger. "Your ex-girlfriend just told me she has no problem going through me to get to you. So yes, Nash. It matters where you were when you talked to her until after two in the morning." Because that's as far as I'd narrowed it down so far. She was here until after two. When I was sound asleep, and probably already dreaming about them making out in front of my locker.

Nash closed his eyes, then opened them and took a long drink from his soda. Then he met my gaze. "Yeah. We were in here."

My chest ached. I don't know why finding out where they'd been made it worse—I knew they'd only talked. But knowing they'd been in his room made it more personal. Made it sting more.

"On the bed?" I asked, when I'd recovered my voice, hating how paranoid I sounded.

"Damn it, Kaylee, nothing happened!"

"Right. I heard. But did this 'nothing' happen on the bed?" I couldn't breathe, waiting for his answer. "Was she on your bed, Nash?"

"For the last time, she's just a friend," he said, his voice low, the wet can slipping lower in his grip. "She's the only friend I have right now who knows more about me than my football stats from last season."

I knew more about him than that. I knew a lot more. But I hadn't come to see him even once while he was working his way through withdrawal, because I couldn't deal with it. The wounds were still too fresh. Too raw. When I thought about Nash, I thought about Avari, and the things they'd each let the other do to me, when I wasn't in control of my own body.

In the painful silence, I popped open my Coke, just to have something to do with my hands. "So...what is she?"

Nash looked up, obviously confused. "I thought Tod told you..."

"He just said she's my worst nightmare. Whatever that means." But frankly, any girl openly trying to steal Nash from me would qualify as my nightmare. "So...what is she?" I repeated, hoping I wouldn't have to say it again. "Siren? Harpy?" I raised both brows at him in sudden comprehension. "She's a harpy, isn't she? She acts like a harpy." Not that I'd ever met one.

Nash laughed out loud. "She'd probably get a kick out of that." But I had my doubts. "She's a Nightmare, like Tod said. Only that's kind of an antiquated term. Now, they're called *maras*."

"There's a politically correct term for Nightmares? Would that make me a death portent?" I joked to cover my own confusion and ignorance, and Nash laughed again to oblige me.

"Sure. We could start a movement. 'Rename the *bean sidhe*.' You make picket signs, I'll call the governor. It's gonna be huge."

"Funny." Only it wasn't. "So what exactly is a *mara?*"

Nash leaned forward and met my gaze with a somber one of his own. "Okay, I'll tell you everything, but you have to promise not to freak out. Remember, it was weird finding out you were a *bean sidhe* at first, too, right?"

*Weird* didn't begin to describe it. "Nash, I just found out she was on your bed at two o'clock this morning. With you. How much worse could this be?"

He gave me an apprehensive look, but didn't deny that

they'd been on his bed together, and another little part of my heart shriveled up and died.

"*Maras* are a rare kind of parasite, and unique in that they aren't native to the Netherworld. At least, according to my mom."

"Did she and your mom get along?"

"Yeah." Nash shrugged. "Sabine didn't know what she was when I met her, and I'd figured out she wasn't human, but that's as far as I'd gotten. But my mom narrowed it down pretty fast. She wanted to help her."

Of course she had. Harmony's heart was too big for her own good. She wanted to help me, too, and I was definitely starting to see a pattern. Nash and his mother shared their hero complex—I should have seen that coming, considering that she was a nurse—and so far, only Tod seemed immune to the family calling to help people.

He killed them instead.

"So she's a parasite? That sounds…gross. If I get in her way, is she going to attach herself to my back and suck me dry like a tick? Or a vampire?"

Nash rolled his eyes. "There are no vampires. And no. *Maras* don't feed physically. They feed psychically. Off of human energy."

Alarms went off in my head. "She eats human energy? Like Avari?"

"No." Nash frowned, like he was mentally organizing his thoughts, and it was a struggle. "Well, kind of. But she's not a hellion. Hellions thrive on pain and chaos, and they're strong enough to take it from the bleed-through of human energy between worlds. Parasites are nowhere near that strong. They have to feed through a direct connection, of one sort or another. And *maras,* specifically, feed from fear."

I blinked. Then blinked again, grasping for a nugget of comprehension from the words he seemed to be throwing at me at random. "She's a fear eater?" I said at last. "So...as long as I don't show her any fear, she can't feed from me?"

Nash took another long drink from his can, then set it on his nightstand. "Not exactly. There's a reason they used to be called Nightmares."

But before he could continue, movement from across the room caught my eye and I looked up to find Tod scowling at me. "You really think this is smart, after what he did?"

Nash obviously could neither see nor hear his brother, but he'd seen me stare off into space often enough to interpret the silence. "Damn it, Tod."

I sighed, glancing from one brother to the other. "I needed answers."

"I would have given them to you." Tod crossed his arms over his chest and glared at Nash, who stared at nothing, two feet from the space Tod actually occupied.

"He *owes* them to me."

"Show yourself or get out," Nash said, finally tired of being ignored. "Better yet, just get out."

Tod's eyes narrowed and he stepped forward, clearly stepping into sight, just to spite his brother. "Did you tell her about the dreams?"

Nash's frown deepened. "I was about to."

*Dreams. Nightmares. Parasite. Sabine kissing Nash in front of my locker.* No! But the pieces of the puzzle fit, so far as I could tell, and there was no denying the picture they formed. "She feeds during nightmares? She fed from *me,* during my sleep last night?"

"Probably," Tod said, while Nash asked, "What did you dream?"

I wasn't going to answer, but they were both looking at me, obviously waiting for a response. "I dreamed you and Sabine were making out in front of my locker. And you dumped me for her, because she 'delivers.'"

Nash flinched, while the reaper only shrugged. "Yeah, that sounds like Sabine."

"I'm sorry, Kay." Nash looked miserable. "I'll make sure she stops."

"Yeah. You will." I didn't even have words for how repulsed and scared I was by the fact that she'd been there while I slept, sucking energy from me through my dream. A very personal, horrifying dream.

"Kay, she didn't just feed from your nightmare," Tod explained, lowering his voice, as if that might soften whatever blow was coming. "She *gave* you that nightmare."

*Huh?* "What does that mean? How do you give someone a nightmare?" Other than scaring the living crap out of them. Which, come to think of it, fit Sabine to a T.

Nash tapped his empty can on the nightstand. "Sabine creates nightmares from a person's existing fear. It's a part of what she is, just like singing for people's souls is a part of who you are."

I felt my eyes go wide, as indignation burned deep inside me. "Yeah, but when I sing, I'm not sucking people dry! I'm trying to save their lives! That's the opposite of parasitic. Sabine and I are polar opposites!"

"Trust me, I know," Nash said. And if that was true, how could he possibly claim to love me, when he'd once loved her?

"Did you tell her how they feed?" Tod crossed the room to sit on the edge of the desk, taking his place at my side like an ally. And I'd never felt more like I needed one.

"Get out, Tod," Nash snapped. "I can handle this myself."

Tod scowled. "I'm not here to help *you*."

"How do they feed?" I demanded, when they both seemed more interested in measuring testosterone levels.

"Are you familiar with astral projection?" Nash asked, and I nodded.

"That's when someone's consciousness leaves the body and can go somewhere else, fully awake. Right?"

"Basically. What Sabine does is similar to that, except when her consciousness goes walking—she calls it Sleepwalking—she crafts people's fears into nightmares while they sleep. She says it's like weaving, only without physical thread." He shrugged. "Then she feeds from the fear laced into the dreams she's woven."

"By sitting on her victim's chest," Tod added, looking simultaneously satisfied and disgusted with his contribution to the explanation.

"Sitting on their...?" On *my* chest. My stomach churned. My horror knew no bounds. "You cannot be serious. While I was sleeping—minding my own business—she came into my room and sat on my chest, weaving some kind of metaphysical quilt out of fears she took right out of my own head?" That sentence sounded so crazy I was half-afraid men in white coats would burst through the door to drag me back to mental health.

"Not all of her. Just the part that was Sleepwalking," Nash insisted miserably.

"Is that supposed to make this any better? How could you not tell me this the minute she showed up at school?" I demanded, and when he had no answer for me, I turned around and stomped out of his room, through the house, and out the front door.

"Kaylee, wait!" he shouted, but I didn't wait. I got in my car and drove straight home, so angry my vision was tinged in red.

Sabine wants a nightmare?

*That's exactly what she's gonna get…*

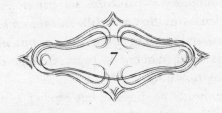

7

NASH IS ON THE *floor watching me. He's not in the bed, and I don't understand why, because he looks sick. His face is pale, and beads of sweat dot his forehead and his bare chest. He should be resting.*

*Instead, he's staring at me, and his eyes hold accusation and pain and shame. His irises swirl with it all, so fast I can't separate one emotion from the others. They blend together, writhing violently, until the definitions no longer matter, because they're all aimed at me. Whatever's wrong with him, it's my fault.*

*My stomach clenches around nothing and suddenly I'm cold. I cross his bedroom and sink onto my knees in front of him, in the corner. His eyes are unfocused. Half-closed. I take his hand, and it's freezing.*

*No! This can't be happening. Not again. He quit!*

*Then I see it. In the corner, the opening pinched between his fingers. A single red balloon, half-deflated. I hate that balloon. In that horrible, irrational moment, I hate all balloons.*

*"Kaylee...?" he whispers, reaching for my face. His other hand stays around the balloon, but that's not safe. Not with him like this. If he lets go, he'll pollute the whole room and probably kill us both.*

*I take the balloon from him, careful not to let the deadly vapor leak out. I twist the end into a knot, gritting my teeth as the unnatural chill seeps into my hands. My knuckles ache with the cold and my fingers are stiff. But the knot holds.*

*"I'm so sorry...."*

*Nash is gone. His body is here and his mouth keeps moving, keeps apologizing, but Elvis has left the building. Abandoned it to the toxin I hate. The poison that is rotting his soul, and corrupting him, and killing us.*

*"I tried," he whispers, and I need to move closer to hear him better. But I can't. I won't. I don't want to breathe what he's exhaling, and I can smell it from here. "I tried," he repeats. "But it was too hard on my own. You didn't come...."*

*Tears form in my eyes. He's right. I didn't come see him while he was getting clean. I didn't help. I could hardly look at him without remembering, and now he hasn't just fallen off the wagon, he's been run over by it.*

*And it's all my fault.*

*I want to get mad. I want to yell at him and scream, demanding to know why he can't just stand and shake it off. He's so strong in every other way. Why can't he do this one thing?*

*But I can't yell. I can't cling to my anger—not when*

*everything I know is falling apart along with Nash. Anger is great. It's powerful, when you need something to hold you up. Something to steel your spine. But in the dark, when you're alone with the truth, anger can't survive. The only thing that can live in the dark with you is fear.*

*And I'm swimming in fear. I'm afraid of Nash when he's like this. Afraid of what he'll do or say. Afraid that he won't listen. That he won't stop. And I'm terrified of Demon's Breath. Of the vapor he loves more than he loves me.*

*Because that's the crux of it. The dark truth. I'm not enough for him. I can't keep him safe from Avari. Safe from himself. He doesn't care enough about me to let me try.*

*"It's okay," I whisper back. "It's gonna be fine." But I can't say it with any strength, because it's a lie.*

*"They're empty," Nash says, as I sink onto the floor next to him, trying to warm his hand in both of mine. But that's a useless battle. His chill comes from within, and I can't fight it.*

*"What's empty?" I ask, and he's shaking now. Not shivering. More like tremors. His bare feet bump into each other over and over, and his empty hand flops on the floor.*

*Convulsions. He took too much. I want to get rid of the balloon, but I can't pop it without polluting the entire room.*

*"Memories…" His head rolls against the wall to face me. "They're empty. Numb."*

*My heart beats too hard. It's going to rupture. Nash*

*has sold the emotions in his memories to pay for this high, and even if he survives, he can never get those feelings back.*

*"Which memories?" I don't really want to know. But I have to ask.*

*"You." His hand tightens around one of mine, but only a little. That's all the strength he has left. "He only wants memories of you."*

*My throat closes and I can't breathe. It's all gone. He can never again look back on our history together and feel what he felt about me then. If there's no memory of love, can there still be love?*

*Finally, I suck in a deep breath, but it tastes bitter. Is this what I'm worth? A single latex balloon full of poison? If someone who loves me could sell me for so little, what value could I possibly have to anyone else?*

*My next breath comes before I can spit the last one out, and the next comes even faster. I'm hyperventilating. I know it, but I can't stop it.*

*I drop Nash's hand, and he stares at it blankly. Then he blinks and turns away from me, reaching for the balloon while I gasp and the room starts to go gray.*

*"It's a relief, really," he says, and I can hear him better now. Somehow he's stronger now, without me. "You're so needy, and clingy, and sealed up tighter than a nun. Too much work for too little payoff."*

*My tears run over, blurring him and the room and my whole pathetic life. His words burn like acid dripped onto my exposed heart. But he's sitting straighter now, like he draws strength from this. The truth is supposed to set you free, but it's killing me. And it is the truth. I can see that in his eyes, and his eyes don't lie. They can't.*

*I truly have no worth. And I don't think I can live with that.*

*"Go ahead and cry." Nash picks at the knot I tied, trying to loosen it. "Your tears are worth more than my memories, anyway. Wonder what I could get for the rest of you? Kaylee Cavanaugh, body and soul. Probably be enough to keep me high for life. Guess you're worth something, after all...."*

I SAT UP IN BED, sticky with sweat. My pillow was damp from tears, and lingering fear pulsed through me, throbbing with each beat of my heart. I wasn't worth loving, or even remembering. I tried too hard, but gave too little. Nash had wasted his time on me, and selling me to Avari was the only way to recoup his loss.

My worst fears, ripped from my own soul and left bleeding like an open wound.

Then the room came into focus through my tears, and I shook off sleep. With awareness came logic. And anger.

Fury, like I'd never felt.

"Sabine, get the hell out of my room!" I snapped through clenched teeth, remembering not to yell at the last minute, to keep from waking my dad. "Stay out of my head and out of my dreams, and stay away from Nash, or I swear your last semester of high school will make you homesick for prison!"

Unfortunately, I wasn't even sure she was still there. But I had no doubt she *had* been. She'd given me the new nightmare, playing on my own fears. And that was the worst part.

Sabine was a horrible, cruel, emotional parasite, but she couldn't have played architect in my dreams if I hadn't given her the building material. The fears were real. Deep down, I was terrified that Nash wouldn't stay clean. That he didn't love me enough to even try. Because I wasn't worth loving. Why else would my father have left me with his brother and let me be hospitalized?

My resolve wavered again, and I clutched at it like a life preserver, refusing to give in. Refusing to wallow in my own fear, which was no doubt what Sabine wanted.

I threw back the covers and grabbed my cell from the nightstand, pacing back and forth on my rug while the phone rang. My alarm clock read 2:09.

"Kaylee?" Nash sounded groggy. "What's wrong?"

"Is she there?" I demanded, stomping all the way to my closet, then turning to stomp the length of my bed.

"Is who here?" As if he didn't know!

"Sabine. Is she there with you? Tell me the truth."

His bedsprings creaked. "You woke me up in the middle of the night to ask if Sabine's with me?"

"It's not like that's a stretch, considering how late she was there last night."

Nash groaned and I heard him roll over. "I sent her home hours ago. Before midnight," he added. "Why?"

"Because she just gave me another nightmare, Nash. She was feeding from me in my sleep, like a great big flea!" Which made me feel a bit like a dog and gave me a huge case of the creeps. "I don't want her in my head, or in my dreams, or in my room." Or in my life, or in his. "If you don't do something about her, I will."

I had no idea what I would do, but I'd come up with something. Fortunately, Nash didn't press for details.

"I will. I'll take care of it, Kaylee. I swear."

"What on earth did you guys talk about? 'Cause it obviously wasn't the fact that *she is not allowed to stalk my dreams!*"

"Kay, I'm sorry. It won't happen again."

"It better not." Sabine had invaded my most private thoughts. "It's almost as bad as having you in my head."

Nash's sigh sounded like it had completely deflated him. "I don't..." He stopped and started over. "I said I was sorry about that. *So* sorry. I wasn't thinking straight." Because he'd been high when he'd tried to Influence me into his bed. "It'll never happen again. Can we please just move on from that? Please?"

"*You* can, obviously. Forgive me if I'm having a little more trouble with that. Especially with your new girl-friend playing dreamweaver in my sleep!"

"She's not my girlfriend, Kaylee."

I sank onto my bed, clenching one fist around a hand-ful of my comforter. "Well, she's not much of a friend to you, either, if this is how she treats your...people you care about."

He sighed again. "You have her at a disadvantage. She thinks she has to use her entire arsenal just to even the odds."

"I have *her* at a disadvantage? Tod says the two of you were attached at the hip. Or was it the crotch?" Yes, I was being petty and unreasonable. That may have had something to do with the fact that I wasn't getting any sleep, and I'd just had my psychic energy drained by my ex-boyfriend's leech of an ex-girlfriend.

Nash's bedsprings creaked again, and the soft click told me he'd just turned on his bedside lamp. "Are you mad at me because I slept with someone else two and a half years ago? Before I even met you?"

"Yes!" I stood again and rubbed my forehead, well aware that my lack of logic wasn't helping my case. But I couldn't help how I felt, and he wasn't doing much to alleviate my worries. "And don't say that's not fair, because 'fair' isn't even in the equation anymore. What you let happen to me wasn't fair, either. And I'm sure Scott would agree."

For a moment, I heard only silence over the line. I'd gone too far. I knew it, but I couldn't help it. I'd never been so mad in my life, and now that the dam had ruptured, I couldn't repair the damage. The overflow of anger wasn't just about Sabine and this nightmare. It was about everything beyond my control that had happened in the past couple of months. Everything I'd never vented about before, but suddenly *had* to address, or I'd explode.

"Are you trying to hurt me? It's okay if you are. I know I deserve it. I just want to be clear on the point of this whole conversation, so I'll know when we've accomplished whatever it is you need."

I had to think about that for a second. "No. I'm not trying to hurt you. I'm trying to heal me."

"Is it working?" He sounded so logical. So frustratingly reasonable, when I wanted to scream and shout and throw things until I felt better, logic be damned.

"I don't know," I had to admit at last, sinking into my desk chair.

More silence. Then, "What was the nightmare about?"

"It doesn't matter," I said, too quickly. I didn't want him to know how scared I was that he'd fall off the wagon. That he'd go back to selling his memories of me and trying to Influence me into things I wasn't ready for. That he might let Avari take over my body again, if that's what it took to get his next high.

Listing my fear—the facts—like that, the logical part of me couldn't even believe I was thinking about forgiving him. The smart thing would be to let Sabine have him. Let the ex-con and the former addict have each other, and wash my hands of the whole mess.

But I couldn't, because of the one truth it didn't hurt for me to think about: the guy who'd done those things to me wasn't the real Nash. *My* Nash was the guy who'd defied my family to save my sanity, and fought hellions alongside me, and put himself in danger just to help protect me.

This other boy—this boy whose addiction was literally the thing of my nightmares—he wasn't even real. It wasn't him doing those things, it was the frost. The Demon's Breath, which had suppressed—maybe even corroded—his soul. Changed who he was with each poisonous breath.

If he'd been human, the damage would have been irreversible. Part of it might be, anyway. But if it wasn't, then Nash was still the first and only guy outside of my family who'd ever loved me. And I couldn't turn my back on him if there was even a possibility of getting that Nash back.

I still wanted that Nash. I still needed to feel his hand in mine. I wanted to see him smile like he had before and know that I was the only thing he craved. I wanted to feel him behind me and know he had my back, whether we faced bitchy cousins or evil, soul-stealing hellions.

"Kay, can I come over?" Nash asked. "Can I please come see you?"

My heart thumped painfully, in spite of my best effort to calm it, and I sat up straight in my chair. "Now?"

"Yeah. I need to see you. We can just sit on the couch and talk. I just… I want to see you without the rest of the student body staring at us."

The ache in my chest spread into my throat, which tried to close around the only answer that made sense. "It's the middle of the night, Nash. My dad would kill you. Then he'd kill me." Just because he'd called to check up on Nash while he was sick didn't mean my dad wanted us back together. If he knew I was even thinking about taking Nash back, he'd make me get my head examined.

"Besides," I continued, standing to pace again before he could protest. "Alec's on the couch, so we wouldn't exactly have privacy."

"What?" Nash's voice went dark and angry with just that one syllable, and I realized I hadn't told him Alec was staying with us. I'd hardly spoken to him at all since the Winter Carnival. "He's there with you, while your dad's asleep? When your dad's not even there? And you didn't tell me?"

I rolled my eyes, though he couldn't see them. "Don't start. Sabine was in your room a couple of hours ago, actively trying to get into your pants while your mom was at work. And don't even get me started on the list of things you didn't tell me."

Another moment of silence. Then, "Fair enough. But I can handle Sabine. I know her. You don't know anything about Alec, except that he spent a quarter of a century working for a hellion. Not exactly a stellar recommendation. Has he tried anything?"

"Gross, Nash, he's forty-five years old."

"That won't matter when you're legal and he still looks nineteen."

I sank onto my bed and let my head thump against the headboard. "You're totally overreacting. He thinks I'm a kid."

"That's not going to stop him from looking."

"You don't even know him."

Nash laughed harshly, like I'd just told him rainbow-colored unicorns had flown through my bedroom window. "I know because he's there, and you're there, and he hasn't seen a girl without tentacles or claws in twenty-six years."

"Wow. You make me sound like such a catch."

"I can't win this argument, can I?"

"Nope. I'm going back to sleep now."

"Lock your bedroom door."

I laughed. I couldn't help it. "Good night, Nash. I'll see you tomorrow." I hung up before he could argue and turned off my lamp.

Unfortunately, I couldn't make myself go back to sleep

for fear that Sabine would be waiting to attack me again from my own subconscious. Every time I closed my eyes, I saw Nash, huddled in a corner, telling me I wasn't worth staying clean for. So I got up and padded into the kitchen, where I found Alec wide-awake, fully dressed, and halfway through a box of snack cakes.

"You, too?" I asked, trudging past him to take a glass from the cabinet.

"Kaylee?" Alec coughed, nearly choking on his snack in surprise.

"Yeah. I live here, remember?" I ran tap water until it turned cold, then filled my glass.

"Of course. I didn't expect you to be awake. At this hour."

I raised one brow at him over my water glass. "You okay? You sound…tired." And less than perfectly coherent. "And Dad's going to kill you for eating all his cupcakes."

An annoyed expression passed over Alec's strong, dark features, but was gone almost before I'd seen it.

"You wanna hear something interesting?" I asked. "And by interesting, I mean terrifying beyond all reason…"

One dark brow rose as Alec closed the end of the snack box. "You have my attention."

I had his attention? "If you're trying to sound your real age, I think you're finally getting it right."

He frowned, like I'd spoken Greek and he was trying to translate.

"Anyway, remember my nightmare last night? I just had another one, but it turns out that they aren't real dreams. Well, not natural dreams, anyway." I leaned against the counter with the sink at my back. "Nash's ex is giving them to me. On purpose. She's a *mara,* if you can believe it. The living personification of a nightmare. How messed up is that?"

"Nash's former lover is a *mara?*" Alec wasn't even looking at me now. He was staring into space as if that little nugget of information took some time to sink in. I knew exactly how he felt.

"Yeah. She wants him back and has decided I'm in her way. But I have news for that little sleep-terrorist—it's going to take more than a couple of bad dreams to scare me off, so I hope she has something bigger up her sleeve."

But as soon as I'd said it, I wanted to take it back. Challenging Sabine felt a little bit like staring a lion in the mouth, daring it to pounce.

"You okay?" my dad asked, pouring coffee into his travel mug as I walked into the kitchen. He wore his usual jeans and steel-toed work boots, his chin scruffy with dark stubble above the collar of a flannel shirt.

"Just tired." I couldn't go back to sleep after my middle-of-the-night chat with Alec, so I'd stretched out on my bed, silently rehashing my argument with Nash, analyzing every word he'd said ad nauseam. "Can I have some of that?"

My father frowned at the pot of coffee, hesitating. Then he gave up and poured a second mug for me. "If you need coffee at sixteen, I hate to think what mornings will be like when you're my age."

Considering how many times I'd nearly died since the

beginning of my junior year, I'd settle for just surviving to his age. But I knew better than to say that out loud.

"Hey, Dad?" I said, pulling a box of cereal from the cabinet overhead.

"Hmm?" He opened his carton of cupcakes—the breakfast of champions—and frowned into it. "Did you eat my snacks?"

"No. Dad, what do you think the chances are of two teachers dying on the same day?"

He looked up from his box, still frowning, but now at me. "I guess that depends on the circumstances. Why?"

"'Cause Mr. Wesner and Mrs. Bennigan both died yesterday. At their desks, at least six hours apart. You didn't see it on the news last night?" The story had been a short, somber community interest piece—a small Dallas suburb mourning the loss of two teachers at once. "There were no signs of foul play, so they're calling it a really weird, tragic coincidence."

"And you don't believe that?" His irises held steady—it took a lot to rattle my father—but unease was clear in the firm line of his jaw.

"I don't know what to think. It probably *is* just a coincidence, but with everything else that's gone down this year…" I couldn't help but wonder. And I could tell my dad was thinking the same thing.

"Well, let's not borrow trouble until we come up short. I can ask around." Meaning he'd talk to Harmony Hudson and my uncle Brendon. "But I want you to stay out of it. Just in case. Got it?"

I nodded and poured milk into my bowl. That's what I was hoping he'd say. And now that I'd been expressly forbidden from investigating the massively coincidental teacher deaths, I should have felt free from the compulsion to do just that. Right? So why was it so hard to get Mrs. Bennigan out of my head? Why did the soft rise and fall of her back haunt my memory?

Alec trudged into the kitchen and I shook off my morbid thoughts and sank into a chair at the table with my cold cereal. He headed straight for the coffeepot.

"You, too?" my dad asked, with one look at the bags under his eyes.

Alec shrugged and scrubbed one hand over his close-cropped curls. "I didn't get much sleep."

My dad's brows furrowed as he glanced from Alec to me, obviously leaping to a very weird conclusion. "Is there something I should know?" he half growled, glaring at Alec as he spooned sugar into his mug, completely oblivious to my father's suspicion and sudden tension.

I could only roll my eyes. "*He's* still adjusting to a human sleep cycle, and *I* had a…bad dream. Two completely separate, unconnected neuroses," I insisted, but my dad looked unconvinced.

He stepped too close to Alec, who looked up in surprise. "I haven't forgotten that you helped get me out of the Netherworld. But if you think that gives you some kind of claim on Kaylee, you're gravely mistaken. You lay one inappropriate finger on my daughter, and you'll learn that Avari isn't the scariest thing you've ever faced."

Alec stumbled backward, away from my father, and winced when his back hit the corner of the counter. "I don't know what you're talking about, Mr. Cavanaugh."

"Dad!" I stood, pushing my chair out of the way with

the backs of my legs. "Back off! Why are men so suspicious? Is it hardwired into your brain? Jeez, he's forty-five years old!"

Alec actually frowned at that, and I felt bad about throwing his lost youth in his face.

"Not that you're not hot…" I backtracked. Totally tall, dark, and crush-worthy, if we'd been anywhere near the same age. Especially with the bonus haunted-past mystique.

Alec dared a faint grin, and my father scowled. "I'm not kidding, Kaylee. I know you and Nash just broke up, but that doesn't mean you need to…"

I dropped my spoon into my half-full bowl and grabbed my mug, already stomping out of the kitchen in humiliation. "I am not having this conversation with you." My dad didn't know exactly what had happened between me and Nash, but he knew Nash had been taking frost and he knew—and loved—that I'd taken a step back, at least while Nash recovered.

My father groaned, then called me back before I'd made it to the hall. "Wait, Kaylee. Please." The magic word. I stopped and turned to face him. "You're right. I'm overreacting. There are so many things I can't protect you from that I tend to go overboard in cases where I can actually make a difference. Come finish your breakfast. I'm sorry."

"You're trying to protect her from *me?*" Alec frowned into his cup of coffee.

Instead of answering, my father changed the subject, already on his way to the front door when he glanced back at Alec. "Don't forget the interview at one. Don't be late." My dad was trying to get Alec a job at the factory where he worked. With better pay and more hours than he got at the theater, Alec could afford his own apartment and really start to get his life back together. "And you owe me four chocolate cupcakes."

"Cupcakes? Is that the fee for getting me an interview?" Alec pulled off a very convincing confused look, and I couldn't quite hide my smile. But there was no way my dad would fall for that.

As soon as the front door closed behind my father, Alec turned to me, coffee mug halfway to his mouth. "You faced down a hellion to rescue three people from the Netherworld. Why the hell is he trying to protect you from me?"

I could only shrug. "He's my dad. That's what he does." And lately, that seemed to be the only normal aspect of my entire life.

I PULLED INTO the parking lot fifteen minutes before the first bell, hoping I'd beaten Nash to school. Hoping he'd find some way to school that didn't include Sabine, after what she'd done the night before. But four minutes after I arrived, her car pulled into a space two rows in front of mine, with a very familiar silhouette showing through the passenger's side window.

Maybe he was telling her to stay away from me. Maybe he was threatening her. Normally, I'm not big on physical threats. But normally, I don't have my dreams invaded by psychotic nightmare demons. Or whatever. I was willing to compromise a little on the former to get rid of the latter.

I followed them toward the building, hanging back so they wouldn't see me. When Sabine turned to brush hair from Nash's forehead, laughing at something he'd said, I dropped into a crouch next to a beat-up old Neon with faded blue paint. It certainly didn't *look* like he was telling her to back off, or else.

I wanted to see more tears. Less laughter and fewer you-light-up-my-life smiles. Nash had dumped countless other girls in his two and a half years at Eastlake, so why was he having trouble getting rid of this one? Had he forgotten how?

When Sabine's laughter was swallowed by the clang of the glass doors swinging shut, I stood, fuming, and kicked the front tire of the car I'd been hiding behind. Inside, I stomped straight to Nash's locker, intending to tell them both off before I lost my nerve. But to my unparalleled relief, Nash was alone, stuffing books from his bag into his locker. I leaned against the locker next to his and crossed my arms over my chest, frowning up at him.

"You really told her off, huh? I could tell by how hard she was laughing."

Nash glanced at me, then turned back to his locker. "I made her promise not to feed off you anymore."

"Just me?" I dropped my bag on the ground at my feet. "What about the rest of the school?" Or the rest of Texas, for that matter. "She can't just go around slurping up fear from the general population while they sleep."

Nash closed his locker door, then drew me into the alcove by the first-floor restrooms and water fountain, where we were less likely to be overheard. "Actually, she kind of has to. If she doesn't feed, she'll starve to death."

Stunned, I blinked at him. "You're serious?"

He frowned. "Why else would she do it?"

"I thought—" *hoped*… "—maybe it was recreational. Something she could quit, if she wanted to."

His frown deepened as my point sank in—a little too close to home. "Kaylee, she's not getting high. She's surviving. It's not her fault that food and water aren't enough to keep her alive."

"You seriously expect me to believe she doesn't enjoy it?"

Nash started to answer, then his mouth snapped shut as two freshmen came out of the girls' restroom, talking about some song one of them had just downloaded. When they were gone, he turned to me again, leaning against the painted cinder-block wall.

"I'm not saying she hates it. I'm just saying she has to do it, whether she likes it or not. Besides, what's wrong with liking what you eat? Don't tell me you hate pizza and chips and ice cream..."

He did *not* just compare me to junk food. My temper flared. "I'm not draining someone's life force every time I have a slice of pepperoni."

"She's a predator, Kaylee. She can't help that, and you can't change it. She has to eat something."

"You mean some*one*," I snapped, and Nash nodded, unfazed by my blunt phrasing. "But it doesn't have to be classmates, right? Why can't she eat bad guys? You know, feed from criminals. She could power up and serve society at the same time."

Nash laughed, and I gritted my teeth in irritation. He'd taken me seriously before she'd shown up, hadn't he? "Great idea, Kay. How would you suggest she identify these bad guys?"

"I'm thinking jail would be a good place to start." She'd probably feel right at home there. "Or Fort Worth gang territories. It can't be too hard to find someone worth scaring the crap out of, either way."

Nash's expression went hard. "I'm not going to tell her to drive downtown by herself in the middle of the night, to look for someone who deserves to be eaten in his sleep! She could get killed."

"But what about that whole astral projection thing? If she doesn't have a physical presence, she can't be hurt, right?"

"What do you want her to do, walk her astral self twenty miles and back? She can't *fly,* even when she's Sleepwalking. Plus, there's a limit to how far her astral form can wander from her actual body, so she'd still be in physical danger."

"Nash, she's a walking Nightmare. She's probably the scariest thing out there, even in the middle of the night."

"That doesn't make her bulletproof!" He ran one hand through his hair and leaned back against the wall, obviously frustrated. "Look, I don't expect you two to braid each other's hair and share lip gloss, but you sound like you're trying to get her killed!"

I crossed my arms over my chest and leaned against the wall next to the water fountain. "I don't want her dead, I swear." *Though I might not object to a light maiming…*

But if she poked one more metaphysical finger into my dreams, I'd probably be singing a different tune.

"Good. Because no matter how tough she talks, she's really not that different from anyone else here." His wide-armed gesture took in the whole school.

"Yeah. Except for that whole creep-into-your-dreams-and-ruin-your-life angle."

Nash studied me, like he was weighing some options I didn't understand. "You know how you got creeped out just from looking at her a couple of times?"

"Like I'm gonna forget."

"She did that on purpose, because she's threatened by you. But she used to have no control over it. Until she learned to quit dripping creepy vibes like a leaky faucet, everyone she ever met had the same reaction to her. Her parents left her on the front steps of some big church in Dallas when she was a toddler. She'd creeped out twelve sets of foster parents before she was fourteen. And she's literally never had a friend, other than me. All because she was born a *mara*."

I blinked, confused. "Wait, why would her parents give her up? Weren't they *maras,* too?"

Nash shook his head, but didn't explain until a throng of girls in matching green–and–white letter jackets crossed between us and into the bathroom.

"It's different for *maras* than it is for us. They are always born to human families. Every seventh daughter of a seventh daughter is a Nightmare, and so is her life, until she figures out what she is and how to feed herself without driving off the rest of humanity. What do you think *your* life would have been like without your family? Or Emma?"

I didn't even want to imagine it. "Fine. I get it. She's had it rough. But that's all in the past. She can control herself now, so if she chooses not to, the consequences are all hers." And those consequences would include whatever happened when she eventually pushed me past my limit.

"I agree," Nash conceded, pulling his bag higher on his shoulder. "But I'm not going to send her to jail or to inner-city Fort Worth to feed. She doesn't deserve to get hurt just because you don't like what she eats." After another moment's hesitation, he exhaled and shrugged, like our argument wasn't worth fighting anymore. "It's not like she's hurting anyone. She'd never take too much."

My inner alarm flared to life inside my head, like a warbling siren. "Too much? What happens if she takes too much?"

"Kaylee, she's not going to…"

"What happens, Nash?" I demanded, stepping closer as the girls jostled their way out of the bathroom and into the hall.

"Not that Sabine's ever done this, but taking too much during a nightmare can leave the sleeper sick, unconscious, or…" He didn't finish. He didn't have to.

"Dead?" Chill bumps popped up on my arms at the memory of the dreams she'd woven for me.

Nash nodded. "But Sabine wouldn't…"

"So you keep saying. But if you're so sure she's not dangerous, how come I don't see you offering up *your* dreams to keep her sated?"

Nash's irises exploded into motion, and his brows rose. "I could do that…" he began. "But I didn't think you'd want Sabine—even her astral form—straddling me in my sleep, literally riding my dreams."

*Damn it.* My cheeks flamed. But I couldn't help being a little relieved by the fact that he hadn't let that happen.

"Fine. Then let's find her something more appropriate to eat. Okay?"

He shrugged. "At least that'll give us something to do, other than think about what we can't have."

I was confused for a moment, until his meaning sank in. "By 'us,' you mean you and Sabine, not you and me, don't you?" Of course he did. I'd just given them another reason to be together. Maybe I should have just let her snack on my cousin's dance team.

"Kaylee, no matter what she thinks she wants from me, what she *needs* is a friend." Traffic had picked up in the hallway, a sure sign the warning bell would soon ring. "You'll just have to believe me when I say her problems are bigger than a bitchy cousin, an absentee dad, and a species identity crisis."

I blinked and felt my face flame.

"I'm sorry…" Nash said, before I could recover from shock enough to even think about responding. "But the truth is that you've got it pretty good right now. Good grades, good friends, a decent place to live, and a dad who loves you so much he hardly wants to let you out of his sight. Sabine doesn't have any of that, and I don't have…" He swallowed, then met my gaze and continued. "I don't have you, and without you, it feels like what I *do* have doesn't matter."

The sudden sentimentality and the yearning clear in his eyes threw me off and dampened my anger. I didn't know how to respond. "I miss you, too," I said finally, and the swirling in his irises became frantic at my admission.

And suddenly we were talking about us.

"Then what's wrong?" Nash asked, trying to read the answer in my eyes.

"I just… I can't help thinking about how much she must mean to you, for you to go through so much trouble for her."

Nash let his bag slide to the floor and stepped close to me. I could feel the delicious heat from his body and had to look up to see the urgent swirling in his eyes.

"I love you, Kaylee. Nothing's going to change that, including Sabine. But she does mean a lot to me—as a friend I thought I'd lost. Sabine and I have a history we can't just erase, and I'm not going to drop her, like everyone else in her life has done. I don't *want* to drop her, because when she looks at me, she doesn't see an addict or a football player, or any of the other labels people keep trying to stick me with. She sees me. She sees what I was before, and she knows I'm trying, and that's enough for her. I really need someone who's okay with me the way I am right now, Kay, and I know that can't be you. So why can't you let it be her?"

I didn't want to answer. I wanted to be able to give him what he wanted—what he needed—to get through this and get back to the person he'd been when we'd met. But it wasn't that simple.

"Because you'll never see her coming, Nash. You think you know her, but you don't know how far she'll go to get what she wants, because back when you knew her, she didn't have to chase you. She already had you. But now she has to work for what she wants, and she's *really good*." That was obvious, based on the fact that she'd seamlessly sewn herself back into his life and he'd accepted her like she'd never been gone.

"You'll just be sitting there one day, alone with her,

talking about someplace you went back in the day, and the next thing you know it, you'll be looking into each other's eyes, and it'll feel just like it used to. She'll kiss you—or maybe you'll kiss her—and it'll feel so good and familiar you won't even remember that you should stop it. So you won't. And then she'll have you, and I'll have lost you, all because I did the right thing, and she was willing to play dirty."

Nash shook his head slowly. "That's not going to happen, Kaylee. I wish you'd let me show you." He leaned into me, watching me so closely he seemed to see right through my eyes and into my soul.

He bent toward me, and my lips parted, my heart and body ready to take him back right then, even while my mind screamed in protest of abandoned logic.

My pulse raced, and his lips touched mine, just the slightest warm contact. Then a familiar voice at my back drenched our rediscovered heat with an auditory bucket of ice water.

"Well, this looks promising!"

I jerked away from Nash and turned to find Emma watching us both, her Cheshire cat grin firmly in place.

"It *was*," Nash mumbled, retrieving his bag from the floor.

"Yeah, well, timing is everything, and Coach Tucker is standing right over there, waiting to bust you for the public display. I just saved you both from detention."

I glanced over her shoulder to see that she was right. The girls' softball coach stood in the doorway across the hall, pink detention pad ready and waiting.

"And…" Em continued, thrusting a thick, worn text-book at me. "I brought you this."

I took my Algebra II book from her, frowning. "Why…?"

She shrugged, looking smug. "I noticed your heart-to-heart, so I stopped by your locker on the way to mine. I had a feeling you wouldn't be done in time to get your books."

Emma and I had known each other's locker combinations since our freshmen year. Just for occasions like this. "And I was right," she added, when the warning bell shrieked from the end of the hall.

In the event of a power outage, her smile could have powered the entire school for a week.

"Thanks, Em."

"You can thank me later by translating our French homework."

"No problem," I said, my heart still beating too hard over the almost-kiss, and the possibility it hinted at. "I better go. See you at lunch?"

Emma and Nash both nodded, and I took off toward first period algebra, while they headed in the opposite direction. Emma got to skip class that morning to meet with the guidance counselor, who wanted to make sure she was still okay, following Doug's death. Thanks to a call from her mom.

But I'd only gone a few feet when Sabine fell into step beside me in a snug polo, ratty jeans, and scuffed-up Converses. On the surface, she was even less Nash's type than I was—at least, Nash as he was known at Eastlake; I didn't know what he'd been like in Fort Worth—but he didn't seem to care. It probably didn't hurt that she was hot no matter what she wore. Sabine's look was overtly gearhead/gamer/troublemaker, but because she owned it, it worked for her.

Despite being new in the middle of her senior year and having no friends to speak of, Sabine had confidence and self-assurance I could only dream about. And that was just one more entry on my ever-growing list of reasons to dislike the *mara*.

"What do you want?" I walked faster, after a quick glance to make sure she wasn't armed. Her dark eyes creeped me out, even more so than before, now that I knew what she really was.

"You've got balls," she said, instead of answering my question, then launched into a high-pitched imperson-ation of me. "'Sabine, get the hell out of my room! Stay away from Nash, or I'll make you homesick for prison!'" she taunted, while I ground my teeth and stomped even faster through the hall. "That's some funny shit! Espe-cially while you're still sitting in sweat-soaked sheets, heart racing from one hell of a nightmare. Though for the record, I was never in prison. The state detention center, halfway houses, and foster homes, sure. But never prison. What do you think I am, a hardened criminal?"

"Go away."

Sabine laughed. "I don't think you're truly getting into the spirit of this rivalry."

"This is not a rivalry. It's your own sad little delusion," I snapped, turning the corner so sharply my foot almost slipped out from under me.

When I paused to regain my balance, Sabine spun

around to stand in front of me, one hand on the wall, effectively blocking my path. She smiled, but her eyes were even darker than usual, the fear they reflected as black as a starless night.

My hand clenched around the strap of my backpack, the other clutching my math book while Sabine leaned in so close her nose almost brushed my cheek. I held my breath, not sure what she was doing. Not sure what *I* should do.

"I'm not into girls, Kaylee," she whispered, her breath warm on my cheek. "But if I were, I think you'd be my type."

My breath froze in my throat, and she laughed, stepping back where I could see her whole face. "I'm starting to see why Nash wanted you. You got a backbone buried in there somewhere." She stepped back again and eyed me from head to toe, like a boxer assessing his opponent. "But if you don't loosen up, you're never gonna uncover enough of it in time."

"He doesn't love you," I said through gritted teeth, determined to maintain eye contact, even though that was about as comfortable as holding a jagged chunk of ice in the palm of my hand.

"I know." Sabine shrugged and crossed her arms over her chest. "But he *wants* me, and that's the first step, and there's nothing you can do about that. Know why?"

I didn't respond, so she answered her own question. "Because you're scared. You're one big ball of fear, wrapped inside a skinny, uptight little body you're not willing to share. But I won't hold back. I'll give him everything, Kaylee." Her gaze burned into mine. "Everything you're afraid to let him have."

My fingers twitched around my book. "Sounds like you already have," I spat, and she grinned, like making me talk was some kind of victory.

"I'm not talking about sex, though that offer's definitely on the table." Her eyes flashed with anticipation, and I hated her just a little more. "I'm talking about my heart, Kaylee. As cheesy as it sounds, I'm willing to give him my heart—everything I am and everything I have— and you're not. You're too scared to trust him, and you can't really love someone you don't trust. So if you care about him at all, you'll let him go, before you screw him up for good."

I forced myself to breathe slowly and evenly, to keep her from seeing how her words affected me. How scared I was—deep down—that she was right.

"You can't scare me away from him." I could see my algebra classroom over her shoulder, the door open, the new sub standing next to it, eyeing the stragglers in the hallway.

Sabine laughed and long dark hair fell over her shoulder. "Yeah, I can. But I don't think I'll have to. I think your conscience is gonna do most of the work for me, because you do care about Nash, and when you're brave enough to be honest with yourself, I think you'll understand that you're not what he needs."

I ground my teeth together, then unclenched my jaw. I didn't want to ask—didn't want to be drawn into her little mind game—but I had to know. "What is it you think he needs?"

Another shrug. "Someone who wants him as he is. Flaws and all. And that's never gonna be you. You're not ready to take him back, but you can't let him go. You're afraid to be with him, and you're afraid to be without him. You're paralyzed with fear, and it's eating you up on the inside and killing whatever you had with Nash."

"You got all that from my dream?"

"I got that from your *eyes*. Well, that, and a little peek into your darkest fears. But it's not like you keep those hidden."

"You don't even know me...."

Sabine laughed again, and I was starting to truly hate the sound. "I know you better than you know yourself. I can see the things you keep buried. The secrets you hide even from your conscious mind. And even if I couldn't, I know your type."

I glared at her, eyes narrowed until I could see nothing else. "I am not a type." Why was I still talking to her? I should have just walked away, but I couldn't help myself. Nash saw something in her. Something he liked. Something he'd once loved—and I wanted to know what that was.

"Oh, you're definitely a type. Self-righteous, like you've never done anything wrong and that gives you the right to point out everyone else's mistakes. You do what it takes to fit in, but not enough to get noticed, because you're afraid of scrutiny and because you think you're above the high school social scene. And frankly, you and I have that last bit in common."

I glanced around, hoping no one was close enough to hear her, and was relieved to find the hall nearly empty.

"You're *obviously* a virgin," Sabine continued, as I stood there, mortified, but unwilling to walk away because some part of me needed to hear this. Needed to hear what she thought of me. What she'd probably been saying about me to Nash. "And you think that makes you pure, but what it really makes you is uptight and scared. You won't admit it, but you think about sex. A lot. But you're not gonna do it, because then you wouldn't be special. You think your virginity is some kind of satin-wrapped, halo-topped gift that, someday, some perfect prince will be honored to receive. But you don't get it, and no one's had the heart to explain it to you yet. Fortunately for you, I'm *full* of heart today. So here's the truth: sex isn't a gift you give Mr. Right in exchange for 'forever' and a white dress. You're selling yourself short and making us all look bad with that kind of naiveté. Sex isn't something you do for *him*. It's something you do for yourself."

I blinked. Then I blinked again, stunned and humiliated. My face was on fire.

How on earth had Sabine's effort to scare me away from Nash become a lecture on sex, and why not to have it? But what was even more disturbing than the surprising turn her lecture had taken was the sincerity obvious on her face.

"Why are you telling me this? I mean, if this little explanation of yours is such valuable information, why waste it on someone you obviously hate?"

Sabine frowned. "I don't hate you. In fact, I kind of like you. I'm just not gonna let you stand between me and Nash."

I felt my brows furrow. "And you seriously think you can just…take him back?"

"Yeah." She nodded, betraying no hint of doubt. "I got this far, didn't I?" When I frowned, confused, she elaborated. "I didn't just *happen* to wind up in your school, Kaylee. Weren't you even a little suspicious of the coincidence?"

Maybe, for just a second… But the truth was that so much weird stuff had happened to me in the past few months that the appearance of an ex-girlfriend had hardly even seemed notable—at first.

"I came here for Nash. It took me a while to find him, and even longer to get myself placed in a foster home in the right district. But I'm here now, and I'm not going anywhere."

I blinked, surprised beyond words. Then impressed, in spite of myself. "You—"

But before I could finish that thought, the front doors of the school burst open behind me, and I whirled around to see two EMTs wheel a stretcher into the hall.

The tardy bell rang, but I barely noticed.

The office door opened and the attendance secretary motioned frantically to the EMTs. "He's in here," she said, her voice so breathy with shock that I could hardly hear her. "We found him a few minutes ago, but I don't think there's anything you can do for him. I think he's been gone for quite a while now."

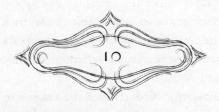

10

"YEAH, IT'S SOME GUY named John Wells," Tod said, sinking onto the bleachers next to me in the gym. No one else could see or hear him, and I was far enough from the other scattered groups of students that no one would be able to hear me, either. And with my earbuds in my ears, hopefully anyone who noticed me would think I was singing along with my iPod or learning to speak German, or something.

"Thanks." I leaned back, and the next bleacher poked into my spine. Tod had just confirmed one aspect of the rumors spreading like brushfire throughout the school.

"Who is he?"

"The vice principal." Found dead in his closed, locked office that morning, according to the rumors. Chelsea Simms had been running copies in the office before first period—the school newspaper's copier was out of toner—when Principal Goody unlocked her V.P.'s door to borrow a file, grumbling about Wells being late for possibly the first time ever. Until she found him, slumped over his desk like he'd fallen asleep, still wearing yesterday's clothes. Only they couldn't wake him up, and he was already cold.

But that's all Chelsea knew, because they'd kicked her out of the office while the secretary dialed 9-1-1.

"You think you can get a look at the list?" I asked, meaning the death list, which told reapers exactly when and to whom reapings were scheduled to occur in any given zone.

"Don't have to." Tod grinned. "I know the guy who works this sector and I already asked. Nothing's scheduled for Eastlake High this week."

Nothing? He'd just blown Nash's coincidence theory out of the water. We'd had three deaths in two days, and not one of them was scheduled....

*Sometimes I really hate being right.*

"Wait, how do you just happen to know the guy who reaps at the high school?" I asked, trying not to be incredibly creeped out that such a position even existed.

"I don't *happen* to know him. I made it my *business* to know him, after what happened with Marg back in September."

Marg was the rogue reaper who'd killed four innocent girls and stolen their souls, which was part of my not-so-gentle introduction to the Netherworld and to the supernatural elements of my own world.

"I don't suppose you have any details about Wells?" I asked, as Tod leaned back next to me, staring across the gym at a bunch of freshmen grumbling their way through calisthenics. Thank goodness I'd already had my required year of P.E.

Tod shrugged. "They took him straight to the morgue, but I got a look at him before they put him on ice."

"Ew." Suddenly I had an image of Mr. Wells, wedged into a giant drink cooler alongside assorted cans of beer and soda, waiting to be consumed at some stupid party.

There hadn't been any parties since Doug Fuller died and Scott Carter got run down by the crazy train. Most of the student body was still in social shock, struggling to deal with conflicting impulses to truly mourn two of our own, and to replace them. Because without someone at the top of the high school social ladder, the rest of the rungs might collapse, and life as we knew it would fall into chaos.

But waiting for the cream to float to the top of the social milk bucket—a rather organic process—took patience, and while a couple of front-runners had emerged—and some splinter faction might yet turn to Nash, once they'd figured out how to approach the last standing member of the former social power trifecta—no clear victor had been declared.

"It's really more like a big refrigerator with a bunch of meat drawers," Tod said, oblivious to the turn my thoughts had taken.

"Thanks. That's a much better visual."

Tod laughed, and I had to remind myself that death didn't affect him the way it affected...anyone else. Anyone living, anyway. He killed people for a living— as ironic as that sounded—and had outgrown the most common reactions to death: fear, sadness, and respect.

"So…notice anything weird about…the body?"

Tod shook his head, blond curls bouncing. "I got a pretty good look at him while they were filling out paperwork, and I didn't see anything noteworthy. No obvious injuries, no blood or bruises. And his eyes were already closed. He looked like he was sleeping."

Yeah. That's what I was afraid of.

I pulled one leg onto the bleacher with me, bent at the knee, and twisted to face Tod, hoping no one was watching me, because now I'd look like I was talking to myself. "I have to ask you something and I don't want you to freak out. Or say anything to Nash."

Tod's pale brows shot up, showcasing his curiosity while his blue eyes flashed in eagerness. "I'm not exactly known for either of those impulses."

Which was exactly what I was counting on. "What happens when a *mara* takes too much? Like, really gluts herself on someone's dream. Worst-case scenario." I'd already asked Nash, but his answer was biased by an intense need to protect Sabine, and was thus potentially unreliable.

Tod just stared at me for a minute, then slowly shook his head. "I know what you're getting at, but she didn't do this."

"That's not what I asked. Worst-case scenario. Could she kill someone?"

The reaper looked like he didn't want to answer, so I just waited, silently demanding a response. "Yeah, but…"

"And would it look like he'd died in his sleep?"

"Kaylee, I'm telling you, Sabine didn't do this. She

and I may not have been best friends, but she's not a murderer."

"She's a thief and a vandal. And an assaulter. Or whatever." Based on her skills with a lunch tray. "It's just a hop, skip, and a jump from there to criminal overindulgence."

"That's not a hop, skip, *or* a jump," Tod insisted. "It's more like a vault over the Grand Canyon."

"Tod, three teachers died in two days. All at their desks, all possibly asleep. The week Sabine moved to town. You seriously think that's a coincidence?"

He shook his head slowly. "There are no coincidences." We'd learned that, if nothing else, during the first half of my insane junior year. "But that doesn't mean she had anything to do with it."

I swallowed a grunt of frustration. Was I the only one who recognized the *mara* as a potential psychopath? Case in point: her obsession with Nash! "Sabine comes here and teachers start dying. It doesn't take a genius to see the pattern."

"What pattern?" Emma dropped onto the bench below mine, staring just to the left of the reaper's head. I hadn't even noticed her climbing the steps. "I assume Tod's around here somewhere. Or else you've progressed to actually arguing with yourself."

"Hey, Em," Tod said, and Emma jumped a little, obviously startled to find him so close when he let her see him. "She thinks Sabine's—"

"Trying to get Nash back," I interrupted, and Tod glanced at me in surprise, then nodded when he understood. Emma didn't know Sabine wasn't human, and

I wanted to keep it that way. At least until we knew whether or not she was a murderer.

"Well, yeah. That's been well-established." Em glanced from Tod to me. "Why? What did I miss?"

She was getting harder and harder to hide things from.

Tod crossed his arms over his snug white T-shirt, silently giving me the floor. Fortunately, I was prepared. "She ambushed me in the hall this morning and gave me a lecture on sex."

Tod's brows rose halfway to his hairline. "I hope you took notes...."

I elbowed his surprisingly solid ribs. "She told me that if I really cared about Nash, I'd let him go. Like he's just gonna fall into her arms if I give him up for good."

Tod and Emma both watched me, like they were waiting for me to clue in to the punch line of some horribly inappropriate joke.

"You think he would?" My heart throbbed with each beat, as if it were suddenly too big for my chest.

"He might fall into her, but he's more likely to land on her lap than in her arms," Tod said, pulling no punches, as usual.

"They have a history, and they're still really close, Kay," Emma said, watching for my reaction before continuing. "You're probably the only thing keeping them apart, and if you tell him he's never gonna get you back, and he should try to get over you, why *wouldn't* he turn to her?"

I had no answer that wouldn't be a lie, and the truth hurt too much to say out loud. "Doesn't matter, I guess," I said finally, studying the wood grain of the tread beneath my hand. "I'm not giving him up."

"Hey, shouldn't you guys be in class?" Tod asked, obviously trying to change the subject.

"I have a free period." And the only thing stopping me from going off campus for a long lunch was the fact that all of my friends had actual third period classes. Speaking of which...

"Are you supposed to be in art?" I asked Em.

She shrugged and held up the giant novelty paintbrush Mr. Bergman used as a bathroom pass. "I *might* be having a really bad menstrual cycle. Bergman's too squeamish to question it."

"That'll get you out of a whole class?" Tod frowned. "No fair using physiology against the entire male gender."

Em grinned. "Says the only person in the building who could put on a one-man version of *The Haunting*. Right, Casper?"

Tod scowled. "I'm a reaper, not a ghost."

"Whatever. Anyway, girl problems are good for fifteen minutes, max. Five, with a female teacher," she said, standing with the giant paintbrush. "So I gotta get back. See you at lunch?"

I nodded.

"Let's go get Chick-fil-A. I'd kill for some waffle fries," Tod said, as Em took the first two steps.

"You'd kill for a lot less than that," she shot over her shoulder.

"You got cash?" I asked, already warming to the idea of lunch off campus. Without Sabine.

Tod scowled. "No, but I can pay you back." He never

had any money, because the reaper gig didn't pay in human currency.

"I'll buy you both lunch, if you bring me something." Emma was on her way up the steps again, already digging into her pocket. But coming back would mean dealing with Sabine at lunch.

Emma handed me a twenty, and I took it hesitantly. Disappoint my best friend with no explanation, or suffer through Sabine's infuriating presence...?

Finally I pocketed the twenty and stood. "What do you want?"

"Nuggets and fries. And a Coke. Thanks, Kay!" With that, she bounded down the steps and out the gym door as Tod and I made our way down the bleachers.

"You know, you could probably make a killing—no pun intended—working at Pizza Hut during your down-time." He worked twelve hours a day at the hospital and had the other twelve free, and he spent most of that time bored, since he didn't need to either eat or sleep. "I mean, you could just blink out of the parking lot and show up wherever the pizza's supposed to go, just like that." I snapped my fingers, then lowered my voice when I realized we were nearing a group of students. "You'd be the fastest delivery guy in history."

Tod huffed. "Like I want to spend my afterlife delivering pizza."

I shrugged. "At least that gig would pay in cash. And probably in pizza."

The reaper looked intrigued for a moment, then shook his head firmly. "Then who'd be around to pop in and drive you nuts when you start getting too serious? I perform an important role in your life, you know."

"Yeah, well, Sabine's starting to give you a run for your money," I whispered, as we headed out of the gym and into the hall.

We passed the closed art and music room doors on the way to the parking lot, but as we approached the library, a sudden shrieking shredded the midday quiet. Tod and I ran into the library to find Chris Metzer, president of the robotics club, standing between a table and the chair he'd obviously been sitting in moments earlier, face scarlet, eyes wide as everyone else in the room stared at him.

"Chris?" The librarian rounded her desk in a series of short, even steps, constricted by her long pencil skirt. "What happened? Are you okay?"

"Fine. Sorry." Chris scooped his books up from the table and I noticed the repeating-line imprint of a spiral-bound notebook on his left cheek. "It was just a stupid dream." Then he hurried past us and into the hall, cheeks still flaming.

I elbowed Tod, and he frowned. "I know, I know."

"Sabine," I whispered, as he followed me into the empty hall. "But when she Sleepwalks, her physical body looks like it's sleeping, right? Where could she go to sleep uninterrupted here at school?" Not the library. Not anymore, anyway...

Tod shrugged. "Storage closet? Locker room?"

I shook my head. During lunch or after school, sure. But those were both actively used during class periods. "Her car," I said, in a sudden stroke of inspiration.

I raced down the main hall and past several open

classroom doors, crossing my fingers against any teachers vigilant enough to notice me. Tod followed, his silent footsteps signaling that no one else could see or hear him.

I shoved open the side exit door just in time to see Sabine get out of her car in the third row. When she noticed me, she smiled and waved, then started around the side of the building toward the quad and the cafeteria. We had to jog to catch up with her, and when we finally did, we were almost to the quad.

"What the hell did you think you were doing?" I demanded, winded, but pleased to realize Tod hadn't deserted me for his waffle fries. Of course, I still had Emma's money.

Sabine shrugged without slowing. "Walking. The most common form of locomotion among American high school students." She glanced at my feet. "Looks like you've mastered the skill."

"I'm talking about Chris Metzer. You can't just Sleepwalk into people's dreams in the middle of the school day."

"I can if they fall asleep at school. Did you know Metzer's afraid of clowns? Like, *seriously* afraid of them. When he was four, he went to his cousin's birthday party and the clown cornered him behind the pool house and—"

"Sabine," Tod said, blessedly interrupting a sentence I desperately didn't want her to complete.

The *mara* blinked in surprise. But she recovered quickly. "Tod! Nash said you were back with us. So... how's the afterlife?"

Tod shrugged, amiable, now that she'd stopped publicly

spewing someone else's darkest fears. "Dull, mostly. But there's no commute, and I don't have to exercise to maintain perfection." He spread his arms, inviting us both to inspect the form he was frozen in.

Sabine arched one eyebrow. "Sounds like a win."

Another shrug. "Death has its advantages."

I glared at them both, but neither noticed. How had I gotten stuck between a grim reaper and a walking nightmare?

"So, you get to see people as they die, right?" Sabine peered around me at Tod. "Do they get scared? Do you ever just sit back and think, 'Damn, I love my job!'"

"Yeah, there's usually some fear. I work at the hospital, so most of the ones I take know they're dying, so they have a little time to get worked up about it."

"Tod!" I snapped, more than fed up with their morbid social hour. "She was just *feeding* from someone in the middle of the school day. Can you at least *pretend* that's not okay?"

The reaper gave me a funny little smile—like he was more amused by my reaction than upset over what she'd done—then turned to the *mara,* plastering a frown over the grin I could still see leaking through.

"She's right, Sabine. You're getting careless. Is this about Nash?"

Sabine sat on the edge of the first picnic table in the quad and shrugged, glancing from one of us to the other. "I don't know *what* this is about. I was just minding my own business, having a little snack, when you two decided to team up on me. And not in the good way."

I rolled my eyes. "This is about you trying to kill

Chris Metzer in the middle of third period, just hours after you drained Mr. Wells at his own desk. You're not just a murderer, you're a pig. Good thing you can't actually gain weight on psychic energy, or we'd have to roll you out of here like a giant marshmallow."

Sabine watched me calmly for a moment, and I became acutely aware that my cheeks were flaming in anger. Then she turned to Tod, completely unruffled by my accusation. "Is she supposed to be on medication, or something? What the hell is she talking about?"

"I'm talking about Wells." I stepped between her and the reaper, so she couldn't ignore me. "The vice principal? And Mr. Wesner. And Mrs. Bennigan. And now Chris Metzer. You can't just walk around killing people every time your stomach growls!"

"I'm not sure where you're getting these delusions, but you need to step *away* from the crack pipe, Cavanaugh. I didn't hurt Metzer. He's never gonna miss what little energy I took, and if I'd wanted him dead, he'd be staring at the inside of a body bag right now. And as for those teachers, I've never even read their fears, much less played around in their dreams. Feeding from old-people fears is like eating tofu when you could have sirloin. I mean, why bother with the geriatric crowd, when guys my own age taste so much better?"

"You're lying," I said through gritted teeth, and Sabine only laughed.

"I've done a lot of things I'm not proud of—okay, I'm not really ashamed of them, either—but lying isn't one of them. Why would I give someone else credit for my hard work? For example, when I have my legs wrapped around your boyfriend, I'm not going to give you credit for losing him. I'm gonna give *me* credit for *taking* him."

My vision bled to red and my hand flew. But I didn't truly realize I'd slapped her until her hand swung up to cover her cheek and my palm started tingling like I'd just grabbed a live wire.

Tod gaped at me, obviously more surprised by how I'd reacted than by what she'd said.

Sabine stared at me, and I relished the shock clear in her eyes, even as a deep thrill of primal satisfaction burned hot in my gut.

But then she smiled and her hand fell to her side, revealing the angry red patch on her left cheek. "Atta girl! *Now* we're playin' the game! I wasn't gonna make this physical, but if you insist…" She pulled her fist back, and I flinched. But then Tod was suddenly between us, holding her back.

"Outta my way, reaper," Sabine growled, and even as my heart throbbed in my throat, I noticed that she looked much less creepy when she wasn't smiling. Anger suited her better, like the grin she usually wore was a weird, ironic mask. "She started it."

"You baited her." Tod shoved her back by both shoulders, and I realized he'd had to become completely corporeal to do it.

"If she wants to fight for him, I say let her. I'll play fair—no fear-reading, I swear."

*Oh, crap.* My pulse raced so fast my vision was starting to go gray. Why the hell had I hit her? Sabine had been to *jail,* and I'd never even thrown a punch.

Yet to my surprise, I realized I didn't regret it. Even

though I'd probably get my jaw broken in front of the whole school. Sabine was a slutty, boyfriend-stealing, murdering Nightmare, and someone had to call her on it.

Evidently that someone was me.

"No, Sabine." Tod stepped to the left when she tried to dodge him, and I stood there like an idiot when she raised both brows at me over his shoulder.

"You gonna let living dead boy protect you, or are you gonna put on your big-girl pants and fight for your boyfriend?"

"This isn't about Nash," I insisted, secure from behind the reaper, at least for the moment. Anger, confusion, and fear swirled inside me like a thick, dark storm. "Okay, that last bit was about Nash. But the rest of it is about you leaving a series of dead bodies in your wake, like slime from a slug's trail."

Sabine stopped struggling with Tod and glanced up at him. "She's crazy. You do realize she's completely, mind-bogglingly insane, right?" And from the way she watched me for my reaction, I knew that she knew.

That righteous, burning feeling in my stomach turned ice cold. "Nash told you?"

"He didn't have to. I know what you're afraid of and why," she said, eyes glittering in satisfaction. "But I don't hold it against you." She shrugged. "We've both spent time in state institutions."

I stood there, shaking with rage, but Sabine wasn't done.

"I don't think you understand, Cavanaugh," she said around Tod's shoulder. Then she glanced up at him and gave him a shove. "Move, reaper, I'm not gonna hurt her." Tod stepped reluctantly out of her way, but stuck close to my side, just in case. For which I was profoundly grateful.

Sabine's attention turned back to me, and her eyes were endless black pits of despair. "Nash and I aren't a thing of the past. We're a thing of *forever.* You're a fleeting fascination for him. The only female *bean sidhe* he's ever met, other than his mom. Of course he's going to be curious, but curiosity's all it is. He'll get over that, and he'll get over *you,* and I'll be there waiting."

"It's not just curiosity," I insisted through clenched teeth, my throat thick with the denial. *It couldn't be.*

"You're right—it's part guilt." She crossed her arms over her chest and stood with her feet spread, guy-tough, yet somehow still hotter than I'd ever be. "You've managed to make him feel guilty for what he is, and for an addiction that's all your fault, even though he's killing himself trying to overcome them both. But he shouldn't have to. If you really cared about him, you'd be the one there with him at night, when he's shaking from needing a hit. When he's sick to his stomach, and sweating, and trying to look like he isn't dying inside."

I swallowed, guilt bubbling up inside me, but she wasn't done.

"If you really cared about him, you wouldn't have told him to stay out of your head. His Influence is part of who and what he is, and you made it clear that he can't be that person when he's with you."

"You don't know what he did…" I started, blinking away tears I refused to let fall. "He didn't tell you that. I *know* he didn't."

"You're so naive it would be cute, if it weren't so pathetic." Sabine shook her head, but her focus never left me. "Nash and I don't have any secrets. He told me. It was this whole big confession for him, and the entire time he's telling me how he lied to you, and pushed you, and let that demon use you, he's looking at me like his fate's in my hands. Like he'll be damned forever if he sees judgment in my eyes. But he won't. He never will, because here's the thing—Nash can tell me anything. He can tell me how guilty he feels for using Influence to try to get into your pants. That's one of his very worst fears, and maybe it should be. He shouldn't have done that to you, because you can't take it. You're too fragile. One push too many, and you'll shatter into a million shards of Kaylee, all sharp and broken, and he'll be left to pick up the pieces.

"But I won't break," she continued. "And guess what else." Her voice dropped into an exaggerated whisper, and she leaned closer as Tod tensed beside me. "This may make me a dirty girl, but I *like* it. Nash's Influence? It's a game of control—a challenge to see who has it, which is a high all on its own for someone like me. Someone who has to be in control of herself for every minute of every single day, to keep from creeping out everyone she ever looks at. After that, letting someone else have control for a few minutes… It's something between a relief and a rush, and it's *fun*. Nash can't hurt me, and I can't hurt him. We can be ourselves around each other, and that's something you and he will never, ever have. Not ever. Because you don't trust him. And you never will. And in his heart, he knows it."

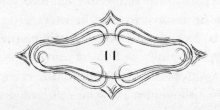

11

At 4:23, someone knocked on my front door. I'd just pulled a bag of popcorn out of the microwave and was about to do some research online, trying to dig up dirt on Sabine. Looking for anything that would make Nash and Tod take my suspicions seriously.

At first, I hesitated to answer the door. What if it was my own personal Nightmare, come to kick my teeth in when Tod wasn't there to stop her? But I shrugged that off. The last thing I needed was something else to be afraid of, and the truth was that in spite of her record, in-your-face violence didn't seem to be Sabine's style. She was much more likely to sneak in at night and make me dream she beat the crap out of me. Then had victory sex with Nash. Or something equally violent and crude.

Still, I peeked through the front window, just in case, and sucked in a surprised breath. *Nash.* I should have guessed from the fact that I hadn't heard a car pull up.

My heart beat a little harder when I opened the door, but I didn't invite him in.

He didn't smile. "Did you really hit Sabine?"

"Yeah." I went back to my homework on the couch and he followed me in, pushing the door shut at his back. "Why?"

I lifted both brows at him and pulled open the popcorn bag from its corners. Fragrant steam puffed up onto my face. "The more logical question might be why I waited so long."

Nash sighed and sank into my father's chair while I dumped popcorn into a bowl on the coffee table. "She wouldn't tell me why."

I faked shock. "I thought you two told each other everything? How could she keep a secret from her soul mate?"

Nash frowned, but looked more frustrated than angry. "If you don't tell me, I'll just ask Tod."

"What makes you think he'll talk?"

"He'll tell me if he thinks it'll help you, or piss her off."

"They sounded pretty chummy this afternoon. All dark and morbid together."

Nash shrugged. "He likes you better." He pulled off his jacket and laid it over the arm of the chair. "Please tell me, Kaylee. What the hell happened in third period?"

Tod and I had left for Chick-fil-A before the lunch bell rang, specifically to avoid Nash and Sabine. We'd texted Em to meet us at the restaurant. I was now considering eating out every day, just to avoid another confrontation. With either one of them.

I shook salt over the popcorn, avoiding his gaze. "She told me she was going to sleep with you. Not a huge surprise—I know what she wants—but it was the way she said it. She's so sure I have nothing to offer you, and she has everything you can't resist."

"And you believe her?"

I closed my laptop and finally looked at him. "I don't know what to believe. You told her things about me. You had no right to talk about me when I wasn't there."

"I wasn't telling her about you. I was telling her about *me*. You just happen to be a big part of my life. And, unfortunately, a big part of everything I've screwed up lately. Kaylee, what I want from her and what I want from you are two completely different things."

"Could you be more vague?" I crunched into the first bite of popcorn, but found it tasteless.

"I want you the same way I've always wanted you."

"The way you used to want her?" He'd love Sabine once—for real—but claimed to have gotten over her. If he was lying, wouldn't he eventually realize he wanted her back? And if he was telling the truth, did that mean he could get over me just as easily as he'd gotten over her?

"Yeah," he said, and I had a moment of panic until I realized he was answering the question I'd actually voiced, not the ones playing over and over in my head. "But now she's just a friend."

"Have you told her that?"

"I tell her all the time."

I pushed the bowl away, my appetite suddenly gone. "She seems to be selectively deaf."

"Well, she's stubborn, and she definitely knows what

she wants." He paused, and I looked up to find him watching me. "I wish I could say the same about you."

I closed my eyes, trying to draw my thoughts and a tangle of emotions I couldn't even describe into some kind of coherent stream. I knew what I wanted. But Sabine was right—I was scared to be with Nash while he was still fighting cravings, because if he gave in, even just once, the Netherworld would have him again. And if it had Nash, it would also have a piece of me. But I couldn't tell him to his face that I didn't have absolute faith in his recovery.

So I said nothing, and there was only silence. Painful, tense silence, like a wire wound so tight it would soon snap and lash us both. And finally Nash spoke, staring at the hands he clasped loosely between his wide-spread knees.

"Kaylee, do you even want me back? Because if you don't, and I make her go, I've lost both my girlfriend and my best friend."

"She's your best friend now?" How was that even possible? She'd only been here for three days! That was an insanely short period of time for everything that had changed!

"She's my best friend *again*. In case you haven't noticed, the other candidates have vacated the position," he snapped, and for just a moment, I saw a glimpse of the bitter, brittle pain he'd kept bottled up since Doug's death and Scott's descent into madness, buried beneath his own dark cravings and wavering willpower. "And as you pointed out, Tod's barely speaking to me."

"Well, then, you need to find a better friend." I stood

and stomped into the kitchen with my bowl of popcorn. "Someone who won't try to carve me out of your life or feed from your friends' fear."

Nash followed me. "You didn't answer the question."

"You're not asking the right one." I set the bowl next to the sink and turned to face him. "Do I want you back? Yes. Desperately. Even though part of me thinks I shouldn't. But wanting you isn't enough anymore. I need to know that it's not going to happen again. Any of it."

"You don't trust me." He crossed his arms over his chest, the line of his jaw tight.

"And she says I never will, right?" I demanded, and Nash nodded. "Do you even realize what she's doing? She's telling you I'll never be able to trust you, while she's tempting you to betray my trust. She's engineering her own predictions."

"Is she right?"

"I don't know!" I crossed the kitchen to throw away my popcorn bag, determined to keep space between us, because when I got close to him, it was hard to remember what I was thinking, even without his Influence. When he was close, all I wanted to do was hold him and remember how that used to feel. How it could still feel, if I could at least forgive, even if I never truly forgot. "You have to earn trust, and you don't do that by hanging out with your ex-girlfriend until all hours of the night."

Nash leaned against the tiled peninsula, watching me. "I wish you would stop thinking of her as my ex and start thinking of her as my friend."

"I wish she would do the same!" I whirled on him and threw my hands in the air, exasperation practically leaking from my pores. He looked miserable, and I was pretty sure I looked crazy, so I took a deep breath and forced my voice back into the realm of reasonable.

"Okay, look." I took a deep breath, bracing myself for what I had to say next. I didn't want to do it this way— I'd wanted to wait until I had some kind of evidence— but waiting no longer seemed to make sense. "This entire conversation is probably pointless, anyway."

He frowned, hazel eyes narrowed. "Why?"

"I think she killed them, Nash. Mr. Wesner and Mrs. Bennigan, and Mr. Wells. Your 'best friend' is a murderer."

"No." Nash shook his head without hesitation, and I almost felt sorry for him. It must be hard to surface from such a sea of denial and finally breathe the bitter truth.

"What, she didn't tell you that, either? Maybe she's the one who can't be trusted."

He crossed the kitchen toward the breakfast table in one corner and pulled out a chair with his brows raised, asking me to sit with him. I nodded reluctantly and sank onto the seat he'd offered. He took the one on my left. "Kaylee, Sabine didn't kill them. I know it's weird, three teachers dying so close together, and it's definitely suspicious. But she had nothing to do with it. Why would you even think that?"

"Because *maras* suck the life force out of people while they dream." I was frustrated and half-embarrassed by my lack of proof, but thoroughly convinced I was right. "Sabine shows up at Eastlake, and suddenly three teachers are dead. And they all died in their sleep. It's not a huge leap in logic."

"Okay, but it's not a slam dunk, either. Sabine doesn't kill people. Why would she, when she can get plenty of energy from a single nightmare? She doesn't even have to feed every night."

"Well, she has been. She's fed from me two nights in a row, and she gave Chris Metzer a nightmare during third period today. That's what started our whole confrontation."

Nash nodded too many times, like his brain was only a word or two ahead of his mouth. "Okay, yeah, she told me about Metzer."

She had? Why would she admit that?

"But that doesn't mean she killed anybody. She didn't do it, Kaylee. I…" He rubbed his forehead, and I was pretty sure I'd given him a headache. "I wish you knew her like I know her. You'd understand then. She likes people to think she's tough—and maybe she is. But she's not a murderer. She's not even really a fighter. The fights she's been in were all self-defense."

All? How many had there been?

"Nash, my dad knows about the teachers." About Mr. Wesner and Mrs. Bennigan, anyway. "And he's looking into their deaths. Something's obviously wrong—I had to tell him. And I'm gonna have to tell him about Sabine, too."

"Wait." Swirls of color exploded in Nash's irises and he grabbed my hand, squeezing it on the tabletop. "Don't tell him about her. Please, Kaylee. If you think she did it, he will, too, but I swear on my soul that she didn't do this." He looked so desperate, so heartbroken, and my chest ached at the reminder of how much he cared about her. "Just give me a couple of days, and I'll prove it."

"How are you gonna do that?" I pulled my hand gently from his grasp, and he suddenly looked lost, clearly grasping at mental straws.

"Hospital records," he said finally. "I'll make Tod get them for me. That'll prove they all died of natural causes."

"Really?" I lifted one brow and crossed my arms over my chest. "So…what would the autopsy report say about someone who was drained by a *mara?*"

Nash frowned as my point sank in. "Probably heart failure." Which was ultimately the cause of any death. "Fine. But I'll find a way to prove it. Just don't tell him about her yet. If he thinks she's dangerous and that I'm hanging out with her, he'll never let me see you again. Give me a couple of days. Please, Kaylee. I don't want to lose you."

"You don't want to lose *her.*"

He took my hand again, and I let him, against my better judgment. "I don't want to lose either of you."

"What about your mom?" I asked. "My dad will ask my uncle and your mom for help looking into this, and your mom knows Sabine's back, right?"

"Yeah, but she *knows* Sabine—she'd never bring her up as a suspect. But if you do, your dad will believe you."

I thought about it and finally nodded. Why not? When he couldn't find any proof that Sabine hadn't murdered Wells, Bennigan, and Wesner, he'd have to finally face the truth. And surely he couldn't possibly still want her once she'd been outed as a murderer.

Right?

"So, how'd it go?" I asked, as Alec closed and locked the front door.

"Oh, you know. Popcorn, soda, candy, scalding-hot butter-flavored oil."

"Not that." I smiled from the couch. It felt good to be talking about something normal. Something other than addict ex-boyfriends, Nightmare ex-girlfriends, and dead teachers. "The interview."

"Oh!" Alec's eyes gleamed like onyx, and I was amazed how different his eyes could look from Sabine's, considering they were nearly the same color. "I got it! I start third shift next week. I gave my notice at Cinemark tonight."

"Awesome! Third shift, though? That's gonna suck."

He shrugged on his way into the kitchen. "I'm not sleeping at night, anyway. How much worse can sleeping in the day be?"

"Yeah, I guess. We'll miss you at the theater, though."

Alec grabbed a Coke from the fridge while I gathered up my homework, preparing to vacate his makeshift bed. He looked tired. "You'll get over it. You don't wanna work with an old man like me, anyway, right?" He grinned, but I couldn't help wondering how much of that was for show.

"Oh, stop it. You may be forty-five on the inside, but outside you're a very young, very hot nineteen, and you have nothing but good things to look forward to."

"Especially with the new job," my dad added, and I

whirled to see him standing in the living room doorway, holding a half-eaten apple.

"Hey, why didn't you tell me he got the job?" My dad had been home for hours and had sat through an entire half a pizza and my recap of the vice principal's death without leaking a word of their good news.

"That's Alec's announcement. And don't call him hot."

I rolled my eyes, but smiled, shoving my folded chemistry homework into the textbook. "I'll leave you two coworkers to celebrate. I'm going to bed."

"So early?" My dad ducked his head to glance at the clock over the stove in the kitchen. It was just past ten-thirty.

"I'm a growing girl. I need my sleep." Actually, I was going to get in bed with my laptop and try again to dig up some dirt on Sabine.

"Common sense looks good on you," my dad declared, as I brushed past him and into the hall.

"Well, apple doesn't look good on you," I said, glancing at the tiny clump of white stuck on his stubble. "Use a napkin." I smiled, then went into my room and closed the door. Twenty minutes later, I was sitting under the covers with my computer on my lap when Tod appeared in the middle of my floor.

"Crap!" I jumped, startled, and nearly dropped the laptop.

"Sorry." Tod reached out to steady it with one hand, then sat on the edge of my bed.

"What are you doing here?" I closed my laptop and set it on the bedside table. "My dad will kill you if…"

He laughed. "The longer I'm dead, the less threat that carries."

"What's going on, Tod?"

He exhaled and reluctantly met my gaze. "I wasn't spying on them. I swear. Not this time, anyway. I went over there looking for my mom. I thought she had to-night off."

"I'm guessing you were wrong?" I was also guessing we were talking about Nash and his ex, and my stomach twisted at the thought.

"Yeah. My mom was leaving just as Sabine pulled up."

"What does this have to do with me?" I already knew they were hanging out, and hopefully Nash was making good on his promise to make her back off.

"I think you should see this."

"Why?" My heart thumped in my throat, and I had to swallow it to speak. "Are they…?" 'Cause I didn't want to see that. Ever.

"It's not what you think. They're just talking. But I think you need to see them together to understand their relationship. To understand why he won't let her go. Because if you take Nash back, I don't think you'll be get-ting just him."

"Tod, I don't wanna…"

"Trust me, Kay."

12

THE NIGHT WAS COLD, and I hadn't brought a jacket. I hadn't thought much beyond making the reaper turn around while I changed out of my pajamas. "So, how do we...?"

"Get in without being seen?" Tod finished for me, and I nodded. I'd sworn Alec to secrecy as I snuck out the kitchen door, then had to walk all the way so my dad wouldn't hear me start my car. And finally Tod and I stood in front of Nash's house, staring at it in the dark. "That's the fun part. I hope."

"Huh?" I glanced at the reaper and he gave a little shrug, but the uncertain gesture made me nervous. "What am I missing?"

"I've only done this a couple of times. I don't exactly have anyone to practice on—"

"Practice on?" I interrupted, but he spoke over me.

"—but you only have to remember a couple of things."

"What things?" I frowned up at him and found his grin highlighted by the streetlight across the road. "What are you talking about?"

"I'm going to blink into Nash's room. With you."

"Is that even possible?" And if so, why hadn't he ever told us? We could have saved so much time and gas money!

"Yeah. But I'm not exactly an expert yet. I can only take one person, and I can't go very far."

"Which is why we had to travel the pedestrian route?"

"Yeah." His grin widened. "Also, I don't have enough strength—or maybe not enough experience—to keep you invisible and inaudible at the same time. So…breathe very softly and don't talk."

"Tod! I can't go in there and spy on Nash! He'll hear us, then it'll get messy, and he'll never trust either of us again!"

His brows rose, and the streetlight glittered off his blue eyes. "You're worried about *him* trusting *us?*"

Okay, obviously that would be the kettle shouting at a couple of black pots, but there was enough distrust in our fractured relationship already.

The real problem wasn't the possibility that Nash might discover us, but the fact that I'd let Tod talk me into spying on him in the first place. However, since we were already playing fast and loose with moral constraints, I saw no reason to make things worse by getting caught.

"What do I have to do?"

"Just take my hand and be quiet. And don't let go, or

you'll suddenly appear in the middle of his room, and then there will be drama. And I hate drama."

"Noted."

"You ready?"

"No." I shook my head for emphasis, shivering from the cold. "But let's go before my teeth start chattering." There was no way I could keep them from hearing that.

He took my hand, and for a moment I could only watch him, getting used to the unfamiliar feel of his warm, dry palm against mine. His fingers wrapped around mine loosely, then squeezed, and I thought I saw the slightest swirling of color in his eyes.

My pulse leaped and I blinked, breaking eye contact, then blinked again, confused by what I'd almost seen.

Tod stared at me for just a second longer, then shook his head, and his ironic grin was back. "Okay, wish me luck!"

"Wish *you* luck!" I gaped at him.

"Just kidding." He put one finger against his lips in the universal signal for "shhhh!" In the next instant, my stomach seemed to drop right out of my body, like it used to on the swings, when I was a kid.

I closed my eyes. An instant later, when my stomach settled, I opened my eyes to see Nash's room coming into focus around us. My mouth fell open, and I would have gasped at the eerie *settling* feeling throughout my body, but Tod squeezed my hand again, a silent reminder to be quiet.

And that's when my ears popped, and suddenly the world had sound again.

"...that time it started pouring, two blocks from your

house?" Sabine asked, and Nash laughed. They lay side by side on his bed, on their stomachs, propped up on their elbows with their sock feet resting on his pillows. A photo album lay open in front of them at the foot of the bed, and Nash turned a clear plastic page as he answered.

"Too bad you don't have pictures of that! We were so soaked my shoes squished for a day."

"Remember how we got warm?" Sabine asked, her voice softer than I'd ever heard it. Nash turned to look at her, and their mouths were inches apart.

I held my breath, and Tod's hand tightened around mine again, another silent warning. But as my teeth ground together, I knew that if he kissed her, I wouldn't be able to quiet my anger and betrayal. Not that it would matter, if that happened. Me and Tod suddenly appearing in Nash's bedroom while he made out with his ex would be the least of Nash's problems.

But he didn't kiss her. Nash only grinned, then stared down at the photo album, the slight ruddiness in his cheeks the only sign that the memory still affected him.

I should have been happy. I should have been giddy with relief to see him actually pass up an opportunity most guys would have pounced on. But instead of relief, I swallowed a bitter, acrid taste on the back of my tongue. The memory—whatever they'd done that day, when they were soaked, cold, and in love—still affected him. Because he hadn't sold it to Avari for another dose of poisoned air. He'd kept the emotional impact of his memories of Sabine intact, and gutted his memories of me instead.

"Like I could forget," Nash said, oblivious to both my

presence and my pain. He flipped another page and she watched him, rather than the pictures.

"Would you, if you could? Forget?" she added, when he looked confused. "Would you forget about me?"

His eyes widened, and I could see the slow churning in them, even from across the room. "No. I wouldn't forget you, or a single moment we spent together, Sabine. You were my first everything, and that still means something, even now that everything's changed. It always will."

Her smile looked painful, like she didn't know whether to laugh or cry. "Did you try to find me, Nash?" she asked at last, after he'd flipped several more pages in silence, and I realized with surprise bordering on amazement that she sounded...bruised. Lost. "Did you even look for me, after you left?"

Nash closed the album and sat up, while she rolled onto her back, staring up at him. "Yeah. I tried to call you at Holser House, to tell you we were moving, but they wouldn't let me through. They wouldn't even take a message."

She nodded, and her hair fell to hang down the side of his bed. "You weren't on my approved calls list, and I lost all my privileges when they found the cell you gave me."

"I tried calling the Harpers after that, but they didn't know anything about your new foster home. The school said you'd transferred, but wouldn't tell me where. And the internet didn't seem to know you even existed."

"Yeah, it took me a while to find you, too." She closed her eyes and let her head roll to one side. "I was stupid to think you'd wait for me."

"Bina..." Nash looked like she'd just ripped out his

heart and shown it to him, still beating, and as badly as I wanted to hate her, I found anger harder to cling to in that moment than ever before. She really was his first everything—including his first broken heart.

"Do you ever wonder what would have happened?" she asked, rolling onto her side to face him again. "If you'd never left? If I hadn't gotten arrested again?"

"I…" Nash exhaled heavily, and I hated the confliction I read in the slow twist of green in his irises. "Yeah, I do. But what-ifs are pointless, Bina. It can't be like it was then. Not anymore."

"It *could* be." She reached up to brush a chunk of thick brown hair from his forehead, and I bit my lip to keep from protesting. I didn't want her to touch him. Ever.

"No." He took her wrist before she could touch his hair again. "It's different now."

"Because of her," Sabine said, staring straight into his eyes. Nash nodded and let go of her. "She thinks I killed those teachers."

"I know."

"Do you believe her?"

"I know you better than that. But you haven't exactly given her a reason to trust you."

Sabine frowned and sat up facing him. "I've never lied to her. And I don't care if she trusts me."

Nash set the album on his pillow. "Yes, you do. I'm not going to be enough, Sabine. You need more than one friend."

She shook her head, and dark hair fell over her cheek. "You're all I need."

I'd never seen her look so vulnerable. In fact, I'd never

seen her look anything short of antagonistic, but she was obviously a completely different person with Nash. I didn't know whether to be relieved that she had a more human side, or pissed off that that side only emerged when she was alone with my boyfriend.

"No," he said. "I was all you had back then. You never had a real shot at any other relationship because you couldn't control yourself. But you can now."

"Shut up. You're making me sound needy just to piss me off."

"I'm telling the truth." He grinned. "Pissing you off is a bonus."

"Oh, you wanna see me mad?" Sabine returned his smile and shoved him back onto the mattress, then threw one leg over him, straddling him. My heart beat so hard it bruised my chest. I tried to pull away from Tod, but he held my hand tight and shook his head, like the ghost of relationships past, demanding I only watch.

Next, would we float through the open window?

Sabine stared down at him, her long hair half hiding them both. "You forget what happens when I lose my temper?" But from the way she was watching him, all flashing eyes and sly smile, I got the feeling she had a rather unconventional, hands-on approach to anger management.

"I haven't forgotten anything, Bina." Nash wrapped his hands around her wrists and gently pushed her back onto her side of the bed. "Including Kaylee. This isn't gonna work if you can't rein it in."

"This is *only* gonna work if I don't rein it in."

"I'm serious." Nash rolled onto his side, propped up on

one elbow. "You should give Kaylee a chance. She knows what you are. She could be a good friend, if you'd let her. If you'd stop trying to scare the shit out of her every time you see her."

Um…no, I could *not* be a good friend to a vengeful Nightmare. Had he lost his mind?

Sabine snorted. She actually snorted and somehow made it look endearing. "I don't have to *try* to scare her. All I have to do is let go. The hard part is not scaring the shit out of everyone else. That took a lot of practice."

I shot Tod a questioning glance. *How much more of this do I need to see?*

He just tossed his head toward the bed, where Sabine watched Nash like he was the only flicker of light in a very dark place.

Nash looked at Sabine like she was some complicated puzzle he was trying to solve, and I knew that look. He'd looked at me that way the first time he saw me sing for someone's soul, before I knew I was a *bean sidhe*. He'd looked at me like that when I was the damsel he felt honor-bound to save from distress, whether I needed saving or not. I used to love that look.

Now I hated it.

"Sabine," he said finally, when she showed no sign of breaking what was obviously a very comfortable silence. "Read me."

"What?" She frowned, looking genuinely uncomfortable for the first time since Tod and I had entered the room. "No."

"I want you to read my fear. For real. Go deep and take a look at what I'm really afraid of."

Her brows furrowed over dark eyes. "Why?" Suspicion was thick in her voice now.

"I think it'll help you understand."

"What if I don't want to understand?"

He leaned closer, looking right into her eyes. "Then you're a coward, and I'm ashamed of you."

Anger, ripe and bitter, passed over Sabine's fine features and her frown deepened. "Now you're trying to piss me off."

"I'm throwing down a challenge. You used to love a challenge. Has that changed?"

A new smile crawled over her lips, slow and dark, like the gleam in her eyes. "Nothing's changed. That's what I keep trying to tell you."

"Then read me."

Sabine sat up, and Nash pushed himself upright to face her. "You want me to make it fun? Like we used to?"

I glanced at Tod again. How could having his worst fear read possibly be fun? But the reaper didn't even look at me.

"Sabine..." Nash said, a very familiar warning in his voice.

She grinned, trying to make light of it, but mostly failing. "You can't blame a girl for trying."

But something told me I would be happy to blame her—if I had any clue what she was talking about.

"Fine. Give me your hand."

Nash held out his hand like he'd shake hers, but instead of a formal hold, Sabine threaded her fingers between his and held their merged grip between them, knuckles pointed toward the ceiling.

I thought they'd close their eyes, but instead, Sabine leaned closer to him, like she was trying to see through his pupils and out the back of his head. For several seconds, they stayed just like that. Nash blinked several times, but the *mara*'s gaze was unwavering.

However, her hand was not. By the time she finally blinked and he closed his eyes, her hand was shaking against his. She pulled her fingers from his and wiped her palm on her pants, like their shared sweat was contaminated by the fear of whatever she'd read inside him.

"What did you see?" he asked, and this time he was the steady one.

"Kaylee…" she whispered, and I nearly pulled my hand from Tod's in surprise.

Nash was afraid of me?

"You're scared of losing her." Sabine dropped her gaze, like it hurt too much to look at him. "You're terrified of it. You dream about it, because that's what he told you would happen. That demon. He said you'd lose her. That you weren't good enough for her now. That you don't deserve her. And you believe it. Your worst fear is that you're not good enough for Kaylee. And that she knows it."

My lips opened, and the breath I hadn't known I was holding slipped silently into the room.

I glanced at Tod, and he nodded. That's what he'd wanted me to see. Or at least something like that. Yet he didn't look happy.

"That doesn't make it any easier, you know," Sabine said. She scooted away from him, but seemed unwilling to get off the bed. "Knowing that."

"No. I'm guessing that makes it harder. But it's the truth, and the truth isn't always easy."

Sabine rolled her eyes. "What are you now, the Zen master? Did Kaylee tell you that?"

"Not in so many words. But you can usually tell what she's thinking just by watching her."

*No, you can't!* I frowned and felt my cheeks color, and suddenly I was extraglad they couldn't see us.

"Yeah, that whole subliminal 'go away and die' message comes through loud and clear." Sabine glanced around the room, and her gaze seemed to linger in the corner where we stood. I knew she couldn't see us, but her eyes creeped me out, anyway.

I'd seen enough. They were just talking now, and she obviously wasn't going to charm him out of his clothes. Or out of me. At least for the night.

*Let's go,* I mouthed silently to Tod, and that time he nodded. He closed his eyes, and I took that as my signal to do the same.

After another stomach-pitching second of existing nowhere, I felt ground beneath my feet and cold air on my cheeks. I opened my eyes to find us in front of Nash's house again, and as soon as I was sure I wasn't going to fall over from disorientation, I let go of Tod's hand. And immediately missed the warmth.

"Well, that was...interesting." I shoved my hands in my pockets, and Tod glanced at me in surprise, like I'd ripped the words off his own tongue. Then he smiled.

"Yeah, it..."

"I mean, how weird that they spent most of the time

talking about me. I guess that should make me feel better, huh?"

His brow furrowed like he wasn't following my logic, and he glanced over his shoulder at the house, as if that would clear it up. "Oh. Yeah." Then he smiled and said, "I have a feeling they do that a lot. So...*does* it make you feel better?"

"Yes, and no." I started walking toward the street, and Tod matched my stride.

"Why no?"

I hesitated. "Because seeing her like that—with him—makes it a little harder to believe she's a murderer." Not impossible. But definitely harder.

Tod shrugged. "So maybe she's not."

I frowned up at him. "She has to be. Who else could it be?" He opened his mouth, but I spoke over him. "And don't say it might not be anyone, because there's no way three of our teachers in two days just happened to die in their sleep, the same week Sabine moves to town."

"I agree. But that doesn't mean she's doing it."

"Then who is?"

"I don't know. But it could be anyone. Or any*thing*. Don't you think it's at least possible that you're fixating on Sabine because she's fixated on Nash?"

I stopped on the sidewalk, almost halfway between Nash's house and mine. He was right. I wasn't ready to dismiss Sabine as a suspect, but as long as I was playing cop, I might as well think like a cop, and a good cop would never rule out all other possibilities because of a personal vendetta against one suspect.

"Help me," I said, peering up at him against the glow of a streetlight.

"What?" Tod frowned.

"Help me. You know way more about Netherworld stuff than I do, and there's no way a human is doing this. If you really think Sabine's innocent, help me rule her out and come up with some other theories. We can't just let this go on. You said yourself that Wells, Bennigan, and Wesner weren't scheduled to die."

"Kaylee, I have to be at work in less than an hour."

I started walking again, and he had to jog to catch up. "When's your first reaping?"

Tod sighed. "Not till two. But I should really at least look like I'd like to keep my job."

"Come on, reaper! There's ice cream—we'll make a night of it."

Tod's brows rose and his eyes sparkled in the street-light. He glanced at my hand, hanging at my side be-tween us, then finally nodded. "You know I can't say no to ice cream."

"Or pizza, or pancakes, or Chick-fil-A…"

"Shut up before I change my mind."

13

WHEN WE GOT BACK to my house, I checked to make
sure my dad was asleep, then dug a half gallon of mint
chocolate chip from the freezer. Tod, Alec, and I ate
straight from the container while they helped me make a
list of every non-human creature who could possibly kill
a person in his sleep.

They seemed to agree that the killer was most likely
some kind of psychic parasite. But while Tod insisted
that, technically, any parasitic species could feed from a
sleeping victim—so we could be dealing with an incubus
or succubus, a *scado,* which feeds from anger, or a *neid,*
which feeds from jealousy—Alec insisted that a *mara* was
the most likely suspect, because Nightmares could *only*
feed from sleeping victims. The reaper scowled a lot at
Alec's conclusion, but couldn't argue.

When Tod had to leave for work, I retreated to my
room with my laptop and a slice of leftover pizza, hoping

that without me there to grill him on creepy-crawly trivia, Alec might actually get some sleep.

Between bites of pizza and gulps from a cold can of soda, I searched the internet for anything to do with Sabine Campbell. But none of the Sabine Campbells I found online were anywhere near the right age. She didn't maintain a profile on any networking sites I could think of—at least, not under her real name—nor did I get any hits on her from school websites. Which meant she wasn't active in sports or clubs, nor was she on the honor roll at her last school.

No surprise there.

And evidently juvenile criminal records aren't searchable, because I couldn't find a single word about her illustrious criminal past.

Then, finally, around two-thirty in the morning, I tripped over a stroke of brilliance. I searched for Nash's old school. The one where he'd met Sabine.

Her name didn't come up in any of the hits, but when I added the word *arrested* to the search, I struck gold.

Two years ago, about three months after Nash started at Eastlake as a sophomore, a fifteen-year-old female sophomore was arrested at his old school for assaulting a teacher. Two months after that, a fifteen-year-old female sophomore was removed from school property for possession of alcohol. The news stories—both from the same online paper—didn't say whether or not the two girls were the same person, but I had no doubt that they were. However, after that, all the trouble at Nash's old school seemed to have been caused by boys.

The logical conclusion? Sabine was either expelled or she moved.

But where did she go between Nash's last school and Eastlake? I knew I'd heard the name of her most recent school—Sabine had told Emma during their first conversation in junior English.

Valley something. Or something Valley. Valleyview? No. Oak Valley? No, but that was closer. It was something to do with nature.

And just like that, I remembered: Valley Cove. Sabine transferred to Eastlake from Valley Cove High School. I remembered Em saying that Sabine had joked that the town sported neither a valley nor any obvious cove.

After a little more searching, I came up with a single, year-old article in the tiny Valley Cove local newspaper—miraculously online—about a female junior who was suspended for vandalizing school property. She was caught in the act of spray painting "lewd images and crude language" on the side of the school building in the middle of the night.

*Yup. Sounds like Sabine.*

By the time I closed my laptop at three in the morning and snuck into the bathroom to brush my teeth, I was thoroughly convinced that Sabine was an unrepentant criminal. But I had absolutely no evidence that her crimes had ever included murder.

*I SIT UP IN BED and unease crawls beneath my skin like an army of tiny spiders. I blink sleep from my eyes and my room comes into focus, dark, but for the glow from a security light outside my window. Something is wrong, but*

*I can't tell what. Not yet. But my scalp feels prickled—my hair wanting to stand on end.*

*I smell it first, even before I hear it, and the spiders beneath my flesh writhe frantically. I know that smell. Once, a squirrel got trapped in the old trash can we rake leaves into, and when Dad found it, it smelled like this. Like rot. Like warm death.*

*My heart thumps painfully and I hold my breath. I don't want to smell that putrid stench, but I want to taste it even less, so I clamp my jaw shut.*

*Next comes the sound—a broken cadence of footsteps, punctuated by a horrible sliding sound. The steps are soft, but they get louder. Coming closer. My pulse races and I scoot back against the headboard, putting a few more worthless inches between me and whatever is step-sliding its way toward my room.*

*I should run. But I can't move. I'm frozen, morbid curiosity and paralyzing dread warring inside me while my door creaks slowly open.*

*My door shouldn't creak. It never has before. But it creaks now, and a gray hand pushes the doorknob.*

*I'm breathing too fast. I want to scream. Screaming has never failed me, but now my voice is as still as the rest of me. Waiting. Terrified.*

*Sweat drips down my spine. I feel it bead on my forehead and in the crooks of my arms. That gray hand leads to a wrist, which leads to an arm, which then leads to a shoulder, and before I know it, she's there. In my doorway. Staring at me through dead, milky eyes.*

*I can't breathe fast enough, and each breath smells like her. Like decay. Like things that should be rotting peacefully in the ground, not dripping thick, foul fluids on my carpet.*

*But the worst part is that though she should be blind, I know she sees me. Though her cracked, colorless lips shouldn't be able to move, they open. And though her throat has already rotted through, raw tendons peeking at me through the holes in her flesh, her voice still works, and I still recognize it.*

*I can never forget it, though I haven't heard it since I was three years old. Since the night she died. Since the night I died, and she took my place.*

*This walking, rotting, stinking corpse is my mother.*

*"I want it back," she says, and at first her voice is a whisper. She hasn't used it in thirteen years. "You squandered it, and I want it back."*

*"Mom?" I don't realize my own voice is back until I hear myself speak. Oh, how I've always wanted the chance to speak to her, just one more time. But not like this. This is wrong, so fundamentally perverse that I can't believe this is happening. Yet I can't deny it, either. Not with her stench in the air, polluting my lungs. Not with her hands reaching, reaching…*

*"You've wasted it. You're not living, you're just dying very slowly." Each word is an obvious effort, but she keeps going. "Give it back to me." She step-hobbles closer, and some part of me understands that her legs don't work right anymore. But the miracle, really, is that they work at all. She should be nothing but bones after thirteen years in the grave.*

*My skin crawls, and fear is the battery keeping my heart beating. I want to run, and I'm sure now that I can, physically. But I can't run from her. She's dead, and smelly, and oddly squishy, but she's my mother.*

*"Mom?" I say it again, waiting for it to sink in. Waiting for her to remember me, like I remember her. But her cloudy eyes show no warmth. No love. They are empty, and her voice is hard.*

*"You whine. You don't listen. You refuse to really live. You don't take risks, you don't make gains, and you're never going to grow up."*

*Terror and revulsion burn within me now, roasting me alive from the inside. Her words bruise like blows. Denial is the only reason I'm still conscious. I hate what she is, because I know it should be me. But I love her, because she's my mother. She gave me life. Twice.*

*"Mom?" It's a question this time, because my mother never spoke to me like this. My mom was kind and gentle, encouraging. I don't remember much, but I remember that.*

*"That would be fine, if you had at least one redeeming quality." She takes an awkward step forward, and I cringe, tears forming in my eyes. "One extraordinary trait, to prove you were worth my sacrifice." Another step, and I blink. Tears scald my cheeks, but still she comes. Still she speaks, shredding my soul with every hateful word. "Beauty. Brains. Talent. But you have none of that. You're mediocrity personified. You don't shine like I did."*

*Another step, and she's at the foot of the bed now. She leans forward, both hands on my blanket. Her fingers split like sausage casings beneath the pressure of her weight. Fluid oozes to stain the purple material, and I suck air in so fast I'm choking on it.*

*"I was the light in your father's life, shining to show him the way. But you don't shine. He gave you away because he couldn't stand to be with you. Because he knows what I know. What you know. That you're not worth it, Kaylee. You're not worth my life, and I want it back."*

*"Mom, no." Tears slide silently down my face, and I swipe at them. She crawls onto the bed. Her knees smear the stains her fingers left, and the stench is unbearable now.*

*Up close, I can see the details. Her skin is damp and gray and flaccid. Her eyelashes and eyebrows are long gone. Clumps of her hair are missing, but that's a mercy, because what's left is thin, brittle, and tangled, caked with dirt and stiff with dried bodily fluids.*

*"I just need your breath. That's all it takes...." she whispers. Her dress has holes, but I recognize it. She was buried in it. It used to be blue, the same shade as her eyes, but now it's faded, and stained, and almost as rotten as she is.*

*"Mom, you don't mean it." I'm scooting to the side now, finally in motion, but in my heart, I know it will do no good. If she can find me here, she can find me anywhere. I haven't lived up to her gift, and now she wants it back.*

*And she will get it. We both know that.*

*"You let my life rot, along with my body. If you ever loved me, give me back what I gave so foolishly...."*

*I pull my knees up to my chest and push myself away*

*from her. The corner of my nightstand pokes into my back. She reaches for my leg. Her fingers squish against my kneecap. More skin splits. Viscous liquid runs over my leg, and the smell is overwhelming.*

*My stomach revolts. Vomit rises in my throat. Tears blur my vision. Terror squeezes my heart with fists of iron.*

*Finally I scream, but it's too late. It is much, much too late.*

14

THAT TIME, I DIDN'T sit up in bed. I pulled the covers over my head like a child, half convinced I was still dreaming. That if I peeked into the room, she would be there waiting for me, that half-rotted perversion of my mother, demanding her life back before I could squander the rest of it.

I stayed like that until I got dizzy from breathing my own used oxygen, and when nothing crawled toward me, when the air never putrefied in my nostrils, I finally pushed back the covers and sat up.

My room looked normal. The door was still closed, but unlocked in spite of paranoid warnings from both Nash and Tod. My comforter was spotless, my knee still clean.

My mother had never stood in this room. She hadn't stood anywhere in more than thirteen years, and deep down I knew that even if she could come see me, she would never demand my life for the privilege.

My mother didn't want me dead. But I *was* afraid I'd wasted her gift. And Sabine obviously knew that.

With that realization came the blazing fury I needed to thaw my icy fear. But there would be no more sleep for me that night. Sabine had done her job very, very well.

"ANOTHER BAD DREAM?" Alec asked, as I tiptoed past the couch on my way to the kitchen. "That's the second one this week."

*Third, but who's counting?*

"Don't you ever sleep?" I demanded, without slowing.

He tossed back the blanket and sat up. "I was gonna ask you the same thing."

"I slept," I insisted, heading straight for the coffeepot. "Now I'm done. Just getting an early start."

The couch springs creaked behind me. "It's four-thirty in the morning."

I knew that, with every exhausted bone in my body. "Thus the word *early*."

"You couldn't have slept more than two hours."

The kitchen floor was cold on my bare feet, and I wished I'd remembered my slippers. "What are you now, a math major?" Or my dad?

"You're doing one hell of a Sophie impersonation this morning." Alec had only met my cousin once, and that was more than enough. "What's wrong?"

After staring at the remnants of the previous day's coffee, I decided making a fresh pot would be too much trouble and opted for a soda from the fridge instead. I popped the tab as I sank into my dad's chair across from the couch, where Alec now sat watching me in nothing but the gym shorts he slept in.

I took a long drink, then met his fatigued, bloodshot gaze. "Sabine's at it again. Or still at it. Or whatever."

"Nash's ex?" Alec rubbed the top of his head with one broad hand. "What's she doing?"

"The usual. Bullying her way into my head and sending nightmares. This has to stop."

"What's the big deal?" Alec shrugged smooth, dark shoulders. "They're just dreams, right? So shake it off and go back to sleep."

I blinked at him, trying to decide whether or not to take him seriously. "They're not just dreams, Alec. They're renderings of my own fears, ripe with life force for her to suck. She's a *mara,* remember?"

Alec's eyes widened, and he sat straighter on the couch. "*Sabine's* the *mara?* Why didn't you tell me?"

"I *did* tell you!"

Alec shook his head firmly. "The other night, you said you dreamed she made out with your ex, then tonight you said you knew a *mara.* But you never mentioned that the *mara* and Sabine are the same damn person!"

I set my can down and frowned at him. "Okay, you seriously need to get more sleep. I told you she was a *mara* last night. In the kitchen, remember?"

Alec looked startled—truly frightened, just for an instant—then his entire expression seemed to simply shut down, like when the power fails and the whole neighborhood goes dark. "Last night?" he repeated, cradling his head in his hands. "Would this have been in the middle of the night?"

"Yeah. While you were working your way through a box of my dad's cupcakes."

He exhaled slowly, then mumbled beneath his breath, "*That's* what he meant about the cupcakes…"

"What?" I leaned forward and studied his face when he finally looked up. "Are you okay?"

"Yeah. I'm just…sleep deprived, I guess. I barely remember last night. So…Sabine's a *mara?* For real?"

"Welcome to the conversation." I turned my head slowly back and forth, stretching out the cramp in my neck. "She's been exploiting my fears to try to scare me away from Nash."

"Wow." Alec whistled and leaned back with his arms crossed over his smooth, bare chest. "That's messed up. I mean, that's bordering on Netherworld-level torture. At least, of the psychological variety."

I picked up the can and took another sip, willing the caffeine into my system. "Yeah, she's not exactly warm and fuzzy."

"So what're you gonna do? You can't just let her walk all over you." Alec looked more awake, and I started to relax a little, now that he was sounding like himself again.

"I know. I thought I had it all taken care of, after I smacked her, and Nash said—"

"Wait, *you* hit someone?"

My fingers clenched around the cold, damp can. "Why does everyone sound so surprised by that?" But Alec only raised both brows at me. "Okay, I'm not exactly a prizefighter. But she had it coming. And anyway, after that, Nash said she promised to stay out of my dreams. Obviously she was lying. Or else he was."

"Which do you think it is?"

I took a long drink to avoid answering. "I honestly don't know. The truth is that I haven't been able to catch Sabine in a lie so far—she's frighteningly blunt—but Nash has lied to me repeatedly. How sad is it that I can trust his serial-killer ex-girlfriend better than I can trust him?"

"Killer…" Alec said, like he was tasting the word. "You really think she killed those teachers?"

"I don't know. She's openly confessed to everything else she's done, so why wouldn't she admit to this, if she's guilty? It's not like the police are going to arrest her for dream-stalking, right? So maybe it's not her." I shrugged and let my head rest on the back of the recliner. "But I don't have any other suspects. And anyway, you said it yourself—a *mara*'s the most likely suspect."

Alec frowned. "Yeah, but that was before I knew you were talking about someone you go to school with."

"What does that matter?"

He shrugged, obviously hesitating. "It's one thing to say that a certain species theoretically fits the bill for what you're looking for. But that doesn't mean that the one member of that species you actually know is definitely the killer. You can't go blaming someone of murdering your teachers without more proof than that, Kaylee."

I flinched. "Too late."

Alec blinked. "Please tell me you did not accuse a

*mara*—to her face—of killing someone. A *mara* who's already not crazy about you."

"Um…yeah. I did."

"Damn." He leaned back and stared at the ceiling. "I can't decide whether you're brave or stupid, Kaylee. No wonder she's playing dreamweaver in your head."

My scowl deepened. "She was doing that already. Besides, this makes sense. She's the only one with motive and opportunity."

Alec leaned forward again and shook his head, eyeing me solemnly. "You watch too much TV. Nothing's ever that cut and dried in real life. Especially when your suspects aren't even human."

I scooted to the edge of my chair, irritated. Why was I the only one who could see what Sabine was really capable of? "She's trying to scare me into backing down, from both Nash and this investigation."

"She wants you to give up on a boyfriend you're not sure you want back, and an investigation that consists entirely of a list of supernatural creatures scribbled on a phone message pad? Sorry, Kay, but it doesn't sound to me like she's the one lacking logic."

Wow. When he put it like that, the whole thing sounded so…insubstantial. And really, really pathetic. Still… "If you were a cop investigating a murder, wouldn't you be most interested in the suspect with a criminal record?"

Alec perked up again. "Wait, Sabine has a record? You didn't tell me that."

"Yes I *did!*" I set my Coke on the end table and studied him more closely. "You seriously need to start paying better attention. I know you're still getting readjusted to the human world, but your memory has so many holes we could strain noodles through it." And this was more than simple forgetfulness. I could tell from the way he refused to look at me, and from the tense line of his shoulders.

A chill developed at the base of my spine and began working its way up slowly. "What's going on, Alec?"

Alec took a long, slow breath, and only after several seconds of silence did he finally meet my gaze, deep brown eyes practically swimming in fear. "Something's wrong, and I think I'm starting to understand what's going on. I need to tell you something, but I need you not to freak out on me, okay?"

Why were people always telling me that?

The chills traveled up my spine and into my arms, where chill bumps burst to life. "Telling me not to freak out pretty much guarantees that I *will* freak out...."

"Sorry." He took a deep breath. "Here's the deal... My memory of the past few days doesn't just have holes in it. It has hollows. Big, gaping blank spots."

*Uh-oh.* "How big is big?"

Alec leaned back on the couch and scrubbed his face with both hands. "Scary big. I wake up and have no idea how I got wherever I am. I can't remember what I was doing. It's very...unsettling."

I would have gone with "bizarre and terrifying." But then, I hadn't spent the past quarter century surrounded by true terror.

"When did this...?" I began, then my voice faded into silence when the rest of what he'd said sank in. "Wait, you said you 'wake up' and have no idea what's going on. So…this happens when you go to sleep?"

The fear churning in my stomach put a bad taste in my mouth. Something strong and foul. Something distressingly familiar…

"Yeah. It's him, Kaylee." Alec's dark gaze held mine captive. "Avari's possessing me."

"No." I shook my head vehemently, even though denial wasn't really an option. "No, no, no. He can't." I made myself put my can down before I could crush it and drench myself in cold soda.

Alec stared back at me from the couch. He looked so vulnerable suddenly. Younger than his nineteen-year-old body, and much younger than his middle-aged mind and soul. "Nothing else makes sense."

"Neither does this," I insisted. "It can't be Avari. He doesn't have the strength. Not without you there to supply extra power."

For years, the hellion had used Alec like a walking snack, drawing energy and nutrition from him to fuel his own evil projects and ambitions. But without Alec at his disposal, Avari shouldn't have enough energy to possess someone in the human world. At least, not so often or for any serious length of time.

Alec sighed, and the weight that sound seemed to carry was unimaginable. "At this point, I'm assuming he's found a new proxy. I can't think of any other way this could be possible."

My head felt like it was about to explode. "You're saying Avari took over your body just to gossip with me and snag some snack cakes? No." He was wrong. He had to be. "Alec, you talked to me. Both of those times, you spoke, and it was your voice, not Avari's. That would have been impossible if he were possessing you."

Alec shook his head slowly. "No, that would have been impossible if he were possessing *you*. Or Emma, or Sophie, or anyone else he doesn't know very well. But I've spent the past twenty-six years with him, and he's been drawing power from me the entire time. He's intimately familiar with my physiology, and it makes sense that he'd know how to work my voice box, along with the rest of my body."

*No. Damn it, no!*

I was breathing too fast and had to focus to keep from hyperventilating. *This cannot be happening.* Avari could not have been so close to us—*inside* Alec—without us knowing! Not now that I knew the signs. The voice was the giveaway. He wasn't supposed to be able to use his puppet's voice!

"This doesn't make any sense, Alec. Why would he burn so much energy just to chat with me and eat some refined sugar? He didn't even tell me what he was doing, so he couldn't have been feeding off my fear and anger. Why would he go to all this trouble, then not take credit for it?"

Alec didn't answer. He propped his elbows on his knees and let his head hang below his shoulders, and all I could see of him then was the rapid rise and fall of his arched back while he breathed too fast and too hard.

"Alec? What are you not telling me?" Because it was obvious by then that there was more. Maybe much, much more.

But he didn't answer.

I left my chair and settled onto the couch next to him, laying one hand on his warm arm. "Alec?" I couldn't decide whether to be mad at him for holding back or sympathize with the obvious pain of whatever he was going through.

Finally he sucked in a shaky breath and looked up. "I think I killed your teachers, Kaylee. I think Avari *used* me to kill them. And I don't know how to make him stop."

My living room suddenly seemed a little darker. I couldn't think. I could barely even breathe. Too many thoughts were flying through my head—too many questions—and I couldn't focus on any one in particular.

"Alec…" I stared at the floor, willing both the carpet and my thoughts to come into focus. "Why… What…" I stopped, took another deep breath, then started over. "How is that even possible? They all died in their sleep, from what we can tell. Tod said there were no marks on them."

When Alec just stared at his feet, I continued, desperate for some concrete information to keep from imagining things were worse than they really were. If that was even possible. "Are you saying Avari can… I don't know. Are you saying he can use his own abilities through you, when he's in your body?"

I couldn't think of a more frightening possibility. Knowing a hellion had been in control of my body was terrifying. But if he could make me kill people, using powers I shouldn't even possess…

There were no words to describe the depth of the horror weighing me down in that moment.

"No," Alec said at last, dragging his gaze up to meet

mine. But my relief was fleeting. "He can't use his abilities outside of the Netherworld, even when he possesses me. But he can sure as hell use *my* abilities."

"What?" My stomach tried to hurl itself up through my chest and out my mouth. "What abilities?"

I'd suspected Alec wasn't human when he'd first contacted me—by possessing Emma from the Netherworld—but so far, he'd shown no nonhuman traits. Nor had he mentioned any.

I stood and backed away from Alec slowly, giving in to the single most logical moment of self-preservation in my entire life. "Please tell me you're human, Alec. I need you to tell me you're human *right now*. Tell me you haven't been hiding something that big from me and my dad for two weeks."

*And please make me believe it…*

Alec remained seated; I think he understood that if he stood, I'd lose what little control I was still clinging to. And that I'd shout for my dad. "I couldn't tell you, Kaylee. I didn't want you to be afraid of me."

"It's a little late for that now, so why don't you just lay it out for me?" I backed around the coffee table and across the room. "What are you?"

Alec sighed and glanced at the couch pillow, like he'd like to rip it to shreds, or maybe clutch it to his chest. "It's a long story."

"It's not like I'm going back to sleep." I sat in the chair again and picked up my soda just to have something to hold.

"My mom's human," he began finally. "Avari caught her half a century ago and used her as a proxy for several years. While she was there, she fell in love. Not with him…" Alec said, anticipating my disgust before I could even ask the question now burning on the end of my tongue. "With someone else. With my father. He helped her sneak away from Avari for short periods of time, usually by distracting him with some plaything newer and shinier than my mom."

My stomach churned harder. "Your dad gave Avari other people to…eat? Or whatever?"

"Not always people. Hellions' interests are very broad and…" But he stopped when he read the horror surely clear on my face. "He did it for my mom. To spare her. To be with her."

And I realized with a start that I could understand that, even if I couldn't excuse it. Tod had done something very similar to be with Addison, after she'd died with her soul in Avari's possession, dooming herself to eternal torment for the hellion's pleasure.

I nodded for Alec to go on.

"Anyway, when she got pregnant, they both realized that my mom had to get out of the Netherworld, and that Avari could never know about me. If he got his hands on a half-breed—a potential proxy who could feed him much more and much longer than a human ever could—he'd be too powerful to fight, and my mom would never get out. So my dad arranged for someone who owed him a favor to ferry her back to the human world. They never saw each other again, and I was raised here, like a human."

"She didn't tell you?" A pang of sympathy rang through me at that thought. I'd been raised the same way, in total

ignorance of who and what I really was, and of what my
differences truly meant. Of what I could really do.

"Not until I was nearly grown and my differences
began to manifest. She told me then because I needed to
know how to control myself. How to keep from hurting anyone accidentally. Her big mistake was contacting
my father for advice. She sent him messages through the
friend who'd gotten her out of the Netherworld, but that
put her on Avari's radar again. He got to the messenger
before my dad did that last time, and…well, I don't know
if he threatened him or paid him or what. But somehow
he convinced the messenger to bring my mother to him,
instead of delivering her message. And once Avari had
her, it didn't take him long to find out about me."

"How did he get you?" I asked, my voice so low I
could barely hear it. Avari had done the same thing to
Nash, and to my dad, and it terrified me to know that
he had the resources to take anyone he wanted from our
world into the Netherworld, any time he wanted.

In fact, I might never sleep again, knowing that.

"He told me I could trade myself for her. He swore
he'd send her back here the minute I turned myself over
to him."

"Did he?" My heart beat so hard I could barely hear
him over it. And I was afraid I already knew the answer.

"Yeah. But what he neglected to mention was that
she was already dead. He used her up in one gluttonous
energy binge, and when I crossed over, he sent her body
back to the human world."

Alec's jaw tensed, and I knew without asking that if he
hadn't already had years to mourn his mother, he might

have broken into tears right then. "I didn't get to go to her funeral. I don't know where she's buried. I don't even know who found her. All I know is that if I have any relatives left, I can't go see them, because I haven't aged since the day she died. And knowing what Avari's been doing with my body…I can't put the rest of my family— whatever's left of it—in danger. You and your dad are all I have here. And if I can't make Avari stop possessing me, I'm going to lose you, too."

I wanted to deny it. I wanted to put my arm around him and comfort him like the brother I'd never had. Or like an uncle, considering our age difference. But I couldn't do that, because he was right. If Avari had that much control over him, no one was safe. Least of all me and my father.

"How did he do it?" I asked. "How did he make you kill them? What are you, Alec?"

Alec looked up at me through shiny brown eyes. "I'm half hypnos."

"What's a hypnos?" I held my breath, waiting for his explanation, but couldn't slow my racing pulse.

"Hypnos are minor Netherworld creatures that feed from the energy of sleeping humans through the barrier between worlds. Full-blood hypnos can't cross into the human world, but obviously I can. I think Avari used me to suck your teachers dry in their sleep." He closed his eyes briefly, then opened them so I could see his raging anger and guilt. "It turns out I'm even more useful to that hellion bastard here than I was in the Netherworld."

15

"YOU'RE A HYPNOS?" I rubbed my hands over the cotton of my pajama pants, needing to feel something real and familiar to assure me that I was still safe in my own living room. That I hadn't accidentally crossed into that world of nightmares—or succumbed to an *actual* nightmare.

"Half hypnos," Alec corrected, scowling at the floor again.

My mind didn't want to accept the concept, and my mouth didn't really want to ask the next question. But I did, anyway. "Minor creature from the Netherworld... Please tell me that 'minor creature' isn't a euphemism for 'monster of titanic proportions.' Your dad isn't some kind of demon, is he? A hellion cousin species?"

"My father is dead." Alec's words were clipped short, yet no hint of emotion showed on his face. "But, no, he wasn't any relation to hellions. Hellions deal in human souls—no other Netherworld creature does that. Hypnos are just another species of Netherworlder, most of which feed from humans in some way. Some absorb the energy that bleeds through from this world to theirs. Some drink human bodily fluids. Some eat flesh. For most species, human by-products are a delicacy—delicious, but unnecessary. Like your dad's cupcakes. However, hypnos are one of the few species that *need* some human energy in their diet to survive. They feed through the barrier."

"How did your dad die?" I asked, pushing aside the information I wasn't ready to deal with yet—the fact that Alec was at least half psychic carnivore.

"Avari killed him when I crossed into the Netherworld, to keep him from trying to send me home."

"I'm so sorry."

Alec only shrugged. "I've had plenty of time to deal. Besides, it's not like I ever actually met him."

Still, I knew what it felt like to lose a parent, and he'd suffered twice my loss. That realization reminded me that Alec had a human side as well as a monster side, which tempered my fear and horror with a bit of empathy.

But what if his Hyde half was stronger than Dr. Jekyll?

"So, do you have to…feed? From humans? Like your dad?" And like Sabine?

Alec shook his head. "I didn't even know I could until I was nearly grown. I inherited the ability to feed from human energy, but not the necessity."

*Thank goodness.* But suddenly another question was poking at my conscious mind. "Alec, did you pull me into the Netherworld in my sleep, that first time I saw you?" He'd been stomping his way through a field of razor wheat, wielding a metal trash can lid like a shield.

"Yeah. Sorry." He looked almost as ashamed about that as he was about hiding his species. "I was just trying to get in touch with you while you slept. Subconsciously. But it didn't go exactly like I'd planned."

Oddly enough, I wasn't angry over his admission. At least now I wouldn't have to worry that I'd dream of death and wake up in the Netherworld again.

"So…how does it work—Avari using you to kill people?"

Alec shrugged miserably. "I don't know. I'm not really in here when he does it." He tapped his skull with one long index finger. "But I can tell you one thing. The energy he's taking from them—and it must be a lot, if it's killing them—must be going straight through me to him, because I'm not getting any of it. I'm almost as worn out now as I was in the Netherworld."

That was a mixed blessing, for sure. The thought of Alec—my new friend and confidant—devouring my teachers' life force made me sick to my stomach. But knowing it was strengthening Avari instead was no better.

"Why teachers?" I asked, and Alec's frown only deepened.

"I don't know. I don't know anything about this, Kaylee. I've never even been to your school—at least, not while I'm in control of my own body."

I frowned at a vague glimmer of light on the dark horizon. "So then…are you sure this is what's happening? 'Cause I'd be perfectly happy to continue pinning this on Sabine." And I was only partly joking.

"I know you want her to be guilty, and I'm not exactly eager to take the blame for something I had no control over. But for the past two nights in a row, I've gone to sleep on the couch, then woken up standing in the middle of the kitchen, fully clothed, with no idea how I got there. Avari's using me to kill people, and I have to make it stop."

"You will. *We* will. I'll help you." But I wasn't sure how to even begin, other than making sure no one fell asleep at school. Ever.

I stood to take my empty can into the kitchen, and his voice followed me. "Thanks, but I don't think there's anything you can do. I'm not sure there's much *either* of us can do."

"Yeah, well, that's what Avari thought last time, and look how that turned out." I tossed the can into the recycle bin and pulled a fresh one from the fridge. "We got you, Nash, and my dad out of the Netherworld and kept Avari from forcibly emigrating the entire population of Eastlake High."

Alec huffed, a harsh sound of skepticism. "Unfortunately, that silver lining is overshadowed by one hell of a gray cloud. You and Nash took a wrong turn on the road to happily ever after, and Avari's practically got on-demand access to my body and my feeding abilities."

"Avari doesn't get credit for driving a wedge between me and Nash," I insisted. "Nash did that himself, and he's only letting Sabine drive that wedge deeper." I popped the tab on my soda as I crossed the living room again, then sank into my dad's recliner. "And as for you... At least now that we know what he's doing, we have a shot at stopping him."

But the truth was that our shot was a long shot at best.

The only thing keeping Avari in check before was the fact that he couldn't cross into the human world. And now that he'd found a way—not to mention a very powerful weapon to wield—he was virtually unstoppable. The hellion was playing by new rules, and we'd have to adapt to them quickly to have any hope of stopping him.

"Kaylee...?" Alec's voice was oddly soft and tentative, drawing me from grim thoughts.

"Yeah?"

"What are you gonna do? I mean... Are you going to tell...people?"

He meant my dad. My father had bent over backward to help Alec, out of gratitude. But if he found out that Alec was being used as Avari's murder weapon—and that he'd kept his species and abilities a secret—my dad would kick him out without a second thought. At the very least. He wouldn't let anyone or anything risk my safety, even if that meant turning his back on a friend.

"I don't have anywhere else to go, Kay." Alec met my gaze frankly. "I spent the past quarter of a century groveling for whatever crumbs of mercy fell from Avari's table, and the pickings were very, very slim. When I got back to the human world, I swore things would be different. Here, I have freedom and self-respect. And friends. But one word from you could take all that away. So I'm begging you, Kaylee."

Alec's eyes watered, and I could see how much it cost him to beg for mercy, when he should have been way past such bruising necessities.

"And I swear, it'll never happen again. I won't let it. I spent two and a half decades trying to get free from

Avari, and I am *not* going to let him use me here like he used me there. But I need your help. I need you to keep this quiet while I figure out how to keep him out of my body. And I swear on my life that I'll never let him use me to kill again."

I wanted so badly to believe him. He looked sincere, and he sounded sincere, and both my heart and my gut believed the agony and determination clear on his face. But what if I was wrong, and he was lying? What if he'd known all along what Avari was doing, and they were working together?

Or what if, in spite of his best efforts, he couldn't stop Avari from using him? What if he knew this was the only thing keeping Avari from calling in every favor owed to him to get his former proxy back? What if Alec was willing to pay this price—to let innocent people die—for his freedom from the Netherworld, and now he was playing me for a fool to keep me quiet?

The soul-searing truth was that I no longer knew who I could trust—my own track record made that painfully clear.

I'd trusted Nash, and he'd lied to me. I'd trusted Tod, and he'd withheld the truth about what could happen to me in the Netherworld. I'd trusted my family, and they had all lied to me about who and what I am, for almost my entire life.

The only person in the whole world—*either* world— that I was sure had never lied to me was Emma, and unfortunately, the reverse could not be said. I'd lied to her countless times, trying to keep her safe from Netherworld elements.

My life was a tower of lies, and I could feel that tower leaning. One day it would fall and crush me, and everyone around me. But until then, all I could do was slap on some more mortar and cling to the framework of trust in humanity that held me upright. Even if I was contributing to my own eventual downfall.

Alec shifted on the couch, waiting in tense silence for my answer.

"No, I'm not going to tell my dad. Yet," I said, and his relief was so palpable I almost hated to ruin it. But the rest had to be said, too. His life was worth no more than the ones I'd be putting at risk by keeping his secret. "But I have to tell Nash." Otherwise, he'd keep trying to prove Sabine innocent. "And if you let anyone else die, I swear I'll drop you off on Avari's doorstep personally."

He shook his head firmly. "It won't come to that. I swear."

*Please, please, please let me be right about Alec.*

"Good. And I think we should sleep in shifts from now on. You know, to watch each other. You can wake me up if I look like I'm having another nightmare, and if Avari possesses you again, I'll expel him through whatever means necessary."

"What means would those be?" Alec asked, his eyes narrowed.

I shrugged. "A good whack on the head seems to do the job. You'll wake up with a headache, but that's better than having more blood on your hands, right?"

Alec nodded. "But how will you know it's him, if he sounds like me?"

I wanted to tell him I'd know. That I'd somehow be

able to look into his eyes and know I was staring at a demon, rather than at my friend, but the truth was that I couldn't be sure. Nash hadn't known the difference between me and Avari once, and I'd already made the same mistake with Alec twice.

"We need a secret code word, or a security question, or something."

"A code word?" Alec chuckled, a release of the tension he'd been buried in, and I frowned at him over my can as I took another drink. "Isn't that a little juvenile?"

I raised both brows in challenge. "You got a better idea?"

After a moment, Alec shook his head.

"Then we go with the security question. It has to be something Avari wouldn't know the answer to. Something like your favorite color, or your mother's maiden name."

"My mom never married. And I don't think there's anything about me that he doesn't know. The question should be about you."

Fine. What would Avari not know about me...? The list had to be endless, but I was coming up with exactly nothing.

"What color was your first bike?" Alec asked

"White, with red ribbons."

He smiled. "That'll be the security question and answer."

"Okay." Makes sense... Assuming I wasn't talking to Avari right now. But that was impossible, right? Avari wasn't *that* good an actor. Still...

"Did he kill anyone tonight? Do you have any new holes in your memory?"

Alec shook his head. "I haven't even been to sleep yet." He glanced over my shoulder at the front window, and I twisted to see faint early-morning sunlight leaking in between the slats in the miniblinds. "And it's looking like the time for that has passed."

Except that he'd gotten Mrs. Bennigan in the middle of the day, when she'd passed out at her desk. Mrs. Bennigan had just gotten back from maternity leave, so no doubt the new baby was contributing to her exhaustion, but she couldn't be the only teacher who ever fell asleep in the middle of the day. And the less sleep Alec got at night, the more likely he'd be to pass out during the day, leaving himself—and any simultaneously napping teachers—at risk.

"You don't have to be at work till eleven, right? Why don't you sleep for a couple of hours while I'm here to watch you?"

He frowned. "You sure?"

"Yeah." I stood and headed for the kitchen. "I'm just going to make some coffee and do some homework." There hadn't exactly been time for it the night before, between spying on Nash and trying to pin the murders on Sabine.

"Thanks, Kay. I really owe you."

I pasted on an uneasy smile. "I'll put it on your tab."

Two and a half hours later, I sat in my car in the school parking lot, waiting for Sabine. Again. And for once, I actually hoped she'd have Nash with her. That way he'd be there to hear that she'd broken a promise to him by invading my dreams. Again.

I'd only been waiting a few minutes when she pulled into the lot and parked one row down, four spots over. I grabbed my backpack and locked the car, wishing that I'd remembered my jacket. But with nightmares, murder, and hostile invasion by a hellion on my mind, the January cold hadn't even ranked among my worries that morning.

"Sabine!" I yelled as I jogged toward her car, and several people turned to look. My resolve wavered for an instant when I realized we'd have an audience, but one glance at the smug look on her face as she stepped onto the pavement was enough to bring my determination back in full force.

"Kaylee?" Nash stood on the other side of her car with one hand on the roof. "What's wrong?"

I stopped closer to Sabine than I really wanted to be, to keep anyone else from overhearing. "Your delinquent Nightmare of a girlfriend was in my head again," I snapped through gritted teeth.

"Did you say head?" Sabine asked, drawing both my anger and my attention from Nash. "'Cause it sounded like you said bed, and I don't think anyone's *ever* been in your bed."

White-hot sparks of anger floated in front of my eyes. "Am I supposed to be embarrassed because I'm not handing it out like Halloween candy?"

"I think you *are* embarrassed, 'cause you're afraid to let anyone have even a little taste of your…candy."

My hand clenched around the strap of my backpack. "You sound like a slut."

"You dress like a prude."

"Whoa, wait a minute." Nash rounded the car in a few steps and grabbed Sabine's arm, pulling her away from me, and I had to wonder which of us he was trying to protect. People were watching us outright now, and Nash turned to yell at them, standing firm between me and Sabine. "Go on in! You're not missing anything." I felt the warm brush of his Influence—not directed at me, fortunately—and probably would have been mad at him for Influencing our classmates, if I weren't so busy being furious with Sabine. But his Influence worked—it always did—and this time no one got hurt. They all just turned and headed for the building, like a herd of human cattle.

When we were no longer the center of attention, Nash turned to Sabine. "You were in her dreams again?"

"Oh, come on. She's such a tease." Sabine shook her head, like I should be ashamed of myself. "Those mommy issues were just crying out for attention."

"Stay out of my head," I demanded, just as Nash said, "Sabine, you promised!"

She turned to him, eyes flashing in anger. "I promised I wouldn't try to scare her away from you, and I didn't. It had nothing to do with you this time. She stuck her nose into my private life, so I responded in kind."

Nash turned to me, rubbing his forehead like it hurt. "What the hell is she talking about?"

"Yeah, Kaylee, what could I possibly be talking about?" Sabine's eyes widened in fake wonder for a second before her gaze hardened into true anger. "Why don't you tell Nash where you were last night?"

My cheeks glowed like sunset on the horizon of my vision. "Kaylee?" Nash asked, but I couldn't say it.

"Even when I can't see you, I can taste your emotions like a shark tastes blood in the water," Sabine whispered, leaning around Nash to make sure I heard her. "You can't sneak up on me. You can't spy on me. I will always know you're there, Kaylee."

My face *burned* now, and I had nothing to put out the flames.

"Someone tell me what the hell you two're talking about!" Nash snapped through clenched teeth, as more students paused to eye us before heading into the building.

Sabine crossed her arms over her chest, smug and satisfied. "Kaylee pulled the Invisible Man routine in your room last night."

Nash turned to me, suspicion and disbelief swirling slowly in his eyes. "Kaylee?"

*Crap.*

"I'm sorry. I just..." I wanted to explain, but I wasn't gonna blame it on Tod. Even if it was his fault. "I don't get what you see in her, and I wanted to see you both together. I needed to understand. To be sure."

"To be sure of what?" Nash demanded, his voice as low and hard as I'd ever heard it. "You spied on me to make sure I'm not sleeping with her?"

"She doesn't trust you," Sabine said, like a snake hissing in his ear. "And she never will. I can't believe you can't see that."

Nash whirled on her. "Shut up!" His irises churned with anger, roiling like storm clouds, but it wasn't all directed at her; a good bit of that anger was for me. "It's my fault she doesn't trust me." He turned back to me. "I know it's my fault, but that doesn't excuse this."

He closed his eyes and took a deep breath, obviously trying to keep a handle on his temper. "I can't believe you spied on me." His eyes flew open and his gaze settled on me with a bitter weight. "Did it make you feel better? I hope whatever you saw justifies you violating Sabine's privacy. And mine."

And just like that, my guilt was overcome by a spark of my own latent rage. "Oh, right. Like you can claim the moral high ground here, after everything you did."

"I'm not claiming anything," Nash insisted. "I just thought you were better than that. Better than *me*. Where were you hiding, anyway? In the closet?"

"I told you, she was invisible," Sabine insisted.

Nash shook his head. "Kaylee can't…" He stopped, and his scowl deepened with understanding. "Tod. Damn it. I take it he's been practicing?"

I could only shrug.

"It's bad enough that he goes around spying on people, but dragging you into it is way over the line."

"Don't blame him," I insisted. "I could have said no."

"I hear you're good at that." Sabine grinned fiercely, bending to pick up her book bag.

"I hear you can't even spell it," I snapped, infuriated by how vulnerable I felt, knowing she knew intimate details of my personal life. Maybe by eavesdropping, I'd evened the score a little bit in that respect.

"Okay, that's enough!" Nash growled. "I've had it with both of you." He pulled his own bag higher on one shoulder and turned to me. "You let me know when you decide what the hell you want from me. I love you, and I miss you, and I'll be waiting, whenever you're ready. But don't spy on me again. Ever."

I nodded miserably as he twisted to face Sabine. "And you... You come find me when you're ready to be my friend, because that's all I have to offer right now. But as badly as I need someone to talk to, I don't need another complication in my life. And as for the two of you..." He stepped away from us, already walking backward toward the school entrance. "Work it out. Or don't work it out. But leave me the hell out of it."

Then, for the first time since our first kiss, he turned around and walked away from me without a single glance back.

"This is all your fault," Sabine snapped, as soon as Nash was out of hearing range.

I rolled my eyes. "We were fine until you showed up."

"Yeah. About as fine as a train wreck."

"We were working things out," I insisted.

"You were pouting and licking your wounds." Sabine pulled open her car door and locked it, then slammed it shut. "You stay out of my way and I'll stay out of yours. Deal?"

"Does that mean you're giving up on him?"

"Hell, no." Sabine's eyes darkened, even as they narrowed at me. "It means I'm giving up on you."

The familiar tap of hard-soled, clunky shoes echoed behind me, and Emma came to a stop at my side. "Hey, what's going on?"

Sabine's predatory gaze snapped from me to Emma,

and Em actually sucked in a startled breath. Then the *mara* turned sharply and marched into the building alone.

"I'm starting to see the creepy," Emma whispered, as we watched her go. And I hoped she'd never have any reason to see the real Sabine—or to feel her fury.

IO

THE REST OF THURSDAY morning was blessedly unevent-
ful. No more teachers turned up dead—Avari hadn't had
a chance to possess Alec the night before—and that was
a mercy, considering the almost universally shell-shocked
faces of both the students and staff members. Avari's latest
evil scheme had proved successful enough to become
obvious to—though still misunderstood by—the local
human populace, and the fact that he didn't care about
the unwanted attention made me very, very nervous.

The only bright spot—though it was more like a dimly
lit spot—in the day was the fact that I got to do my unfinished homework during algebra, which was still being
treated like study hall by the long-term sub.

I went out during my free period again and bought
lunch for me and Emma, and when I got back, I found
Sabine sitting at one of the tables in the quad, talking

to my cousin, Sophie, and a couple of her dance team friends like they were long-lost sisters.

That might have been believable—if she hadn't just brushed her arm against Sophie's hand when she reached for a packet of mustard. Sabine wasn't just spreading her social wings—she was reading their fears.

My mood instantly soured as I crossed the quad toward them, fast-food bag in hand. "What's going on?" I asked, glaring at Sabine from behind Laura Bell, the reigning Snow Queen and Sophie's best friend. Sabine was up to no good, as usual.

I could tell because she was breathing.

"This is a private conversation," Sophie snapped. "Go peddle weird somewhere else."

"Sabine?" I said through clenched teeth, and she looked up at me with those weird, dark eyes, sporting a faux friendly smile the three blind mice would have seen through. "Can I talk to you for a minute?"

"I'm kind of busy now, Kay," she said, raising one brow at me in challenge. "Sophie and Laura were just telling me all about the dance team. Seems they're short one team member."

As if Sabine would ever even consider trying to replace the dancer whose life I'd failed to save from a rogue reaper a few months earlier.

I fought to keep from grinding my teeth. "I brought you a hamburger."

Sabine cocked her head in interest. "I never could say no to a good piece of meat."

She stood, and Sophie put a hand on the *mara*'s arm, as if to stop her—whether she wanted Sabine there or not, she'd do anything to keep me from getting what I wanted. But then Sabine looked down at her and Sophie froze when their gazes locked. When the *mara* looked away a second later, my cousin silently withdrew her hand and turned back to her teammates, obviously upset by whatever she'd seen in her new "friend's" eyes.

At least I wasn't the only one. Sabine seemed to be letting her creepiness leak out for everyone to see lately, and I credited myself with shaking her off her foundation.

"I thought we were going to stay out of each other's way," I whispered angrily to Sabine as we wound our way through the quad to our usual table.

"You're the one dragging me away from the only healthy relationship I've attempted in years," Sabine snapped. "I'd say that's you getting in my way."

"Sophie's my cousin," I said, but the satisfaction on Sabine's face said she already knew that.

"So?"

"So...leave her alone. She may be a pain, but she's not food," I insisted, pulling the first burger from my bag. "Got it?"

"She hates you," Sabine said. "For real. Her fears are a bit bland, except for a vague, inexplicable fear of you, which is interesting all on its own. But she has plenty of energy to spare, and it all tastes like spite and insecurity. Why do you care if I take a little sip? I'd really be doing you a favor."

"Just because I don't like her doesn't mean I want you feeding from her."

Sabine frowned as I handed her the burger I'd bought for myself. "I don't get you, Kaylee."

"That's painfully obvious." I took a fry from the carton, glad I hadn't included those in my bribe. "Just stay away from my family and my friends."

"Oh, real food!" Emma said, jogging the last few steps toward our table. She pointed to the *mara* and gave me a questioning look, but I couldn't explain, because she didn't know what Sabine was. "This is why I love you, Kaylee!"

I pushed the greasy bag toward Em when she sat.

"This is why we all love her." Sabine shot an ironic, predatory smile at me. "Because she feeds us."

I glared at Sabine, hoping she'd wander off, now that she had my lunch, but she seemed content to stay just to bug me, even though Nash obviously wouldn't be joining us. And since I had nothing civil to say to the *mara,* lunch would have been either really quiet or really ugly, if not for my best friend. Fortunately, Emma was a never-ending fount of pointless gossip.

"Did you hear that Chelsea Simms ratted out Mona Barker for smoking pot behind the gym during second period?" Emma said, a ketchup-dipped fry halfway to her mouth.

"Why would she do that?" I asked, cracking the lid on my bottle of Coke. "They've been best friends since, what? Preschool?"

"Mmm-hmm." Emma nodded. "And Mona always shared."

"Chelsea Simms?" Sabine looked unconvinced. "The newspaper chick? I can't picture her smoking anything. She looks too…uptight." She shot a pointed glance my way, but I just glared and ate another fry.

"Yeah, she thinks it gives her some kind of hippie, free-speech, peace-rally quality."

"Turning in her best friend doesn't sound much like peace to me," I said, and Em waved her burger for emphasis while she spoke.

"I heard Chelsea flipped out because she got demoted from editor of the school paper, for running that conspiracy theory story connecting Bennigan's death with Wells's and Wesner's. She found out first period that her best friend got the job. By second period, Mona was starin' out the back window of a cop car."

"Da-yum." Sabine whistled, looking decidedly impressed. I kind of wanted to slap her again.

I finished my fries while they discussed Mona's chances of surviving jail for even one night—Sabine provided the insider's perspective—then her chances of surviving her parents the following night, and I'd just stood to throw my trash away when the cafeteria door flew open and Principal Goody stomped outside, her flat-soled shoes clacking on the concrete steps.

Both campus security guards came right behind her.

Emma's last sentence faded into nothing and I sat back down on the bench as a hush settled over the quad. All gazes tracked Goody and the school cops, who headed straight for the last table on the left, two spots down from us. It was the football table, where Brant Williams sat with several teammates and their girlfriends—all friends of Nash's who didn't quite know how to be around him without Scott and Doug at his side.

"Zachary Green?" Principal Goody said, her drill sergeant voice almost comical, coming from such a small, prim woman. "Come with us, please."

"Come with you where?" Zach demanded, and I couldn't help but notice that he hadn't asked what he'd done wrong.

"To my office, then home with your parents. They've already been called."

"What for?"

*Oh,* now *he asks, when his ignorance is too late to be believable.*

"For vandalism of school property."

Instead of demanding specifics, Zach stood and let the old guard tug him toward the cafeteria, and he only dragged his feet long enough to throw a satisfied look over his shoulder at one of the other players still staring after him in surprise.

As the guard hauled Zach up the first step, the cafeteria door flew open again, and Leah-the-pom-girl nearly collided with the entire principal parade. She bounced down the stairs to make room for them to pass, and as soon as the door swung shut, she raced across the half-dead grass toward the seat Zach had just vacated.

"Did you guys see?" she demanded, sliding onto the bench seat next to Laura Bell. "He did it in neon pink. It looks like a flamingo bled all over the lockers."

"What lockers?" Brant asked, and Leah's gaze narrowed on the player Zach had glanced back at.

"Yours." She nodded to Tanner Abbot. "And Peyton's." Her focus skipped to his girlfriend—who also happened to be Zach's ex-girlfriend, after a very messy breakup right before the winter break.

"Ouch. I thought Zach was over that," Emma whispered, as talk among the players built to a startling crescendo.

"Jealousy festers..." Sabine said, and I nearly choked on the last gulp of Coke from my bottle when she stood, facing the other table. "What'd he write on them?" she called across the quad, and every voice went silent as all heads turned our way.

I wanted to melt into the ground just to escape all the stares, but Sabine stood tall, silently demanding an answer.

Leah hesitated, glancing at Peyton—her friend—in sympathy. But in the end, the spotlight called to her; she could not disappoint her audience. "He wrote, 'skanky nympho whore' on hers, and 'limp-dick traitor' on Tanner's."

For one more, long moment, silence reigned. Then the entire quad broke into laughter and loud, eager commentary, while Peyton and Tanner huddled together in humiliation.

"Never a dull day around here, is there?" Sabine asked, sinking onto the bench again with a huge smile on her face.

She was right about that—nothing had been the same since she'd come to Eastlake.

AFTER SCHOOL, I RODE to work with Emma and Alec, glad she had offered to drive, because I wasn't sure I could have stayed awake behind the wheel.

Alec looked just as tired, and when I asked, he admitted he hadn't let himself sleep at all that day, for fear of waking up somewhere other than on my couch, with mud on his shoes and a new hole in his memory.

The Thursday night crowd was enough to keep me awake and on my feet for the first half of the evening at the Cinemark, but during my break, I went to check on Alec and discovered that he'd already gone on his. I started my search in the parking lot, where he usually napped in the car on his breaks.

Unfortunately, Emma's car was empty.

When I didn't find him anywhere else in the lot, I headed back inside and glanced into the break room, then called his name outside of all the men's rooms. But Alec was gone, and he wouldn't have wandered off without telling me. Not after what we'd figured out the night before.

*Think, Kaylee!* I demanded, leaning against the closed door of theater two. My heart was beating too hard, and I was starting to sweat, in spite of the enthusiastic air-conditioning. *If Avari really has him, he'll be looking for someone sleeping.* But why would anyone pay to sleep in a movie theater, when you could sleep at home for free?

Maybe he'd left. Maybe Avari knew we were on to him, so he'd hijacked Alec's body the first chance he got, then simply ditched the theater? Surely a hellion wouldn't care whether or not his host got fired....

I'd taken two steps—on my way to tell my boss I had to leave—when the door to theater two opened so suddenly it slammed into my shoulder. The two college-age men who emerged didn't even notice me in the shadows.

"I swear, I'm gonna fall asleep in there if I don't get some more caffeine and sugar," the shorter, rounder of the pair said, running one hand through pale hair. "This better pay off."

"It will," the taller man said, as they headed toward the lobby and the concession stand. "Dana always leaves these tearjerkers all mushy and willing, 'cause she's grateful her life doesn't suck like the chick in the movie. Don't fall asleep, though. That'll piss them both off, then we'll have sat through an hour and a half of women bonding on screen for nothing."

And as they walked off toward the land of caffeine and sugar, what they were saying truly sank into my exhausted, frustrated brain. If a chick flick could bore them to sleep, it could bore some other poor jerk to sleep. Which made theater two my best bet for finding Alec, assuming Avari had actually caught him asleep at the wheel. Literally.

I pulled open the doors and rushed up the steeply inclined walkway toward the front of the theater, then had to pause to let my eyes adjust to the darkness. Fortunately, theater two was one of the smaller spaces, so it didn't take me long to find a familiar, close-cropped head of curls about two-thirds of the way up, several seats from the right-hand aisle.

I made my way up the steps slowly, but he saw me before I got there. Unfortunately, in the dark, I couldn't see his expression, so I had no clue whether I was looking at Avari or Alec. Or whether lights would have made any difference.

"Hey," Alec's voice said, as I sank into the chair next to him, and I took a deep, silent breath. My heart raced. It was Avari. It had to be. Why else would Alec waste his dinner break watching a six-week-old movie about middle-aged women rediscovering their lost youth?

I was even more convinced when I noticed that the man in front of him was snoring softly, while his wife munched on popcorn, oblivious.

But I had to be sure.

"What color was my first bike?" I whispered.

Alec's head turned toward me slowly, and my pulse tripped faster. "I'm sorry?"

My heart leaped into my throat, and I had to swallow it to speak. "I know it's you. Let Alec go. Now."

Alec only blinked, and my hands clenched around the armrests. Then, finally, he nodded, and the voice that replied was all hellion, oddly muted but rendered no less terrifying by the whispered volume.

"Ms. Cavanaugh, how delightful to see you again, without all the pretense."

Hearing his voice left no room for doubt—it was really Avari. I'd known that, deep down. But knowing it and experiencing it were two completely different things, which I didn't discover until I found myself staring into the unfamiliar depths of a familiar pair of deep brown eyes, lit only by the flicker of the big screen.

"Get out," I repeated, whispering through clenched teeth.

"Oh, I don't think so." Avari leaned Alec's head so close his lips brushed my ear, and my skin crawled. But I didn't dare pull away, for fear that he'd only come closer. "Alec has been very difficult to get ahold of lately, and I'm disinclined to let him go, now that I finally have him."

"You can't stay in there forever," I insisted softly, resisting the urge to rub the chill bumps popping up on my arms.

His hand settled over my wrist, as if he knew what I was thinking. "No, not forever. But I have quite a bit of energy stored up at the moment—thanks to our friend Alec—so I can hang on more than long enough to replace the meal you've interrupted." He waved one dark hand toward the man sleeping in front of him in an eerily graceful motion, which looked very wrong on Alec's strong young body.

I jerked my hand from beneath his in horror. He'd already been feeding. But with any luck, my interruption had saved the poor idiot's life, if nothing else.

"Get out!" I demanded, forgetting to whisper, and the lady in front of me turned to glare.

"Or you'll what?" Avari leaned close again. "Dump popcorn all over this badly tailored, ill-fitting uniform?"

And that's when I realized I had no idea what to do next.

My plan only went far enough to expose the hellion's presence. How the hell was I supposed to get rid of Avari? I didn't have anything to hit him with, and I couldn't afford to make a scene in the theater, anyway.

Or could I?

"Is this really what my proxy has been reduced to?" he asked. "Serving greasy concessions to the masses in ugly shirts and pleated pants. I think he was better off in the Nether. With me."

"Well, I don't think so, and neither does he."

The hellion chuckled, and the smooth, dark sound

wound its way up my spine, promising me pain and pleasure so hopelessly intertwined that I knew if I gave into it, at least I'd die smiling. "Is that what he told you? That he's the victim here, rather than a full partner? He didn't happen to mention the fee he gets for renting out his body?"

"Fee?" He was lying. He had to be. Alec didn't have to tell me anything about Avari's new hobby, but he'd volunteered the information. He wouldn't have done that if he were a willing participant, right?

"He didn't tell you he gets a portion of the energy from each one?"

In fact, he'd claimed the exact opposite. "You're lying."

Another laugh, and this time his breath stirred my hair, warm and damp on my earlobe. "Ms. Cavanaugh, you are charming, even in your ignorance. I have many, many talents. Some that defy description in any human vocabulary, and more's the pity. But lying is not among them. Hellions cannot lie."

But if that were a lie itself, wouldn't that mean that everything else he'd said was, too?

I shook my head, confused. So I clung to what I knew without a doubt. I wasn't sure I could trust Alec, but I was sure I *couldn't* trust Avari.

"Get out right now, or I'll scream for security," I hissed, leaning into him this time, in spite of the discomfort crawling up my spine. "I'll tell them you assaulted me, and you can spend the rest of your time here in jail, getting to know an entirely different portion of the 'masses.'"

I had Sabine and her criminal history to thank for that little stroke of genius.

Alec's thick, dark brows arched dramatically in the flickering light from the screen. "I don't believe you'd do that to your friend."

"Believe it. Alec would rather wake up in jail when you've exhausted your resources than be an unwilling participant in another of your murders."

Plus, I could always recant my accusation later, without hurting anything but my own credibility.

"So what'll it be? Home sweet Netherworld, or the inside of the Tarrant County jail?"

"People have to sleep in jail, right?" Avari smiled, and I decided to call his bluff.

"Maybe. But I hear most people are bailed out pretty quickly, so you'd probably be the only overnight guest." No need to mention that my knowledge of the inner workings of the adult justice system came entirely from television. "And considering that you haven't had a good meal recently, I'm guessing you won't be able to hold out that long. Am I right?"

Avari's borrowed smile faded slowly. "You know I will be back."

I shrugged, trying to look like I wasn't scared out of my mind and sweating beneath my "ill-fitting" uniform. "Not if I can help it."

"But you cannot help—not Alec, and not yourself. You're in over your head, little *bean sidhe,* and if you are not careful, I'd venture that someone will be happy to relieve you of that pretty little head entirely. In just… one…bite."

I clutched the seat between us to keep my hand from shaking as his eyes flashed with malice and the promise of pain, in the sudden bright glow from the movie screen.

"Until next time, Ms. Cavanaugh…"

Then Alec's eyes closed. His hands relaxed and his head fell onto the cushioned back of his chair. He snored lightly.

I sucked in a deep breath, then let it out slowly, trying to purge my fear with the used air. Then I shook him awake.

Alec sat upright in a single, startled movement. His eyes widened, and he glanced around the darkened theater in wild panic, gripping the armrests almost hard enough to crack the cup holders.

"It's okay," I whispered, and he whirled in his chair to face me, shocked eyes still round, pupils drastically dilated.

"Kaylee?" He swallowed, and his Adam's apple bobbed. "It happened again?"

I nodded. "First, what color was my first bike?"

Alec blinked. "White, with red ribbons."

My whole body relaxed with my next exhale, though I knew I'd already used up my entire break, plus some. "Thank goodness. Yeah, it happened again. Let's get out of here." I stood and pulled him down the steps by one hand, moving so fast I almost tripped us both. In the wide hallway between theaters, I tugged him into a corner of the unused secondary concession stand.

"I'm late, so here's the short version—you must have fallen asleep on your break, and Avari got in. He found some guy sleeping during the chick flick in theater two and was chowing down on some human life force when I found you. Er...*him*. I threatened to have him arrested if he didn't vacate your personal premises immediately."

"And that worked?"

I shrugged. "I may have exaggerated how long he'd be in jail, and how alone he'd be, with no one to feed on."

Alec frowned. "What were you going to have him arrested for?"

I glanced at the sticky ground beneath my feet, avoiding his eyes. "Inappropriate, unwelcome contact with a minor."

*"Sexual assault?"* Alec hissed. "You were going to get me arrested for groping a sixteen-year-old girl in the back of a theater? Are you *insane?*"

I bristled over his use of my least favorite nonmedical descriptor, but I had to admit that hearing it aloud made it sound pretty bad. "It was just a bluff," I insisted, staring up into his horrified eyes. "And anyway, I would have recanted."

"Kaylee..."

"What else was I supposed to do?" I demanded. "I didn't have anything to hit you with, and I couldn't just let him use you to kill that poor man."

"Fine." But he didn't look like it was fine, and the longer he stared at me in horror, the guiltier I felt. "Just promise me you'll come up with some better threats. Preferably nothing that'll get me arrested."

"I swear. And you have to promise not to fall asleep by yourself."

"That's a lot harder than it sounds, you know."

"I remember. I spent days trying to stay awake, to

keep you from dragging me into the Netherworld in my dreams."

"I *said* I was sorry about that." Alec groaned.

"And I'm sorry about this. But I gotta go. I spent my whole break talking to a hellion in the back of the theater."

Alec flinched. "I'll make it up to you."

But I didn't see how that was even possible. I started walking back toward the concession stand, where my shift was tragically Emma-less—she'd gotten stuck in one of the ticket booths—then stopped when something else occurred to me.

"Alec?"

"Yeah?" He turned, halfway to the break room, and followed when I gestured toward the shadowed alcove housing a supply closet.

"Avari said you're in on this. That you're his partner, and that you're getting a portion of the energy from each of his kills."

Alec frowned. "Kay, would I be this exhausted if I were getting any of that energy?"

*Oh, yeah.* Still, exhaustion could be faked… "He also said hellions can't lie. That's total BS, right?" I asked, trying in vain to think of a time Avari had lied to me. But I came up blank.

Alec's frown deepened. "Actually, that part's true."

"Then how could he say…?"

"That I was his partner in this new serial slaying?" Alec finished for me, and I nodded. "He probably didn't. Hellions can't tell an outright lie, but they're very, very good at implying things and letting people draw their own conclusions. Did he actually *say* I was in on it? Or did he just ask leading questions, then fail to correct your assumption?"

I thought hard, but I couldn't remember. The whole encounter was indistinct now, but for the memory of his hand over my arm, the sickening warmth of his breath on my ear, and the skin-crawling revulsion I'd felt over both.

What kind of world was I living in, where the only people who never lied to me were the ones out to steal either my soul or my boyfriend?

17

THAT NIGHT, AFTER my father went to sleep, Alec came into my room and we took turns sleeping in two-hour shifts. True to her word, Sabine stayed out of my head, but because Avari had made no such deal with Alec, and especially since I'd evicted him from his earlier occupation, I shook him awake every time he so much as grunted in his sleep, and every single time, I made him tell me what color my first bicycle was.

He passed the test each time. We'd dodged a bullet, but I was far from sure we'd be able to do the same thing night after night. Especially considering how exhausted I was the next morning, after nearly a week without a decent night's sleep.

Friday was a blur of desks, textbooks, and piercing school bells, made even more miserable because Nash ignored both me and Sabine again. All day long. And I have to admit that once I was sure no more teachers had died, I kind of mentally checked out of the school day. I was just too tired to concentrate.

Until some sophomore, bitter over not making the basketball season cheerleading squad, was caught dumping bleach from the custodian's closet all over the cheerleader uniforms hanging at the back of the team sponsor's classroom during lunch. That woke the whole school up.

As Principal Goody escorted a gaggle of pissed-off cheerleaders to the office to call their parents, she stopped in the hall and I heard her tell the team coach she'd be glad when this week was over.

I knew exactly how she felt.

That night, I had to work, with neither Emma nor Alec to keep me company. After my shift, I checked my phone for missed calls and found a voice mail from Nash. I listened to it in my car, in the dark, with nothing to distract me from the intimate sound of his voice in my ear.

"Hey, it's me," he said, and just hearing from Nash made my chest ache, after two days of near-silence from him. "I'm sorry about the other day. Are you working? You wanna come over tonight? Just to talk? We could order a pizza, and Mom made some of those fudge cookies before she left for work."

He paused, and my sigh was the most pathetic sound I'd ever heard.

"Anyway, I figured if I invited you, you wouldn't feel like you had to sneak in under the cover of...Tod. Give me a call?"

Then the phone went silent in my hand.

I dropped my cell onto the passenger seat and started

the engine. Then I turned the car off and stared out the windshield.

Nothing had changed. Nash was still recovering from a serious frost addiction, I was still trying to forgive him for what he'd done, and his ex was still marching toward a very messy boyfriend coup.

But then again, maybe nothing *would* change until I gave him a real chance to make things better. Maybe I never would be able to move on until I either forgave him or let him go.

And I desperately didn't want to let him go.

*I'll just stay for a few minutes. I'll have one slice of pizza. And maybe a cookie. A cookie never hurt anyone, right?*

Besides, I hadn't had a chance yet to tell him what was going on with Alec, because he'd been avoiding both me and Sabine at school. So I'd stay for a few minutes. An hour, tops.

I'd definitely be home before curfew....

TWENTY-FIVE MINUTES later, I knocked on Nash's door, suddenly wishing I'd changed out of my uniform shirt. I'd considered it during the drive, but in the end I dismissed the thought—dressing up might send the wrong message.

If I came in my uniform, he'd know I was just there to talk. That I wasn't trying to look good or to take things beyond that first crucial private conversation. I'd made the right choice.

But I still wished I'd changed.

Nash opened the door in nothing but a pair of jeans,

and suddenly I wished *he'd* changed. He was really hard to talk to when he wasn't fully clothed.

A relieved smile lit up his face when he saw me, and I couldn't resist a small grin of my own. "I didn't think you were coming." He stepped back to let me in. "I called three hours ago."

"I was at work. They make us leave our phones in our lockers." But even after my shift, I hadn't called to let him know I was coming because I wasn't sure I'd actually go through with it until I rang the doorbell. Being alone with Nash was hard. Even without his Influence working in his favor—which he'd sworn would never happen again—he was temptation on two feet. When I was with him, I wanted to touch him, and when I touched him, I wanted to touch him some more, but that would lead to all things sweaty and illogical, and logic was the only weapon I could deploy against the lure that was Nash, and the traitor that was my own heart.

He closed the door at my back, then leaned against it, and my pulse rushed in my ears as I pulled off my jacket and dropped it on the back of a chair. "Did you eat?" he asked, while I stood there like an idiot in the middle of his living room.

"Just some popcorn on my break."

"I'll call for pizza."

While he dialed, I sat on the couch and tried to get comfortable. We'd never really hung out in his living room, but I wanted to make it clear that I had no business in his bedroom. Not tonight. Not while we were still feeling things out. Figuratively.

When he hung up, Nash sat next to me, and I twisted

to face him, leaning against the arm of the couch with my back to the end table lamp. Light from over my shoulder lit his face enough for me to see the browns and greens in his eyes, alternately twisting contentedly and churning with nerves.

I was relieved to realize he was nervous, too. He understood that he was getting a second chance, and he obviously didn't want to mess it up.

"Hey, I thought you should know you were right about Sabine."

He shook his head slowly. "I don't want to talk about Sabine."

"I'm just saying, she didn't kill them."

"I know. I still don't want to talk about her."

I smiled. "Looks like we still have things in common."

"I sure hope so." He reached out for my hand and curled his fingers around mine, and my pulse leaped just like it had the first time we'd touched. How could it possibly feel just like that still?

I hesitated, tempted to drop the subject and continue exploring a potential reunion. But Nash deserved to know the truth, and frankly, I didn't like the pressure or responsibility that came with being the only one who knew Alec's secret. "Wait, there's more," I insisted.

"I like more..." His eyes flashed, and my heart beat harder.

"It's Alec," I said, and Nash froze.

"What's Alec?" He pulled his fingers from my light grip and scowled. "You and Alec...?"

"No!" I rolled my eyes and crossed my arms over my chest. "Why does everyone keep saying that? He's *old,* no matter how young he looks!" And he had much more important things on his mind than dating. I took a deep breath. "Alec killed them. The teachers." I frowned. "Well, not him, exactly. It was actually Avari, but he was using Alec's body. It's kind of a long story."

"Then you should probably talk fast." Nash's irises churned too fast for me to isolate individual emotions, but his lips were pressed thin, his hand clenched around the back of the couch.

"Okay. It turns out that Alec's only half human. His other half is hypnos, and Avari somehow scraped together enough power to possess Alec and feed through him. Which only gives him more power. And evidently kills people."

Guess that wasn't such a long story, after all.

Nash's frown could have blotted out the sun. "And he's sleeping on your couch?"

Actually, now he was sleeping half the night in my bedroom, where I could watch him for signs of possession. But all I said was, "He's not really sleeping much at all, since we figured out what was going on."

"Kaylee, you have to tell your dad."

I shook my head. "He'll kick him out."

"That's kind of the point."

"No, Nash. If my dad kicks Alec out, who's going to make sure he doesn't get possessed and kill someone else?"

"Let your dad worry about that." I started to shake my head again, but Nash cut me off. "If you don't tell him, I will. This is too dangerous, Kay. Swear you'll tell him. Tonight."

And finally I nodded, feeling almost as relieved to be free from the responsibility as I felt guilty over having to break a promise to Alec. "Fine. I swear."

Nash's hand relaxed on the back of the couch and he slouched a little, obviously more at ease now that he had my promise.

"So...how are you?" I asked, ready for a subject change. I didn't want to bring up the issue that had separated us in the first place, but I felt like I should know how he was doing. For real. I *wanted* to know.

"I'm better now." Now that I was here. He didn't say it, but we both heard it. Then the heat in his gaze gave way to a different kind of intensity. "Kaylee, I'm so sorry for everything that happened. I wish I could take it all back. I wish I could do so many things differently...."

I squeezed his hand. "Nash, you can stop apologizing."

"But you haven't forgiven me."

"Not for lack of apologies." I glanced at our intertwined fingers, enjoying the familiar warmth and the way our palms seemed to fit together. "It's just a lot to deal with. Doug died because we did too little, and we did it too late. And Scott probably wishes he were dead."

Surely lifeless oblivion would be better than living with Avari's voice constantly in your head, telling you things you don't want to know, demanding you do things no sane person would do....

His hand tightened around mine, and his gaze seemed to burn a hole right through me. "What else can I do?"

"I don't think there's anything else you *can* do," I whispered. "It'll just take time. And for now, this is nice." I tried on a small smile and held up our linked hands, but Nash only frowned.

"Nice is good, but it's not enough. I want you back for real. I want to talk to you at lunch, instead of staring at you while you eat. I want to see the smile on your face and know I put it there. I want to hear your dad's voice get all low and pissed off, like it only does when I've stayed over too late."

I grinned. No one could piss off my dad like Nash.

Except for Tod.

"You know why he sounds like that, don't you?" Nash asked. "It's because he knows how I feel about you, and it scares him. He knows that he's missed most of your life, and you're not a little girl anymore, and I'm proof of that. He knows what I know, and what you'll let yourself know some day—that you love me. And it scares the shit out of him."

I couldn't breathe around the fist-size lump in my throat. That lump was all the words I was dying to say but shouldn't, all rolled up into one word clog, refusing to move. I couldn't let them out—couldn't expose so much of what I really felt while I still wasn't sure I could completely trust him—but I couldn't swallow them, either. Not anymore. Because whether I wanted to say them or not, whether they would actually change anything or not, they were true.

"Kaylee?" Nash's focus shifted between my eyes, searching for something inside me. "You can't tell me there's nothing left for me in there. I know there is. I can see it in your eyes."

"No fair peeking," I mumbled, and he chuckled.

"Nothing about this is fair." He hesitated, swallowing thickly, like he needed something to drink all of a sudden. "I know I don't deserve a second chance, but I'm asking for one. Let me prove how serious I am. Just one more chance."

I stared at him, studying his eyes. And all I found in them was sincerity and heart-bruising need. He meant it.

So instead of answering, instead of *thinking,* I leaned forward and kissed him. For once in my life, I let my heart lead the way, while the rest of me held on tight, helpless and scared, along for the ride.

Nash kissed me back, and it was like we'd never broken up. And for the first time, it seemed possible that we could just pick up where we'd left off and forget all about that messy little pit stop on the path to forever.

But that wasn't right, was it? Was forgetting even possible?

In that moment, I just didn't care about roadblocks thrown up by my brain—my heart and my body were committed to crashing through them. So I set the hard questions aside and focused on Nash. On the way he tasted, and the way he felt. Of the warmth of his fingers wrapped around mine and his free hand sliding up my arm and over my shoulder to cup the back of my head.

My mouth opened against his, and I welcomed him back, while my body welcomed back the heat he awoke in me, which had lain largely dormant over the past three weeks. But Nash was very careful, his eagerness very controlled. He was hyperaware of my boundaries, and reluctant to even approach them after what had happened the last time.

His caution was both blessing and curse. It was like trying to scratch an itch with gloves on—his passive caresses only made me want more. And maybe that was the point. Maybe he was leaving it all up to me, how far we went and when. Which would have been awesome, if I weren't trying to quench a thirst for him which had been building for the past twenty-one days.

"Nash..." I groaned, when his mouth finally left mine to travel down my neck.

"Too fast?" He started to pull back, but I wouldn't let him.

"No. I just wanted to say your name without being mad."

He grinned and leaned with his forehead against mine. "That's my favorite way to hear it. But this *is* too fast. We have to slow down, or we're going to wind up in the same position again—without the frost. Or the Influence," he added, when I frowned.

"But you're not..."

"Kaylee, *I* need to slow down."

"Oh." I tried to banish disappointment from my voice, but he heard it, anyway, and I think that made it worse for him—knowing that I wanted more. But he was doing the right thing, and so should I. "Um...okay. I'm gonna get a Coke. You want one?" I stood, straightening my shirt.

"Yeah. There's some in the fridge."

I'd made it halfway across the room when a car rumbled to a stop outside, and a wash of bright light traveled across the living room through the front window. "Must be the pizza." Nash stood, already digging his wallet from his back pocket, and I shoved open the swinging door into the kitchen, pleasantly surprised by the quick delivery.

But when I pulled open the fridge, a familiar, disembodied voice spoke to me from the other side of the door. "It's not the pizza," Tod said, and I slammed the door shut without grabbing the cans. But the kitchen was completely empty.

"Where are you?" I demanded in a whisper, as the front door creaked open from the living room. "And how do you know it's not the delivery guy?"

Tod suddenly appeared between me and his mom's small kitchen table, wearing a royal blue polo with a stylized pizza—missing one slice—embroidered on the left side of his chest. "Because I have your pizza right here, and I didn't drive."

I laughed. I couldn't help it. An undead reaper was one thing. But an undead pizza delivery driver? The jokes wouldn't stop coming.

"It's not funny!" Tod snapped. "This was your idea."

"I was joking!" I hissed, opening the fridge again.

"Well, I wasn't. Being dead doesn't have to mean mooching off all my friends, right?" he said, and I shrugged, pulling two cold cans from the top shelf. "Plus, you were right about the free pizza."

I couldn't resist another grin. "So…is there a family discount?"

"Hell, no. Nash is paying full price. Plus tip."

Before I could reply, hushed voices from the living room caught my attention. "Who's that?" I demanded, setting the sodas on the table. I headed for the swinging door, but Tod grabbed my arm before I'd made it two steps.

"It's her, isn't it? That's Sabine's car? You saw her?"

He nodded reluctantly, brushing a curl from his forehead. I started forward again, and again he pulled me back. "Let go. What, you're on her side now?"

"I'm just trying to keep this from going bad, fast."

"Shh…" I said, when I realized I could make out words from the other room.

"Kaylee's here?" Sabine said, obviously refusing to be shushed by Nash. And it's not like she didn't know I was there—my car was in the driveway! "I thought it was just going to be us."

"I didn't think she'd come. Bina, *please* go before she hears you."

I couldn't hear what came next, so I snuck closer to the door. Tod clenched his jaw, but let me go.

"Sabine, no! I'll make it up to you, but you have to go n—"

Then there was no more talking from either of them, and my blood boiled.

I shoved open the swinging kitchen door and froze with my foot holding it open, unable to truly process what I saw. Sabine Campbell had her shirt off, and she'd latched onto Nash like the parasite she really was. She had him pressed against his own front door, her tongue surely halfway down his throat. But the worst part…

He held her shirt, dangling from one fist—and he was kissing her back.

I couldn't speak. I couldn't even form a coherent

thought until Tod cleared his throat at my back, and Sabine reluctantly peeled herself off my boyfriend.

Nash's face flamed, but Sabine only grinned. "Hey, Kay. Sorry I'm late to the party, but the more the merrier, right?"

"You two look merry enough without me," I snapped through clenched teeth. Then I stepped forward and let the kitchen door swing through Tod, who barely seemed to notice.

"Kaylee, wait…" Nash pushed Sabine away from him. "I didn't… She…"

"I know. She was all over you like a tick on blood." But I also knew that he hadn't pushed her away. He may not have started it, but he'd let it happen, and I couldn't help wondering, if I hadn't been there, how much farther he would have let it go.

I glanced pointedly at the shirt he still held in one hand, and his cheeks flushed nearly scarlet.

Nash whirled on Sabine and shoved the shirt at her and she took it, reluctantly covering herself. Then he pulled open the front door, grabbed her arm, and shoved her onto the porch, still clutching the material to her chest. "Don't come back," he growled, an instant before slamming the door in her face.

"Kaylee…" He turned to face me, leaning against the door.

"You didn't stop her."

"I was about to…"

"Yeah. You can tell from how far down her throat your tongue was…" Tod said, sarcasm threaded boldly through each word.

Nash turned on him. "This is none of your business. What are you even doing here?"

"You owe me $15.99. Plus tip."

Nash looked confused until he noticed Tod's uniform. "I'll owe you," he finally snapped. "Get out."

"I'm going, too." I headed for the door as Sabine's car started in the driveway.

"Kaylee, wait."

"Where's her bra?" I asked, my hand already on the doorknob.

Nash closed his eyes and exhaled slowly, miserably. "She wasn't wearing one."

16

"KAYLEE!"

Someone grabbed my shoulder and my head flopped forward as he shook me.

My eyes flew open. Alec stood over me, his hair rendered even darker by the halo of light shining around his skull from the fixture overhead. His brown eyes were wide and worried, his generous lips thinned into a tight frown.

"What?" I wasn't even dreaming, much less having a nightmare. In fact, he'd interrupted the first almost-peaceful sleep I could remember getting in the past few days.

And even as that thought faded, I realized the problem—I was supposed to be watching him, not dozing. I'd insisted that he take the first shift sleeping under the assumption that my dad would get back from my uncle's house—where they were conferring about the sudden spike in the teacher mortality rate at Eastlake—while Alec was still asleep. That way I could explain about Avari's murder-by-proxy without having to break my promise to Alec to his face.

Obviously I'd underestimated my own exhaustion.

"Sorry." I sat up and wiped an embarrassing dribble from the corner of my mouth. "Is my dad home yet?"

"No," Alec said, and I glanced at my alarm clock in surprise. It was just after midnight. "Kaylee, this isn't going to work." He sank onto the edge of my rumpled bedspread, broad shoulders sagging in frustration and obvious fatigue. "How are we supposed to watch each other if neither of us can stay awake?"

"I'm fine," I insisted, standing to stretch. "I just need some coffee."

"If you guzzle caffeine, you won't be able to sleep when it's your turn, either, and that'll just make everything worse." Alec hesitated, and I read dread clearly in his expression. "You're gonna have to tie me up."

"What? No." I sat on the edge of my desk and pushed tangled hair back from my face, hoping I'd heard him wrong. "I'm not going to tie you up, or down, or any other direction!"

"Kay, I don't think we have any choice. Avari's just waiting for a chance to get back into my head, and how happy do you think Sabine's going to be with you, after her little stunt tonight failed?"

I'd given him the short version of my visit with Nash, skipping my promise to fill my dad in on everything.

"If either of us falls asleep at the wrong time, things are going to get a whole lot worse."

My tired brain whirred, trying to come up with a viable alternative, but in the end, I was too worn out to think clearly, much less argue. Survival and a good night's sleep trumped my deep-seated aversion to restraints—born of my week-long stay in the mental health ward—so I finally relented and trudged into the garage for the coil of nylon rope looped over a long nail on the wall.

In my room again, I turned my stereo on and cranked the volume, hoping the noise would keep me awake. Then Alec helped me cut the rope into workable sections and showed me how to tie a proper knot. Evidently he'd had practice restraining…things…for Avari in the Netherworld.

I bet the hellion never thought that particular skill could be used against him, and that thought made me smile, in spite of encroaching exhaustion, and the disturbing reality of what I was about to do.

The plan was for me to tie Alec to the chair in one corner of my room—the one I'd woken up in—but the back was one solid, padded, curved piece of wood, with nothing to tie his hands to. The desk chair was no better, and since I wasn't willing to tie him up in the living room, where my dad would see him before I'd had a chance to explain, our only other option was my bed.

I cannot begin to describe my mortification—or the flames burning beneath every square inch of my skin—when I knelt at the head of my bed to secure Alec's right arm to my headboard. "It's okay, Kaylee," he insisted, head craned so he could watch me while he voluntarily submitted to something that would have sent me into a blind panic. "This'll keep us both safe."

"I know." But I didn't like it, and my revulsion didn't fade when I tied his other hand, or bound his first foot to the metal frame beneath the end of my mattress. I had trouble with the final knot, but had almost secured his right ankle when a sudden hair-prickling feeling and a subtle shift in the light told me that someone was behind me.

"What in the hell are you doing?" my father demanded, his voice low and dark.

I whirled around so fast I fell onto one knee, and the end of the rope trailed through my fingers to hang slack. My dad stood in my doorway, his irises swirling furiously in some perilous combination of anger and bewilderment.

The music had covered his footsteps, and evidently the sound of his car.

"Maybe this wasn't such a good idea," Alec mumbled at my back, and my father's harsh laugh sounded more like an angry bark.

"Considering your current predicament, I'm betting that's the first smart thing you've said all night!"

"This isn't what it looks like." I frowned and shoved myself to my feet, then glanced back at Alec, who could only stare at me in humiliation. "Actually, I'm not sure what it looks like," I admitted, turning back to my father. "It's to keep us both safe…" I ended lamely, wishing I could just melt into my bedroom carpet and disappear.

"Safe from what?" my father demanded softly.

"From…" I closed my eyes and took a deep breath, then met his stare again and started over. "I was gonna tell you everything when you got home. Nash made me promise."

Behind me, Alec shifted on the bed—as best he could, with three limbs bound to it—and I could practically taste his anxiety.

"What does Nash have to do with you tying Alec to your bed?" But honestly, he looked like he didn't really want to know the answer to that.

I perched on the corner of my desk and turned off my stereo. "I'm assuming you want the short version...."

"That would be good."

So I sucked in another deep breath, then spat the whole thing out. "Avari's been possessing Alec and killing my teachers—we have no idea why he picked teachers—so we've been sleeping in shifts for the past couple of nights, to stop it from happening again. But now I'm so tired that I can't stay awake—" no need to tell him about Sabine just yet, since she wasn't immediately relevant to the hellion or the dead teachers "—so Alec thought I should tie him up, in case I fall asleep and Avari gets back into his body. You know, to keep everybody safe." I shrugged miserably, then watched my father, waiting for the fireworks.

"I don't even know where to start," he said. But he got over that pretty quickly. "Avari's the one killing teachers?" he said, and I nodded. "And he's using Alec to do it?" Another nod from me. "And you've known this for two days without telling me?"

"I was afraid you'd kick him out. And even if it were okay to do that to a friend—and it's not—if you kick him out, there won't be anyone around to make sure Avari can't use him as a murder weapon again," I finished, proud of my own coherence, considering how incredibly tired I was.

For several moments, my father stood mute, obviously thinking. Then his focus shifted from me to Alec. "Those teachers died without a mark on them," he said, and I could see in the angry, frustrated line of his jaw that he'd come to the right conclusion, with far fewer clues than I'd needed. "What are you?"

"I'm half hypnos." Alec met my father's gaze unflinchingly—his species wasn't his fault, after all—but looked genuinely sorry for the danger he'd involuntarily exposed us all to.

"Please tell me your other half is human," my father said, and Alec and I both nodded.

My dad sighed and pulled a folding knife from his back pocket. "Well, Kaylee, you're right about one thing—we can't leave him on his own. Not unless we want the next blood spilled to fall on our hands."

My relief was almost as strong as my confusion when he strode forward purposefully and cut Alec's left ankle free.

"Mr. Cavanaugh, it's not safe to let me sleep free," Alec insisted, as my father rounded toward the head of the bed.

"Which is precisely why you won't be sleeping in my daughter's room." He slashed the rope around Alec's left arm, then leaned over him to repeat the process with the remaining knot. "Ever."

A few minutes later, we all stood in the living room, my father unwinding a new rope he'd produced from a pile of not-yet-unpacked cardboard boxes in the garage.

Alec sank into my dad's recliner and positioned a pillow beneath his head, then my father tied his feet to the metal frame of the foldout ottoman. While I spread a blanket over our poor houseguest, my dad pulled Alec's arms toward the back of the recliner, where he tied his wrists to each other, linked by a taut length of nylon spanning the back of the chair.

But even with this new precaution and my dad's much sturdier knot work, he wasn't willing to let Alec sleep alone, just in case. So when I finally headed to bed at almost one in the morning, my father was settling onto the couch with his pillow and a throw blanket, determined to protect us all from the most recent Netherworld threat. Even in his sleep.

"HE KICKED HER OUT topless?" Emma shoved her spoon into the pint of Phish Food and dug out a chocolate fish, her brown eyes shining in the light pouring in through the kitchen window. After a long, mostly sleepless night, Saturday morning had dawned bright and clear, in blatant disrespect of my foul mood.

Fortunately, Emma had come bearing ice cream. Two reserve pints sat in the freezer.

I nodded, letting my bite melt in my mouth. Chocolate may not cure everything, but it goes down a lot better than any other medicine I've ever tasted.

The front door opened before I could respond, and Alec walked in, carrying a newspaper under one arm, nose dripping from the cold. He closed the door, then noticed us in the kitchen.

Before he could speak, I pointed the business end

of my spoon at him and said, "Where were you? You weren't on the schedule today." He'd been gone when I woke up, both the ropes and bedding stowed somewhere out of sight.

Alec dropped the newspaper on the kitchen counter. "Apartment shopping."

My eyes narrowed. "I thought you didn't have the money yet."

"I don't. But I will soon, thanks to the new job." And I had a feeling that after the big revelation, my father had suggested Alec move forward with his plans for financial and residential independence.

*Still…* I wasn't taking any chances after meeting Avari at the theater. "Just humor me. What color was my first bicycle?"

"White, with red ribbons," he replied, without hesitation.

"What's with the twenty questions?" Em asked, scraping the inside edge of the carton with her spoon.

I shoved another bite in my mouth, buying time to think. But Alec was faster. "It's this stupid trivia game." He winked at me. "I'm winning."

"Oh, I wanna play!" Em said, sitting straighter. "What was the name of my first bra?"

I nearly choked on my bite. "You named your first bra?"

She frowned. "You didn't?" When I could only laugh, she turned to Alec. "You gonna guess?"

He hesitated, pretending to think. "I gotta go with Helga."

She threw the ice cream lid at him. Alec laughed, then

dropped it into the trash. "One carton of Ben & Jerry's, two girls, two spoons. I'm guessing this is about Nash?"

Emma nodded, watching as Alec took off his jacket and draped it over the half wall between the kitchen and the entry. She'd made no secret of the fact that she thought he was hot, and I couldn't exactly tell her he was nearly three times her age.

Alec raised one brow and grinned. "Isn't the ice cream therapy thing kinda cliché?"

I shook my head. "It's a classic for a reason."

"And that reason is 'cause we're underage," Em insisted. "If I could've gotten my hands on anything stronger last night, we'd be recovering from strawberry daiquiri therapy this very moment."

He laughed, heading for the silverware drawer. "So, is this girl-only ice cream, or can a sympathetic guy get a bite?"

Emma leaned over the table much farther than she had to for her next bite, to be sure he could see down her shirt. "What's mine is yours."

I kicked her under the table, as Alec dug in the fridge for a soda. He was older than her mother! And he was currently being used as the murder weapon for a Netherworld demon. Not that she knew any of that.

One more point in favor of full disclosure. I was probably going to have to tell Emma soon....

"What?" Em pouted, then licked ice cream from her spoon with it inverted over her tongue.

"That's *all* you're gonna share with him," I whispered

She stuck her tongue out at me, then took another bite.

"What were you doing at Nash's, anyway?" Alec

asked, taking the chair on my other side. I think Emma scared him. Thank goodness.

"Makin' up."

Em grinned. "More like makin' out."

"Not that it matters now."

"Why?" Alec dug in, his small spoon dwarfed by both of ours. Obviously an ice cream drama rookie. "If *she* kissed *him,* what's the problem?"

I stared at him like he'd just volunteered for a lobotomy. "He kissed her back. I saw it. He didn't push her away. He let her take her shirt off and stick her tongue down his throat."

Alec licked his spoon, then set it on the table and popped his drink open. "Okay, I may be breaking some kind of girl-bonding rule or something, but can I offer you a guy's perspective on this?"

I frowned, my spoon halfway to my mouth. "Is this gonna make me want to hit you?"

He shrugged. "Maybe. But it's the truth. Here goes: kissing back is instinct. Unless the girl smells like a sewer or has tentacles feeling you up independently, a guy's first instinct is to kiss back. That's how it works. What's important is how long that kissing back lasted. So…how long?"

"You can't be serious." I could feel my temper building like the first spark in what could soon be a roaring blaze. "You think it's *okay* for him to kiss her back just because she isn't hideous? Aesthetically speaking." I was no suffragette, but I was pretty sure the he-can't-control-himself defense was a big, stinky load of horseshit.

"No." Alec held up one hand defensively. "But I also

don't think it's okay for you to condemn him, if he was the innocent kissee, rather than the instigator of said kiss."

I rolled my eyes. "Fine. He wasn't the instigator."

Alec nodded, obviously pleased with the progress. "Did she know you were there?"

"She parked right behind my car."

"And he kicked her out, right?" Emma added, catching on.

"Yeah. And he told her not to come back."

Alec turned to Emma, and she couldn't resist another grin. "Are you hearing what I'm hearing?"

"Yup." Alec met my gaze. "This was for your benefit, not his. She set you both up, and did everything she could to make you think he wanted it. And *you*…"

My frown deepened. "You think I'm overreacting?"

Alec shrugged again and dug in for another bite. "I wasn't there. But it sounds to me like you at least owe him a chance to explain."

I hesitated. Long enough for two more bites. "Maybe." But I just wasn't sure I had any more chances for Nash left in me.

*I'M AT MY DESK with my laptop open, scouring the internet for a good price on a spray can of mara repellent, when the room suddenly feels wrong at my back. I don't turn. I don't even look up, because I know neither one will help. For several long seconds, we both pretend I don't know he's there. That the back of my neck isn't prickling with fear.*

*Finally he says my name and I can't ignore him. I*

*slowly close my laptop and swivel in my rolling desk chair to confront the impossible.*

*"You can't be here." Yet me knowing that hasn't prevented it from happening.*

*"Surprise," Avari says, and he sounds truly thrilled. Somehow he's managed to cross into the human world in his own body, and as far as I'm concerned, he brought hell with him.*

*The hellion looks different than I remember him, but that's no surprise. Hellions can look like whatever they want, with one exception: they cannot replicate the exact form of any other living or deceased being. There will always be some small difference—finding that difference is the key.*

*At least, that used to be the rule. But if he can cross over now, do any of the other rules still apply?*

*Avari is now shorter than I remember him, with lighter hair. But he hasn't bothered to change his voice, and his eyes are still the featureless ebony orbs I can't forget—spheres of chaos and infinity. Madness at a glance.*

*"Get out." It's all my overwhelmed brain can come up with while the rest of me fights the waves of fear and despair emanating from him like radiation from ground zero.*

*"Not until I have what I want."*

*I don't ask, because I know what he wants: me. But I don't know why, and he's never felt inclined to explain. Hellions can be bargained with—I've seen that firsthand—but they never give information for free, and I'm not willing to pay.*

*"So how does this work?"*

*He takes a step toward me, and I stand, my heart beating frantically. I want to retreat, but there's nowhere to go. My desk is already cutting into my spine. "I grab you, then I drag you kicking and screaming into the Nether, where I'll take good care of you—until the next new toy comes along."*

*"And how are you planning to keep me there?" I'm impressed by my own nerve. I was stalling—for what? The cavalry? A brilliant idea?—but also digging for important information.*

*"Oh, after a couple of hours with me, you won't have the strength to cross over. You won't sleep and you won't eat until I've broken your mind as well as your body, and after that... Well, it simply won't matter what happens to you after that. You'll never know the difference."*

*"You won't break me." I sound much more sure than I really am. I have this strange calm now. It almost feels like acceptance. I can't fight him, and I won't scream for help and doom my would-be hero. And that means he's won, before the fight even begins. So what's the point in fighting?*

*Then he's in front of me, and his hands have become wicked claws. He grabs my arm and his claws sink through my wrist, and suddenly I remember the point in fighting.*

*Pain, the moment he touches me, and not just where he rips through my flesh. I double over, struggling to breathe through an agony like electricity being run through me. He is the lightning and I am the rod, and the strike never ends.*

*Pain everywhere. I smell my skin cooking, hear my hair crackle as the follicles pop from the heat. In the mirror, I see no change, but I feel every single bit of it, like life is fire and I am the fuel, forever burning but never quite consumed. He can make me hurt in every cell of my body with a single touch. He will do this for eternity, if I go with him.*

*And he hasn't even started on my mind yet.*

*NO! I'm screaming now, the magic word. They teach us in preschool. If something bad happens, shout NO! and parents will come running. If a stranger touches you, shout NO! and the police will take him away. You can always shout NO! and there will always be someone there to protect you.*

*But that's a lie. No one comes. NO! is a lie, and safety is a lie, and the only truths are pain and forever, and pain is everywhere, and forever has already begun.*

*He pulls my arm, and the pain doubles, though that shouldn't be possible, because how can you double infinity? I fall to the ground, because I can no longer stand. I can no longer think. I can only feel, and hurt, and scream, and know that it will never end. And that my grand delusions of resistance are like wielding a breath of air against a brick wall. There is nothing I can do. Giving in will not stop the pain. Begging will not stop the pain. In the end, even dying will not stop the pain.*

*And as my world fades beneath a swirl of gray fog, I know that I am lost, and that I will never, ever be found....*

IT WAS STILL DARK when I opened my eyes, and the only sound I could hear was my own breathing, too hard and too fast. Still panicked from the nightmare. I stared up at the ceiling without seeing it, more afraid of the understanding now burrowing its way into my head than the dream I'd just escaped.

It wasn't Sabine. My nightmare about Avari didn't feel like her work—which I was definitely starting to recognize. It wasn't personal enough. There was no angst and no self-doubt, the primary colors of her dream palette.

This dream felt like...Avari. Like the hellion was playing with my mind, messing with my very psyche. But that was impossible, right? Hellions couldn't give people nightmares. Could they?

In the dark, as my breathing gradually slowed and my pulse calmed, I became aware of another sound, soft and even. Someone else was breathing. In my room.

I turned my head slowly, my heart thumping painfully, and could barely make out a familiar silhouette outlined by the creepy red glow from my alarm clock.

Alec sat in the corner chair. Silent. Watching me, like he'd *been* watching me for quite a while.

*Why* was he watching me? Why wasn't he tied to the recliner in the living room, which is how he'd started the second night in a row? Where was my dad?

Uh-oh.

"Alec?" But I knew before he answered. I knew from the creepy smile Alec would never wear, and the way his eyes seemed to focus on something *inside* me.

"Bad dream?" he asked, leaning forward to study me closer in the dim light, and I froze at the sound of his voice. Because it wasn't his voice. It was Avari's.

No pretense this time; the hellion was all business. Just like in my dream.

"How did you…?" I started, clenching the top of my comforter.

"How did I get Alec free from those sad little ropes?" Avari finished, and I nodded. I didn't bother ordering him to leave, because I didn't have anything to threaten him with this time without involving—and endangering—my dad. Who'd probably already been both involved and endangered, considering that Avari had somehow gotten past both him and the restraints.

"Waking up bound was a bit of a surprise, I must concede," the hellion said, leaning forward to peer at me through my friend's eyes. "Regrettably, this body does not come with extraordinary strength. Fortunately, your father—or rather, his unconscious form—proved quite useful."

"You possessed my dad?" My hands were damp, and I resisted the urge to wipe cold sweat on my covers. My father was eligible for hellion possession by virtue of having spent time in the Netherworld when Avari had him kidnapped the month before.

"Only long enough to free our dear Alec in his sleep. Your father is now unconscious, and both bound and gagged with his own restraints for my convenience. But he is otherwise unharmed, and I suggest you give me no reason to change that."

My chest ached, and each breath felt like a knife to my heart. There was no one left to help me, and very few ways for me to help myself, without making things worse for both my dad and Alec. Even if I'd been willing to leave my dad, I couldn't run, because if the hellion knew Alec's physiology well enough to make his voice work, he could certainly catch me in the older, stronger body.

Why had he stayed to watch me sleep instead of going out for his usual murder-by-proxy? He couldn't really drag me back to the Netherworld. Not using Alec's body, anyway.

"You did that? My dream?" I asked, stalling for time to come up with a plan as my heart thudded in my ears. My only real hope was to knock Alec unconscious, which would expel the hellion from his body. But I'd never hit anyone that hard in my entire life. At least, not without a weapon to wield…

The hellion nodded magnanimously, an artist reluctantly taking credit for his masterpiece. "What did you think? Dreams are a new medium for me, and I may have used just a bit too much terror, when a little suspense would have sufficed."

Fear and fury coiled within me, a startled snake about to strike, but I'd have to time my move perfectly to disable him with one unpracticed blow. "How?"

Avari shrugged nonchalantly, and it was almost as disturbing to see him in Alec as it had been to see him in Emma less than a month before. "There is a bit of a learning curve, but I'm sure I will get the recipe right next time."

"How did you get into my head?" I snapped. "And there won't be a next time." There wasn't supposed to be a *this* time. Depriving Avari of his proxy was supposed to keep him too weak to possess anyone. But not only did he clearly have the strength, he'd somehow picked up a new skill set!

"I've discovered several new talents since your last visit to the Nether, Ms. Cavanaugh. And there certainly *will* be a next time. Talents unpracticed are talents wasted, you know."

"What do you want?" I asked, fully aware that this confrontation was now mirroring my bad dream. But that was the best I could do with the memory of the nightmare-hellion's hands on me, his claws digging through my flesh, his power singeing my every nerve ending.

Avari cocked Alec's head to one side, lending him a look of vacant curiosity. "You know, I've never had trouble answering that question in the past. And now it seems I want so many things that I can't decide what to take first."

I nodded, going for bravado. "Makes sense, considering you're a demon of greed."

"Lately, that's not as much fun as it sounds like. What I really want to do is shove my hand down your throat and rip your heart out the long way. But I'm not sure if this body can accomplish such a physically demanding feat. And even if it can, if I give in to such immediate gratification, I'll lose your precious, innocent little soul. And I think I might want that even more than I want your deliciously painful death."

*Don't show him fear. Don't shake and don't sweat. Hold on to your anger, Kaylee.* But that was all much easier said than done. "Lucky me."

"Not in the slightest. Once I have your soul, I'll be

able to kill you over, and over, and over. It's immensely entertaining—for me. Just ask Ms. Page."

Addison. My chest ached just thinking about her and the very real torture she endured daily at Avari's hands, er…claws. Because she'd sold him her soul, and we hadn't been able to get it back for her.

"So, while I'm not quite ready to kill *you* yet, and I rather like having Alec on this side of the barrier now that I've had time to consider the benefits, I have no reason at all to leave your father breathing, if I cannot bring him into the Nether."

*No!* A jolt of adrenaline shot through my chest. I lurched toward the door, all thoughts of patience and timing forgotten. But I didn't even make it to the end of the bed before Alec's hand closed around my arm. He jerked me backward with more strength than a human should have had, and I had half a moment to disagree with the hellion's assessment of Alec's power before Avari threw me back onto the mattress. My head slammed into the headboard, and he was on me in an instant.

He pinned me with his weight, propped on his elbows with my wrists trapped in his fists.

"Get off me!" I fought the suffocating panic building inside me as I struggled to free my arms. Flashes of four-point restraints and men in hospital scrubs played in my memory, with an all new fear born of the sheer delight in not-Alec's eyes.

"Shhhh…" Avari whispered, as Alec's cheek brushed mine. "Your father is fine, for the moment. I simply haven't yet decided what to do with him."

And that had to be true, because a hellion couldn't lie....

I went still, my heart racing, terror lapping at my fragile control.

"Would you believe that while I'm in this body, I can feel everything it feels? And it *likes* this arrangement." He shifted over me, and I bit my lip against a scream, knowing Avari enjoyed every single moment of my fear. "Have you and my Alec done this before?"

I couldn't talk. I couldn't do anything but ride the horror in silence, desperately hoping I was still dreaming. That this was part of the nightmare.

He let go of my left wrist to brush hair from my face, then wedged one leg between my knees.

Pulse racing in panic, I acted without thinking. Without stopping to consider what would happen if my rash plan didn't work. My free arm shot out. I grabbed the first thing my hand landed on. My alarm clock.

I swung as hard as I could. The cord ripped from the wall. The clock slammed into Alec's head. Avari blinked, stunned. So I did it again, grunting with the effort.

His eyes fluttered shut and he collapsed on top of me.

Tears of relief and belated terror blurred my view of the ceiling. I shoved him off of me and scuttled off the bed into one corner of my room. Alec rolled over the edge of the mattress and thumped to the floor on the other side.

For several long moments, I could only breathe, fighting not to hyperventilate. My legs shook when I stood, and my hand trembled as I wiped my eyes, determined not to give in to sobs. I crossed my room slowly, watching

Alec, half convinced Avari was playing possum just so he could catch me again, and start the whole sadistic game all over. But he didn't move, other than the steady, slow rise and fall of his chest.

Once I'd crossed the threshold of my room, I raced down the hall and into the living room, where I dropped onto the floor next to my dad. He lay on the carpet on his left side, with his back to the couch, his ankles tied together, wrists bound at his back. There was a piece of duct tape over his mouth, and when I ripped it off—hoping in vain that the pain would wake him up—I found an entire ratty dish rag stuffed into his mouth.

I couldn't find my dad's pocket knife—there was no telling what the hellion had done with it—so I got a steak knife from the kitchen and carefully cut the ropes, but my father's eyes wouldn't open. And I had no idea what to do.

I should do something. I should call someone, but an ambulance seemed risky. What would I tell the police? Technically, Alec had attacked us both, but even if I denied that, the evidence wouldn't support whatever desperate lie I made up.

But I didn't want to be alone in the house with two unconscious men, both of whom had been possessed by a vengeful hellion in the past hour. So I fumbled for the phone on the nearest end table and speed-dialed the second number on the list.

I hadn't forgiven Nash, and I did *not* want to go groveling back to him when I needed help. But I did want to hear his voice. And welcome a touch that could replace the feel of Avari's unwelcome, surrogate hands on me.

The phone rang and rang, and when Nash finally answered, I sank onto the floor in relief. "Hello?" He was still half-asleep, and I wished I could join him. Just curl up next to him and forget about the constant terror my own nights had become.

"I need help." I was proud of how steady my voice sounded, but he knew me too well.

"What happened?" Bedsprings creaked and a light switch clicked softly. "Are you okay?"

"Yeah. Just a little freaked out, and I don't really want to be alone. Could you... Would you come over?"

"Give me five minutes." The phone clicked in my ear, then buzzed with a dial tone. He didn't even know what had happened, and it didn't matter. If I needed him, he would come. No matter what.

I sat there for a moment, still reeling from the trauma of the past few minutes. Then I stood and did the only thing I could think of to protect myself while I waited: I grabbed the duct tape lying on the floor near my father's head, then headed into my room, where I rolled Alec onto his side and taped his hands together behind his back and his feet together at the ankles. It wasn't a perfect solution, but it was all I had. Duct tape, and the desperate hope that Avari wouldn't have the strength or the opportunity to possess either Alec or my dad again before the end of the longest night in history.

Then I unlocked the front door and sat on the floor next to my father's head. And waited.

A minute and a half later, my front door flew open. Nash stood on the porch, panting, wearing only jeans, a short-sleeve tee, and sockless sneakers. He stepped inside and shoved the door closed, and I stood. "You ran the whole way?"

"Mom has the car." He folded his arms around me, and I let him, even though his chilled limbs stole my warmth and made me shiver.

I was warm on the inside.

"What the hell happened?" he asked finally, pulling away to kneel beside my dad, two fingers pressed against the pulse in his neck.

"Avari. Dad's been making Alec sleep tied to the recliner, so tonight Avari used my dad to cut Alec free, then he possessed Alec and…"

"And what?" Evidently satisfied by my dad's pulse, Nash stood, his irises churning with green twists of fear and amber swirls of protective anger.

"Nothing." I shrugged miserably. "Nothing happened. I hit him with my alarm clock, and now I might need a new alarm clock, but I think Alec's okay."

"I don't give a shit about Alec." More fierce colors flashed in his eyes. "What about you? Are you okay?"

"Yeah. Just a couple of bruises." I held up my arms so he could see the faint handprints around my wrists, and Nash clenched his teeth so hard I was afraid he'd crack them. "I taped him up, so I think we're pretty safe. I just… I didn't want to be alone."

Nash wrapped one arm around me, and his hands felt warm now, through the tee I slept in. "Where is he?"

I pointed toward my room, and Nash stomped off down the hall. A second later, he reappeared, dragging a still-bound and unconscious Alec behind him. He dropped Alec on the floor and stared at him, and I understood that he was fighting a violent impulse I could only vaguely understand. He wanted to kick Alec while he was down—I could see it in his eyes.

"Nash, none of this is his fault. He hates Avari as much as we do. Maybe more."

"No. More isn't possible. Not after that," Nash insisted, gesturing toward my bruised arms. He helped me lay my father on the couch, then we curled up together in the recliner and watched them both, waiting for morning.

NASH STAYED UNTIL my father finally woke up around dawn and thanked him, then sent him home. Over coffee, I explained what had happened—my dad didn't remember anything—then I tried to pretend I couldn't see the slow swirl of fear in his eyes. If Avari had the power to possess him—a one-hundred-thirty-year-old *bean sidhe*—then his limits were few. And that was enough to scare anyone.

Alec woke up half an hour later, while my dad was in the shower.

"Kaylee?"

I rubbed sleep from my eyes, but stayed in my chair, across the room from where he still lay on the floor. "Are you...you?"

"Yeah. Shit. My arm's asleep." He tried to move, but could only shrug awkwardly with his hands bound, his forehead wrinkled in confusion. "What happened?"

I brushed hair back from my face, but stayed in my corner. "What color was my first bike?"

Guilt flooded his features when he saw my face and

recognized the remnants of my recent trauma. "Kaylee, what happened?"

"Just answer the question. What color?"

"Red. No!" He shook his head when my eyes widened in panic. "White, with red ribbons. Sorry."

My gaze narrowed on him. I wanted to trust him, but I couldn't. I couldn't fully trust anyone who was in a position to actually help me. I'd never felt more alone in my life.

"Give me a break, Kaylee, please. My head feels like it's the size of a pumpkin and I'm tied up on the floor and I don't know how I got here. I'm not exactly thinking straight."

I exhaled slowly, fighting for calm. Avari had fooled me too many times. "What did you guess Emma named her first bra?"

A flicker of amusement lit his features for just an instant. "Helga," he said, and I finally stood. "What the hell happened?"

I crossed the room carrying the steak knife, but hesitated to cut him free. I was sure it was Alec now, but when I looked at him, I saw Avari staring down at me through Alec's eyes, pinning me. And every time I thought about that, fear gave way to a miniburst of panic, deep in my chest.

"Kay?"

"You…" I stopped and started over, squatting to cut the tape so I wouldn't have to look at him. It wasn't Alec's fault. "*He*… He tied up my dad, then came into my room and…" I couldn't finish, so I finally just showed him one bruised arm.

"Oh, damn, Kaylee, I'm so sorry." Alec looked like someone had just punched him in the face. Then followed up with a kick to the groin. "You know I'd never…"

"I know." I sank onto the floor and leaned against the couch with my knees pulled up to my chest. "I don't know what to do. He'll come back. I don't think we can stop him."

"Yes, we can." Alec sat up and used the knife to free his feet. "We'll find a way." He peeled off the last piece of tape, then his hand rose to the back of his head and came away smeared with blood. Alec winced. "I guess your dad's pissed?"

I forced an uneasy grin at that. "Yeah, but I did that. Also, I'd steer clear of Nash for a while. And you should probably stay away from Tod, for good measure." Because one way or another, the reaper would hear about what happened.

And that's when I noticed the dark red stain on the carpet. I could have killed Alec. And none of this was his fault.

"This has to stop."

"I know. We'll find a way. I swear, Kaylee, this will never happen again."

But it was hard to take heart in his words, because they sounded more and more hollow every time I heard them.

19

SABINE WAS SITTING in the passenger seat of my car when I tried to leave for work at nine-thirty Sunday morning. I saw her the moment I stepped onto the front porch, and for a second, I considered simply marching back into the kitchen, where my father was cleaning Alec's head wound, trying to figure out how to keep Avari out of our lives for good. To my surprise, he was more sympathetic to Alec's dilemma this morning, rather than less, since he'd now personally fallen victim to possession.

But ignoring her would only be prolonging the inevitable. And Sabine's presence *was* starting to feel inevitable, though I'd only known her a week. The *mara* was a force of nature—a tidal wave of fear, and pain, and need—and the only way I knew to survive her was to grab the nearest tree and ride out the surge.

She didn't look up as I jogged down the porch steps; she just stared out the window, long dark hair covering the only visible side of her face. A glance up and down the street showed no sign of her car, and I decided right then not to even ask how she'd gotten to my house.

I exhaled slowly as I walked down the driveway, struggling to contain the sudden white-hot flare of my temper, determined to face my latest problem head-on.

Despite her obvious B and E, the driver's side door was locked, and Sabine didn't turn to face me when I tried the handle. Nor did she unlock the door and let me into my own car, though she'd clearly gone through some effort to let *herself* in. If I couldn't see the back of her rib cage expanding with each breath, I might have thought she was dead.

That'd be just like Sabine, to die in my car—one last trauma for me before she'd probably haunt me for the rest of my life.

Gritting my teeth, I unlocked the door myself and slid into the driver's seat. "What are you doing in my car?" I demanded, still clutching my keys for fear that if I put them in the ignition, she'd grab them and run, as the next part of whatever stunt she obviously had planned.

"Waiting," she said, and her voice was oddly nasal.

My spine tingled. Had Avari somehow gotten ahold of her, too? Had he found another body to wear while he tortured me?

But then she turned, and I understood. She wasn't possessed—she'd been crying.

Great. A bawling Nightmare. *What's next? A schizophrenic Minotaur?*

"How did you get in here?" I asked, not sure I really wanted the answer. I should have just kicked her out and headed to work—I'd probably be late as it was. But I so rarely had the upper hand with Sabine that I couldn't resist the opportunity to find out what could possibly make the big bad *mara* cry.

Sabine reached between her seat and the passenger's side door and held up a long, thin strip of metal with a hook on one end. A slim jim.

My fist clenched around my keys. "I don't even want to know how you learned to use that." My curiosity—not to mention my patience—was fading by the second. "If you expect me to feel sorry for you, you're out of luck," I said, trying not to stare at her swollen eyes, flushed face, and tear-streaked cheeks.

"I don't want your sympathy." She sniffled, then grabbed a tissue from the minipack in my center console and wiped her face. It didn't help. "I want you to fix this."

"Fix what?"

"This!" She spread her arms, as if to encompass her entire screwed-up life. "Nash won't talk to me. I went back last night, and he just kicked me out again. He won't even listen."

I have to admit, I took a little joy in her pain; she'd certainly dished out enough for me. "I'm surprised he let you in in the first place."

Sabine frowned like I wasn't making sense. "I went in through a window."

"You broke into his house!" But then, why not? She'd broken into both my dreams and my car....

She shrugged. "Harmony always forgets to check the windows."

"That's not the point." Though I made a note to mention that little security lapse to Nash. "You can't just break into his house and expect him to be happy to see you!"

Her frown deepened. "He always was before. We never could stay mad at each other, and after we had a fight, one of us would sneak into the other's room, and instead of apologizing, we'd—"

"Stop!" I shouted, louder than I'd intended to in the confines of my car. For a couple of endless moments, I could only blink at her, trying to process what she'd almost said, while subconsciously denying that we were even having this conversation. "I get the picture, and I *don't* need to hear about it." Or think about it, or ever, *ever* get stuck with a visual. "And anyway, that's not normal, Sabine. In fact, it's messed up. Sounds like you two had nothing in common but sex."

Hurt flickered across her tear-streaked expression, and again, my heart beat a little faster in satisfaction. But she recovered quickly. "I don't think you *know* what's normal, Kay. Sometimes messed up is just the way things are. And even if we weren't a normal couple, so what? *Screw* normal. Normal is dull, and Nash and I were lightning in a bottle. We burned hard and fast, but never burned up."

I started to argue, but she spoke over me. "And it's none of anyone's else business what our relationship is built on, but just so you understand, I know Nash better than you ever will. You can't truly know someone until you've seen what he's afraid of, and even if he tells you all his deep dark secrets, you can never understand them like I do. You can never understand *him* like I do."

"Get out." I'd heard enough.

"No." She locked the passenger's side door with her elbow and crossed both arms over her chest. "Not until you fix this."

"Why should I? You haven't even apologized."

She frowned, looking genuinely confused. "I can't apologize."

My hands clenched around the wheel. "Why not?"

"Because I'm not sorry!" She sat straighter, eyes wide and earnest. "I did what I had to do. It didn't work, and now I wish I'd done something else, but I had to try, and I'm not sorry for that. I'll do whatever it takes to get him back. I thought you'd understand that."

"I do." I exhaled heavily and stared at the dashboard, then made myself meet her pained gaze. "That's exactly why I'm not going to help you. Now get out of my car. I have to go to work."

Her gaze went dark, her full lips pressed into a thin, angry line. "Damn it, Kaylee, you're going to fix this, or I swear I'll be in your head all night long, every night for the rest of your life."

My jaw clenched so hard lights started flashing in front of my eyes. I shoved the key into the ignition and turned it, and when the engine rumbled to life, I twisted in my seat to check out the rear windshield as I backed down the drive. "Fine. If you won't get out, consider yourself along for the ride. And don't ask me how you're getting home, 'cause this is a one-way argument."

"I can do it, you know," she insisted a couple of

minutes later, like I hadn't spoken at all. Like I wasn't halfway to the highway in my stupid Cinemark polo and pants. "Those other nightmares only ended because I let them. I can ride your dreams all night long—as long as I want—and you won't be able to wake up until I decide you've had enough. And that won't be until you make things right between me and Nash."

I swallowed thickly as I swerved onto the on-ramp, trying to pretend her threat hadn't scared the crap out of me. But it had. Aside from the terror she could inspire, my very worst fear was of not being in control of myself. I couldn't stand the thought of being at someone else's mercy. And she knew that. But I wouldn't bend to her threats—not even the big one.

"Threatening me isn't going to make me help you, you know," I said, wishing I could watch for her reaction, instead of staring at the road. Because frankly, I wasn't sure which was more dangerous, the highway traffic, or the *mara* in my passenger seat.

"Then what will?" She sniffled again, and wiped her face with both hands this time.

"Nothing! I don't owe you anything, and I'm glad Nash isn't talking to you! You half stripped and jumped my boyfriend, right in front of me, and you wanted to get caught. The whole thing was just another part of your mind game!"

"Well, *yeah*," Sabine said, and I glanced away from the road to see her frowning, apparently surprised by my statement of the obvious. "You knew I was coming after him—I told you that up front. It's nothing personal. But you're wrong about that last part. This isn't a game. This is my *life,* and he's the only good thing in it. He's all I've thought about in the two years I spent trying to get back to him, and I'm not going to lose him now. You have to help me, Kaylee. *Please.*"

Her voice cracked on the last word, and I glanced at her again in surprise. She obviously hated asking for my help, but she'd do anything to get Nash back, and I knew how she felt.

Nash and I had made up, but not because I'd forgiven him. I missed him so much that we'd made up *in spite* of me not forgiving him. Which meant that Sabine was totally barking up the wrong ex-girlfriend.

"No, I *don't* have to help you," I said at last, and the words sounded so foreign coming from my own mouth that I actually had to repeat them in my head, to reinforce the certainty.

"You are such a selfish *bitch!* You have everything!" she shouted, and I nearly swerved into the next lane. "You could find someone else to love you—hell, all you'd have to do is open your eyes—but I can't. Nash is all I have. He's all I'll *ever* have, and I put everything I am into finding him again." She stopped yelling and swallowed thickly, staring out the windshield for a long moment while we both tried to catch our breath.

Then she turned to me again, calmer now, but no less intense. "Kaylee, I'm not asking you to shove him at me. I'm not even asking you to step aside. I just need you to stop pulling him away from me."

I flicked my right blinker on and veered smoothly off the highway at my exit, and when I didn't answer, Sabine tried again.

"What do you want?" she demanded. "You want me to beg?"

The theater was up ahead, and I picked a spot near the back of the lot. "I want you to get out of my car! I couldn't help you even if I wanted to. Nash made up his own mind."

"I know, and he's mad now, but he'll get over it. I'm pretty sure it'll take longer without makeup sex, but he *will* get over it. But he won't tell either of us that unless you get over it, too. If you forgive me, he'll forgive me, and we can go back to the way things were."

"I don't *like* the way things were!" I shut off the engine and pulled the key from the ignition. "And he doesn't, either."

"Ask him." She grabbed my arm when I tried to get out of the car. "Ask him if he really wants to be rid of me, Kaylee. He'll tell you the truth. And if he says he doesn't want to lose me—at least as a friend—and you still won't help me, then you're intentionally trying to make him unhappy. Why would you do that if you really love him?"

"That doesn't even make any sense! I…" But I didn't have anything logical to follow that up with, so I could only groan and let my head fall back against the headrest. "You are the most infuriating person I've ever met."

She lifted one brow, half-amused, even with tears still standing in her eyes. "I'm going to take that as a compliment."

"It's really not."

"Yet you haven't kicked me out of your car."

"Not for lack of *trying!*" I sighed again, but recognized

the sound of futility in that breath. It was so much harder to hate her when she wasn't kissing my boyfriend or stalking my dreams. "Sabine, I have to be on the clock in five minutes. And this isn't going to happen. You can't seriously expect me to forgive you for a topless make-out session with Nash. Much less sanction your friendship."

"Why are you always telling me what I can't do? There's *nothing* I can't do, and the same goes for you, whether you know it or not. And if you weren't so threatened by me, you'd have no problem with this."

"That's it. I'm done." I shoved open my door and got out. "Lock the doors when you go. And stay out of my car." *And out of my life.*

MY SHIFT ENDED at two, and I was relieved to find my car empty. And not so relieved to find all four doors unlocked—a metaphorical middle finger from Sabine. Fortunately, I didn't keep anything in my car, so there was nothing to be stolen except the car itself, which probably would have happened if I'd been working a night shift.

When I walked through my front door half an hour later, I found a note from my father in the empty candy dish on an end table, where I usually dropped my keys. The note repeated what his voice mail had already told me: he'd driven Alec to the factory for a preliminary drug test and training video, and he'd be back by six with dinner.

What the note didn't say, but I'd heard in my father's voice, was that he was unwilling to leave Alec alone if at all possible, after last night's demon-roping marathon.

So for the first time in weeks, I found myself alone

in my house. I would have loved a nap, or even just a couple of hours spent staring at the TV, with no one else around to fight me for the remote. Unfortunately, I couldn't really relax until I knew how to keep Avari out of my dreams, and out of Alec's body.

By my best guess, the only reason he hadn't tried to steal *my* body was that I couldn't feed him like Alec could. But it was only a matter of time before I made him mad enough that he'd take me over just to hurt or humiliate me. Or worse. Because if he had the power to possess a half hypnos, he had the power to possess me, and it wouldn't take him long to figure out how to use my own abilities to cross me into the Netherworld. And I couldn't just sit around with that thought eating at me like acid.

Unfortunately, I had no idea where to start looking for solutions. My dad and uncle—and probably Harmony Hudson—were already burning their respective candles at both ends, so far without a thing to show for their efforts.

My only idea—some of that weird Netherworld dreamless-sleeping herb Harmony had given Nash while he was sick—was shot down before I'd even fully expressed it. Nash said that the herb would keep Sabine from giving me nightmares—she can't mess with dreams that aren't there—but wouldn't even slow Avari down. He didn't need us to dream; he only needed us to sleep.

And I already knew from experience that the internet had nothing about hellions. At least, not about real hellions. There was plenty of info on comic book and video game hellions. But nothing of use, unless I had an enchanted sword hanging from my belt or a gang of mismatched but powerful superheroes at my back.

And even then, there were no guarantees.

I was staring at my Betty Boop phone message pad— still blank—when the doorbell rang. Surprised, I dropped my pen and pad on the coffee table and crossed the room to glance out the front window, where I found Tod standing on the porch, his hands behind his back.

*Huh. Weird.*

I pulled open the door and looked up at him. "What's with the doorbell?"

He grinned, and a blond curl fell over his forehead. "Just tryin' on some manners."

"Why? Who died?" I meant it as a joke, but when his smile faded, I frowned. "Please tell me no one died...."

"Well, I'm sure someone, *somewhere,* died. But no one I know." He hesitated, and I stared at him, still trying to figure out what the reaper was doing on my porch. "Can I come in?"

I shrugged and stepped back to clear the way. "You don't usually ask permission. Or use the door. So...what are you delivering today—pizza or death?"

"Both, actually." He pulled his arms out from behind his back as he stepped over the threshold, and his right hand held a grease-stained medium pizza box. "Pepperoni for you now, and a fatal aneurism to the woman in room 408, in about ten hours."

"Thanks." I took the box and closed the door behind him, a little disturbed that I was only a little disturbed by the mention of his night job. "What's the occasion?"

"No occasion. I need to talk to you, and I was hungry."

*Okaaay...* "What do we need to talk about?" I set the pizza box on the coffee table and flipped open the lid to find the pie still steaming and gooey with cheese.

But instead of flopping into my dad's favorite chair, Tod stood in the middle of my living room, watching me like he wasn't sure what to do next. "Are you alone?"

"Not as alone as I was a minute ago," I said, and at that, he cracked a smile—but a small one. "What's up, Tod? Is something wrong?"

"We need to talk about Nash. And Sabine."

I dropped onto the couch and grabbed a slice of pizza, then gestured for him to help himself. "Pizza isn't enough to get me to talk about Sabine. You should have brought chocolate." I chewed my first bite as he sank onto the opposite end of the couch, but made no move on the pizza. "She broke into my car this morning and wouldn't get out, so I had to take her to work with me. Then she left my car unlocked, like a tribute to suburban crime statistics."

Tod's mouth quirked in a half smile. "You're lucky she didn't take a bat to it."

"So I hear. That girl is seriously damaged."

"I know. She came to see me after she left the theater."

"At work?"

"Yeah. She's hurting, Kaylee."

"I know. Now explain the part where that's my fault."

"It's not. But she's not the only one. I talked to Nash after that."

I frowned and swallowed another bite. "You have too much free time. Two jobs, yet you're never at either of them. I'm in the wrong line of work."

He shrugged and glanced at the pizza, but didn't take a slice. "I have a lot of 'driving' time to kill, so I stopped by home—" by which he meant *Nash's* home "—on the way to a delivery address."

"Convenient."

"Yeah." He frowned. "It almost makes up for the whole walking corpse thing, huh?"

"Anyway…"

"Anyway, Nash is in bad shape, Kaylee. On Friday, he had been reunited with a good friend and was a couple of steps from getting back together with his girlfriend. Today he has neither one of those."

"He has me," I insisted. "We kinda made up. He even came over last night." *Or early this morning…*

"Yeah. You 'kinda' made up. In the sense that he'll drop everything to come running when you call, but you still haven't forgiven him enough to deal with his problems. Which means that he's still alone in every way that counts. And being alone is really hard on his willpower."

I made myself swallow another bite. "By willpower, are we talking about resisting certain Netherworld addictive substances, or certain willing ex-girlfriends?"

"I'm talking about frost, Kaylee. Demon's Breath. He can't do this on his own, and Mom and I can't be there all the time. Especially now that I have two jobs."

"When were you ever there?"

"I was around. He just didn't know it. But I'm not gonna let my brother start using again." He looked right into my eyes then, and I saw a hint of true turmoil flicker in the cerulean depths of his eyes. Turmoil and…something else. Something even more aching and suppressed.

"Being alone and in pain makes everything harder to resist, and right now Nash is hurting because he knows you can't forgive him. And he's resisting something that already has a hold on him. He's fighting the undertow, Kaylee, and he needs your help."

Nash hadn't said anything to me about that. He didn't talk to me about his cravings or the lingering effects of withdrawal, because he knew I wanted nothing to do with that part of his life.

"You think I should forgive him?" Like it was just that easy.

Tod blinked and met my gaze. "I think you should give him up. You need to let Sabine have him."

20

"I NEED TO WHAT?" Tod was kidding. He had to be.

The reaper held two hands up in a defensive gesture. "Okay, just hear me out before you start yelling, okay?"

I nodded, because the truth was that I could barely speak, much less yell. My vocal cords were paralyzed by shock. Which almost never happens to a *bean sidhe*.

"Kay, you and Nash are no good for each other," Tod said. I tried to interrupt, but he spoke over my inarticulate mumble. "You know it, even if you won't admit it. He needs you, but you don't need him."

"That's not true." I shook my head, emphasizing my denial. "I do need him. I needed him last night."

"No, you didn't. He said that by the time he got there, you'd already expelled the hellion, tied up the host, and cut your dad loose, all by yourself. You're so strong, and smart, and you never hesitate when something needs to be done, and that's all...amazing." Tod's irises sparked with a sharp twist of bright blue before going suddenly still. "But Nash needs to be needed. You both *want* each other—even a dead man could see that—but you've changed, and he has nothing to offer you anymore, and eventually you're going to realize that on your own. But probably not before you've wasted years of your life—and his—with the wrong guy."

My chest throbbed like one big bruise, like my heart was trying to pound its way out through my ribs. But above that steady beat of pain, my indignation roared, drowning out everything else, demanding to be heard.

"What gives you the right to tell me who I shouldn't be with? What, you think being a few years older than me means you know everything?"

Tod's irises pulsed with a quick beat of anger, then went still when he got control of them. "No. But I think being dead for a couple of those years gives me a perspective most people don't have. I know how short life really is, and I can see things you and Nash don't understand yet. Like, maybe there's someone better out there for him. And maybe there's someone better for you."

I dropped my half-eaten slice of pizza into the box and stared at him in disbelief. "Being dead doesn't qualify you to play matchmaker between my boyfriend and his *ex*-girlfriend. Maybe she's an ex for a very good reason."

"Or maybe she's an ex because my death got in the way of their relationship. Maybe they never should have been separated. And then you two never would have met, and this whole thing would have played out differently."

Shocked silent, I could only blink for several seconds, as what he was really saying sank in. "Then he wouldn't be an addict, right? Because if he'd never met me, he would never have been exposed." I could barely breathe through the sting in his words.

"No." Tod reached for me, looking both stunned and confused, but I pulled away from him. "Kaylee, I swear that's not what I meant. I'm not even sure how you got that out of what I was trying to say..."

"Then what did you mean?"

"I just meant that if you and Nash had never met..." He stopped and closed his eyes, like he was trying to gather his thoughts. "If you hadn't met, you wouldn't have to deal with letting each other go now."

"I'm not letting him go."

"If you give a damn about him, you will. As bad as it probably hurts to think about this right now, Nash and Sabine are right for each other. Maybe more so now than they ever were before, because now they need each other. They're both messed up pretty bad, but together, their two halves make a whole, while the most you and Nash are ever gonna add up to is one and a half."

"One and a half?" I repeated, like a brain-damaged parrot. I heard what he was saying, but I just couldn't believe that some manipulative, antagonistic, dream-pirate could possibly be better for Nash than I was.

Tod nodded solemnly. "It's an improper fraction. Sad, but true."

"Actually, it's a mixed number," I said, slowly going numb as his words continued to sink in. "Fourth-grade math."

"Whatever." He glanced down, then met my gaze again and let me see a sad little swirl of color in his eyes.

"My point stands, and I have to side with Sabine on this one. If you really care about him, you have to let her have him. That's the only way either of them are ever going to be whole. If you try to keep Nash for yourself, you'll only ever really have half of him."

"But he loves me." I felt like I'd just turned in a hundred circles and the room wouldn't stop spinning.

Then Tod put his hand on my arm, and the world went still.

"Yeah. He does. And it'll hurt like hell for him to get over you. But he *will* get over you. And she'll help make that happen."

"What if I don't want him to get over me?"

"Then you're being selfish." Tod leaned back and ran his hand through his hair again. "Kaylee, you're never going to be able to truly forgive him for what he did, and honestly, I don't know that you should. But my point is that if you can't forgive him, he won't be able to forgive himself. Which means that as long as the two of you are together, he's going to be living with this, trying to make up for it and failing over and over again, because he has nothing left to offer you. Do you really want to watch him suffer like that?"

I shook my head, not in answer, but in denial and confusion. "Being with Sabine won't fix that. She can't undo it, and she can't make me get over it."

"No, but she can help him forgive himself. Your relationship with Nash was all shiny and clean, but it's tainted now. It's like a stain you can never wash out. A constant reminder. But their relationship...well, it was messed up from day one, so that's kind of their status quo. It'll work between them, Kaylee. If you let it."

I could only stare at him in mounting shock and pain. And when my anger reached its crest, my temper exploded. "What is *wrong* with you?" I demanded. "How can you stand there and tell me that two people who love each other shouldn't be together? That I should just shove him into the arms of his slut of an ex-girlfriend and call it a day?"

"This is the truth, Kaylee." Tod put his hands up, palms out, in another defensive gesture. "You can't get mad at me for telling the truth."

"Oh, yes, I can." I stood and flipped the pizza box closed, then slammed my hand down on it for good measure. "Get out." I picked up the smooshed box and shoved it at him.

"Kaylee…"

"Just go away, Tod. I have enough to worry about without adding 'taking stupid advice from a dead guy' to the list."

Tod blinked at me, and the smallest cobalt tremor of emotion rippled through his irises before he regained control. Before I could interpret what I'd seen. Then he sighed and blinked out of the room, pizza box and all.

Alone in my house again, I sank onto the couch and buried my head in my hands, my fingers pressed into my eyes so hard that red spots formed behind my eyelids. I refused to let the tears fall. Tod was wrong. So what if I didn't need Nash anymore? Wanting him was enough.

But as I lay awake that night, listening to Alec snore in

the recliner he was now handcuffed to, doubt ate at me, one vicious bite at a time.

What if Tod was right? What if wanting Nash wasn't enough?

BY MONDAY MORNING, exhaustion had become my state of normalcy. Even with Alec well secured, none of us had gotten much sleep for fear that Avari would possess my dad and tear up the house looking for keys to the cuffs Tod had commandeered from the local police station's supply room. For our safety, neither Alec nor I knew where my dad had hidden the keys.

But beyond all that, I was afraid that if I let myself sleep deeply enough to actually get any rest, Avari would find me again in my dreams. And lying awake only gave me more time to obsess over dead teachers, vengeful hellions, and a boyfriend who may or may not be better off with a walking Nightmare than with me.

Thanks to another largely sleepless night, I pulled into the school parking lot just five minutes before the final bell and had to park near the back, both my scattered thoughts and flagging energy focused on finding Emma, so I could ask for advice about Nash. I was halfway to the building when a scream ripped through the parking lot, and all random snatches of conversation ended in startled silence. Heads turned toward the human but obviously agonized wail, now accompanied by other enraged shouts, and the sickening thunk of some blunt instrument into solid flesh.

I shouldn't have gone; I didn't really want to know. But horror and curiosity are overpowering lures on their own, and together, they're virtually irresistible. So I found myself in the thin flow of bodies streaming toward sounds of anger and pain, fully aware that there was probably nothing I could do to stop whatever was happening.

When the crowd stopped moving, I elbowed my way to the front, then sucked in a sharp breath when what I saw sank in.

In the main aisle, Trace Dennison, one of the basketball team starters, clutched a golf club in both hands, huge feet spread for balance, cheeks flushed in obvious outrage. He pulled the club up over his head, and the crowd around me gasped.

"No, man, wait!" Derek Rogers, the captain of the basketball team, leaned against a dusty blue four-door car, clutching his left arm to the big *E* on the front of his green-and-white letter jacket. His face was ashen beneath a smooth, dark complexion, his jaw clenched in pain, and he held his right arm over his head in defense against the golf club ready to swing at him again.

"Whoa, Trace!" Two of the other team members stepped out of the crowd, palms up in identical defensive gestures, intense, cautious gazes trained on Trace. "What are you doing? Put the club down!" the first player said, nervously running one hand through a head full of soft brown waves.

Trace didn't even seem to hear him.

The second player—Michael something?—moved in boldly, while around me, the entire crowd seemed to stop breathing. "Dennison, do *not* make me kick your ass. Put that thing down before I shove it someplace graphic."

Trace never even turned. Instead, he gripped the golf club—a putter?—like a baseball bat, and as we watched, frozen in horror and anticipation, he swung overhead again, grunting with effort and with what sounded like primal rage.

Michael lunged for the club and missed. Derek shouted. Onlookers sucked in sharp breaths. And over all that, I heard the muted thud of impact and the crunch of breaking bone.

Derek's shouts became high-pitched screams, and his right arm fell to his side, useless.

Tears blurred my vision, but shock held me in place. I didn't know what to do. *No one* seemed to know what to do, except Michael, who looked determined to put this insanity to an end, despite the obvious danger to himself.

"You're crazy!" Derek shouted between pain-filled gasps, edging down the length of the car and away from the club as Trace lifted it again.

"Trace…" Michael said, hands outstretched now, and Trace whirled on him, club held high. The crowd shuffled backward as one, but Michael didn't seem to notice. "What's the problem, man? What's this about?"

"He's my problem," Trace said through clenched teeth, glancing over at Derek, who'd clenched his jaw shut— probably to keep from screaming—clutching both ruined arms to his chest. "Seventeen point average and an MVP nomination doesn't mean you walk on water. If he wasn't such a ball hog, maybe people'd realize there's more than one man on the court!"

A ripple was working its way through the rapidly growing crowd—a single capped head sticking up above most of the others. Coach Rundell and both security guards stepped into the clearing as Trace started to turn back to Derek, already pulling the club high again, ready for another swing. Michael must have seen them, because he moved closer to Derek, dragging Trace's gaze with him, distracting him from the newly arrived authorities.

Coach Rundell wrapped one meaty hand around the neck of the club and neatly plucked it from Trace's grip, jerking him backward in the process.

When Trace turned, his face scarlet with rage, the security guards each grabbed one of his arms.

"Call an ambulance," Rundell growled, after one look at Derek's misshapen right arm, obvious even beneath his thick jacket sleeve. The younger of the two guards pulled a portable radio from his belt and spoke into it, passing along the coach's orders to the attendance secretary as they hauled a belligerent Trace Dennison toward the building. But by then, at least a dozen students were already dialing 9-1-1 directly.

Rundell helped Derek out of his jacket carefully, but the senior screamed as the sleeves slid over his arms. "Oh, shit," Rundell said. Derek's arms were both obviously broken, but his right sleeve was torn and oozing blood, the white end of a bone sticking up through both flesh and stained material.

"Okay, let's get you inside." Coach waved Michael forward to help him get Derek to the school building, both basketball players towering over the shorter, thicker football coach as several other teachers arrived and began to disburse the onlookers.

"Hey, Coach!" another voice called from the crowd,

and I turned to find a freckled sophomore member of the golf team holding up the club Rundell had dropped, a long black golf bag hanging from his opposite shoulder. "Can I have this back now?"

Rundell stopped and turned toward the kid, and Derek groaned. "What was Trace doing with it?"

The kid shrugged. "He grabbed it right out of my bag and just started swinging."

"Well, I think it's evidence now. Have your dad call me." Rundell held out his hand, and the kid jogged forward to hand him the club, then the coach marched toward the building with one hand on Derek's shoulder.

"What happened?" Emma asked from behind me, and I turned to see her rounding the car on my right.

"Trace Dennison went homicidal, and now the basketball team's down two starters. He broke both of Derek Rogers's arms."

"Damn." Emma whistled as we headed toward the building.

"Yeah. It was pretty brutal." I was oddly relieved to realize that even after everything I'd seen in the Netherworld, human-on-human violence still truly bothered me.

We followed the crowd toward the side entrance, and gossip buzzed all around us, people rehashing Trace's psychotic breakdown, Mona's arrest for possession with intent, and Tanner's locker vandalism, which had been largely outshined by the rest of the chaos. Then the shrill ring of the final bell cut through the animated chatter, and the foot traffic sped up.

*Great. Another tardy.* Maybe Mr. Wesner's sub wouldn't notice.

As we jogged toward the building, a car pulled into the parking lot, and distantly, I noticed that it was Jeff Ryan's rebuilt '72 Chevelle. Nash had helped him work on it a couple of times, and Jeff had let him borrow it once, as a thank-you.

I waved to Jeff as I crossed the aisle, practically dragging Em along with me. We were only feet from the school door when an engine growled behind us. Tires squealed, and I turned toward the sound to see a sleek, low-slung black car racing down the center aisle. I sucked in a breath to shout a warning, but I was too late.

The black car slammed into the passenger side of Jeff's Chevelle with the horrible *squealcrunchpop* of bending metal. I flinched and grabbed Emma's arm. And for a second or two, a thick, shocked silence reigned complete in the parking lot.

Then Jeff's door creaked open and he crawled out of his car, the passenger side of which was now wrapped around the crunched front of the other vehicle.

People raced toward the wreck. The other driver got out and started yelling at Jeff, but I couldn't understand much of what he said. Jeff was wobbly and too stunned to reply, but after one good look at his ruined masterpiece, he blinked and shook his head, then jumped into the shouting match full-strength.

Teachers came running. Some gestured for onlookers to get to class while others tried to break up the fight that had erupted between Jeff and the other driver, who were still shouting between blows.

"Holy shit, what's that all about?" Emma asked, walking backward as slowly as possible, reluctant to tear her gaze from the latest violent outburst .

"That's Robbie Scates," someone said from my left, and I glanced over to see a guy I didn't know staring longingly at Emma. "He and Jeff entered some kind of hot-rod show in Dallas on Saturday, and Jeff placed higher. His picture was in the Sunday paper. Guess Robbie's a sore loser."

"A stupid one, too," I mumbled. At least fifty people had seen him T-bone Jeff's car.

"Damn…" Emma breathed. "An arrest on Friday, and now two fights and a wreck today, before school even started!"

"Technically, school's started," I noted, dragging her by one arm toward the entrance. "We just missed the first few minutes."

"I don't think we're the ones missing anything," Em said, turning reluctantly to follow me to algebra, where our dead teacher's desk was now occupied by a clueless long-term sub.

IN SPITE OF THE BUSY work the sub handed out—along with our tardy slips—Emma managed to fill the rest of the class in on the parking lot chaos, through a combination of whispered sentences and passed notes, until the sub finally gave up and pretended not to notice the crowd gathered around our desks.

"It's the pressure," Brant Williams opined, dark brows drawn low. "Trace needed that scholarship, otherwise he'll end up at TCJC. But he fumbled twice in the first quarter, and the recruiter never even looked at him after that."

"Well, they're sure not gonna recruit him now," Leah-the-pom-squad-girl added. "Unless maybe the golf team's really hard up."

But whether it was senior year pressure or something dumped into the school's water supply, the truth was that half the student body seemed to have gone insane over the weekend.

During second period, the fire alarm went off right about the time we started smelling smoke, and when we filed into the parking lot, the most prevalent rumor was that Camilla Edwards's science fair project—brought to school so the yearbook staff could get pictures of the first state finalist in nearly a decade—had been doused with something flammable and lit on fire in one of the chemistry labs. Now those pictures were all that remained of a project she'd started more than eight months earlier.

"This is insane," Emma said, when I snuck away from my class huddle to meet her by her car. The red and blue lights from the fire trucks and police cars flashed over her face, giving her expression a look of urgency, on top of the standard bewilderment. "Why would anyone trash Cammie's project? Just to get out of second period?"

But I had no answer. All I knew for sure was that Eastlake High had lost its collective mind, and the timing was too precise to be a coincidence. I was already dealing with a new Nightmare of a student, dead teachers, and a hellion with more strength and abilities than he should have. And now some kind of violent mental defect was sweeping the student body.

It was all related. I could feel the connection in my gut, even if I couldn't make sense of it. There was something I wasn't seeing. Some piece of the puzzle I hadn't yet found. And the only thing I knew for sure was that until I put the whole thing together, no one at Eastlake High School would be safe.

21

WHEN I WOKE UP at 2:24 a.m. on Tuesday, something lay on my pillow, two inches from my face. I sat up, fumbling for my bedside lamp, instantly alert. It was a purple sticky note, taken from my own desk.

Ice surged through my veins as I reached for it, raising chill bumps all over my body, and those chill bumps blossomed into chill *mountains* when I read the note.

Three words. Infinite possibilities.

*And sleeping, wake.*

There was no signature, and the handwriting was unfamiliar, with an old-fashioned, curly look to it.

Avari was back. And he wanted to play.

And that's when I realized the house around me was silent. No snoring. No groaning couch springs or squealing metal recliner frame as someone shifted in sleep.

Swimming in panic, I pulled on the jeans I'd worn the day before and raced into the living room—then froze when I squinted into the dark and made out the empty recliner and the pillow lying next to it on the floor. Alec was gone.

I whirled toward the couch, but it was empty, too, except for my dad's bedding, and for one long, horrible moment, I thought he was gone, too. Then something shifted in the shadows between the couch and coffee table, and I realized it was the rise and fall of my father's chest.

Shoving the coffee table out of my way, I clicked on the end table lamp and dropped to my knees next to my dad. His hands were cuffed at his back and blood had pooled beneath his head, and when I brushed back his hair, I found a sticky lump above his left temple.

Avari had found the keys. He'd possessed my dad in his sleep, found the handcuff keys, then released Alec and restrained my father. My dad had obviously woken up at some point after Avari had taken Alec's body—otherwise, why hit him? But I'd slept through the whole thing.

And now someone innocent would die, because I couldn't master the art of defensive insomnia.

Well, that, and because Avari was a vindictive, soul-sucking demon with an appetite for chaos and a yen for my complete destruction. But I couldn't help blaming myself, at least in part, because I'd failed to stop him. Again.

But maybe I could catch him. The others had all died at the school.

Since my father was safe for the moment, I pulled on my jacket, grabbed my car keys, then headed for the front door, where I froze with my hand on the knob. Stuck to the wood, half covering the peephole, was a second purple sticky note, displaying that same antiquated writing.

*A walk I take.*

If it was a riddle, it was a very bad one. I already knew he'd gone somewhere. Probably to kill someone. So why start a new game now?

He wouldn't, unless he was planning to feed from my pain, as well as from whatever energy he funneled through Alec. Which meant he was going after someone connected to me. And that narrowed things down. As did the fact that he was on foot.

But even knowing that, I could think of at least half a dozen people he might target, and I didn't have time to check on them all individually.

As I stepped into my shoes, panic-fueled, anger-driven plans of action tumbled through my brain, their unfinished edges making mincemeat of my upper level logic. In the driveway, I slid into my driver's seat and shoved the key into the ignition, and when the interior lights flared to life, I found myself staring at another sticky note in the middle of my steering wheel. My heart thumped painfully. Four words this time, in that antiquated scrolling print.

*Fair maid to break.*

It was more poem than riddle, but hardly brilliant, either way.

*And sleeping, wake*
*A walk I take*
*Fair maid to break*
Emma.

No, wait. What if he meant Sophie? My cousin and best friend were the only two human girls I knew for a fact that he knew how to find. My hands clenched around the steering wheel in frustration. Emma was my refuge from all things twisted and non-human. Sophie was my own flesh and blood. I couldn't lose either of them. But I couldn't save them both; they each lived about a mile from me, but in opposite directions.

I slammed the gearshift into Reverse, anger at Avari burning bright beneath aching fear for my cousin and my best friend. I backed down the driveway and onto the road, then shifted into Drive and took off, dialing as I drove.

Nash answered on the third ring.

"Mmm… Hello?" He sounded groggy, and bedsprings creaked as he rolled over.

"Wake up, Nash. I need help." I ran the first stop sign, confident by the lack of headlights that no one else was on the road in my neighborhood at two-thirty in the morning.

"Kaylee? Are you in the car?"

"Yeah. I need you to call Sophie and make sure she's okay." She wouldn't answer the phone if she saw my number on the display, especially in the middle of the night.

"Avari?"

"He found the handcuff key, knocked my dad out, and left me this stupid, cryptic riddle about breaking a 'fair maid.' I'm on my way to Emma's to check on her. So can you please call Sophie?"

"Yeah. I'll call you right back."

I got to Emma's two minutes later, driving way over the suburban speed limit. There were two cars in the driveway and another parked at the curb, and I recognized them all. One was Emma's, one her mother's, and the third belonged to one of Em's two older sisters. I saw no sign of Alec, or Avari, or evil of any kind.

I closed my car door softly and studied Emma's house. The front rooms were dark, except for the lamp they always left on, and since I didn't have a key, I wouldn't be able to get in without waking someone up. But then, neither would Avari, unless Alec had some kind of walk-through-walls power I didn't know about.

I practically tiptoed across the lawn and onto the front porch, where my hand hovered over the doorknob. An unlocked door would mean that Avari had beat me there. But a locked door didn't eliminate that possibility—he could have gone in through the backdoor or a window.

Holding my breath, I twisted the knob. It turned, and the door creaked open.

Uh-oh.

I stepped inside, and my blood rushed so fast the dimly lit living room seemed to swim around me. A few steps later, I could see down the hall, where a thin line of yellow light shone beneath the second door on the right. Emma's room.

My sneakers made no sound on the carpet as I crept toward her door, and when I was close enough to touch it, I heard voices whispering from inside, one deep and soft, the other higher in pitch.

Wrapping determination around myself like a security

blanket, I turned the knob and pushed the door all the way open. Then blinked in surprise.

Emma sat on her bed in a tank top and Tweety print pajama bottoms, her straight blond hair secured with an old scrunchy. Alec sat in her desk chair, pulled close to her nightstand. Neither of them looked surprised to see me.

"'Bout time!" Emma said, waving me inside. "Shut the door so we don't wake my mom up."

Bewildered, and more than a little suspicious, I closed the door, but hovered near it, unwilling to move too far from the exit until I was sure it was safe. I studied Alec, looking for any sign that he wasn't…himself. "What color was my first bike?" I asked, and Emma laughed.

"You guys are obsessed with this game!"

But Alec knew it was no game. "White, with red ribbons," he said, right on cue, and only then could I relax. Kind of.

"What's going on?" My eyes narrowed as I ventured a little farther into the room. Even if he was Alec now, he'd been Avari when he planted those notes and left my house. Something felt wrong. How on earth had he explained this to Emma?

But before either of them could answer, my phone rang. I pulled it from my pocket and flipped it open when I saw Nash's number. "Your cousin's not a morning person," he said, before I had a chance to say hi. "But she's fine."

"Thanks. I found Alec, and he and Em both seem okay. Do you think you could run over to my house and…look for that key?" Without it, I wasn't sure how we'd ever get my father out of the cuffs. "If my dad wakes up, tell him I'll be back in a few minutes, and I'm fine."

"Yeah. See you in a few."

I flipped my phone closed and slid it into my pocket, then looked up to find Emma watching me.

"Alec came to check on me," she said, in answer to my question. "He said you'd be right behind him, and here you are. *He* brought ice cream, though." She gestured to two spoons and a pint of Ben & Jerry's on the nightstand. One of the very pints she'd left in my freezer, no doubt. "Just FYI, Kay, if you're going to wake me up in the middle of the night for my own protection, then refuse to explain exactly what I'm in danger from, bringing ice cream is a good way to soothe my sleep-fuddled anger."

"Huh?" Considering the time, my lack of sleep, and the fear-laced adrenaline still half buzzing in my system, that was as articulate a response as I could manage.

Alec leaned back in his chair. "Emma, would you mind bringing another spoon?"

Em frowned, then glanced from me to Alec. "You know, if there's something you don't want me to hear, you can just say, 'Em, there's something we don't want you to hear.'"

He smiled, and I could practically see my best friend melt beneath the full power of his attention. "Em, there are things we don't want you to hear. Also, we need another spoon."

Emma sighed, but stood. "Whisper fast," she said, then headed into the hall.

"There are notes all over my house and car from

Avari," I whispered as softly as I could, the minute her footsteps faded. "What the hell happened?"

"It sounds like he found the key." Alec sat up straight, facing me as I sank onto Emma's bed. "I was here, alone, not ten minutes ago. Then she came in with two spoons. Evidently he brought her ice cream, but I'm not fool enough to believe that's the only reason for this little excursion."

"You told her I'd be coming, too?"

Alec shrugged. "He must have said that…before."

"So…he left notes for me and brought ice cream for Emma." I closed my eyes, trying to think through exhaustion, anger, and an encroaching headache. "How did you get rid of him?"

Alec shrugged. "I didn't."

"He vacated on his own…" I mumbled, as Em's muted, bare footsteps echoed toward us. "He never planned to kill her. He's just playing some kind of twisted game." But why?

Emma came back into the room before he could answer, but even if she hadn't, I doubt he'd have had anything to say. Though he'd lived with the hellion for a quarter of a century, he seemed no more privy to Avari's thought process than I was.

"So…what's up?" Emma asked, handing me the spoon. She sank onto the bed and pulled the lid from the carton of ice cream. "What's the latest cloud on the horizon of my pathetic existence?"

"Dramatic, Em?" But I had to grin. Nothing ever seemed to get Emma down. Even being told she was in danger from some mysterious force she probably would never understand.

"It's poetic. I like it," Alec said, and I swear I saw Emma flush, which hadn't happened much since the night she'd snuck into my room at one in the morning to tell me all about losing her virginity.

"You're not pathetic, and you're not in danger." *Any-more…* "We had a scare, but it seems to be over."

"A scare of the Netherworld variety?" Emma's smile faltered. She knew just enough about the non-human side of my life to be scared senseless every time it was mentioned. And I intended to keep it that way. If she was scared, she was much less likely to dig for information. Her fear was keeping her safe. Or at least safer than she'd have been otherwise.

"Yeah, but it's fine now." I stood, eyeing Alec. "You ready?"

"Wait!" Em waved the spoons at him slowly, like she could hypnotize him with the lure of shiny metal. "Stay and have some ice cream."

"Em, it's almost three in the morning." And I had to get back to my dad.

"Hey, you two woke me up from some very pleasant dreams. The least you can do is mollify me with ice cream."

One look at Em—who only had eyes for Alec—and I knew I was fighting a losing battle. So I stayed for just a few bites, if only to keep her from making any beyond-friendship overtures toward a man three times her age.

Then Alec and I headed home, where I cleaned my father's head wound while Nash called his mom at the hospital and asked her to send Tod to the police station for another handcuff key.

We never found the one Avari had taken.

22

AFTER ANOTHER MOSTLY sleepless night and an early breakfast spent watching Harmony stitch the gash on my dad's head, I held my breath as I walked into the school on Tuesday morning, half-afraid of what I'd find. I knew better than to believe that yesterday's campus chaos had faded into the ether.

I was right.

I'd made it halfway to my locker when the door to the girls' bathroom flew open and slammed against the wall right in front of me. I lurched out of the way as two bodies stumbled into the hall and collided with a stretch of lockers, ringing the metal doors like a gong. Hair flew, too wild and fast for me to identify either of the fighters as I scrambled out of the immediate impact zone.

A crowd formed quickly—a living boxing ring—as each girl tore at the other's hair and clothes, clawing at exposed skin. They screeched and grunted, a primal racket of pain and rage, punctuated with just enough profanity-riddled half sentences for me to understand the cause.

They were fighting over a guy. Someone's boyfriend, or ex-boyfriend, or stupid, unwitting crush.

A couple of teachers came running to break up the fight, already haggard before eight in the morning, and as I bypassed the action, I noticed two of the school's larger coaches hauling a boy apiece down the hall in my direction. The student on the left had a split lip and a black eye. The one on the right was bleeding from a head wound and a totally *crunched* nose.

In spite of their injuries, it was everything the coaches could do to keep them apart.

"Did you hear?" Emma asked, when I finally slid into the seat next to her in algebra.

"About the fights in the hall? Caught the live show and nearly got flattened. It's like going to school in a war zone."

"Not that." Emma looked just as put together as always, in spite of her interrupted sleep. Obviously middle-of-the-night ice cream was the cure for dark under-eye circles. "They took Coach Peterson away in handcuffs this morning. The custodian caught him trashing Rundell's office, shouting that he would have been the head football coach if Rundell hadn't married the superintendent's daughter." Emma leaned closer to me, not that it mattered. Everyone else was busy passing the same news. "I swear, Kaylee, the entire school's gone insane!"

Yeah. Including the teachers, which was a new development.

By third period, there had been four more fights and another teacher removed from school grounds, for undisclosed reasons. Whatever she'd done, she'd done in the teachers' lounge, and the rest of the staff wasn't talking. Which left us to interpret her crimes as we saw fit. And there was no shortage of rumors.

After third period—my free hour—I headed across the deserted gym toward the cafeteria, but stopped short when I heard a screech from the girls' locker room. "Sophie, no!"

I dropped my books on the polished wood floor and raced for the locker room, then threw open the door and froze in surprise at what I saw.

In one hand, Sophie held a huge pair of metal scissors with jagged blades. The ones she'd been using for her Life Skills project—pinking shears, Aunt Val had called them. In the other hand, my cousin held a thick chunk of Laura Bell's long, shiny brown hair.

Laura was bawling hysterically, her face already red from the effort, one hand clutching the back of her scalp.

"I'm…I'm so sorry!" Sophie screeched, her hand shaking violently, and a second later, she burst into tears, too.

"Give me that!" I jerked the scissors from her grasp by the closed blades, then spun Laura around to assess the damage. The center section of her hair had been clipped so close to her head I could see scalp showing through.

Great. A half-bald beauty queen. Laura was going to need therapy—I could already tell.

"Go to the office and have them call your mom," I said, unsure if Laura could even hear me over her own snot-strangled tears. "I'm sure they can get you some kind of emergency salon appointment. Or something."

Not that there was anything they'd be able to do for her, short of shearing the rest of it to match.

Laura wiped tears from her face with one sleeve, then wandered out of the bathroom in a traumatized daze, rendered virtually useless by a bad haircut. Not that I couldn't sympathize.

"Sophie, what the hell?" I demanded, as soon as the door closed, but my cousin just stood there, clutching a handful of her best friend's hair.

"I don't know!" she screeched, her words so painfully high-pitched I wanted to slap both hands over my ears. Maybe she was part *bean sidhe,* after all… "She was working on her hair, going on and on about being Snow Queen, and I just kept thinking that she never should have won. Then I just…snapped, and the next thing I know, I'm holding half her hair, and she's screaming, and all I can think is that it should have been me. It *would* have been me, if you hadn't trashed my dress. I didn't even get to compete after that!"

Her eyes widened, then narrowed in sudden understanding. And fury.

"This is *your* fault. I would have been Snow Queen if you hadn't ruined everything, like you always do! Luck of the Irish, my ass. You're like an agent of darkness. I swear, you have horns growing under all that stringy hair."

"Sounds like you found the family resemblance." I scowled and stepped closer to her, and Sophie backed up until her hip hit the sink. "I ought to cut your hair to match hers, and if you open your mouth one more time, that's exactly what I'll do." With that, I dropped her shears into the big covered trash can and stomped out of the locker room, leaving Sophie to her guilt and tears.

I was almost out of the gym—Sophie had yet to emerge—when a familiar voice shredded my remaining self-control like wood through a chipper.

"So you actually died, and she just...let it happen?"

*Sabine.* My pulse spiked with irritation. What the hell was she doing?

"Well, I don't think she could have stopped it..." another, softer voice said, and my anger was a white-hot ball of fury flaming in my gut. *Emma.* Sabine had Emma, and they were talking about...things they shouldn't be talking about.

"But you don't know for sure, right? I mean, you don't actually know what she's capable of, do you? All you really know is that she's not human and she screeches louder than a police siren. Right?"

I spun silently, trying to pinpoint the voices, but the gym looked empty.

"Yeah, I guess..." Em finally answered, and confusion slowed her words, like the first drink of the night.

"Don't you ever worry about the next time? I mean, being best friends with a *bean sidhe* should come with hazard pay, right? You're always in the line of fire, thanks to her."

"Actually...yeah. Something went down last night, and she and Alec wouldn't tell me what. Again." She paused as I crossed one corner of the basketball court quietly. "But everything turned out fine."

"But what if it hadn't? What if you'd become collateral damage again? Do you ever worry that she might…"

"Just let me die?" Emma asked, and I could hear the fear in her voice. My blood boiled. Sabine was goading her, reading and manipulating her fears with every word, but the actual fears were all Em's. Things she'd never told me about.

"Yeah," Emma continued. "Kaylee and Nash can't save someone without letting someone else die. One of these days, it'll be my time to go, and I'm afraid that Kaylee will just…let it happen. Or that they'll save someone else and end up killing me by accident."

"It could definitely happen," Sabine said, as I rounded the edge of the bleachers to see her smiling at me over Emma's shoulder. She'd known I was there the whole time. My hands curled into fists and my jaw clenched so hard my whole face ached.

"Sabine, what the hell are you doing?" My voice sounded lower and darker than I'd ever heard it.

"Just getting to know Em a little better."

Emma was watching me now, a familiar edge of irritation in her narrowed eyes. "Why didn't you tell me Sabine isn't human? And don't tell me this is more *bean sidhe* business—she's not a *bean sidhe*. And why do you and Alec have Netherworld secrets now? Are you just using any excuse to lock me out of your life?"

I raised a brow at Sabine. Clearly I was late to the conversation—Em had obviously confided *several* fears.

Sabine only shrugged and grinned, so I turned back to Emma, my arms crossed over my chest.

"Did she tell you what she is?"

"More than *you* told me. She's a *mara*."

I nodded. "And did she tell you what that means?"

Emma frowned. *That's what I thought.* "She's a Nightmare, Em. Literally. She reads people's fears and exploits them for her own entertainment." Or nutrition. I was still a bit fuzzy on that detail. "And that's what she's doing to you right now. Exploiting your fears."

And that's when it hit me. The school chaos. The fights and jealousy. They had nothing to do with Avari—what did he care if a few kids got arrested or expelled?

It was Sabine. All of it. I'd heard her talking to Sophie and Laura about the Snow Queen title last week. She'd chatted with the basketball team at lunch. And now she was moving in on Emma. She was feeding from their fears and insecurities. And it had to stop.

I took a deep breath, then faced my best friend, without letting Sabine out of my sight. "Em, I swear I'm not going to let you die. No matter what. Your life is definitely a priority, so you can stop worrying about that." I closed my eyes, weighing pros and cons in my head, then met Emma's suspicious gaze again. "And I'm going to tell you everything. I promise." It wasn't fair for me to keep her in the dark—I, of all people, should have known that. "But right now, I have to deal with the mess Sabine's gotten us all into. I'll meet you in the cafeteria, okay?"

Without waiting for her answer, I grabbed Sabine by the arm and hauled her across the gym. She just laughed and let me pull her. "Where are we going?"

"To find Nash." If anyone could reason with an out of control *mara,* it would be our mutual ex. Her one true love, according to Tod.

My anger burned even brighter at that thought.

"Oh, good!" she said, as I hesitated in the middle of the basketball court, debating the shortcut to the quad through the cafeteria. But pulling Sabine through a crowd of students she'd already worked into some kind of fear-fed frenzy would be a very bad idea. So I turned right and headed for the gym exit. "But you should probably know he's not speaking to me."

"Fortunately, he is speaking to me."

"So, what, you're gonna tattle on me for telling Emma I'm not human? That wasn't your secret to keep, Kaylee. Totally my call. And if blowing my own cover happens to poke holes in your credibility...well, we'll call that a big fat bonus!"

"You are *such* a bitch." I shoved open the heavy exterior door and pulled Sabine into the parking lot, then took an immediate left, circling the building toward the quad.

"That's hardly breaking news."

"Yet the headlines just keep coming." I tightened my grip on her arm. The quad was in sight by then, but I saw no sign of Nash. In fact, all the tables were empty, which was weird, considering we were ten minutes into lunch.

"Okay, this has been real fun," Sabine said, as I stopped next to the first empty table. She jerked her arm from my grasp and faced me, her goading grin gone, true anger flashing in her eyes. "But if it isn't gonna get Nash to talk to me, I'm done with this."

She started to stomp off toward the cafeteria, but I grabbed her wrist. "Get back here." Nash would have been *so* much better at talking some sense into her, but since he wasn't there, it was up to me.

Sabine jerked her arm away again. "The novelty of your badass act is wearing off quickly."

And suddenly I realized that the lack of a crowd was as much disadvantage as advantage—she probably wouldn't hesitate to punch me if there was no one around to see it. "How could you pull Emma into this? She has nothing to do with your sad little obsession with Nash."

Sabine rolled her eyes. "I didn't hurt her. I barely even got a taste of her fear. And as for my disclosure, you of all people should know how scary it is when you don't understand the world around you. I would have thought you'd want to spare your own best friend from such painful ignorance."

I couldn't fault her logic and I'd already decided to tell Emma everything. But even if Sabine's argument was sound, her intentions were not. She'd been using an innocent bystander to piss me off, and it worked. "Just leave Emma alone."

"I don't answer to you about anything, Kaylee. Including my dinner plans."

Fresh flames of rage licked at my skin; I felt like I was standing too close to a bonfire, and if I didn't back up, I was going to get roasted. And I was fine with that—so long as Sabine got singed, too.

"You can*not* just go around feeding from people! You've turned this school into a war zone, and people are getting hurt."

Sabine rolled her eyes and crossed her arms over her chest. "I told you I didn't kill those teachers. And I'm not responsible for how a bunch of human sheep deal with the loss of a couple of shepherds."

"They're people, not sheep!" Even if they did tend to follow the herd and stand around bleating uselessly at times... "And no matter what you call them, you don't have the right to turn them against one another and get people thrown in jail, or sent to the hospital!"

Sabine frowned. "Okay, you can't even *see* sanity from where you're standing. I had nothing to do with any of that."

"Right." I stepped closer, shoving my fear of a broken jaw—or worse—to the back of my mind. "I heard you talking to Sophie and Laura the other day, and today Laura's missing a chunk of hair from the back of her head."

"Sophie sheared her BFF?" Sabine looked genuinely surprised—like she didn't already know. "Wow. Good one..."

"Shut up. Laura's bad hair day is the least of what you've done. Jeff's car. Derek's broken arms. Coach Rundell's trashed office. Cammie's torched mold spores... This school is the only safe, normal thing in my life, and Eastlake does *not* deserve to go down like this!"

"I know. That's why I'm not doing it." Sabine shrugged. "I could if I wanted to, but I kinda like it here. The food sucks, but I'm passing with minimal effort and I have friends..." She gestured to me, and my mouth actually dropped open.

"I am not your friend."

She gave me an infuriatingly good-natured roll of her

dark eyes. "I think the definition of 'friendship' is open to a little interpretation from the fringe groups, Kaylee."

I crossed my arms. "It's really not."

"Whatever. My point is that none of that stuff is my fault."

I shook my head, thoroughly disgusted. "I *saw* you talking with half the people who've gone psycho!" And there was no telling how many private conversations I'd missed.

"Yeah. I was reading their fears. For later." The *mara* uncrossed her arms and shrugged. "A girl's gotta eat." She sat on the edge of the nearest table, leaning forward with her palms against the wood. "I've been in your head. I've been *all over* your boyfriend. And I was messing with your best friend in the gym. But I didn't hurt anybody. And I didn't do any of that crazy shit you're talking about."

"And I should believe you because you're just such a joy to be around?"

"Think about it, Kaylee. This isn't fear-based. From what I can tell, all these newly converted psychos are running on pure jealousy, and that's just not palatable for a *mara,* no matter how hungry I get."

Crap. I hadn't thought of that. But then, she couldn't directly benefit from making Em distrust me, either, and that hadn't stopped her.

"Fine. So you're doing it for fun."

Sabine's grin was back, and I wanted to slap it off her face. But I wasn't stupid enough to indulge that impulse. Again. "Well, there's definitely a slapstick sort of low-brow entertainment value involved in watching your school fall apart at the seams. But a few laughs aren't worth the effort it would take to orchestrate something like this myself. And anyway, my nightmares aren't just food—they're art. I take pride in that. But this isn't art, Kaylee." She spread her arms to take in the school around us. "This is nothing but...chaos. And as much as I enjoy upsetting the balance of your sad little existence, believe it or not, I don't thrive on chaos."

*Chaos...*

She was right. *Maras* don't thrive on chaos—but hellions do.

Yet the violent frenzy all around us didn't feel like Avari's work—jealousy wasn't his medium—and the only suspect that left was Sabine, no matter how artfully she wielded logic against me.

"So, what, you expect your pristine record to speak for itself? You've been arrested at least twice, expelled from two different schools, and were handed off from one foster family to the next for years. I think that says pretty clearly what you're capable of."

Sabine's eyes narrowed and darkened. She stood and stepped closer, putting her face inches from mine, and for the first time, I notice that she was at least a couple of inches taller than I was. And now thoroughly pissed. "You Googled me?"

I shrugged. "I thought I should know what I was dealing with."

"Then you should have asked me," she growled through clenched teeth. "I got expelled the first time for punching a teacher who called me stupid in front of the whole class. He had it coming, and everyone knew it. Which is why he got fired and never pressed charges.

I got expelled the second time for breaking into some stuck-up bitch's locker to take back the cell phone she stole from my jacket pocket and used to send dirty emails to the entire school from my account."

"You really expect me to believe that?" Her story actually made sense, and I might really have believed it—if she hadn't spent every moment since we'd met trying to make my life miserable. Logic said that I probably wasn't her first victim.

"I don't care what you believe. But just in case you still have a brain cell functioning behind that inch-thick skull, listen up. I've never lied to you, Kaylee. Not once. I may not always say what you want to hear, but it's always the truth."

With her last word, the first wave of fear slammed into me, so cold and strong I had to fight to suck in a breath. She'd opened her mental gates, and now the full force of the terror *maras* emanated naturally was washing over me in wave after bitter wave.

"It's *your* version of the truth," I insisted, taking an involuntary step back when the black weight of my own fear threatened to drive me to my knees. "And that's about as reliable as a politician's promise."

"Well, how 'bout a few truths you can trust?" She stepped forward again, and again I stepped back, watching shadows twist in her eyes, the silent reflection of every fear I'd ever felt. "Nash belongs with me, whether he knows it or not. You were nothing but a fleeting curiosity, and he's already started getting over you."

"Pathetic…" I spat, gasping for breath as the dark oblivion in her eyes swelled, threatening to swallow me whole. "You're in denial, and it's pathetic. And so are you. What, can't you handle one little *bean sidhe* without channeling Freddy Krueger?"

Sabine's brows arched high over black irises swimming around bottomless pupils. "You think I can't rein it in?" Without waiting for me to answer, she closed her eyes, and a second later the dark cloud of fear lifted. I could breathe again, and even the sun looked a little brighter.

"Better?" she snapped, malice sharp in her voice and in her gaze. She'd pulled it in, but that only meant that the concentration of anger inside her had doubled. Sabine was an angry dog on a leash—if I kept goading her, she'd pull free, and next time she might not be able to control it. "I can play nice if that's all you can handle, but that won't change the facts." She took another step, and this time when I backed up, my spine hit the corner of another picnic table. "If I'm in denial, why are *you* the one he gave up, memory by memory?"

"He had no other choice…" I made myself stand straighter and maintain eye contact.

"There are always choices. The truth is that you're what he was willing to give up."

"No." I shook my head. I couldn't believe that. I just… couldn't.

"Oh, yeah? Then why is it he can't remember what it felt like to kiss you for the first time, but he can relive every single time he touched me, whenever he wants? I'm still up there." She touched her temple, eyes narrowed in fury, hand steady with conviction. "And I'm still in here." She laid that hand over her own heart, and I felt mine crack a little. "And I've been other places you were too scared to go when you had the chance. And now it's too late."

I couldn't breathe, and this time that had nothing to do with any fear leaking from her abusive, rotting soul. I couldn't breathe because she was right. He'd given me up, but he'd kept her. All of her.

Why would he do that?

Sabine's brows arched again, and she leaned down to peer into my eyes. "You get it now, don't you? He can still feel that initial thrill from the very first time we touched."

She ran her hand slowly down from my shoulder, and my chest felt like it was caving in. I jerked back, but she only laughed. "It was innocent, at first. Fresh and new. Exciting, like if my heart beat any faster, it'd explode. And he still feels that, every time he thinks about it."

I shook my head and backed around the corner of the table.

"What does he feel when he thinks about you, Kay? You should ask him. Or I could just tell you. He feels nothing. You're a big numb spot on his heart, and all he feels now when you're around is guilt and pain. You're killing him, and for what? So you can cling to something he didn't care enough about to preserve? You should let him go so he can find peace."

And with that, my anger flared to life again, incinerating doubt and self-pity. "I don't know how to be any clearer about this. *Nash doesn't want you.* Not like you want him. And getting me out of your way isn't going to change that, because I'm not the obstacle in your path, Sabine. You're standing in your own way."

That one great truth strengthened me, and I stood taller, itching to show her what she refused to see. "You're obsessed with him. And not even with the real Nash. You're in love with the memory of someone you knew two and a half years ago, but you're both different people now, and here's the thing that's killing you: he's moved on. You want to believe that he never really got over you. That if you could just push me out of the way, he'd remember what the two of you had together. But you said it yourself, Sabine—he never forgot. He remembers exactly what it was like to touch you, and love you, and know you loved him back. And he still picked me."

Sabine flushed bright red. Shadows swam over her eyes, and my skin prickled with the cold concentration of terror accumulating inside her, like a balloon, about to explode. Her right hand curled into a fist, and I braced myself for the blow. But before she could swing, the lunch room door burst open and students flooded the quad, carrying trays and drinks, and talking about whatever cafeteria disaster had cut our lunch time in half.

I wasn't sure the sudden crowd would actually stop either her physical or psychological blows, but Sabine dropped her fist and glared at me like she could see right past my heart and into my soul. "You're right," she whispered, anger shining along with something deeper and more haunted in her eyes. "We're not friends." Then she spun around and stomped toward the building.

And the really weird thing was that as the rest of the lunch crowd spread out around me, I could only watch Sabine go, fighting a deep bruising ache in my chest, just like the one I felt every time I lied to my dad.

23

"Hey," Nash said, pulling even with me in the hall on the way to my fifth period French class. "We need to—"

"I don't want to talk about it."

He frowned and reached for me, but I pulled away. "Talk about what? Did something happen?"

I clutched my books and kept walking. "Doesn't something always happen?" After four months of hellion-induced pandemonium, I could hardly remember what my life had been like before I'd known about the Netherworld.

"Specifically…?"

I sighed and stopped to lean against the nearest locker. I was exhausted, physically and emotionally, and I was too worried about Alec's serial body snatcher and the unchecked series of school disasters to concentrate on class work. Or to dwell on Sabine, and whether or not

I'd falsely accused her of trying to bring the school to its knees.

"I had a fight with Sabine."

"Again?" Nash forced a grin, but I wasn't buying it. "It couldn't have been too bad—your face is intact. What happened?"

But if the past week had taught me anything, it was that if I accused her of something, he would automatically come to her defense—another point in favor of Tod's "they're meant for each other" conviction. So I tried a different tactic. "Don't you think this is weird? I mean, the school's in total chaos. Everyone's gone crazy." I hesitated, giving him time to infer my point. But he only frowned harder. "Something's wrong, Nash, and I don't think it's human in origin."

And the truth was that I had no idea how to even trace the source of the problem on my own. Of my two prime suspects, one was physically inaccessible by virtue of a hellish alternate reality, and the other was socially inaccessible, due to the fact that she now wanted to knock my head clean off my body.

"Agreed," he said at last, and I actually sighed with relief.

"Okay, I'm not saying Sabine's behind all of it, necessarily." Though that's what I'd believed an hour earlier. "But she's definitely involved somehow."

"Kaylee…"

"Just listen. I *saw* her talking to several of the kids who've gone off the deep end, and she's not exactly a social butterfly." Sabine was more like a social cockroach, skittering around in the dark, making trouble. "She has

Coach Peterson for geography." I'd verified that during English, with one of her classmates. "Also, I swear I saw her in Mrs. Cook's class the other day, on my way to the bathroom."

Mrs. Cook was the teacher who'd lost it in the teachers' lounge.

"Kaylee, there could be a hundred people who have both Cook and Coach Peterson. That doesn't prove anything."

"No, but this didn't start until she came to Eastlake," I insisted.

Nash put a hand on my arm and stared straight down into my eyes. "Your turn to listen. This has nothing to do with Sabine." He glanced around the hall, then pulled me into the alcove near the restroom entrances. "This is a blitz. It has to be. I've never personally seen one, but my mom says they're not that uncommon. The news usually reports them as mass suicides—like that Jonestown thing back in the seventies?—or mass hysteria, or mob mentality. There've been witch hunts and lynchings and riots. And if this one goes unchecked, eventually Eastlake will devour itself whole and the building will crumble into a pile of smoldering bricks. Or something less dramatic, but equally bad."

"Wait." I blinked, struggling to absorb so much information so fast. "You told your mom about this?"

"No, I didn't figure it out until lunch. She told me all about blitzes when we studied herd behavior in psychology."

"So...what exactly is a blitz?"

"It's a full-scale assault on a specific population by

some force in the Netherworld. In this case, that specific population is our school, obviously. But it has to be driven by a *big* force, because... Well, you know how hellions and some of the minor Netherworld creatures feed on the bleed-through of human energy?"

"Yeah." Unfortunately, I was intimately familiar with that process.

"Well, to support a blitz, this Netherworld force has to be able to do the opposite. He has to push enough energy into our world to affect human behavior. Or at least our state of mind."

Which sounded exactly like what was happening here.

"So...who could have that kind of power? A hellion?" Avari was the obvious suspect.

"Not on his own. But with help, yeah. I think it's possible." Nash sighed and glanced at his feet before looking up to meet my gaze. "Avari's the dominant hellion in our area—well, the Netherworld version of our area—and his entire existence is powered by greed. There's no way he'd let something like this go down without at least getting in on the profit. Which means he's involved, but not acting alone."

"What kind of profit are we talking about?" I asked, as pieces of the puzzle floated around in my head, looking for some place to fit.

"Energy, probably. There'd be lots of it to go around, with this large an operation. And with energy comes power."

"Would this blitz be enough to...boost his abilities?" I asked, thinking of his recent cameo in my nightmare.

"Yeah, I guess. Why?" When I didn't answer, Nash

stepped closer, glancing around to make sure no one was near. The bell would ring any second, but another tardy seemed pretty petty compared to an entire school under attack by at least one hellion.

"I think Avari's had an upgrade. He was in my nightmare. And I don't mean that I had a dream about him. He was *there*. Controlling it. Hurting me. And I think he was feeding from my fear."

"Kaylee, that's impossible. Hellions can't mess with your dreams, and that's not how they feed."

I shrugged. "The only other person who can do that is Sabine. But this nightmare didn't feel like her and she hasn't claimed credit, which seems to be a point of pride with her. So who else could it be?"

Nash scowled as he thought, and I saw the exact moment understanding washed over him. "Shit. It was Sabine. Well, it was Avari *using* Sabine. If he can possess a hypnos, he can possess a *mara,* and he'd have access to anything she can do while he occupies her body. The tricky part would be catching her while she sleeps."

"Uh-oh." Avari was getting too strong, too fast, and we had no clue how to stop him. "Why didn't she say anything?"

"I don't think she knows. If she did, she'd tell me," Nash insisted. "She'd be beyond pissed, and out for blood."

I couldn't blame her there. Avari was using Sabine, just like he'd used me. As badly as I hated to absolve her of any guilt, she was a victim in this—a selfish, deluded, boyfriend-stealing victim, but a victim nonetheless.

"What I can't figure out is how he even knew she was there to use…" Nash wondered aloud.

*Crap.* "Um...that part's my fault." I shrugged miserably at the realization that I'd accidentally dragged the *mara* into this, then blamed the whole thing on her. "He masqueraded as Alec a couple of times before we figured it out, and one of those times, he heard me and Emma... complaining about Sabine."

Nash's eyebrows rose, like he might ask for details, then he apparently thought better of it. "Okay, I guess that's understandable."

"So, if he can possess her and feed through nightmares, or possess Alec and feed through any kind of sleep... would that give him enough energy to power this blitz?"

"I doubt it. He'd probably recoup the energy possession requires by feeding while he's in the host body, but that's not going to be enough for something this big." Nash's widespread arms took in the whole school.

"So, how is he running this thing?"

"Well, once he got it started, it would be self-sustaining. The chaos he causes would bleed through even stronger than regular human energy, and he could easily feed from it. But as for how he got it going in the first place..." Nash could only shrug. "I don't know. But we have to make it stop."

I KNEW FIFTH PERIOD was going to suck the moment Mrs. Brown turned off the lights. Because of the chaos—which everyone had noticed, but no one could explain—she'd decided to ditch her lesson plan in favor of something requiring a little less concentration from her half-traumatized students. The class let loose a universal groan when she pulled out an old documentary on the history of French architecture.

It was all I could do to keep my eyes open when the monotonous narration began.

*THE NARRATOR DRONES ON about art nouveau, complete with pictures and clips of buildings I've never even heard of. I don't care about art nouveau. I don't care about art old-school, either. I care about staying awake and surviving another school day, so I can find and eliminate the source of the pandemonium.*

*And suddenly, my exhausted mind finds that word hilarious. Pandemonium roughly translates to "all demons," and that seems weirdly fitting, considering Avari's relentless intrusion into my life, and into my body, and now into my school.*

*All demons, all the time. That's what my headstone will read, if Avari ever gets his way.*

*Mrs. Brown stands at the front of the room, and for a second, I'm convinced she's read my mind. Or noticed that I'm not paying attention. But instead of yelling at me in French, she stares at the back of the room, her eyes oddly unfocused.*

*And that's when the scream explodes from my mouth. It's too hard and too fast to stop this time, and I am strangling on the vicious sound. Choking on it, as it scrapes my throat raw.*

*I taste blood on the back of my tongue and everyone stares at me. I can't hear the film anymore. Can't hear whatever they're shouting as some gather around me and others back away. I can only hear my own screech.*

*No one notices Mrs. Brown. No one else is watching when she collapses, and finally I understand. She's dead, and her soul cries out to me, clinging to the life she no longer has, begging to be held in place.*

*I want to help her, but I can't. Not without damning someone else. So I try to close my mouth, but the scream is too strong, and my jaw too weak. I claw at my throat in desperation. My fingers come away bloody, and there is a new layer of pain. But still I scream, and now I can see Mrs. Brown's soul, hovering over her body, a slowly swirling grayish form—just a representation of her actual soul, Harmony explained to me once. You can't see a real soul, and you probably wouldn't want to, she'd insisted.*

*But then the fog rolls in, and the real terror begins. Gray mist rises all around me. My heart trips over some beats, skipping others entirely. The fog obscures dingy floor tiles and scratched desk legs. I slap one hand over my mouth, but the sound leaks out, anyway. Thirty sets of shoes disappear into the gray. I try to back away from it, but there's nowhere to go. It's everywhere.*

*NO! I won't cross over. I won't!*

*But the scream has a mind of its own. The scream wants me to go and the fog is too thick to fight, so I close my eyes and pretend it's not real. And only once my voice fades to an ineffective croak do I open my eyes again.*

*This time when I scream, nothing comes out.*

I KEPT MY EYES squeezed shut, afraid to look. The desktop was cold beneath my folded arms, and I could feel the crack in the seat of my chair that pinched my leg when I wore shorts. Both of those facts should have meant everything was fine. That I was still in my darkened classroom, with twenty-nine other students feigning interest in the history of French architecture.

But silence doesn't lie.

There was no tapping of Courtney Webber's feet as she listened to her iPod instead of watching the film. No scratching of Gary Yates's pencil against paper as he scrambled to finish his history essay before last period. And certainly no criminally dull narrator droning on about angles and perspective and rebellion against classical architecture.

My heart thudded against my sternum. I sat up, gripping the sides of my desk with my eyes still squeezed shut. I didn't want to look. But not looking would be stupid. Not looking could get me killed. So I opened my eyes and took in the differences—the things that hadn't bled through the barrier into this warped, twisted version of my own world.

An empty classroom. The thirty-two empty desks, devoid of scratches and names scribbled in permanent marker, gave the room an abandoned feel—the high school version of a ghost town. A barren metal teacher's desk sat up front, by the door. There was no whiteboard. No posters of le Louvre, la tour Eiffel, or le Centre Pompidou. There was no ancient television on a cart, playing an outdated, staticky video cassette.

*The Netherworld.* If I'd had any doubt, it disappeared with my first glance at the educational void surrounding me. I'd crossed over. In my sleep.

*No!* It takes intent to cross into the Netherworld, and I

had no intent. I had the *opposite* of intent. Yet there I was, of someone else's volition.

*Sabine.*

She was mad at me. She was *pissed,* and I couldn't blame her. And she alone had the ability to mess with my dreams. Well, she and Avari, but this felt like Sabine. It was cruel on a personal level—making me dream that my wail wanted me to cross over—and she knew my fears. She knew there was little in either world that scared me more than winding up in the Netherworld.

*Focus, Kaylee.* I had to get back to my own world, but I couldn't just cross over again in the middle of class. It was entirely possible that no one had seen me disappear from French, thanks to the darkened classroom and bored or sleeping students. Assuming I hadn't actually screamed my head off, in life as in my dream. But the chances of thirty people also missing my reentry were slim to none, and I wasn't exactly swimming in good luck.

I'd have to find someplace unpopulated in both worlds before I could cross over. And I'd have to find that place without being eaten, captured, or ritualistically dismembered by any of the Netherworld natives.

*No problem.* The last time I'd been in the Netherworld version of my high school—less than a month before—it had been completely unpopulated. Surely I could just jog down the hall and around the corner, into the nearest supply closet, then scream my way back into my own world, completely unnoticed by the Nether-freaks.

Taking deep, slow breaths to control my racing pulse, I stood and walked silently to the classroom door, only feet from Mrs. Brown's unoccupied desk. Fingers crossed against surprises, I twisted the knob, pulled open the door—wincing at the creak—then stepped into the doorway.

And froze in terror.

The walls were red. And they were moving.

It took one long, terrifying moment for me to understand what I was seeing, but understanding only made it worse. The walls themselves weren't red. I couldn't tell what color they were because they were covered—completely *obscured*—with thick red vines, pulsing, coiling, constantly twisting in one huge tangle.

My hands clenched around the door frame and three of my fingernails snapped off at the quick. Panic tightened my chest, constricting my lungs. I couldn't breathe. I couldn't move. I could only stare in horror so profound it swallowed the rest of me whole.

Some sections of the vine were as thin as a pencil, others as thick as my bicep. The larger sections were striated with every possible shade from dried-blood red to a softer, watercolor cherry, like thinned paint. The ends of the vines, very fine and limber, sported needle-thin thorns and sharply variegated leaves, greenish in the center, bleeding to maroon on the edges.

I gasped, then clasped one hand over my mouth. I knew those leaves.

Crimson Creeper.

The entire hallway was *crawling* with it. A few months before, I'd been pricked by several thorns from an infant vine growing through cracked concrete, and that had been enough to nearly kill me. What clung to walls and lockers now was probably enough to take out half of Dallas.

As I stood frozen, staring, trying to overcome fear too thick to breathe through, something brushed my right index finger. I jerked my hand away from the door frame and turned to see a thin cord of vine slowly slithering down the metal jamb, leaves the size of half-dollars reaching for me like petals toward the sun.

I swallowed a startled shout and stumbled away from the door—and into the hall. Too late, I realized my mistake, but when I turned back toward the classroom, I found that one curious vine stretching across the opening at waist height, blocking my entrance. Deliberately.

Sparing one moment for a string of silent curses—most aimed at Sabine—I stepped carefully into the center of the hallway. There was no turning back now.

I walked slowly, eyes peeled for reaching vines, while soft, dry slithering sounds accompanied my whispered footsteps. A thicker vine slid toward my right foot. Skin crawling, I backed out of the way—only to step on a small tangle of leaves and thorns.

Several steps later, I noticed a break in the ever-shifting plant life—an open classroom door. A metallic scraping sound screeched from the opening, and I jumped, my heart pounding fiercely. I swallowed the new lump of panic and went still, willing myself to go unseen, hoping that whatever was in that room hadn't heard me. Eyes closed, I sucked in a deep breath through my nose—and nearly gagged on it.

And that's when I realized something warm and wet was soaking into the back of my shirt.

Barely suppressing a squeal of disgust, I darted forward and glanced up to find something foul and goopy and vaguely orange in color, dripping from the ceiling. From a large, tightly wrapped coil of vines, almost directly overhead. The creeper had caught something, and it was being slowly digested by tiny pores in the plant—but for the bit of Nether-slime that had leaked down my shirt.

Revulsion shuddered through me and it took every bit of self-control I had not to pull my shirt over my head and drop it where I stood, as fears of Netherworld poison and weird biological contamination threw my logic circuits into overload.

Another harsh, heavy scraping sound echoed from the classroom ahead, and I edged forward a little more. Then stopped again when a deep, rough voice slid over me, like sandpaper against bare skin.

The words sounded familiar, but the speech pattern was so foreign I couldn't decipher any meaning from sounds and syllables I felt like I should know. When no one came thundering into the hall to grab me, I silently released the breath I'd been holding and crept forward again until I stood inches from the open door.

A second voice spoke, higher in pitch, but his meaning was no easier to grasp. I could hear them moving around inside the room—a second-floor math class, in the human world—and my muscles were so tense I was starting to ache all over.

If I ever made it back to the human world, I was going to *kill* Sabine.

After a pause in the bizarre conversation, the scraping sounds resumed, and I gathered my battered courage around me like the remains of badly beaten armor. Then, using the scrapes to disguise the sound of my movement, I lurched across the open doorway and deeper into the vine-tangled hall, my heart racing erratically.

As I passed, I got a fleeting look at the backs of two tall, hairless creatures with skin so wrinkled and voluminous they looked like overgrown shar-peis. They had smooth, shiny skulls—the only unwrinkled parts of their bodies—and long, black claws tipping too many fingers to count. But even weirder than the creatures themselves was the huge stack of school desks they were both studying, puzzled, like chess players searching for their next moves.

From there, I walked on softly, concentrating on silence and speed, trying to ignore the cooling patch of fetid wetness on my back as I dodged grasping creeper vines. The next few doors I passed were closed, the classrooms quiet and presumably empty.

I was about fifteen feet from the T-shaped hallway junction when a mad scrabbling sound sent chills skittering up my spine. It sounded like a hundred cat claws scrambling for purchase on a slick floor, the whole thing accompanied by a high-pitched, foreign-sounding voice.

My arms prickled with chills, I tiptoed toward the door, which stood open about four inches. The closer I got, the louder the sounds became, and when I was less than a foot away, a chorus of younger, sharper voices joined the first in a frenzy of eager inhuman cries.

Sweat broke out over my forehead. I took a deep, silent breath and peeked around the vine-choked doorjamb and into the classroom. My throat tightened around a gasp as waves of terror and revulsion washed over me, freezing me in place for several eternal moments.

At first, I couldn't understand what I saw. There were too many limbs, gray like death, but short and dimpled like toddlers. Too many round, smooth heads, covered in soft, translucent peach-fuzz hair. Too many tiny violet eyes. Too many gaping mouths full of needle-teeth, snapping and whining eagerly.

And in the midst of what could only be a nest of pint-size Netherworld monster children stood a single adult, darker and smoother in color, but no less terrifying. As I watched, my pulse rushing in my ears, she held up an ordinary cardboard box, extended over the crowd around her. The children stilled, staring at the box in reverent silence.

The adult paused, and her smile chilled the blood in my veins. Then she overturned the box, and half a dozen round, fleshy things fell from it.

The children pounced. The air crackled with their hisses and snarls, and with the scratching of their clawed feet on tile. They fought for the bloodied treats, snatching quick, gory bites before another set of clawed hands ripped the prize away. Crimson sprays arced through the air. Teeth gleamed red beneath black gums.

It was a preschool free-for-all—a child-size slaughter—and the one adult watched, a proud, gruesome smile warping the bottom half of her round face.

Shuddering, I stepped past the door and only released the breath I'd been holding when nothing burst from the room to devour me.

Breathing hard now, I took a second to get myself back

together, then I started walking again. The storage closet was right around the corner from the bathroom. Surely I could make it that far.

But I'd only taken a couple of steps when a commanding, glacier-cold voice sent chills the length of my body. I froze.

*Avari.* He was right around the corner.

*Damndamndamn!* What were they all doing here? The school had been empty just weeks before! Sabine's life expectancy had just shrunk to a matter of minutes from the time I got back to the human world. Assuming that actually happened.

Riding a fresh wave of fear, I raced down the hall—*toward* the sound of his voice—and ducked into a bathroom niche, thick with shadows. The walls were blessedly free of vines, but covered with a thick, smelly, slowly oozing fluid.

I pressed as close to the wall as I could get without actually touching it, and stared out at the empty hall from the shadows hopefully hiding me.

"...very close now..." Avari said from around the corner, as I sucked in a silent breath tasting of fear and smelling of my own sweat. "When you have yours, and I have mine, this affiliation is over. You will slink back to your own corner of oblivion, and we shall see each other no more. Agreed?"

"Agreed," said a second voice, smooth and seductive, like the first sweet taste of a chocolate-dipped pepper, before the fire inside it roasts you alive. "I shall have the lovely Nightmare child, and you shall have your little *bean sidhe,* and we shall feast on their souls for all of eternity...."

## 24

As they rounded the corner, I breathed shallowly through my mouth to keep from smelling whatever oozed down the wall behind me. Wishing with every single cell in my body that I was anywhere in the world but where I stood in that moment.

Avari stepped into sight, and I willed my heart to stop beating for a few seconds, afraid that even that small noise—plus the stench of my terror—would give me away. But he never even glanced at the restroom alcove. Evidently the flood of human emotion from the blitz in progress disguised my individual fear. And he was obviously too irritated at the creature who walked on his other side to bother checking the shadows for humans accidentally stranded in the Nether.

Lucky me.

The woman with him was shorter than Avari, and very thin, her hands a tangle of swollen joints and skeletal fingers beneath the tattered sleeves of a black velvet dress. Her cheeks were sharply pronounced, the hollows beneath them dark and deep. Her black orb eyes reflected a faint green glow in the little available light, and since she had no obvious pupils or irises, I couldn't tell whether or not she was even looking in my direction.

But her most prominent feature by far was her hair— an ever-dripping flow of noxious liquid, streaming over her head and down her back in distinct currents and waves. The flow was thick and black, except where the light overhead gave it a dark green tint. As I watched, she brushed a streaming strand back from her hawkish face and several drops splattered on the floor at her back, sizzling in green-tinted fizz on the grimy tiles.

I'd never seen anything like her river of hair, and I had no doubt that if it splashed me, the drops would eat the flesh right off my bones.

I shivered in my shadows, fighting to keep my teeth from chattering, but the two hellions just walked on slowly, talking, and I strained to hear every word.

"My beautiful Nightmare is ripe for the plucking—so full of luscious envy," the woman said, her words sliding over me like the seductive warmth of a fireplace. Suddenly I wanted her voice for myself, to replace the screeching abomination my own throat spewed into the world. Why should a monster like that get such a beautiful voice, when I got a shriek that could drive grown men home to their mommies? "And I would pluck her *now*," she continued, oblivious to how badly I wanted to rip her voice box from her emaciated throat and stomp it into the ground, to deny her what I couldn't have for myself.

The thought that I might be capable of such a violent act should have shocked and scared me, but it didn't. It felt...justified. Why should someone else—*anyone* else— have something I couldn't have?

"Your impatience is tiresome, Invidia," Avari said, drawing my thoughts from the wrong I ached to right. "I've readied both hosts, but pushing them into slumber in the same moment is rather an exact science, and one rash act could bring this whole tower tumbling down on top of us."

"Nonsense." Invidia tossed her hair again as she passed out of my sight, and several vines shrank away from the drops sizzling on the tiles. "You exhausted them for just this purpose, and this flow of youthful energy will not last forever. We should strike now, while the iron is hot, lest our hosts have time to cool their heels."

"Soon, Invidia. I give my word, it will be soon...."

I didn't release my breath until I was sure they'd turned the next corner and passed out of both sight and hearing range. Their conversation played over in my head as I tried to make sense of antiquated phrasing, using what little I knew of the Netherworld and the continuing catastrophe my school had become.

The "flow of youthful energy" seemed the most obvious: the increased bleed-through of human life force the blitz provided. But as for the rest...I needed a second, more enlightened opinion. All I knew for sure was that Avari and this Invidia—clearly a fellow hellion—were planning to somehow claim me and Sabine, body and soul, with the help of a couple of preselected "hosts." And we didn't have much time to defend against whatever they were about to throw at us.

Considering the seemingly steady flow of traffic in the Netherworld version of my school hall, I decided to risk crossing over in the bathroom instead of pressing on to the storage closet, which may or may not be locked from the outside in the human world.

I eased the door open slowly, and when I saw no sign of any Netherworldly occupants, I slipped inside and let the door close behind me. The row of sinks looked just like the sinks in my world, except that the one in the middle was steadily dripping a viscous-looking yellow fluid in place of water.

Swallowing my disgust, I knelt to peek beneath the doors of the two closed stalls, glad most of them stood open. On the human side of the crossing, the second to last stall was out of order. The toilet had been broken since we got back from the winter break, and a sign hung on the outside of the locked door.

That stall held my best chance of crossing over without being seen.

The door on this side of the barrier was open, so I went in and closed it, then stepped up onto the slimy-looking toilet seat to keep a set of feet from suddenly appearing in the human world version of the stall when I crossed over. I braced my hands on either side of the stall, careful not to slip. I did *not* want to land in the goopy yellow liquid putrefying in the bowl beneath me.

Then I took a deep breath and closed my eyes, concentrating on the memory of death to summon my *bean sidhe* wail and my intent to cross back over.

I thought about Doug dropping the clip from Nash's bright red balloon, the night of his own party. He'd inhaled as I raced toward him, but I was too late; that one hit was all it took. Doug's eyes had rolled back into his head and he'd collapsed to the ground. The balloon had fallen with him, and I'd nearly choked on the scream trying to rip free from my body.

And with that memory, the wail came again, as real and as painful as it had been the first time. My throat burned like I'd swallowed fire. The scream bounced around in my skull and in my heart, demanding to be set free. Pain echoed everywhere the trapped wail slammed into me, but I clenched my jaw shut, letting only the thinnest thread of sound out, desperately hoping it would be enough.

I closed my eyes and clung to the sides of the stall when the fog began to roll in, roiling around the base of the filthy toilet and over my ankles, though I couldn't feel it. I ignored the intense need to open my mouth, to scream for that remembered soul—one I hadn't been able to help, in real life.

And now, in memory, Doug and his soul would help me. They would send me back so I could save myself and Sabine from eternal torture, and the rest of the school from the energy blitz that would soon be its ruin.

When I heard water running—the first sound not produced by my tortured throat—I glanced down to find the toilet beneath me clean and white, the water in its bowl clear and odorless. Only then did I let that thread of sound recede within me, like winding up an unrolled ball of twine. A very thorny, scalding ball of twine.

"What was that?" a girl's voice asked from outside the stall, and I nearly groaned out loud. The broken stall was empty, which I'd been counting on, but the bathroom itself was not. Either someone was skipping class, or I'd crossed over between bells.

"What was what?" another voice asked.

I considered hiding out until they left, but I had to find Sabine and Nash before they made it to sixth period, or I might not get another chance until it was too late.

Bracing myself for embarrassment, I hopped down from the toilet and unlocked the stall. When I stepped out, all four girls in front of the mirror turned to stare at me.

"Can't you read the sign?"

"Gross. That one's *out of order.*"

"That's Sophie Cavanaugh's sister."

"Cousin," I corrected on my way into the hall, and before the door closed behind me, the fourth girl made a disgusted sound in the back of her throat. "Ew! She didn't even wash her hands!"

"Or flush!"

I speed-walked through the hall, sidestepping students and teachers alike, scanning dozens of familiar faces for the two I needed. I couldn't stop Avari and Invidia on my own. I needed Nash and Sabine.

But what I found was Tod. Where I least expected him.

After glancing into Sabine's sixth period classroom with no luck, I ducked into the first-floor girls' restroom in search of her. I'd checked three of the four stalls and found them all empty when Tod suddenly appeared in front of the door to the fourth.

I shrieked a shrill profanity and jumped back so hard my elbow slammed into the third stall. "You can't be in here!"

Tod stuck his head through the last stall door, then backed up and shrugged. "It's all clear."

"Well, it might not be for long. What are you doing here?"

"Nash called me."

He had? Emma must have told him I'd disappeared from fifth period.

"Oh. Well, thanks, but I'm more than capable of sneaking around the Netherworld on my own for a few minutes." Even if I almost got devoured by man-eating plants and carnivorous kindergarteners… "So you can go polish your shining armor for someone else to admire."

I *might* have been a little irritated at him for telling me to give up Nash.

Tod frowned and brushed a curl from his forehead. "You went to the Netherworld? Why the hell would you do that?"

"I didn't do it on purpose!" I propped my hands on my hips, impatient to continue my search, but I wasn't going to be seen talking to an invisible friend in the hall. Not so soon after the recent bathroom weirdness. "Sabine took her anger issues out on me when I fell asleep in French."

"Hell hath no fury like a *mara* falsely accused."

"Nash told you? What'd he do, call you at work?"

Todd shook his head and pulled a small, slim phone from his back pocket. "Mom put me on her cell plan, now that I can pay for the additional line. Got it a couple of days ago."

"And you didn't give me the number?" I swallowed a bitter, unexpected wash of disappointment.

The reaper grinned and leaned with one hip on the nearest sink. "I was waiting for you to ask."

A flash of irritation burned in my cheeks. "That might have actually happened, if I'd known you had a phone."

His brows arched in surprise. "I figured Nash would tell you."

"Well, he didn't," I snapped.

Tod slid the phone back into his pocket. "So...you're still mad about the other day?"

"Wouldn't you be mad if I told you to give up on someone you care about? Just...hand her over to someone who doesn't even deserve her?"

Tod gave me a strange, sad look I couldn't interpret, and the blues in his irises shifted subtly for a moment before he got control of them. "Yeah. I guess I would."

And obviously that was as much of an apology as I was going to get.

"Anyway, if you didn't come to rescue me from the Netherworld, what are you doing here?"

Tod blinked, and I could almost see him refocusing on the crisis at hand. "Nash just called to tell me that Sabine sensed someone sleeping in the hall—you know *maras* can feel slumber, like we'd feel heat from a fire, right?"

I nodded, creeped out by the comparison. "So what?"

"So there was no one sleeping in the hall. Everyone was up and moving, on the way to class."

"So maybe her spidey senses are all messed up." I

shrugged. "Karmic payback for sending me to the Netherworld in my sleep."

"I doubt it's that simple. Or that satisfying," he said. So did I. "The only way I know of for a sleeping person to function like he's awake is if he's…"

"Possessed," I finished for him, as the implication began to sink in and dread settled through me like lead, pinning me in place. Avari had taken control of his "host." Or maybe Invidia had taken control of hers. "Did Sabine mention the lucky victim's name?"

Tod shrugged. "She said the hall was too crowded and no one was snoring."

"Great. She's always *so* much help." I closed my eyes, trying to gather my thoughts, then looked up at him. But before I could tell him what I'd overheard in the Netherworld, the sixth period bell rang, and I nearly jumped out of my shoes.

"You gonna be in trouble?" Tod asked, glancing at the ceiling like he could actually see the bell.

I reached for the door and gripped the handle. "Nowhere near as much trouble as we'll all be in if Avari gets his way. He's playing with a friend this time, and they're up to something big."

"You mean the blitz?"

"The blitz is just a means to an end. He and his partner are trying to drag me and Sabine into the Netherworld, and they've each picked out a body here in the human world to give them hands-on involvement in the process. We have to find out who they've possessed before they can make their move."

There weren't many possibilities to choose from. A

person had to have some connection to the Netherworld to even qualify for hellion possession, and I couldn't think of a single eligible party, other than me, Nash, and Emma.

And Sophie…

*Shit!*

Tod's blue eyes went hard and angry on my behalf—and probably on Sabine's. "What can I do?" He followed me into the hall, where I lowered my voice to avoid notice by the stragglers still making their way to class.

"Find Sophie and make her talk. If she doesn't sound like herself, knock her out. Then meet me in the quad."

Tod's lips turned up in a grim smile. "You know I never pass up an opportunity to smack your cousin."

25

Tod DISAPPEARED, and I headed straight for the gym, where Nash hung out during last period, now that football season was over.

I scanned the bleachers, glancing over several groups of students talking and watching the basketball team practice, but Nash found me before I spotted him. "Hey," he called, and I turned to see him walking toward me from the boys' locker room. "What happened?" he asked, falling into step with me when I gestured for him to follow me toward the gym doors, where we wouldn't be overheard. "Emma said you disappeared during French. Like, literally disappeared."

"Unscheduled trip to the Netherworld, courtesy of everyone's least favorite *mara*."

"Damn it, Kaylee, I'm so sorry." He ran one hand through his hair in frustration. "Are you okay?"

I shrugged, trying not to show how pissed off I was,

or how scared I'd been. Like it was no big deal that his ex had nearly gotten me killed. A lot.

"A little sticky…" I plucked at the drying gunk stuck to the back of my shirt. "But still in one piece. And I *did* accuse her of trying to incite a school-wide riot. Though for the record, I think the interdimensional field trip constitutes gross overkill."

"I'll talk to her…" he said, shrugging his backpack higher on his shoulders, and suddenly it felt weird for me to be whispering to Nash in the middle of class, carrying nothing but the weight of my own guilt and fear. I'd left my stuff in French class, after my involuntary departure from the human world.

"Don't bother. We have bigger hellions to fry, before one of them drops me into the hot oil. Or Sabine."

"What?"

"I'll explain when we find Sabine," I said, leaning back against the side of the bleachers. "For now, please tell me you found the sleepwalker."

"Not even close."

"Great." I shoved a flyaway strand of hair back from my face. "Well, now we're looking for two puppets. One will sound like Avari, the other like this demon chick named Invidia. I heard them plotting when I crossed over. I'm guessing she's a hellion of envy."

Nash's brows arched halfway up his forehead. "Based on…?"

"Based on the fact that she's obsessed with Sabine, because of the amount of jealousy she's evidently festering with."

"Envy. Shit," Nash said, leaning against the wall by the

first set of doors, and I could practically read his thoughts on his face as he put the puzzle together for himself. "So…this Invidia helped power the blitz?"

"Yeah." I shrugged and glanced through the glass door into the hall, itching to get moving. But discussing Netherworld business in the empty school halls in the middle of last period would not only get us in trouble, it might just get us committed. The noisy gym was a much better place to go unnoticed. "My guess is that the power she shoved into our world to get the ball rolling came through as violent jealous impulses."

"Thus, all the fights and property damage."

"Exactly. And I'm pretty sure they *wanted* me to blame the whole thing on Sabine."

"Because you're jealous of her?" Nash said, nodding like he understood, and I bristled.

"I'm not jealous of her! I just don't think she belongs on your bed at two o'clock in the morning." Okay, maybe I was a *little* jealous of that part. "What I mean is that they framed her. I'm guessing Sabine's envy drew this new hellion into the area, and Avari saw his chance. He probably knew your ex was here before we did. He killed the teachers in their sleep to make me think she was doing it, and Invidia overloaded the kids I saw Sabine reading fears from, so I'd think she was doing that, too."

"Why?" Nash frowned. "Why do they care who you blame this on?"

"I haven't figured that part out yet. Maybe to divert attention from Alec?" I glanced at the huge clock over the far set of bleachers, and my heart thudded harder. A quarter of last period was gone. We were running out of time. "I need you to get Sabine and meet me and Tod in the quad. We need to figure out who the hellions are possessing, and evict them."

"No problem. We'll be right there."

Nash and I parted ways in the hall, where he headed right, toward Sabine's sixth period class, and I went to the left, headed toward the French class I'd missed half of, where Mrs. Brown handed me my books, along with a pink detention slip.

Funny how "teenage hero" translates to "teenage delinquent" on my permanent record.

Next I headed toward my history class, approaching from the right, so I could check on Emma without being seen by Coach Rundell, who rarely left his desk during class. Like several of the other teachers, Rundell was showing a video instead of actually teaching, but I could hardly blame him, considering that his office had been trashed that morning and the inexplicable chaos had only gotten worse.

Emma was in her usual seat with her arms crossed over her chest, staring blankly at a television I couldn't see. The entire classroom flickered with a familiar bluish light, and half the students had fallen asleep sitting up.

Satisfied that Emma was safe, I dropped my books off in my locker, then slipped outside through the parking lot exit and made my way around the building from the outside. The quad looked empty when I got there, but before I could take a seat at the nearest table, Tod appeared several feet away.

"It's not Sophie," he said, by way of a greeting. "She's

in the office, cryin' like a baby, trying to explain why she cut some chick's hair off."

"Good." At least that would keep her out of Avari's grip for the time being.

More footsteps crunched on the grass behind me, and I turned to find Nash headed across the quad toward us. Alone.

"Where's Sabine?" I asked, sliding onto the nearest bench seat.

Nash frowned, but sat down across from me. "Sabine's a no-show."

"From geography?"

"From school, as far as I can tell." He stared at his hands, clasped together on the table, his jaw clenched in frustration, eyes swirling in true fear. For her. "I looked everywhere I could think of, and she's just gone. Her books are in her locker—not that that's any indication of…anything—and her car's in the lot. And she definitely wouldn't leave campus without her car."

"You have her locker combination?" I asked, and they both just stared at me until I rolled my eyes. "It was a valid question!"

"You think she crossed over?" Tod asked, sitting on the end of the table next to ours, his legs hanging.

"I seriously doubt it," Nash said. "She *can* cross, of course, being a *mara*. But she'd be just as vulnerable there as we are. And no matter what else you think about her, she's not stupid."

"No argument there," I said reluctantly. If she were stupid, she'd be *so* much easier to deal with. "But if she didn't cross…" My words faded into uneasy silence as a horrifying possibility occurred to me. "Avari can possess her," I said, glancing from brother to brother.

"We've established this," Nash said. "He used her to give you that nightmare about him pulling you into the Netherworld."

Which was now starting to sound prophetic.

"That's my point." I stood, my thoughts racing too fast for me to process without freedom of movement. "When he possessed her, he had control of her abilities. So...does that mean he could possess her again and make her cross over?"

That thought was scary enough to make the fine hairs on my arms stand up. But even worse was the knowledge that if he could make Sabine cross over that way, he could make me do the same thing.

So why hadn't he? Why would he need human hosts, if he could just make us cross over on our own?

"I don't think that would work," Tod said, and my relief came almost before I'd heard his rationale. "You have to have intent to cross over, and even when he's in control of your body, he's not in control of your will-power. He can't make you want to cross over."

"Sabine did," I pointed out, frowning over the incon-sistency—yet grateful for it.

"Sabine made you dream that you wanted to cross, right?" Nash asked, and I nodded. "She's had a lot of prac-tice weaving nightmares. Avari hasn't. For the moment, I think you're safe from that. But we have to find a way to keep him from possessing us, or this is going to keep happening."

Tod shrugged. "Being dead seems to do the trick."

I glanced at him, arms crossed over my chest. "I think we're looking for something a little less drastic."

Nash cleared his throat, bringing us back on target. "Okay, we have to find Sabine. And whoever else they're planning to grab."

"Any idea who that could be?" Tod asked.

I shook my head. "All I know is that Avari claims to have prepared both the hosts. Which I'm guessing means that he wore them out somehow, so they'd be tired enough to fall asleep at school today."

"Well, then, the joke's on him," Nash said. "Everyone I know could fall asleep at school *every* day."

"That doesn't exactly narrow it down," I snapped, as the pressure to *do something* started to overwhelm me. "And the fact that it has to be someone with a connection to the Netherworld narrows it down too much. I can't think of anyone else who qualifies."

"I could tell you…" a nauseatingly familiar, glacier-cold voice said from my left, and I turned slowly to find Alec watching us from the entrance to the quad. "But that would ruin the surprise."

I stood so fast I nearly tripped over my own feet. "Let him go," I demanded, wishing my own voice held half the authority the hellion's did.

Avari sauntered toward us in Alec's tall, lanky body, moving much too smoothly for a human. Or even a half human. "I've been in here for almost twelve hours now— thanks to the energy produced by the cesspool of envy that is your school—and I've grown much too comfortable to give him up now."

"Twelve hours…?" But twelve hours ago, Alec was…

Dark rage washed over me, igniting tiny fires in my veins. "It was you the whole time, in Emma's room. With the ice cream."

Tod and Nash glanced at me nervously, eyes narrowed in identical questioning expressions, but I ignored them.

"You only pretended you'd let him go."

Avari shrugged. "You've made it difficult to gain access to this body lately, so why give it up once I had it?"

"But the password... How did you know about my bike?" I asked, and both Hudson brothers frowned in confusion.

"Ahh, Ms. Marshall is a veritable fount of information."

He'd tricked Emma into playing what she thought was a trivia game, then had manually hacked our password. Damn it! That never would have happened if I'd told her what was going on.

But... "I saw you." I stepped closer, and Nash and Tod moved up to stand at my sides. "An hour ago, in the Netherworld. Talking to Invidia. You didn't have Alec then."

Avari smiled with Alec's full lips, and the effect was too creepy to bear. "I had him in...what would you call it today? Limbo?"

"Paused? You had him *paused?*" Somehow, that sounded almost worse than being actively possessed. Where had Alec been, when neither he nor Avari were using his body? Some sort of mindless, metaphysical holding cell?

"Precisely. And that would never have been possible, if this generous educational institution hadn't provided me with the power to control both his body and my own simultaneously."

"Let him go." Nash stepped forward when my horror proved too much to fight through for the moment. But Avari had come to make a deal, and he wouldn't leave until he'd gotten what he wanted.

Or been physically evicted from his host.

"What do you want?" I demanded, trying to gather my thoughts and come up with a plan.

"I want you." The brown eyes that stared at me were Alec's but their expression was all hellion. "You come with me now, of your own free will, and I give you my word that I'll never possess any of your friends again."

"Stall him," Tod said, and that's when I realized Avari could neither see nor hear the reaper. And Tod had a plan. "Keep him talking. Blink if you understand," he said, and I blinked, careful not to look at him and give away his presence.

"I'll be right back," he said. I blinked again, and Tod disappeared.

"No way," I said to the hellion, hating every second that I was forced to address him in my friend's body. "You're gonna have to do better than that if you expect me to just hand myself over to you."

Alec's head cocked to the side, like he was studying a particularly interesting insect. "This isn't a negotiation, Ms. Cavanaugh. If you don't cooperate, you'll be to blame every time I feed through this body, or try on Ms. Marshall's form and find out exactly what she has to offer."

I swallowed, fighting through horror and revulsion just to be able to speak. "You're psychotic."

"We don't utilize that term in the Nether. The very concept is considered both obvious and redundant. Now, if you don't cross over this instant, I swear I will take the reins of your boyfriend's subconscious the next time he succumbs to slumber, and we'll see how well you like him when *I'm* in control."

"Don't listen to him, Kaylee," Nash insisted. "I'll never let that happen."

Avari laughed, and the cold, sterile joy sounded foreign and harsh coming from Alec's throat. "We all know you can't stop me."

"But *I* can."

I heard Tod before he appeared, and he appeared just a fraction of a second before he swung a big aluminum toaster in a two-handed grip—at the back of Alec's head.

Alec's eyes fluttered, then closed, and he collapsed to the ground, unconscious but still breathing, and at least temporarily free from the Netherworld body snatcher.

"One down," Tod said, grinning over the still form on the grass. "Let's go evict the other one."

26

Tod stared at me over Alec's unmoving form on the grass, still holding the toaster, the flat left side of which was now massively dented. "Kaylee? You okay?"

"Not even kind of." I shoved hair back from my face and glanced from Tod to Nash, then back. "But having known you both for several months now, I'm starting to see 'okay' as a relative term."

Nash gave me a grim, confident smile, and Tod actually chuckled without letting go of the toaster.

"Okay. I need you to check Sabine's house, and if you find her, call us," I said, and Tod nodded. I didn't think she'd left campus, since her car was still in the lot, but with Sabine, I'd learned to expect the unexpected. And the impulsive. And the vindictive. And the just plain crazy.

"If she's not at her house, try mine," Nash added, just before his brother blinked out of sight. "I've already checked everywhere she hangs out when she skips class," he said, as we headed toward the cafeteria entrance.

I shrugged. "So we'll check again. And if we don't find her here, we're gonna have to cross over."

Nash nodded reluctantly, obviously much more willing to put us both in danger to save Sabine than he'd been for Addison.

He pulled open the door and held it for me, and I stepped past him into the lunchroom—where I could only stare. The cafeteria was *trashed*.

"What happened?" My gaze wandered the food-smeared walls, then snagged on a huge plastic jug of nacho cheese that lay busted open on the floor, oozing smooth orange processed cheese product a couple of feet from my shoes.

"Giant food fight. I'm not sure who started it, but a couple dozen people trashed the place before Goody could get it under control. She suspended thirty-eight kids. The cafeteria staff got pissed when she told them to clean it up, so they walked out, and now all those suspended kids have to spend tomorrow scrubbing the walls. Which is why they sold pizza for lunch in the hall. You didn't see any of that?"

I shook my head, still stunned. "I was busy falsely accusing Sabine during lunch." Then I'd sat in my car to cool off until the bell rang for fourth period. Somehow I'd missed the entire spectacular disaster.

Normally, I would have assumed that food fights were a little juvenile for high school, but based on the number of dented pots and busted food containers, I'd say this one was really more of a riot than anything. "This isn't going to smell any better tomorrow..." I said, stepping over the busted cheese container, on my way to the main entrance. "Let's go."

But I'd only taken a few steps when Nash's hand landed on my arm. "Wait. Did you hear that?"

I'd only heard the sticky squeak of my shoes on the filthy floor, so I stopped and listened. And I heard it, too. A voice, soft and smooth, and feminine, in spite of the low pitch.

My chest seemed to constrict around my heart. I knew that voice, though I'd only heard it once. "Invidia," I whispered. "She's already here." And Sabine would be with her.

Suddenly I wished I hadn't divided our resources by sending Tod to look for her.

Nash held one finger to his lips and I nodded as I followed him toward the kitchen, carefully sidestepping most of the mess. We followed the empty serving lane past the glass-topped ice cream freezer and into the heart of the Eastlake cafeteria, a maze of commercial-size stoves, dishwashers, and deep stainless-steel sinks. And there at the back, between one of the sinks and a tall metal shelf filled with commercial-size cans, stood Sabine.

And Emma.

"Em?" I asked

She smiled at me slowly with a foreign tilt of her head, and that's when I understood. Emma had fallen asleep in history during the video, and Invidia had made her move. My best friend was the second host.

Emma's body stood half-behind Sabine, pressed against

the *mara*'s right side, her mouth inches from Sabine's ear. She watched me closely, a predatory gleam in her normally bright brown eyes, lips half-parted, like I'd interrupted her in midsentence.

"Is this the sweet little *bean sidhe?*" Invidia's voice asked, while Emma's hand stroked Sabine's bare arm. "See how she taunts you? How she flaunts the boy in front of you? She knows how you feel. She knows how *he* feels, and she doesn't need him, yet she clings to him, just to keep him from you."

"Sabine, that's not true…" I moved closer slowly, scanning my peripheral vision for anything I could use against Invidia without permanently injuring Emma.

"Hellions can't lie," Sabine said, and her gaze blazed with hatred. With envy so bitter I could practically taste it on the air between us. How could she suddenly hate me, when she'd called me a friend a few hours ago? Was this because of my false accusation—which I'd actually believed at the time? Or was some of it because of Invidia, and the storm of envy she'd unleashed in our school?

Surely the lure of it was even thicker, so close to the hellion who controlled it.

"Hellions can't *intentionally* lie," Nash corrected, stepping up on my right. "But they're free to guess and make assumptions, just like anyone else."

"Look how they work together to subvert you…" Emma's long blond hair fell over Sabine's shoulder, standing out against the dark strands as the hellion's voice slid over me, sweet and smooth as honey on my tongue. If *I* could hardly resist her pull, how was Sabine supposed to, considering how badly she actually wanted what I had?

"She's changed him. Lessened him," Invidia continued, and I could see that Sabine was listening. That the hellions words were hitting their target—not Sabine's ears, but her heart. "But with her gone, you could fix him. You could have him back, and it would be like it was before. Without the meddlesome little female *bean sidhe* to get in your way…"

"Sabine, don't do this," I begged, taking a single step toward them. "Make her leave Emma alone. Em has nothing to do with this."

"This Emma-body?" Invidia looked surprised, then she exhaled a languid, seductive laugh from my best friend's throat. "Emma Marshall has everything to do with this," the hellion insisted, leaning closer to whisper directly into Sabine's ear, though we could all hear her. "She is part of the problem. Part of the effortless existence simply handed to this little *bean sidhe,* while life has given you only battles to be fought."

"Bina, please…" Nash begged, and Sabine's conflicted gaze flicked his way. But that made things worse, because she couldn't see him without seeing me, and seeing us together only reinforced the poison the hellion dripped straight into her ear.

"He's part of it, too. Part of her gilded privilege." Emma's hand reached Sabine's fingers, then trailed slowly upward again, and the *mara*'s arm twitched. "The loving boyfriend, the loyal friends, the protective father. She has everything, and you have only hunger. Insatiable, unbearable hunger, clawing, devouring you from the inside, night and day."

I edged forward again, and Nash came with me.

"Sabine, you can have all that, too!" I insisted. Well, maybe not the father, but that wasn't my fault. "And you don't need to bargain with a hellion to make it happen!"

"She lies," Invidia purred, and Sabine shuddered when Emma's lips brushed her ear. "People are drawn to the sweet little *bean sidhe,* to bathe in her bright innocence. When you enter a room, they tremble and shrink back. You must work to hide the horrors they see in your eyes, and she has only to smile. You cannot have what she has—not *any* of it—on your own. But *I* can give it to you. I can give you love, and acceptance, and a smile brighter than the sun. I can give you people, and attention, and a steady stream of sleeping mortals, just waiting to scream in their slumber for you."

"She can't do it, Sabine," I insisted, stepping past a stainless-steel counter, now less than ten feet from them. "Even if she thinks she can, it won't really be what you want. She can't change your species, and she can't give you real friends. No matter what she promises."

"What does she know of your pain? Of your isolation?" Invidia hissed, and a deep chill traveled through me at the sibilance in her voice. "She knows nothing of your darkness, yet she would extinguish the one flame glowing on your horizon." Em's gaze flicked to Nash at my side, and Sabine's followed.

"You need only cross into the Nether..." The hellion slid Emma's arm around Sabine's waist in a possessive gesture. "Deliver me this young, ripe Emma-body and sign away your soul. Such a small price, for a lifetime of peace and pleasure."

"Sabine, no!" Nash cried, and when I glanced at him, I saw his irises *churning* with fear and rage. "If you cross over, you'll never make it back. She won't let you."

"Smart *bean sidhe* boy…" Invidia purred. "He still wants to protect you. If not for *her,* he would be yours. Cross over now, and I give you my word you will return, the moment you sign. You will live out your full lifeline here, with everything she has, but you truly deserve."

My thoughts raced so fast the room was starting to spin. Invidia might be able to give things to Sabine, but she couldn't take them from me. Could she?

I saw the decision in Sabine's eyes a moment before she disappeared. She loved Nash too much—and evidently envied me too much—to resist the offer. "No!" I lunged for Emma, desperate to pull her away from Sabine before the *mara* crossed over. But I was too late. My fingers barely brushed the fine hairs on Emma's arm, then they were both gone.

"No!" Nash took me by both arms and made me look at him, forcing me to see through my own encroaching shock.

Emma was in the Netherworld. And I had let it happen. Humans couldn't survive in the Netherworld, and even if Em proved to be the exception, she'd never be the same. How could she be, if she saw even a fraction of the grotesque, horrifying creatures who lived there, every last one of them waiting to devour her in one way or another?

"Kaylee, we have to get them back. You have to cross us over. Now!"

And that's when I understood the depth of Invidia's plan. She couldn't take what I had from me and give it to Sabine. Surely that was beyond her power. But if I went to the Netherworld, she—or Avari—could enslave me for the rest of my life. Or they could just kill me and take my soul, which was what they probably had in mind for Emma. Eventually, anyway.

We'd been set up. Invidia had meant for us to hear her talking to Sabine, and she meant for us to see them cross over. And she wanted us to follow.

But even knowing that, knowing both hellions would be there waiting for us, we had to cross. I couldn't leave Emma—or even the terminally conflicted *mara*—to the hellions' mercy. Not and live with myself afterward.

"I know," I whispered, my voice having succumbed to terror and shock. *Get it together, Kaylee.* "Okay, let's think about this."

"No, let's go get them back. I can't cross over without you, Kaylee. Come on…"

"Wait a second." I pulled Nash to the opposite side of the room, careful not to get too close to the walls in case the Crimson Creeper invasion had spread to the kitchen. "We'd be stupid to cross over in the same spot they last saw us. They'll be right there waiting to grab us."

A current of surprise and relief twisted through the fear churning in his irises. "Good thinking."

"Thanks."

Nash was usually the calm, cool one, but he wasn't thinking clearly at all this time. *It's Sabine.* He wanted her back as badly as I wanted Emma back, and I couldn't help wondering if Tod was right. Were Nash and Sabine meant to be together? Was I the only thing standing in their way.

*No time for that now…* "Give me your hand."

His fingers tightened around mine and a lump formed in my throat. I'd held his hand so many times before, but it had never felt this…bittersweet. Sabine needed him, and he needed to go save her. And he needed me to get him there. But what did I need from him?

"Kay?" Nash's forehead furrowed in fear and concern. "You ready?"

I exhaled heavily. "Nope. Let's go."

Calling forth my wail was much too simple that time, because of how easy it was to picture Emma dying—again. I'd promised her I wouldn't let that happen, no matter what. And I was *not* going to break my promise.

When the wail faded from my ears and the pain in my throat subsided, my eyes flew open and I scanned the Netherworld-version kitchen around us. Thin tendrils of creeper vine had snaked in from the cafeteria but, though they reached for us, slowly slithering along the walls and floor, they hadn't grown enough to completely overwhelm the room yet.

The sink faucets dripped typically rank, gloppy substances, but few of the other appliances had bled through the barrier.

Emma and Sabine stood in the middle of the kitchen, exactly where they'd crossed over, only now my best friend was back in her own body—and obviously in shock. Sabine held Em's forearm, and I couldn't tell whether the *mara* was trying to protect her or control her.

Avari and Invidia faced them from separate sides of the

room, so that Sabine couldn't keep an eye on both hellions at once.

"Kaylee...?" Emma's brown eyes were wide, but not truly focused when her gaze slid to me from Invidia, whose long, sizzling hair flowed rapidly now with excitement. Drops of it rolled down her clothes without damaging the material, then fell to bubble and burn little holes in the linoleum tile. Emma winced at the sizzle. "Where are we? This is hell, right? I'm in hell?"

"It's the Netherworld, Em." My version of hell. "It's gonna be fine. I'm going to get you out of here."

"Am I dead, Kay?" Her words were slurred with shock, and my heart broke. She'd fallen asleep in history class and woken up in hell, and she thought I'd let it happen. That I'd let her die when I could have saved her.

"Soon, my dear..." Invidia crooned. "Very, very soon."

"Don't listen to her, Emma. Don't even look at her," I insisted, and for the first time, I wondered why neither hellion had simply charged them both. Or us.

"Sabine, cross back," Nash said. "Take Emma back to the human world, and we can all work this out there. You don't have to sell your soul to get your life back together."

"He's wrong," Invidia insisted, her green-tinted eyes flashing, while Avari stood silently by, apparently content to wait and see how things played out, at least for now. "You've tried it on your own, and how well did that go?"

"It went fine!" Nash shouted, irises churning furiously as he stepped forward. I followed him, reluctant to let him out of arm's reach in case I had to cross over quickly.

He turned back to Sabine. "You can do this on your own, and I'll help. I've *been* helping."

"You threw me out." Her hand tightened around Emma's arm, and Em flinched, but didn't try to pull away. "You kicked me out of your house and told me not to come back."

Nash hesitated, and I read confliction on his face. He couldn't deny what we all knew had happened, but passing the blame on to Sabine, where it rightfully belonged, would only push her further toward making a proverbial—and almost literal—deal with the devil. "I take it back," he finally said. "I was frustrated and angry, and I acted on impulse, when there was probably a better way to handle the situation," he said, and I wondered if that was a direct quote from his mother.

"He'll do it again." Invidia swept a rivulet of hair over her shoulder, and drops of it splattered the floor behind her. "As long as *she's* in the way, he'll abandon you again and again. Sign over your soul, and I'll make all that go away. I'll make *her* go away."

And suddenly I was out of patience.

"Okay, look," I started, and when all heads turned my way, I had to swallow the lump in my throat before continuing. "Your soul is your business, Sabine."

"Kaylee…" Nash started, warning me with his tone.

"She's a big girl, Nash," I insisted. "She can handle the truth." I turned back to Sabine, uncomfortably aware that I also had the full attention of two hellions. "What you do with your soul is up to you. I personally think you'd be an idiot to sign it over to someone who plans to torture you for all of eternity, and that *is* what she's planning. Ask her, if you don't believe me. But I won't let you drag Emma down with you."

I propped my hands on my hips and shot Sabine a challenging glance. "You let her go right now, and then if you still want to sell your soul I'll prick your finger myself, so you can sign in blood. How's that?"

"Kaylee!" Nash snapped, but I could only shrug, hoping my attempt at reverse psychology didn't backfire. Sabine typically did exactly what I wanted her not to, so maybe if she thought I wanted her to sell her soul—or at least that it wouldn't bother me—she'd run in the opposite direction.

"Let her speak," Avari said, hands in the pockets of his suit jacket. "I find her honesty...blissfully chaotic." He was dressed like any human corporate monkey, which should have made him look harmless and...normal. But his eyes...

I couldn't stand to look at those solid black orbs; they seemed to suck the light out of the room, rather than reflect it. His eyes were windows not into his soul—he didn't have one—but into a void so deep and dark it was the very definition of despair.

"Good. Here, let's get this over with." I marched toward Sabine, hoping a show of aggression on my part would push her into action.

Sabine took a step back, pulling Emma with her. Nash called my name, but I didn't stop. And when I was half-way between him and Sabine, a sudden wink of motion drew my attention to my right. My head swiveled, eyes searching for the anomaly.

Avari was gone.

Nash yelped behind me. I spun to find Avari holding him by one arm, and suddenly I understood why neither hellion had made a move until that moment—I'd gotten pretty damn good at crossing over in a hurry, and based on what I'd seen minutes earlier, Sabine could do it nearly instantly. Neither hellion was willing to risk us crossing over and depriving them of four victims.

But once Nash was out of my reach, he was fair game.

I froze, stuck between my maybe-boyfriend and my definitely best friend, unsure what to do.

"One move, and I'll kill him," Avari said, and since hellions can't lie, I was pretty sure he wasn't bluffing.

"Kaylee, go!" Nash shouted, face already twisted with pain, and I understood that he was feeling exactly what I'd felt in the nightmare Avari had given me. "Take them and go!"

But I'd no more leave him than I'd leave Emma, and the hellion obviously knew that.

Avari glanced past me at Sabine. "Let's make a deal, Ms. Campbell."

"No!" Invidia screeched, and Emma gave a startled yip. I followed her gaze to see that the hellion of envy now sported several rows of razor-sharp, needle-thin teeth, the yellowish white of aged bone. "No deals. The *mara* is mine, and so is the lovely Emma-body. *Mine!*"

"Kaylee...!" Em moaned, and now she was clinging to Sabine.

"Sabine, get her out of here!" I snapped, splitting my attention between Invidia, Sabine and Em, and Avari and Nash.

"If you go, you'll never see him again," Avari said, and

Sabine's eyes widened in panic. She wouldn't let Nash die, and as grateful as I was for that impulse, I was terrified to even think what she'd do to save him.

"What's your offer?" Sabine asked, and a horrible screech of fury erupted from Invidia's inhuman throat.

"No! Mine! I found her. I fed her. I cultivated her envy into a fragrant bouquet of desire and bitterness and rage, and she is perfectly ripe right now, and *I will pluck her!*"

Avari's gaze never wavered from Sabine. "A trade. Mine—" he shoved Nash forward, without letting go of him, and Nash moaned "—for yours." And that's when I understood that Avari was feeding from him. Draining his energy, like he'd done for more than a day, the last time Nash was in the Netherworld.

"No, Sabine," Nash gasped, as his face drained of all color. "Kaylee, don't let her do it."

I didn't know what to say. I couldn't choose between Nash and Emma. I *couldn't!*

"You'd give up a *bean sidhe* for a human?" Sabine aimed a suspicious look at Avari. "Why?"

"All you need to know is that if I get the girl, you may take your lover and cross back over."

But I understood what he wasn't saying. He wasn't giving up Nash for Emma. He was giving up Nash for me. Because if he got Emma, he could force me to trade my freedom for hers.

"Kaylee…?" Em was shaking with full-body tremors, her eyes glazing over with shock.

"No!" Invidia was wild with fury now. Her hair flowed so fast a sizzling puddle was forming on the ground at her feet. Her eyes glowed bright green, and her hands had become claws, sharp and hooked on the ends.

Sabine glanced from Invidia, to me, to Avari, then back to me, and I could see the confliction written all over her face. She didn't want to damn Emma. But she didn't want to lose Nash, either, and Avari's deal was obviously much more beneficial than the one Invidia had offered.

Then she looked at Nash and saw pain shifting the colors in his eyes, and I knew what she'd say before she could even form the words.

"Fine. Here." Sabine pushed Emma to her right. Avari let go of Nash and shoved him in the opposite direction. I raced toward Emma. She stumbled and fell to her knees. Across the room, Nash half collapsed from pain. Sabine ran toward him, arms outstretched.

And before either of us reached our goal, a dark blur flew across the edge of my vision. Invidia screeched. I turned to see her racing toward me—I was closest to her—claws bared, needle teeth snapping together, so long and curved she couldn't even close her mouth.

I dodged to the left, and she mirrored my movement from ten feet away, hissing in fury, hair sizzling in a trail behind her.

Avari let loose an inhuman roar, enraged to see another hellion so close to his prize. He stopped—just feet from Emma—and planted his right foot firmly on the ground, like a giant determined to shake the earth. Tendrils of frost shot across the tile from his ordinary black dress shoe, racing toward Invidia, growing thicker and stronger with every inch of ground they covered. They reached her as she lunged for me. I scrambled backward in terror, and she froze. For real.

A blue sheen covered her skin. Her hair stopped dripping, instantly frozen into overlapping, green-tinted icicles. Her claws still reached for me, a foot from my face, frozen in time.

"Kaylee!" Tod shouted, and I looked up to see him standing across the room, surprised by what he'd found, but ready for action.

"Get Em!" I yelled. He nodded, then disappeared. Avari reached for Emma again, and she stumbled away from him. Tod reappeared at her side and she clutched at him. Another instant later, they were both gone.

Avari roared again, and his gaze narrowed on me from my left. On my right, something crackled sharply—Invidia was fighting the ice. Avari stalked toward me. I closed my eyes to summon my wail. But before I could produce any sound, Nash shouted from across the room.

"Come get us!"

I opened my eyes to see him holding Sabine at arm's length, refusing to let her cross them over until he knew I was safe.

Avari stood and straightened his jacket. He glanced at me on his right, then at Nash and Sabine, on his left, and I recognized the look on his face.

Greed. Pure, concentrated avarice. He wanted us all. But even a hellion couldn't be two places at once. He'd have to choose.

But then more ice crackled on my other side, and I knew he wouldn't get the chance.

Invidia's left claw shot toward me. The ice glaze over her arm cracked and shattered on the floor. I kicked out on instinct. My foot slammed into her stomach, and she fell to her knees, still half-frozen. I kicked her again, and she fell onto her side. When her face hit the ground, three long, sharp teeth broke off of her lower jaw and clattered on the ground, as long as my little finger. Several frozen hair-cicles snapped off of her head and skittered across the floor toward Nash and Sabine.

"Sabine, cross!" I shouted. She glanced at Avari, then knelt and plucked one of the poison-cicles from the ground, holding it between her thumb and forefinger. Then she nodded at me and grabbed Nash's arm.

"No!" Nash shouted, as she crossed over with him in her grip.

I tried to summon my wail. Avari ran for me. Invidia's thawed claw wrapped around my ankle, ripping through my jeans. I jerked my foot, but she wouldn't let go. So I grabbed one of her broken teeth, my pulse racing in my ears. Avari roared in fury, feet away. Invidia's grip on my ankle tightened.

I shoved the tooth through her left eye.

Invidia screamed and let go of my foot, slapping both claws over her injury. I scrambled backward, trying desperately to call up my wail. But it wouldn't come. I was too scared to think of any death but my own.

Then strong, warm arms wrapped around me from behind. "I've got you," Tod whispered in my ear, as Avari charged us.

An instant later, we stood in the Eastlake kitchen, Tod

still holding me from behind. My right foot stood in white glop from a busted bottle of mayonnaise. Emma stared at me from three feet away, eyes wide with shock.

Across the room, Nash was hunched over in pain and exhaustion, wrapped in Sabine's arms. On the floor at her feet stood a clear plastic cup with the melting poison hair-cicle inside. I didn't even want to know why she'd taken it.

Tod squeezed me, then let me go, and I whirled around to face him. "Thanks. I totally owe you."

"No. You don't," he said, and the blues in his eyes shifted slowly.

Then Emma was there, wrapping me in a hug.

"Are you okay?" I asked her, pulling my foot from the mayo.

"I think so." She let go of me and pushed strands of blond hair from her face. Her eyes were still wide and her skin was pale, but being back in familiar surroundings went a long way toward calming her down. "That was the Netherworld?"

"In all its many-splendored horror." I grabbed an apron hanging from a hook on the wall and wiped as much of the gunk off my shoe as I could.

"What the hell happened? I was in history one minute, and the next thing I know, I'm staring at some man in a suit and some…thing with rancid water for hair, who looked like she wanted to eat me whole."

"It's a long story, Em. I promise I'll tell you the whole thing. But I need just a second to…breathe."

Emma nodded, and I sat down on a stool, blessedly

free of splattered condiments. And for a moment, the five of us just stared at one another.

Shocked. Relieved. And very much alive.

"So, the one with the hair?" Emma said, pulling the pan from the oven.

"The poison hair, dripping and fizzing everywhere?" I asked, laying a hand towel across the counter.

Em nodded and set the pan on the towel, then inhaled deeply through her nose. To try to make up for her trauma the day before, I'd promised to answer every Netherworld question she could throw at me over homemade brownies, chosen for the inherent comfort-power of chocolate.

"That was Invidia. She's a hellion of envy."

She dropped the pot holders on the counter. "The one who put the whammy on you and Sabine?"

"And half the school." I shoved the pot holders into the drawer to the left of the stove. "It was part of the blitz, remember?" Emma nodded, but didn't look very sure, so I elaborated. "Okay, think of it like a waterwheel. Once it gets going, it produces lots of power, right? But you have to put in an initial effort to get it set up. The setup in this case was one big burst of energy shoved into our school by Avari, a hellion of greed, and Invidia, a hellion of envy. That one burst irritated already existing frictions between people, and since it was powered by greed and envy, it paid off in greed and envy."

"So…Sophie cut off Laura's hair because she was jealous of that stupid Snow Queen crown."

"Exactly." I reached into the fridge and pulled out a gallon of milk, while Em got down two short glasses.

"And it made Sabine crazy jealous of you, and it made you determined to blame everything that went wrong on her."

I huffed and handed her the first glass. "Sort of. But Avari and Invidia went through some special effort to play the two of us against each other, because we were the payoff."

"That's creepy, Kay."

"At the very least." I sipped from my glass, watching her closely.

For the most part, Emma had dealt pretty well with what she'd seen, and subsequently been told. Her reaction to finding out she'd been possessed—"Did my head spin around?"—was her typical humor defense, but I saw the fear beneath. I knew what she was feeling—out of control and terrified and *used*—because I'd been there.

And I would be there to help her deal. And to fight back.

We all would.

When the doorbell rang, I answered it while Em cut

the brownies. Nash stood in the circle of light on my front porch, and the moment our gazes met, the colors in his irises started swirling and my heart beat a little harder.

"Hey."

"Hey," I said, then I let him fold me into a warm hug, punctuated by a kiss. I ached for more, but it wasn't the time. I couldn't help wondering if that time would ever come, because...

"So, are you gonna make us stand out here all night?" Sabine asked, stepping onto the porch behind him. "I'm freezing my ass off, and I need to talk to Emma."

I stepped aside to let them in, then closed the door and took Nash's hand when he offered it. He'd asked me out for Friday night—a real date, guaranteed free from all Netherworld interruptions and *mara* scheming—and I'd accepted. Though I had no idea how I'd talk my dad into letting me go. Nash was willing to earn back my trust, and I was willing to let him try, so long as he stayed clean. But my dad was staunchly con, regarding the possibility of a Kaylee/Nash reunion.

It might actually be easier to make Sabine give up on Nash than to make my dad accept him.

Sabine stomped past us into the kitchen, where Emma had yet to look up from her brownies. The *mara* had already apologized for sending me to the Netherworld, then almost selling me to Avari. I accepted her apology because I knew she meant it—she wouldn't have said it otherwise. And I'd apologized for blaming the murder of our teachers and near-destruction of our school on her. So in her warped world view, we were even, and the status quo was secure. She would keep trying to claw her way into Nash's heart—unsatisfied with the role of good friend—and I would continue to push her back every time she went too far.

But because Em refused to accept her apology and didn't owe Sabine one, the *mara* had become obsessed with making Emma forgive her.

It was not going well.

"Em?" Sabine launched into another round of apologies, while Nash and I sat on the couch.

"Feeling okay?" I asked, staring into his eyes to see the truth. It had been more than a day, but he was just now regaining color after being drained by Avari. Again. Of course, it helped that he no longer had to worry about me and Sabine being actively pitted against each other by a pair of evil Netherworld hellions. We weren't best friends—I'd probably never actually *like* the *mara*—but we could be in the same room without needing a referee now.

Most of the time.

"I'm better." After a lengthy pause, during which Emma tried to get rid of Sabine by offering her chocolate, Nash said, "Mom should be here any minute."

"She's on her way," Tod confirmed, and I looked up to see him sitting in my dad's favorite chair. Watching us.

"Shouldn't you be delivering pizza?" Nash asked.

The reaper shrugged. "Like I'm gonna miss this."

I frowned. "You've already seen it?"

"Um…yeah. And heard it, and smelled it, and…"

"What is it?" Nash asked, but his brother only grinned.

Harmony had been looking for a way to keep us from getting possessed ever since she found out what had happened to me a month ago, and we'd gotten a call that morning saying she'd finally come up with something. Which was the only reason Sabine and Emma had wound up in the same room so soon after Em's first trip to the Netherworld.

"Where's your dad?" Tod glanced down the hall, like my father might materialize any moment.

"Helping Alec get settled." Alec and my father had struck up an odd sort of friendship, thanks to their mutual lack of humanity and abject hatred of the hellion who'd possessed them both multiple times. My dad had even cleaned out our meager savings to lend Alec his first month's rent and security deposit.

"Knock, knock!" Harmony called from the front porch, then came in without waiting for me to open the door, carrying a large cardboard box. "Tod, give me a hand, please."

The reaper stood reluctantly and took the box from his mother. As soon as he touched it, the box started to shake and erupted into a chorus of squeals and odd, high-pitched growls.

"What's that?" I asked, standing as Tod set the box on my coffee table. Em and Sabine wandered in from the kitchen to stare suspiciously at the weird, yipping box.

"That..." Harmony began, "is part of what's going to keep you from playing host to a hellion ever again. But first..." She stuck one hand into her coat pocket and pulled out a plastic sandwich bag filled with odd, blue, stiff-looking strands of...something. "Emma, give me your wrist."

Em stuck her arm out hesitantly, while Harmony

pulled out one of the cords, which turned out to be braided lengths of something fibrous.

"This is silk from a Netherworld plant called *dissimulatus*. It's very rare, which is why it took me so long to find it, but it's also very sturdy." She tied braided silk into a loop around Emma's wrist, then double and triple knotted it. The bracelet was too small to slip off, but too loose to cut off her circulation. "It won't shrink, stain, or tear, so you can wear it all the time. Even in the shower."

*"Dissimulatus?"* Em asked, twisting the loop around her wrist while Harmony dug in her bag for another one.

"It means 'disguise.' As long as you wear them, the silk will disguise your energy signature, both here and in the Netherworld."

"What does that mean?" Emma asked. And if she hadn't, I would have.

"Think of yourself as a cell phone," Harmony began, tying the second bracelet on Sabine's left wrist. "Constantly broadcasting a signal—your energy signature. That signal identifies you as a human female, about sixteen years old. Specifically, it identifies you as Emma Dawn Marshall. This bracelet—" she held up another one and waved me forward, as Sabine frowned at her new accessory "—is like a jammer. It's going to jam your signal. And for the rest of you—" Harmony glanced at me, Nash, and Sabine in turn as she wrapped the stiff length of cord around my arm "—it will disguise your species, as well."

"So…no one will know I'm a *bean sidhe*?" I asked, as she tied the first knot.

"Not just from tasting your energy signature."

"And that'll keep Avari from possessing us?" Nash said, holding his arm out for his bracelet.

"It'll keep him from identifying you. And if he can't find you, he can't possess you. Right?"

"But he knows where we live," Sabine pointed out, frowning skeptically. "It's not gonna be hard to find us, if he's looking in the right place."

Harmony nodded solemnly. "And that's where these come in." Without further explanation, she opened the box on the coffee table, reached inside, and pulled out a small, quaking ball of fur.

I frowned at the creature, and at the faint gamey smell emanating from it. And when Harmony shoved it toward me, I took a step back.

"He won't hurt you," she insisted, and pushed it toward me again. This time I held out both hands, and she deposited the furball in them. "This is your new best friend." She brushed blond curls back from her face, then reached into the box again and pulled out another ball of fur, and handed this one to Nash. "They don't have a name that I can actually pronounce, so you may as well just think of them as puppies. Very special puppies."

"They're dogs?" Emma asked, and Harmony smiled.

"Not fully. They're a mix of a Pomeranian and a small Netherworld critter. They're very expensive and difficult to breed. So don't take this responsibility lightly."

"Responsibility?" Sabine said, holding her "dog" at arm's length.

"Yes. It's very important that you bond with them over the next couple of weeks."

"So, what?" Emma said. "Hellions are allergic to fur?"

Harmony laughed and stroked the small creature in my hands, which had begun to sniff my fingers with a tiny, wet nose. "No. These little guys are Netherworld guard dogs. If they sense a hellion anywhere near you, on the other side of the world barrier, of course, they'll start yipping up a storm. So…if you sleep with him in your room, he'll wake you up before you can possibly be possessed."

"So…the cure for hellion possession is a pet?" I asked, running one finger down the creature's thin, trembling spine.

"Well, it's more preventative than actual cure, but it's the best I could come up with."

"My mom won't let me have a dog," Emma said, looking worried as she cradled hers to her chest.

Harmony was unconcerned. "Tod can talk her into it, can't you, Tod?" The reaper nodded. "And, Sabine, I'm sure Nash can talk to your foster mother for you." Their Influence should pave the way toward pet ownership before the poor mothers even knew what hit them.

"But I don't want a dog," Sabine said, still staring at hers like it might bite her. Or vice versa. "I didn't even want a bracelet."

Harmony frowned. "Do you want Avari in your body?"

"No."

"Then you want this bracelet, and you definitely want this dog. Name him. Feed him. Bond with him. He's the only thing standing between you and serial possession. Got it?"

Sabine nodded hesitantly, and I laughed out loud. I couldn't help it. She couldn't have looked less comfortable if Harmony had demanded she cha-cha in a pair of three-inch heels.

"What about Alec?" I asked, pushing my new bracelet up my arm, to keep the pup from chewing on it.

"I dropped his off at his new place. Sophie's getting one, too, though I don't know how her dad's going to explain it."

"So…this is it?" Nash asked. "We're using jewelry and puppies to ward off evil?"

Harmony nodded. "Right now, guys, these puppies and bracelets are all you have standing between you and the Netherworld. Well, these little guys, and one another. For whatever reason, the dominant hellion of this area has literally moved into your high school, just across the world barrier from where you spend most of your waking hours. And he's not alone. Such a concentration of power is like a lighthouse in the dark. It's going to attract others, and your school is going to be at the heart of whatever trouble moves into the neighborhood.

"If you're going to take on the entire Netherworld population, as some of you seem determined to do, you need to at least know what you have going for you. So take a look around this room. This is it. These are the people in your corner. So I suggest you all find a way to get along. I have a feeling someday your lives are going to depend on it."

I glanced around my living room, one face at a time, thinking of everything we'd been through together. Everything we'd fought and survived. Hellions. Possession. Toxic vines. Demon's Breath. Walking nightmares. Was Harmony saying it would get worse from there?

A chill shot through me at the very thought.

But as I watched Sabine watching Nash watch me, I realized something I should have understood much sooner—as horrifying a threat as the Netherworld represented, learning to trust again in my own world might just be the scariest thing I'd ever had to do.

★ ★ ★ ★ ★

# Netherworld Survival Guide

A collection of entries salvaged from
Alec's personal journal during his
twenty-six year captivity in the Nether...

# COMMON HAZARDOUS PLANTS

**Note:** Flora in the Netherworld is eighty-eight per cent carnivorous, ten per cent omnivorous, and less than two per cent docile. So keep in mind that if you see a plant, it probably wants to eat you.

## Razor Wheat
- **Location** – Rural areas with little foot traffic.
- **Description** – Fields full of dense vegetation similar to wheat in structure, ranging in colour from deep red stalks to olive-hued seed clusters. Over six feet tall at mature height.
- **Dangers** – Razor wheat stalks shatters upon contact, raining tiny, sharp shards of plant that can slice through clothing and shred bare flesh.
- **Best Precaution** – Complete avoidance.
- **Second Best Precaution** – Long sleeves, full-length rubber waders and fishing boots, metal trash-can lid wielded like a shield.

## Crimson Creeper
- **Location** – Anywhere it can get a foothold. Creeper can take root in as little as a quarter-inch wide crack in concrete and will grow to split the pavement open. It grows quickly and spreads voraciously, climbing walls, towers, trees and anything else that can be made to hold still.
- **Description** – A deep green vine growing up to four inches in diameter, bearing alternating leaves bleeding to crimson or blood red on variegated edges. Vines also sport needle-thin thorns between the leaves.
- **Dangers** – Though anchored by strong, deep roots, which have hallucinogenic properties when consumed, creeper vines slither autonomously and will actually wind around prey, injecting pre-digestive venom through its thorns. The vine will then coil around its meal and wait while the creature is slowly dissolved into liquid fertiliser from the inside out.
- **Best Precaution** – Complete avoidance.

- **Second Best Precaution** – Crimson creeper blooms can be made into a tea which acts as one of two known antidotes to the creeper venom; however, the vine blooms only once every three years. Blooms can be dried and preserved for up to two decades.

## COMMON DANGEROUS CREATURES

**Note:** Whether it intends to consume your mind, body or soul, fauna in the Netherworld is ninety-nine per cent carnivorous, in one form or another. So keep in mind that if you see a creature, it probably wants to eat you.

### Hellions
- **Location** – Everywhere. Anywhere. Never close your eyes.
- **Description** – Hellions can look like anything they want.They can be any size, shape or colour. Their only physical limitation is that they cannot exactly duplicate any other creature, living or dead.
- **Dangers** – Hellions feed from chaos in general, and individual emotions in particular. But what they really want is your soul—a never-ending buffet. Since souls cannot be stolen from the living, a hellion will try to bargain for or con you out of it. If you refuse—and even sometimes if you don't—the hellion will either kill you for your soul or torture you, *then* kill you for your soul.
- **Best Precaution** – Complete avoidance.
- **Second Best Precaution** – Pray.

### Harpies
- **Location** – Found in large numbers near thin spots in the barrier between worlds, but individual harpies can live anywhere they choose, in either the human world or the Netherworld.
- **Description** – In the human world, harpies can pass for human at a glance, as long as they brush hair over their pointed ears and hide their compact, bat-like wings beneath clothing. In the Netherworld, harpies

appear less human, with mouths full of sharp, thin teeth, claws instead of hands and bird-like, clawed talons instead of feet.

- **Dangers** – Harpies are snatchers. Collectors. They will dive out of the air with no warning to grab whatever catches their eye, which can be anything from broken pots and pans to shiny rings—often still attached to human fingers. Also, they're carnivores and they don't distinguish between human and animal flesh.
- **Best Precaution** – Complete avoidance.
- **Second Best Precaution** – Stay inside or keep one eye trained on the sky and get ready to run.

## ESCAPE AND EVASION

**Note:** The best way to escape a Netherworld threat is to leave the Netherworld, though that won't keep certain species, such as harpies, from crossing into the human world after you. If you are incapable of leaving under your own power, eventually something *will* eat you. But to help put that moment off as long as possible, here is a list of the most effective evasion tactics:

- Find shelter in rural areas. Netherworld creatures are attracted to heavily populated areas, where the overflow of human energy they feed from is most concentrated.
- Fibres from the *dissimulatus* plant can be woven together and worn to disguise your energy signature and keep predators from identifying you as human and thus edible.

# Something is wrong with Kaylee Cavanaugh...

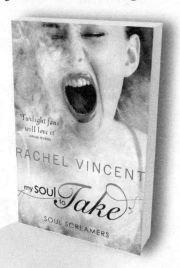

She can sense when someone near her is about to die. And when that happens, an uncontrollable force compels her to scream bloody murder. Literally.

Kaylee just wants to enjoy having caught the attention of the hottest boy in school. But when classmates start dropping dead for no reason and only Kaylee knows who'll be next, finding a boyfriend is the least of her worries!

*Book one in the* Soul Screamers *series.*

**www.miraink.co.uk**

# When Kaylee Cavanaugh screams, someone dies

When teen pop star Eden croaks onstage and Kaylee doesn't wail, she knows something is wrong. She can't cry for someone with no soul.

Starry-eyed teens are trading a flickering lifetime of fame and fortune for eternity in the Netherworld.

Kaylee can't let that happen, even if trying to save their souls means putting hers at risk…

*Book two in the unmissable* Soul Screamers *series.*

www.miraink.co.uk